DRAGON: OUT OF THE BOX 27

The Girl in the Box, Book 37

ROBERT J. CRANE

Ostiagard Press

DRAGON
The Girl in the Box, Book 37
(Out of the Box, Book 27)

Robert J. Crane

1st Edition.

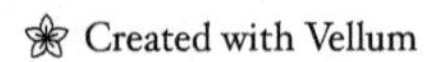

PROLOGUE

Jaime Chapman
Mountain View, California

The ink was drying, the deal was done, and the handshakes were being exchanged. Jaime Chapman couldn't imagine himself being any happier unless Gwen had been here.

Smiling for the cameras hurt. Not a big smiler, Jaime nonetheless plastered one on his face and steeled himself against the seemingly endless flashes. Everyone was here – the *Times*, the *Post*, the *Washington Free Press*, plus every single nightly news, cable channel, and even a ton of internet outfits like Davey Kory's Flashforce. The phosphorescent bursts hurt Jaime's eyes, too, had him running his palm over the smooth grain of the conference table's wood. He gripped the sleek plastic of the pen they'd done the signing with. It was like his security blanket in the face of the flashbulbs, the cell phone cameras.

"In China," Wu Huang said, leaning over to whisper in Jaime's ear, his hand still gripping Jaime's tightly, "this would be smaller, more organized. One outlet, not this many. And we would be done by now." Huang was in his forties, a touch of steel color lacing through his otherwise black hair, cheeks puffy and wide, fixed in a smile as his eyes glittered with slightly less amusement than the smile would indicate.

"In America we have to feed the beast," Jaime said, keeping that smile going as the flashbulbs continued to assail his eyes. Sensory overload was not far off, but he'd learned to manage it. The CEO of the largest tech company in the world couldn't just collapse under the weight of his neuroses, after all. That'd be bad for the stock price. "Still..." He raised his voice. "All right, people, that's enough trying to trigger latent epilepsy for a few minutes."

That prompted a laugh from the reporters in attendance.

"Mr. Chapman!" Chapman blinked through the purple spots in his vision to squint at the reporter. They'd planned to take questions in the next room, in a few minutes, but leave it to the nimrod from Flashforce to try and squeeze one in early. "What led you to this deal?"

Well, at least it was a good question. And he had a perfect, boilerplate answer for it. "We've long wanted to increase our business ties to China," Chapman said, hitting the bullet points, "and when Mr. Huang came to us with this proposal, it just made sense. He gets to become one of the largest stakeholders in our business, and we get to roll out Socialite in China starting next year. Over a billion potential new users," now Chapman's smile was real, "with a FindIt search engine product specifically tailored to China to follow shortly thereafter. Instaphoto, Cashfer, our entire portfolio of companies will all be entering the largest market in the world, bringing Silicon Valley engineering to the most populous country in the world." He hit the talking points with gusto, because this deal was a slam-dunk, no brainer. Selling a little bit of his equity to Huang and then facilitating him buying shares on the open market to make him the second largest shareholder in exchange for nearly-full access to Chinese markets?

Only an idiot wouldn't take that deal. And Jaime Chapman was no idiot.

"Mr. Huang?" The question came from a slightly older, more grizzled-looking reporter. Looked like he'd been on the beat awhile. "How do you respond to allegations that your company is backed and owned by the Chinese government?"

Chapman felt his blood go cold. "I'm sorry, we're not meant to be taking questions right n–"

"It's fine." Huang held up a hand to stay him. Still, there was a tightness around Huang's eyes that suggested he was not entirely pleased to receive the question. "I have long enjoyed good relations with the party and the Chinese government, which allows this merger to be advantageous for all parties. I hope to facilitate a new level of cooperation between our countries, with better understanding through our greater business and technological ties."

"Thank you," Jaime said, cutting off the next volley of questions. Eight reporters tried, but he and Huang turned away, flashbulbs ringing out madly in the conference room.

"I hate your press," Huang said as the PR people herded the reporters out the door.

"They're a bunch of filthy savages," Chapman agreed. His phone was buzzing in his pocket, and he fished it out to take a look, frowning when he saw the screen.

IT'S TIME TO PLAY!

"If you'll excuse me for just a moment..." Jaime said.

"Quickly, first," Huang said, catching him by the elbow. "I have several engineers from my company ready to start interfacing with yours so we can start design on the China-specific products."

"Right, right," Chapman said, feeling the pull of his phone. The Network was meeting, and he was going to miss it if he didn't get away soon.

"I'd like to 'get the ball rolling,'" Huang said, and there was a flicker of something in his eyes, "with your Lineage affiliate."

Chapman held in a frown. Lineage? He'd bought that company on a whim, a DNA testing and family tree tech company that he'd tried, unsuccessfully, to mate with Socialite's capabilities and data. It had led to some embarrassing viral stories about unknown siblings that were the product of infidelity suddenly being contacted through Socialite. It had spawned a couple heart-warming puff pieces, too, but the bad had outweighed the good and he'd scuttled the integration plans. It wasn't a core competency of Socialite, he'd decided, so now Lineage just sat there on his balance sheet, making a few bucks for the company and that was about it. "Sure," he said. "I'll clear your people for full access to the product right away, just get their names to my assistant."

"Excellent," Huang said, and now he settled into a much more easy smile, that little flash in his eyes gone. "I think this is going be a fruitful partnership."

"I agree," Jaime said, with a smile of his own. "Now if you'll excuse me..."

"Absolutely." Huang nodded and left him, barking at one of his assistants in Mandarin.

Jaime keyed in his password quickly, flipping right to the Escapade app and jumping in mid-conversation. For security reasons, Chapman's people made it so only the most recent ten lines of text were retained, the rest immediately deleted from the secure network it traveled on and stored absolutely nowhere on the internet. The app even disabled the screenshot function during use, as a precaution.

RUSS BILSON: I'd like you all to welcome our newest member, Chris Byrd! I'm sure you've all heard of him. Chris's politics and news forum is watched by the people who matter most in Washington.

Chapman snorted. Byrd had the lowest rated evening show on cable news, but Bilson wasn't wrong – it was watched by more congressional staffers and politicians than any other, mostly because it was the most inside-baseball show on DC's inner workings out there. Not meant to feed the proles outside the beltway, it catered to the Acela corridor. That was something, but still...being in last place after CNN in the cable news rankings was a special sort of hilarious to Chapman.

HEATHER CHALKE: Welcome, Chris.

TYRUS FLANAGAN: Welcome.

DAVE KORY: Glad to have you.

Chapman rolled his eyes as the salutations filled the screen, not bothering to add an anodyne greeting of his own. It'd be lost in the shuffle in any case, and he was indifferent to Byrd's entry to the group. His philosophy was that there ought to be a reason to add anybody. Byrd's influence seemed limited to him, but maybe he'd be of more use to the DC based members, like Chalke and Bilson. Chapman couldn't imagine much use for the cable TV host. In terms of their press contacts, he ranked behind Kory's Flashforce or Johannsen's *Free Press* in his view.

CHRIS BYRD: Hey u guys russ told me things were lit AF in here so glad to be part of the team

Chapman cringed. Didn't it just figure that Byrd's typing would fit neatly into the "Aging Boomer, bereft of texting skills" style.

Whatever. He turned, keeping the app open on the off chance something interesting emerged, but took a moment to survey the boardroom, thinking about what he'd wrought today.

New access to China in a way that no US tech company had ever managed. An inside track via Huang to the Chinese government, and a chance to develop inside that market with their tacit approval. It would deliver billions in market cap to his stock, and already the alerts were pinging to his phone showing him that, yes, Wall Street liked – no, *loved* – this deal.

It was a crowning triumph in his business career, which had been replete with doing things no one had ever done before. Dethroning tech giants that had captured first-mover advantage. Making deals in countries few others could.

The only downside was that it was too bad Gwen couldn't be here to witness it. That was the life of busy CEOs, though. He could sympathize, her being up to her eyeballs in some project or another, but still, it bothered him a little. He was about to become the world's richest man, thanks to this, and she was off piddling with her cute little startup. Sure, he'd been there – the constant grinds of programming, checking, debugging, managerial business – but now he was in a much more elevated position. Other people handled that low-grade bullshit.

Maybe her startup would go belly up, he sometimes secretly wished. Then he could hire her to do something here, with him. That way he could see her every day instead of this catch-as-can bullshit her work schedule currently provided.

"Mr. Chapman?" One of the PR people called to him, quiet, respectful – but urgent.

"Right," Chapman said, forcing that smile back onto his face. Not the real one, from when he thought of Gwen. The fake one, the one that wouldn't fade as he concentrated back on the job at hand – publicizing this new venture to the whole world.

CHAPTER ONE

One Month Later
Yorkshire, Virginia

The coffee in Cathy Jang-Peters's tumbler was warm and good, and almost made this drive tolerable. It was certainly necessary, she reflected, blotting at her eyes delicately with a dark sleeve of her jacket, avoiding smearing her makeup but dabbing at the sleepiness pushing her lids down. It was just after 5:30 in the morning, after all, a damned uncivilized hour to be on the road.

Blinking as the rural scenery of Virginia State Road 28 passed her by, green fields covered in the darkness of lingering night broken by the occasional tree. Cathy Jang-Peters took a sip of her coffee. The tumbler was good, solid, and a cold brew lingered within. Her husband had made it for her starting the day before, giving the grounds time to seep into the filtered water. It was less acidic than hot coffee, and he made it with some fancy stuff she didn't really pay much attention to. It was good, though, and smooth, and she could drink it right away as she walked out the door of their Manassas home in the mornings with nothing but a kiss and the tumbler to speed her on her way.

Blinking her eyes again, her BMW's headlights chased away the early morning shadows as she cruised down the highway. It wasn't bumper to bumper yet, but give it an hour or so and it'd start to fill up; two hours and VA-28, this two-lane road, would be just another logjammed thoroughfare, even some 25 miles from Washington DC.

Oh, how she missed living in DC. She and her husband had moved out to Manassas only six months ago. Six months she'd been doing this commute and she was already over the drive. Three days a week she went into DC, to Georgetown University, where she was an adjunct professor of Chinese history. Three interminable driving days.

Cathy let out a little sigh. But at least it was only three days a week. Plenty of their neighbors commuted to Arlington or all the way to DC. Hell, one even went to somewhere on the outskirts of Baltimore – five days a week! And during rush hour. At least her schedule permitted her to get in early and leave before the afternoon rush.

Still, this was getting to be a bit much. She took another sip of the smooth, cool coffee. The other nice thing about her husband's cold brew was that he didn't dilute it too much, so it had twice the kick of a hot cup. She needed that caffeine for this drive. Cathy was not, by disposition, an early riser. Nor was she a country person, and yet, as she looked out the window and saw a deer raising its head to look at her from out in the field, here she was, in the countryside of Virginia.

She missed DC. She missed the shorter commute. But everything was so expensive in DC. Shane had suggested moving out, and she'd acceded after some argument. Maybe it wouldn't be so bad, she'd reflected. They could get a bigger house, have some more space to start a family. The pace of life could be a little calmer.

Six months and she was ready to teach at the local community college if it meant she could stop this murderous commute and go back to sleeping in again.

Fighting to keep her eyes open, Cathy Jang-Peters quietly cursed her husband's brilliant, pragmatic idea. At least the school term was getting close to finished. As an adjunct, she wasn't going to be needed during the summer. So she'd have a few months off to figure things out before next school year. What was she going to do? She looked behind her; a big panel van took up the entire rearview. Shifting her gaze out the window again, she saw she was passing a shadowy patch of trees that looked alarmingly skeletal as they breezed by the windows of her BMW.

Well, she didn't know yet. But she'd figure it out. With less than two weeks to go to the end of term, she was ready for the break and a chance to consider the next phase of her life. It wasn't as if she had the brain power to think it through during these commutes. She took another sip of coffee. Maybe in the afternoons heading home, but definitely not the mornings, when she was entirely too focused on just staying alive and not crashing into one of these endless fields that surrounded the road she moved along in the early morning darkness.

CHAPTER TWO

Fred Brooks had been making the commute from his home in Nokesville, Virginia to Arlington, just outside DC, for almost twenty years. Back when he'd started, it had been a fairly easy thing. Smooth ride over open roads, right into Arlington proper where he worked. Easy shot out at the end of the day, too, a peaceful drive out I-66 to Virginia State Road 28, then follow through Manassas back home.

Well, the times had changed. Fred had noticed, a little slow to adapt, but he got there eventually. Nowadays, if he left at the same time he'd left back when he'd started at work, he'd show up about 9:30 in the morning. Fred was a steady sort of guy, but even he knew when to adjust things up. So he'd started getting up earlier. Prepared himself for spending more time in the car.

His coping mechanism was audiobooks. Time was, all you had was the stupid radio. Half commercials, thirty percent DJs blathering on, twenty percent music, and only ten percent of it he liked. His kids had shown him the way to salvation on this: first, music apps. Then, the audiobooks.

Fred liked to read, but he didn't have much time for it anymore. Trying to squeeze in an hour before bed these days was an exercise in futility. He'd drift off early, because he woke up early.

But the audiobook! He'd start it off on his phone when he

got in the car, and it'd keep him going through Manassas and Centreville, all through his journey along I-66 into Arlington. End of the day he'd repeat, listening to the words of the narrator over the honking horns and background engine noise that surrounded his crawl back to Nokesville.

This morning he was listening to a book— non-fiction – about the mystery of Polynesian settlement in the Pacific. Fred liked to mix things up. His last had been the latest Dan Brown novel, but switching over to non-fiction kept things interesting. This book was not up his usual alley, but he had no complaints. He could tell it was good because it kept him at rapt attention. When a book was boring he'd find himself sliding into the doldrums of sleepiness, staring out the window and remembering little.

He was really into this one, though, cruising along VA-28 and nodding in interest as he went. He was paying such careful attention that he almost missed the subtle flash across the field to his right – almost.

But not quite.

It was followed, a moment later, by a quiet popping noise somewhere ahead of him, and then the flash of crimson brake lights in the early morning dark. The big Mercedes Sprinter in front of him was slowing, and Fred tapped his brakes, too, slowing his car as his mind left Polynesia behind and started to focus on putting together the pieces of what he'd just seen.

CHAPTER THREE

Cathy Jang-Peters

"Dammit!" Cathy hurriedly put her tumbler down, managing to thumb the lid closed as she braked, the car threatening to slew to the right.

It was a flat tire. She'd heard it go, but couldn't believe it. The pop had not been subtle. Nor had the sudden jerk of the wheel as her car threatened to go off road and down the abrupt drop to the field below the shoulder.

A few years ago VA-28 had been a rural road. The continued, rapid expansion of Washington DC had pushed people out into places like Manassas in order to afford to live here, and now the road carried thousands of people per day. Infrastructure hadn't quite caught up with the needs, and so as Cathy pulled over, she felt the also-not-subtle thump of her tires leaving the pavement, the shoulder ending abruptly.

"No, no, no," Cathy moaned as she let the BMW drift to a stop on the shoulder. Damn.

Figured. Just a couple weeks to go and she'd picked up a nail in her tire or something. Well, there was nothing for it. She'd have to give Shane a call and–

A flash of headlamps in her rearview mirror made her stop halfway to reaching for her purse and the cell phone within. That big van had pulled in behind her, slightly more on the road than she was. In her sideview mirror she could see a shadowed figure get out and stop behind her.

One nice thing about moving out here? The people were pretty decent. She'd lost count of the number of times she'd seen someone pulled over and another person pulling in behind them or slowing beside them to make sure they were all right.

Cathy opened her door as another car pulled slowly by. There were actually two vehicles stopped behind her, she noted as she got out. The van, and an older sedan just behind it. "I'm fine," she said, waving to the man standing just outside the van. "Just picked a flat or something."

"Do you need any help?" he asked. He had a little bit of an accent, and familiar at that. Cathy's parents were Chinese; she'd recognize the accent anywhere.

"I'm just going to call my husband once I make sure it's a flat," she said, nodding at the shadowed man, who kept his distance. That was nice of him. She circled around to the rear passenger side. Yep, the rim was buried in the dirt, the rubber flattened entirely on the bottom side. "Damn," she muttered to herself. Well, she'd have to call Georgetown, too–

Cathy looked up, a sudden flash of motion sending a tingling feeling down her spine. The guy – that shadowy guy – he was standing behind her. "Hey, wha–"

That was all she got out before he stuffed something – cloth, stinking of a heavy chemical scent – in her face.

The darkened sky swirled around Cathy, and all the energy left her limbs. She swayed, fell, and the man caught her as the sky closed in.

CHAPTER FOUR

Fred Brooks

"What in the poxy pits of hell...?"

Fred had pulled in well behind the Mercedes van, killing his lights as he did so. He could see just fine by the bright white ones that the van was sending out, illuminating the BMW ahead, the one that had lost its tire. Fred had mostly pulled in as a courtesy. He always did, when he saw someone on the side of the road, just in case they didn't have cell phone service. That was an artifact of his upbringing, back before cell phones.

He'd done just that, here, and was about ready to pull out once he saw the gentleman get out of the van to go help. Still, something had held him in place. Maybe that flash across the field he'd seen right before the BMW lost the tire and started to swerve.

Fred Brooks had done twenty in the Marine Corps, retired at age 38, then embarked on his second career as a database administrator. He hadn't started as that, but he'd grown into the role. He had the full Marine pension, and was heading rapidly toward his second retirement. He was looking forward to it, at 58, fully aware that he had more days behind him at this point than ahead.

But old habits died hard, and Fred had been a Marine gunnery sergeant. He'd fought in Desert Storm. Still carried a 1911, his preferred sidearm of choice, in the glove box. Just in case. Arlington wasn't the same as it had been twenty years ago, after all.

He was parked far enough back to see the lady get out and check her car. He saw the man from the van zip up to her, too, almost too fast to be believed. One of those metahumans, his brain informed him, as he went for the glove box. He saw the white cloth dangle from the man's hand, saw the door of the van open on the passenger side, a couple more shadows getting out–

Fred was out in a hot second himself, adrenaline firing, old instincts, all that training coming back to him. He circled around behind his own Buick and got into cover behind the trunk. He may have been getting old, but his hands didn't shake when he raised his 1911. "Put the lady down!" he shouted, drawing a bead on the fellow who had grabbed her. She was limp in his arms.

The other men, the ones that had just come out of the van, both looked at him. Only for a second, though, and then they went for their weapons–

Fred aimed for center mass, giving the trigger a squeeze. He'd taught a generation of Marines at Camp Pendleton how to shoot, and it had not left him, though it had been about six months since his last range trip. Two shots ripped into the chest of the nearest target, then he switched and drilled two more into the second. That man had pulled out a pistol from his waistband, but didn't even have a chance to clear it before he dropped.

Fred kept in cover, but drew his bead on the third man, the one with the woman in his arms. Here he had to be more careful. There was a hostage, after all–

The third man dropped the woman from the BMW, throwing his hands up. A flare of light made Fred duck, instinctively. It was orange and bright, and that fellow's silhouette seemed to change. Fred fired off a high shot as he went into cover behind his trunk.

Fred didn't sink all the way down, just squatted with his

sights still on target, at the shadowed man. That orange flash grew for a moment – two flashes, then, the man's eyes going bright and fiery like his eyeballs were about to explode into flames–

Then they faded, and he turned and fled, bolting across the field to their right so quickly that Fred could barely keep his pistol on target. Ten seconds and the man – demon, maybe, with that fire coming out of his eyes – had disappeared into the woods across the field, to about where that shot had come from.

Fred circled back to his driver's side, keeping the vehicle between him and the woods. He ducked all the way over, not wanting to provide a target for the sniper over there. They were probably gone, given they hadn't shot at him during the action, but they could come back. He didn't want a bullet in his chest to be his warning.

Once he was safely behind cover, Fred snatched his cell phone out of his open door. Traffic had stopped in both directions on VA-28 now, and he huddled behind his vehicle. Hopefully that woman up there was okay. He'd try and check on her in a minute, but first he needed to do this, the most important thing he could, now that the shooting had stopped.

The phone was in his hand and dialed in a hot second. Now the shaking was starting, the adrenaline wearing off. Still, he got the phone up to his ear and squeezed it there, bringing his hand back to his pistol to steady in case he had to take another shot.

"911, what's your emergency?"

Fred tried to think of what he needed to say. There was a lot. A metahuman. Men with guns. A kidnapping. How was he going to get all that out, plus check on the woman? "I need police," Fred said, finally, "and an ambulance. We got a woman down. Someone tried to kidnap her." He swallowed, heavily, huddled behind the hood of his car. "I think it was a metahuman."

CHAPTER FIVE

Sienna Nealon

Driving out of Washington DC against morning traffic was my idea of heaven. Getting out of DC at all was actually my idea of heaven, especially since it was now mid-May, and the humidity was starting to settle on the former – and honestly, current – swampland that was our nation's capital.

Doing so with Kerry Hilton in the passenger seat, chattering her little millennial heart out as I drove?

A little less heavenly.

"So this guy, like, didn't even ask me out," Kerry said, shaking her head, face all askew. "DC guys, like, don't ask. They come at it all low-key, like, 'Hey, what are you up to tonight? There are some people getting together. Maybe you could come out.' And then you get there, and boom – no one's there but you and him. Have you noticed that?"

"I have not noticed that, no," I said, so glad my reflective aviator glasses could shield my eyes so as not to give away the fact they were rolling furiously. "I haven't exactly been in the dating pool here, though."

"You should stay out, definitely," Kerry said, evincing her

obvious disgust. "It's a toxic pool. Like radioactive. The men are all chicken shits and bullshit artists."

"Well, it is DC," I said. "Maybe they're all future politicians."

"Yes, I think that's it," Kerry said, nodding along. "All worried about their downside risk of humiliation. It's all about saving face. I mean, it's a little different on Tinder–"

"Yeah, I don't really care," I said, but she went on anyway as I took exit 53A off interstate 66 onto Virginia State Highway 28 south, green trees blowing soundlessly in the wind as my millennial sidekick went on.

She talked my ear off as the traffic slowed, clotting on the four-lane road. I hit the lights and siren myself, because she was too involved in telling me a story about some sexual non-conquest, and I rolled along the shoulder at about thirty to avoid smoking anyone who opened a door. I went as fast as I deemed safe, because there was not a chance in hell I was going to spend one minute more in the car with Kerry Hilton than I had to.

Seeing flashing lights ahead came as a great relief. The local police had closed one side of the highway, and thus the traffic jam. A sheriff's deputy was managing traffic as the four lanes merged to two, creating a zipper-merging mess in both directions. Driving on the grass, I was immune to all that. I pulled off next to an ambulance in the middle of the cluster of law enforcement vehicles, killed the siren but left the flashers going, and bailed out in the middle of one of Hilton's sentences. Something about a malfunctioning diaphragm that I really didn't need overshared.

The scene was a hot mess, both literally and figuratively. Even though it was May, summer was well underway in Northern Virginia, and I felt it as I strode across the highway, cars honking as the sheriff's deputy stopped them to let me pass. Kerry Hilton struggled along behind me, prompting a fresh bevy of honks as the already strained patience reached critical mass and found an auditory outlet.

"Could you slow down just a little?" Kerry called to me as I made my way over to the plainclothes officer standing in the middle of it all. She was in charge and it was obvious, hair a little gray over her ears, watching my approach cool as a cucumber.

"Nealon, FBI," I said, going formal as I offered my hand to her.

"Stacks, Prince William County Sheriff's Department," she said, giving me a brisk shake.

"Hilton," Kerry said, rushing to get her hand in there.

Stacks gave her a once-over, found her lacking, then turned to me. "911 call at about 5:30 this morning from a Fred Brooks," she nodded to an older, African-American gentleman in a shirt and tie who was standing by the side of the road with a couple local deputies talking, "who witnessed the occupants of this van pull over next to this BMW," she nodded at each exhibit in turn, "which developed a flat tire after Brooks said he observed what appeared to be muzzle flash across that field." She pointed helpfully.

I raised an eyebrow. "Was it really muzzle flash?"

"We did find disturbed ground where he pointed us," Stacks said, as though having to concede something painful. "But no shell casings, and we haven't found a bullet yet."

"Wow," I said, looking at the BMW. "That's strange. But I was promised metahumans, so tell me how this involves me."

Stacks evinced a little annoyance at me rushing her along. "When the driver got out of the car, she was chloroformed by the occupants of the van." She nodded at a rag that was on the ground, marked by a yellow evidence tent bearing a 1. "Mr. Brooks pulled his gun and asked them to stop. They tried to draw on him," she nodded to a couple bodies covered by white sheets on the side of the van, "he dropped them. Third suspect had fire coming out of his eyes," she nodded to Brooks, "according to the witness, then sprinted across the field and disappeared in ten seconds flat."

I looked over the field. It was a hundred yards, easy. "That's a metahuman sprint time all right. The fire eyes thing is interesting, too."

"What type is that, you think?" Hilton was all up at my elbow like an eager little puppy.

"Who's the vic?" I asked, ignoring my partner in hopes she'd control her bladder if I didn't give her attention. "And where is she?"

"One Cathy Jang-Peters," Stacks said, nodding at an ambulance parked on the shoulder. "Adjunct professor at Georgetown. Chinese history, I think." She fished out a little notebook, flipped to the middle and read for a second. "Yes. That's it."

"Huh," I said, and looked at the sheet-covered bodies before making my way over. The van was big, white, one of those models used as work trucks for electricians or for delivery services. "Got a registration on this?"

"Tags are stolen," Stacks said. "VIN suggests it's registered to a corporation in Delaware: HDRKVC Corp."

"Front company for somebody?" I asked, squatting to lift one of the stained sheets. "Or do they actually do something?"

"No website, the storefront is empty," Stacks said. "Ten other companies are registered to the same address."

"So it's a front," I said, and looked at one of the downed kidnappers. "Curiouser and curiouser." I took a step over and lifted the second sheet. "I don't mean to be a racist, but I think I detect an ethnic pattern among these perpetrators."

"They're Asian," Hilton said, still dangerously close to my shoulder.

"As is the vic," Stacks said coolly, looking at Hilton. She was black, Stacks and I were white. It was just safer for her to make that observation aloud.

"Any ID on these guys?" I asked.

"Nope," Stacks said.

"Hm," I said, dropping the second sheet. I beckoned to a guy standing a little ways off with a gurney. "You can have the ME take them away now. I'm curious about tattoos and other identifying marks."

"Aren't we all," Stacks said dryly, and nodded at the guys I'd beckoned to.

"Victim know these guys at all?" I asked, making my way back to Stacks.

She shook her head. "I took a picture of their faces and showed her. She said she didn't recognize them. She's pretty disoriented, though, even now. Chloroform does a real number on you."

"Anything else of interest before I start making my rounds?" I asked.

"Perps had Glocks," Stacks said, reading off her notebook. "Model 19's, if that helps. Stolen."

"Common as dirt. Your people take a look at that tire yet?" I pointed at the BMW.

"It's definitely popped," Stacks said. "It'll take ballistics work, but preliminary suggests it was probably shot out. Small caliber, either .22 or .223 is what our guy says. Oh – and there was duct tape and zip ties in the van."

"Oh my," I said, glancing at the van again. It looked new. "Sounds like one of your dates, Hilton." She made a noise of irritation behind me. "Does the van have a GPS?"

Stacks gave me a ghost of a smile for the first time since I'd arrived. "Yeah. We're getting a warrant to release the GPS records."

I made a fist and raised it. "Rock on, Stacks. Great work. Let me talk to the witnesses and tell me immediately if that warrant comes through."

Stacks just nodded. "Sure," and she peeled off to go do her thing.

CHAPTER SIX

"Sir," I said, approaching the older black gentleman who'd been talking to the sheriff's deputies before he saw me coming and cut it off. "I'm Sienna Nealon."

"I know you," he said, offering me a hand and shaking. "Fred Brooks."

"Well, I'm glad to meet you," I said. "You called this in?"

"A-yep," he said, slow drawl coming out as he hooked his thumbs in his belt loops. He had a little belly on him, a bit past his prime, but he still looked like the kind of guy you wouldn't want to tangle with unless you had superpowers. "Saw the whole thing while I was driving. Pulled over to see if I could help with the flat tire. Didn't quite connect the flash to the flat, at least at first. Then those fellas popped out and tried to grab the lady, and I just...well, old habits die hard, you know?"

I knew. "You retired from the service?"

"Yes, ma'am," he said, and his chest puffed out a little. "I was a gunnery sergeant. Marine Corps."

"Semper Fi, gunny," I said. "I took a look at your handiwork. Were you back here by your car when you opened fire?"

"Yes, ma'am," Brooks said, and pointed to his vehicle's trunk. "I was behind cover right there."

"Nicely done." I eyeballed it; it was a good thirty feet and he'd pegged both those guys in the 10 ring. "What were you shooting?"

"Colt 1911," he said with a trace of pride. "Used it in the service when I first went in, before they switched to those damned Berettas. Never could accustom myself to those."

"A classicist, huh?" I smiled. "Really good work there."

Brooks puffed up a little more. "Thank you."

"Did you follow this van for long?" I asked.

"I don't rightly know," Brooks said. "Probably been behind them since at least Yorkshire. I was really into my audiobook so I didn't much take notice. I was in the right lane the whole way. They were ahead of me for a bit, but I couldn't say how long."

I nodded, giving it a little thought. "Did you hear a gunshot when you saw the flash?"

Brooks thought about it a second. "No. No, I would have known if I'd heard a shot. My book wasn't turned up that loud."

That was interesting. I looked across the field again; he would have heard the crack of a rifle, even in his car, unless it was turned down. Most likely a suppressor plus a subsonic round. Unless it was something else entirely, as in not a bullet. "I'd say you did your good deed for the day, sir." I gave him a smile. "Let the officers know if you think of anything else?"

"Yes, ma'am," he said, offering me a thumbs up.

I walked away, almost bumping into Hilton as she hurried to clear out of my path. She leaned in to whisper to me. "You think he's telling the truth?"

I waited a few steps until we were well out of Brooks's earshot before answering, mostly because I didn't want him to feel insulted by Hilton's question. "Yeah, he seems on the level to me. No signs of lying, and he gets the presumption of good faith from me because of his service." We went past the dead bodies, red stains starting to spread on the white sheets that covered them over. The medical examiner was preparing his gurney to pick them up, and the smell was already getting a little ripe.

"But he shot these guys," Hilton said in a hushed whisper.

"And if he hadn't, he'd have gotten drilled himself," I said, making my way toward the open ambulance where our victim waited, looking a little woozy. She had a plastic oxygen mask in her hand, like she'd used it some recently, and I caught hints of the chloroform even at this distance and after the paramedics had surely cleaned her off. She'd gotten a stiff dose, I gauged, if that much was lingering in the air even after this long. "Plus, our vic would have been kidnapped."

"I guess," Hilton said. "It just weirds me out when citizens try to do our job for us."

"He served and protected better than we could have," I said. "We're cleanup and investigation, Hilton. Cops are barely ever there when things go down and it's lucky if we are. We catch the bad guys after the fact – if at all. I say good for Gunny Brooks. He probably saved this lady's life."

We cut it off as we approached the victim. She'd locked eyes with me as I came up, head bobbing slightly, eyes looking a little watery.

"Hey," I said, "how are you feeling?"

"Like I took a snort of Drano right up the nose," she said, blinking a few times at me. "Hey, aren't you...?"

"Yeah," I said. "Are you Cathy?"

She nodded slowly. "Cathy Jang-Peters." She looked around dazedly. "Have you seen my husband? He's supposed to be on the way."

I made a show of looking around, then settled my gaze on the line of cars logjammed in our lane. "If I had to guess, he's probably stuck in traffic." Turning back to her, I asked, "Mind if we talk real quick?"

She took a quick snort of the oxygen. "Sure, but I don't know if there's anything I can tell you that I didn't already tell the other detective."

"Can you think of a reason anyone would want to kidnap you?" I asked, going for the basics anyway.

Cathy Jang-Peters shook her head slowly. "I'm an adjunct college professor at Georgetown. Unless one of my students commissioned someone to kidnap me because I graded them too harshly, I honestly have no idea."

"Are there any students you can think of that'd have an axe to grind?" I asked, maintaining eye contact and giving her a gentle smile. I was coaxing, trying to get her to give me anything. If she knew literally nothing about why this was happening, it'd probably be obvious, because it was much harder to lie or be guileful under the influence of chloroform.

"No, not really," she said. "I teach mostly juniors and seniors, and have a very limited class load. I'm not sure I even have anyone failing my classes at present." She gave it a moment's thought. "No. No, I don't think...no one's failing."

Scratch that one. "Is there anyone professionally that you're having a problem with? Or personally?" I glanced back down the slow-moving line of cars. "Everything going all right at home?"

Cathy snorted a laugh. "Other than my husband convincing me to move out to the sticks, everything's fine at home. And no, I can't think of any enemies that would sic a group of kidnappers on me."

"Family money?" I asked. "Shot in the dark, but..."

She shook her head again. "My parents are first generation immigrants from China. They came over after Tiananmen Square with nothing. Both are college professors. My in-laws are farmers a few hours southwest of here. They have good years and bad, and have made it through a lot, but they're not exactly running a huge agribusiness. So...no to your question."

"Hm," I said, trying to think of anything I'd missed. Money was the biggest motive for kidnapping, followed by personal reasons. If no one in her family had money or an axe to grind, I was hard pressed to figure out why she had a professional kidnapping squad complete with a metahuman come after her. "If you think of anything else, let the officers know."

"Sure," she said, then raised her eyes, a little sluggishly, to meet mine. "Have you ever heard of anything happening like this before? Metahumans kidnapping a regular person?"

I paused, really trying to give it some thought before answering. "It's unusual, but metahumans are people like any other. It seems like this is a well-planned attempt, though. Professional to the max, and it only failed because there was a retired Marine that just happened to be behind you today. So, to answer your question – no, this is new. But we're going to find out why it happened, don't worry." I forced a tight smile. "Until then, it's probably best if you have local police watching out for you." I caught Stacks's eye from across the scene. She was beckoning.

With a last nod, I disengaged from my conversation with Cathy and headed toward Stacks. When I got close enough, she arched her eyebrows. "A couple things just came through – first, the warrant is approved. We should have GPS data on where that van has been in the next little while."

I nodded. "What else?"

"We sent searchers into the woods," Stacks said, nodding in the direction where the putative shot had come from to pop Cathy Jang-Peters's tire. "They found fresh tire tracks on a dirt path about a mile away. Looks like our sniper and metahuman had an escape vehicle waiting."

CHAPTER SEVEN

I hiked across the field under the hot morning sun, Hilton struggling along in my wake. I wasn't a forensic guru, but I did want to see for myself both the scene of the sniper's nest and the dirt road where the getaway car had been parked. A helicopter chopped overhead, sweeping the area and hopefully ensuring that our perps were not still close at hand.

"Can you just...wait up?" Hilton puffed from behind me.

"No," I said. "Go get the car and find the entry to the dirt road Stacks mentioned, will you? I might need a quick pickup from there."

"I don't have the keys," Hilton whined.

Barely looking back, I turned and tossed her the keys. She fumbled them, of course, in spite of my perfect throw. I might have put a little heat on them, but only because she was both annoying and deserved it.

That settled, I broke into a metahuman-speed jog and left Hilton behind, disappearing under the canopy of trees in seconds. The shade brought the temperature down by at least ten degrees, but I was already sweating and the air was heavy with moisture. I found the cops hanging around the sniper's spot and gave it a quick look.

It looked like someone had gone prone here. Eyeing the

distance to the BMW, I thought the shot was decent, but not exactly professional quality. I didn't take Stacks at her word about there being no visible shell casing, but after a couple good minutes of looking, I had to concede that she was probably right. Most likely, the shooter had used a bolt action and not chambered a second round. No ballistics to be found here. They might still turn up the bullet, which had either lodged in Cathy Jang-Peters's car or traveled beyond. I had my doubts they'd ever find it if it hadn't stopped in the BMW.

Getting a quick directional point from the officers at the scene, I trotted off toward the dirt road where they'd found the tire tracks. I marked it on my map and sent the location to Hilton via phone. She didn't acknowledge, presumably because she was driving. Not that she was the sort to put down her phone while driving.

Jogging through the woods was surprisingly peaceful, if a little steamy. My boots were laced nice and tight, and the topography was mild hills, changes of altitude no more than about twenty-five feet, total, from hilltop to gully. I crossed three or four of those sort of slopes on my traversal, stopping and checking my GPS every couple hundred yards to adjust my course.

It was a lovely forest of aging pines, sweet scent filling the air, needles covering the ground along with the decayed remnants of whatever had been left over from last fall. My boots crunched as I went. I broke a heavy sweat about halfway to the road. Not because of the exertion of the hills, but because of the warmth. I checked my weather app and it informed me that it was 85 degrees Fahrenheit but felt like 92. The humidity was thick and only getting worse as the sun rose higher.

About two hundred feet from the road I came out of the cover of trees and found a couple sheriff's cars parked ahead, khaki-uniformed deputies holding court just outside of a yellow taped-up crime scene. I slowed when I got close and ducked under to take a peek at the tire tracks.

Well, they were tire tracks, all right. A cursory examination suggested to me a sedan, though it was just a guess. It looked like someone had parked here when the ground was still wet from morning dew or a light rain that had come in the night, very clear indications from when they'd driven in on the right side of the road. They'd driven out under slightly less damp conditions on the left side of the road, and those tracks were less clear.

My big government SUV appeared ahead, turning the corner through a densely packed copse. I heard it coming a little before I saw it, Hilton taking her sweet time, like she was afraid she'd run off the road into a ditch and get assaulted by hillbillies or something.

The deputies just nodded to me as I passed and I returned the courtesy. A text lit up my phone.

GPS data – Stacks.

With it came a file that I opened. It popped up a map, with lines drawn all over the Northern Virginia and DC metro. The finish was obvious, a blue line terminating on VA-28 just out there across the woods I'd just traversed.

I zoomed in, peering at the most recent destination. It seemed to be a residential area a little farther south, in Manassas. A flag there suggested the van had been idle in that location for just under an hour. I texted Stacks a quick inquiry, snapshotting it and sending it along, then continued following the trail on my screen.

The blue line led back to DC, to some commercial zone therein. A flag on the map suggested the van had been parked at a location in that area for twelve hours. Looking closer, I switched to my own mapping app as Hilton rattled the SUV to a stop beside me.

"These are rough roads," Hilton said as I swung into the passenger side and closed the door. My phone buzzed with a response from Stacks.

Jang-Peters says the location where the van waited is at the end of her driveway.

That was interesting. I flipped back to my mapping app, inputting the second address, where the van had spent twelve hours the previous day and into last night.

It popped up quickly: *Save Much Furniture Store*. In DC proper.

"What?" Hilton asked as I hit the button to *Get Directions*.

"What is it?"

"Our next stop," I said, as the GPS voice chimed in and told us to turn around. "Let's go."

CHAPTER EIGHT

Driving back into DC was not nearly as heavenly as leaving, but at least we'd managed to avoid rush hour. We hit the Key bridge over the Potomac just before 10 a.m., and followed the GPS to a commercial development that was technically just over the DC boundary in Maryland, reaching the Save Much Furniture Store just after 10:30.

"Drop me around back," I said, casing the place as we went through the parking lot. It was a decaying strip mall of the kind you could find in almost every suburban area: bright paint colors that had faded with seasonal wear, empty spaces punctuated by the usual assortment of coffee shops and overnight gyms farther down the line. "I want you to go in and look around. Don't flash your badge unless you have to."

"What are you going to do?" Hilton asked with just a little alarm as we pulled around the back. The Save Much was an anchor tenant of this particular strip center, with the largest retail space in the building and taking up the far left side of it. Behind the furniture store was a wooded area, and the parking lot had three whole cars in it, indicating this was not a hotly trafficked place.

"So little trust from my associates," I said, checking my sidearm as I opened the door, as though it had vanished in transit. Of course it was still there, still loaded. One of the cars back here was an older model Ford Taurus, a sedan that would easily fit the vague and fuzzy mold we had for the getaway car. I looked at the tires; they were a little dusty, but not out of line with what you'd find on any car, really. No proof there.

"Maybe it's you checking your gun as you get out of the car that instills so very little faith in me," Hilton said.

"That should absolutely instill confidence in you," I said, flashing a grin as I eyed the loading dock at the back of the store. "It says, 'I'm not going to get blindsided.' Which is important for you, too, partner, since without me you're a lot more likely to get wiped out by a stray meta."

Hilton cringed, and I shut the door on her as I leapt up onto the loading dock. There was an overhead metal cargo door, and a standard swing-open person one. I tested the handled one first.

Unlocked. Lucky me.

Slipping into the back of the furniture store, I found myself in a darkened storeroom. Dim lamps were lit overhead, giving me a hazy view of a seemingly never-ending canvas of furniture, furniture, and more furniture. Couches lay to my left, dining room tables to my right. Beds and mattresses stood in order like files in a cabinet at my two o'clock. Rows of end tables were stacked neatly at my ten o'clock.

Not a soul in sight, I reflected, checking the shape of the building. It ended a couple hundred feet ahead of me, big swinging doors leading out to the showroom, where light flowed in as though the rest of the building was a normally lit space instead of being on power reserve like this room was. To my right, past the dining room tables, there seemed to be a room built into the corner, likely for the break room and employee bathrooms.

I headed in that direction, my jacket pulled back so I could draw my pistol quickly if need be.

There was a lot of furniture in this place, but most of it seemed to be of the same exact product lines. I passed eight of the same dining room table in a row, clueing me in that it was definitely mass manufactured. The room was a little too dim and my eye for aesthetics a little too weak to tell, but I suspected that the rest of the furniture in the place was of a similar bent.

Save Much had very few manufacturers, and just kept in stock the most popular SKUs of furniture, but in bulk.

I listened in the dark, but the only sound I heard was the sound of muzak playing out in the showroom. Hopefully Hilton was in by now, casing the place and maybe even kicking up a little attention. If she caught anyone's interest in a bad way, I suspected I'd see a corresponding flurry of activity as someone came back here into the break room area to warn whoever was in charge.

I paused, looking around again. There was no manager's office back here. Maybe it was out front?

What did I know about furniture store design? Maybe there was no manager's office. Either way, I kept on target, making sure my footsteps stayed soft and quiet.

When I was about twenty feet from the "break room," I started to hear voices. They were raised, and not speaking English.

I kept my hand on my pistol, but I didn't draw it yet. Technically, I was out of bounds here, though them not locking their door was hardly my fault. I didn't have probable cause, but this wasn't exactly trespassing, either. All a store employee had to do was ask me to leave and I'd be compelled to do just that, bounced until I got a warrant to search the place. Since all I'd seen so far was tons of furniture, I didn't have a lot of legal ground to stand on. Maybe a judge would nod and approve a warrant based on the thin gruel of the van being parked here overnight, but maybe not. The kidnappers could have just as easily decided to sleep in the van and picked the most convenient parking lot they could find.

So I needed to confirm or deny that this place was linked to the crime, and quickly, before I got caught. Relying on the kindness of strangers as I prowled around the back room of their store may have worked for Blanche DuBois, but Sienna Nealon didn't tend to put her faith in that. I counted on the viciousness of people, and had seldom been disappointed.

The voices grew louder as I got closer, but my ability to interpret whatever language they were speaking was still nil, so the increased volume didn't help me a bit. Someone was mad, but whether it was a kidnapper's boss for the failure of his hires or just a furniture store owner mad about low sales was up in the air. I wasn't much of a linguist, either, but I was able to rule out Spanish, German and a few Western European languages from being in play here.

My foot hung on something, and I nearly tripped. Stopping just in time, I looked down to find a rolled-up rug that had been felled from a plastic-wrapped, stacked forest of them. Lacking meta reflexes, I would have gone down like a tree. As it was, the tip of my shoe squeaked on the plastic.

I paused, listening, but heard nothing save for the angry imprecations of whoever was in the room ahead. They'd left the door very slightly open, just a crack, and light flooded out into the dim storeroom. I stayed very, very still just a few more seconds to make sure that, no, they hadn't stopped whatever was going on in there while I minded my footing.

Beginning my creep anew, I sidled up to the door. This part of the store didn't seem to have air conditioning, but a residual trace must have seeped in from the showroom floor, because it wasn't as desperately hot and stuffy as outside. I stacked up outside the door, debating whether to draw my gun. I really couldn't, though; legally I would be on quicksand to do so before I had a reasonable element of threat presented, especially given the legally questionable circumstances of my search here.

So I put my back to the wall, feeling the sweat dotting my back press into my blouse as I listened to the angry, foreign words of the ranting speaker within. I listened, listened...

I was getting nothing from this except older. After about ten seconds, I decided to just press on. Planting a hand on the door, I shoved it open and stepped inside.

CHAPTER NINE

I stepped into a room that did indeed have the characteristics one might find in a break room. The muffled speaker I'd heard from outside was one of three guys inside. They were clustered around a beaten-up circular table that looked like it was remaindered from World War II era furniture. An old fridge waited in the corner, and gray, beaten cabinets lined two walls.

That was where the comparisons to a break room stopped, however.

There was a bulletin board to my left, but instead of the normal, OSHA-approved notices, there were pushpins securing full color pictures of a house in the country, a familiar BMW, and head shots of our victim, Cathy Jang-Peters.

"That's probable cause," I said, drawing my Glock as the three men in the break room exploded into action around me.

The two to my left – the ones listening – were dressed in suits, a little too high-class to be furniture salesmen in this joint. They both went for their belts, and it didn't take a genius law-woman to figure out they were going for their guns.

I got to mine first.

"No!" I shouted at both of them, my Glock aimed at the chest of the first one. "Don't do it!"

The last thing I needed was an agent-involved shooting right now, but the good news was that I'd pulled before either of them.

The bad news was that the boss man, standing to my right, didn't go for a gun.

The worse news? His eyes started to glow.

Like fire.

"Oh, sh–"

I didn't even get the entire word out before the guy snapped toward me, his body distorting like something out of a horror movie.

Out of the corner of my eye I could see the guys to my left taking advantage of the distraction and drawing their guns; to my right the metahuman was charging. My pistol was pointed in the wrong direction to deal with him, both hands on it, ready to fire, and I split my decision just a second too long–

The metahuman kidnapper, now looking like a dark silhouette in the middle of the well-lit room, barreled into me before I could even raise an arm in defense. I felt the power of the strike run through my body as my feet left the ground and I flew through the air. I smashed through the drywall and tumbled into the darkness of the warehouse, my only guide the light spilling in from the break room.

CHAPTER TEN

My landing was hard, but broken by a couple of recliners. Still hurt, pain spasming down my back, but I retained consciousness.

I lost my gun, though. Pretty typical for when one has been thrown through a wall, I would imagine.

This wasn't the kind of hit one just popped up from. Something in the vicinity of my rib cage was badly bruised, if not broken, though I hadn't heard anything snap during my tumble or landing, probably because the sound of me crashing through furniture covered it up.

Numbness danced down the fingertips of my left hand. There was a clouded darkness around me, and not just from the lack of light in the storeroom. I'd taken a bump to the head and was probably concussed. I recognized the sensation. I should, by now; I'd certainly been hit in the head enough.

Something dark and inky appeared out of the darkness, punctuated by two bright spots of fire, like torches glowing in the night.

It was the bad guy, standing atop a footstool.

"Oh, look," I said, "it's the Sultan of the Ottoman Empire."

He cocked his head at me, distracted by my brilliant banter and terrible punning. Then he looked down and realized he was standing on an ottoman. As the recognition dawned in his fiery eyes, I kicked it out from under him.

The big guy took a tumble, slamming to the ground. Either the clarity of my vision improved, or his closeness made it easier to see him, but either way, suddenly I knew what I was looking at.

He'd transformed – transmogrified, really – from a normal-looking dude into some sort of Kafka-esque beetle with flame eyes. He had blackened shell plates across his chest, and the same sort of material formed a helm on his head. I couldn't see the rest of him, but I suspected he was similarly clad all over, his metahuman power apparently to grow armor plating.

As he hit the ground, I swung a kick at him. It didn't do much against that armor – it made a solid noise, like I'd banged my steel-toed boot against a metal drum – but it did send him sliding away into the legs of a dining table that promptly broke, thumping the tabletop into him.

"Gonna squash you like the cockroach you are," I muttered, ears still ringing. I swung an arm down and planted a hand to throw myself back to my feet.

Thudding footsteps in the dark prompted me to abandon that plan. The two other guys were just beyond my landing zone, and I could see them raising their guns in the dark.

I flung myself over and behind a nearby armoire. The gunshots exploded in the cavernous storeroom like summer thunder ripping off next to my ear. The flashes were like lightning in the dark, strobing brightly, blinding me. I had my fingers in my ears, huddled behind a thick piece of furniture, getting showered by splinters thrown off by each shot.

"Nothing is ever easy," I said, fumbling at the small of my back for my spare pistol. It was a personal weapon, a Sig Sauer P365 I'd bought after getting a chance to try the weapon out in Nashville. It was fully loaded with the twelve-round magazine, ready to rock. I waited for the fire to subside enough that I could lean out and take my shot.

It didn't subside.

The gunmen had training. One was keeping the pressure on me, and as soon as he stopped to reload, the other guy started pouring it on. I could tell they were circling around, trying to flank my cover so they could bust a cap in my ass without an armoire to stop them. It was good tactics.

It was also not the sort of thing your typical street thug kidnapper would do without having to at least yell out the plan first.

These guys did it without a word spoken between them. Unless there was a telepath linking their minds, I was dealing with professional soldiers. Ex-cops, at least. Someone with training that was not to be found on your garden-variety crook.

I had to think fast, and unfortunately, thanks to the fuzz in my brain, I came up with nothing good. I'd need to open up on whoever came into my line of fire, and I'd have to do it quickly because his partner would be lining up a second or so later. I'd need to make a split shot; kill one of them or at least drive him behind cover, then bring my gun around one hundred and eighty degrees and take out the second attacker.

Oh, and there was still a beetle-shelled, fire-eyed metahuman somewhere in the mix, probably getting up from where I'd waylaid him with nothing but some irritation to show for my gambit.

"Just another day in the life," I muttered, listening to the gunfire coming from my right. My guess was the guy to my left was just about to circle into view, and I made ready, preparing myself to switch fields of fire in case I judged wrong. Hopefully my metahuman speed would save me here.

It didn't.

As the guy came around to my left, I lined up my shot, putting the three dots on the sight in perfect alignment and squeezing the Sig's trigger. He jumped back before my first shot even left the barrel, though, wary and wise to my game. My bullets went harmlessly past him, my targeting lined up with where he should have been, now desperately off from where he actually was.

Once I knew he was committed to jumping back, and that he'd land off balance, I swung my gun around to deal with the other guy.

I didn't make it.

The armoire shattered as the metahuman in the equation, Mr. Firebeetle Bailey, smashed through it and wrapped a thick, armored wrist around my neck. An oily smell flooded my nasal passages as he gripped me tight in a choke hold. Out of the corner of my eye I caught motion as the flanker lined up his own shot.

It was easy. He was ten feet away and I was pinned against Firebeetle Bailey.

I was as good as dead.

CHAPTER ELEVEN

When you've got a hard arm pressed against your windpipe, there's not a lot you can do about it, especially if you're seated. Sure, there were a range of solid Jiu-Jitsu type throws and holds I could – and would – employ given a few seconds of time to act, but the tightness around my throat and the gun pointed straight at me told me I did not have seconds.

Without anything else to enter the equation, *X* plus *Y* equaled *I'm cooked*.

Staccato bursts of gunfire lit the room and I tensed unintentionally, girding myself uselessly against the bullets that were coming my way.

But they didn't come my way. The flashes of the gunshots went off, illuminating the scene in stark colors.

The gunman in front of me danced like someone had hooked a car battery up to his junk and was giving him the full jolt. He dropped a couple seconds later, but the gunfire continued unabated as I swept my gaze toward the source of the shots–

Hilton, coming into the room like a boss. Shit yeah, millennial. You show them.

I took advantage of the momentary distraction posed by my gun-toting colleague and reached up, planting my Sig against the head of Firebeetle Bailey. I shot twice before he smacked the gun out of my hand. Then he started to tighten his grip around my neck, and I had a bad feeling I knew what was next.

Decapitation. Or a broken spine.

That wouldn't do at all.

I reached up, grabbing him firmly by the back of his neck, and jerked it down with all my weight. He was braced for pressure on his arm; a sudden, desperate, full-force yank on the top of his head? Well, he wasn't balanced for that.

He countered by trying to drag me back up, but I was ready for it. He lifted me off the ground just enough for me to get my feet beneath me. As soon as I did, I let the natural pendulum swing of momentum drop me back until all my weight and part of his was on the balls of my feet.

Then I leapt with everything I had, and suddenly he was riding the rocket of Sienna Nealon as we flew across the room.

I wasn't sitting idle as we launched through the storeroom, though. He still had a death grip on my neck, though it loosened somewhat in surprise when I sent us both flying. He had the most leverage, and all I had was a momentary distraction. I used it by adjusting my grip, shoving my hands between his arm and my throat, ramming my fingers up with all my meta strength.

I did a little cosmetic damage to the skin around my throat, but nothing too serious, and my fingers had snaked inside his chokehold, creating a small barrier to him choking me by the time we came in for a landing.

And by landing, I mean we hit the back wall of the building, Firebeetle Bailey first.

I slammed into him a second later, feeling absolutely zero give in his armored hide. He didn't so much as grunt as he absorbed the impact of me. Another second, and we started to tumble down.

Taking full advantage of this shift in the momentum, I thrust my feet out again and hit the wall behind us with both heels, pushing us both off. This time we tumbled, and Firebeetle did an unwitting somersault, putting him beneath me as we crashed into a pile of dressers. Wood shattered and groaned.

He did not let go of me, though. He kept that arm anchored around my neck, that same oily scent filling my nose.

That was okay. I ignored the initial landing pain as his steely carapace rammed into my back, thighs, even my left calf. As soon as we started to settle, I rolled my whole body and flipped, shoving hard with my hands to break his death grip as I did so.

Either because of the hard landing or because I caught him by surprise, he let go – barely. I safely rolled backward out of his grip and caught myself, albeit unsteadily, on my own two feet. I bobbled back a few steps, putting my dukes up and staring at the twin burning coals of his eyes.

"Yeah," I said, about two good seconds from keeling over from the battering I'd just taken trying to escape his death grip. "How do you like them apples?" I caught myself on an end table, barely keeping from keeling over in a pile of foot stools.

He must have thought them apples were just fine, because his response was to flip from his back to all fours and stare at me with those flaming eyes for about a second before throwing himself at the far wall again. He crashed through and daylight flooded in as he disappeared beyond that boundary.

"Oh, hell," I muttered, and hobbled toward the door at top speed. I just about shinned myself on a low table, shattering the glass and not giving the least of a damn. I burst out of the doors onto the loading dock to find–

He was gone. Sweat poured down my forehead, my back, my chest, which heaved taking in big breaths.

"You see him?" Hilton burst out of the doors behind me, gun in hand, sweeping left to right with squinted eyes against the sudden, invasive daylight.

"No," I said, looking to the expansive wood line to the left, pretty sure that if he'd run, I wasn't catching him, at least not in my current condition. Hell, I didn't even know if I could run him down on foot, nor if I could beat him if I caught him, given I was having a little trouble standing without swaying at present. His oily smell still hung in the air, though he was long gone. "He got away."

CHAPTER TWELVE

"That was some excellent timing," I said to Hilton in the midst of the swirl of police and FBI agents combing through the furniture store in the aftermath of our battle. "Not too shabby shooting, either."

"Thanks," Hilton said. She'd been pretty reserved after we'd called in backup. Something about killing a fellow human being brought on a heady air of reality, like a sudden pressure on your chest.

Or so I thought. It had been a long time since my first kill, and I'd left a rather long trail since, so the feeling didn't really come up on me anymore.

"We've got two furniture store employees up front for questioning, ma'am," Agent Santos of the FBI said. He'd shown up about ten minutes after the local police, dispatched from headquarters. Our other backup, Agent Holloway, had yet to show for whatever reason. Possibly hangover-related. Some rank and file agents like Santos, not from our division, had shown up, so the FBI was clearly flying the flag here.

"Thanks," I said, sitting next to Hilton on our SUV's open hatchback. "Can I question them?"

He nodded, then directed a look at Hilton. "You two need to separate anyway. Until we get statements, you know."

"It was a righteous shoot," I said, giving Hilton as close to an affirming look as I could. "Agent Hilton just saved my life."

"That's nice," Santos said. "But you're not allowed to talk to her again until we get both your statements, okay?"

"Yeah, yeah," I said, giving Hilton a last nod of encouragement as I headed into the store. Lucky for me I was such an important asset to the FBI that they didn't make me go through the post-shooting suspension and removal from duty that was common to most law enforcement agencies. Being just about the only person capable of doing my job had certain advantages, and not getting benched during crises just because I fired my weapon at people and occasionally killed them was definitely one of them, at least from my perspective.

Santos trailed behind me as I entered the store. My earlier suspicion was confirmed; they definitely put on the AC in the customer portion of the store, while leaving the back room in a nearly sweltering natural state.

"Here's our guys," Santos said, trying to catch up and overtake me so he could do the leading. I almost laughed under my breath at his little dominance game, but instead I just sped up my pace so he would have had to run to succeed at passing me. The look on his face when he realized what I did was hilarious.

"Hey guys," I said casually as I came up on the store employees. They were both Asian, just like all three perps we'd encountered in the back room and the two out in Virginia as well as the vic, which I found interesting. "How's everybody doing today? Good?"

I didn't expect much response to that, and boy did I get it. Hangdog looks from both of them. They wore dress shirts and ties fully buttoned with dress slacks, every piece of their ensembles off-the-rack and a size too big for them. They were both very slender, and the looks in their eyes as they took in my approach reeked of defeat.

Picking which of them to talk to first was an exercise in eenie meenie miney moe. There was roughly no difference in their attitudes; both looked to be in their early twenties, with black hair cut in almost the same style, and both seemed about a quarter second from hurling themselves over a bridge if a sufficiently high one suddenly presented itself.

"All right, you're with me," I said to the nearest, gently seizing his wrist and pulling him my way.

He offered no resistance, coming along like a whipped dog as I pulled him out of earshot of his colleague, who watched him go with marked disinterest, as though keeping an eye on a small argument between co-workers as it unfolded during lunch.

"What's your name?" I asked, trying to keep my voice in the range of "compassionate, yet tough," as I made him walk toward the storeroom. He complied easily.

"Ru Sung," he said in a low, dead voice. He hung his head as he walked.

"You know who I am, Ru?" I asked. He nodded pitifully, and that was it. "Do you know why I'm here?"

He lifted his head. We passed through the swinging doors into the back room, and he looked around as we did so, taking swift note of the giant hole in the break room wall. FBI agents and local PD were inside poking around, but he seemed unsurprised and not particularly reactive to this turn of events. "It's about our new arrivals," he said at last, in a voice heavily accented.

"Yep," I said. "How long have these guys been here?"

"Two weeks," Ru said, completely miserable.

I nodded. "What else do you know about these guys?"

"I don't know anything," he said. "Not their names, nothing. I have not met them or talked to them, just seen them. They don't tell me anything. They don't allow us in that room." He pointed to the break room. "All I do is my job – sell furniture. Then sell more furniture. Every day, so they don't send me back to China."

I raised an eyebrow at that. "Why would they send you back to China?"

The slump of his shoulders suggested there was not a lot of guile to be found in Ru. "I am here on an H-2B visa. Save Much sponsored me. Without their backing, I have to return."

"What's so bad about going home?" I asked, more because I was fishing than because I didn't know. I read pretty extensively about foreign affairs, and of all the big powers, China made me the most uneasy.

Ru stiffened, looking around like he was being watched. "Nothing," he said robotically, eyes flitting about looking for cameras or listeners. "I just...like it here."

I didn't feel like pressing the poor guy, so I let that one go. "How long have you been here?" I asked. "And how long have you been working for Save Much?"

"Twelve months," Ru said, back to quiet despair. "For both. I studied English in Tianjin and signed up with Save Much to bring me over." He looked around again. "Do you know if I can transfer to another Save Much location?"

"That's really a question for your boss," I said, pressing on. "Speaking of – who is your boss?"

"The store manager is Jiahao Lam," Ru said miserably. "He's not here today."

"You know where he lives?" Ru shook his head, so I asked another question. "Where do you live?"

He pointed toward the far wall. "Company apartment. Two miles that way. We all live there together. The workers, I mean."

That was unsurprising given his H-2B status. "How many of you?"

"Fifteen," Ru said. "In two apartments."

"You guys must be sleeping on mattresses on the floor," I said. "Do you know the address?"

He nodded, and I offered him my pad. He wrote down an address and I passed it to a local officer moving through from the break room. "Can you send a squad car over there and detain the occupants for questioning? It's where the store workers all live. H-2B visas, company housing."

The officer nodded and disappeared out the door, and I turned my attention back to Ru. "How are the working conditions here?" I asked.

Ru stiffened again. "Fine," he answered, a little too quickly.

"Mmhm," I said, again not pressing. I jotted a couple nothings down in my notebook. "What do you do in your off time?" I asked, looking back up at him.

Again, Ru froze. "Not...much," he finally said.

"How much do they pay you here?" I asked.

Ru stiffened further, making him look like his entire musculoskeletal system had gotten a good jolt of electricity. No answer was forthcoming.

"Where's your passport?" I asked, figuring I'd ease off on him on one vector of attack and see what I could pull up from another.

Once more he sagged, and his answer came mumbled, his eyes locked to the storeroom's dull concrete floor. "I...don't know."

I squeezed the notepad between my fingertips, leaving a nice impression of my thumb at the bottom corner. "The manager took your passport, didn't he?" I asked, trying to look him dead in the eyes. "This Jiahao Lam, right? As soon as you came over?"

If Ru had sagged any further, he would have melted into a pool on the floor. But he nodded, and I knew he wasn't lying.

"Okay," I said, giving him a pat on the arm. "You can go on back out there with your friend." I pointed him toward the doors. "Just–"

"Ma'am?" I turned to find a tall, black agent standing at the door to the break room. "You might want to come take a look at this."

I snagged a nearby chair and dragged it over, gesturing for Ru to have a seat. "Wait here," I said, and he sat down meekly. I made my way through the aisles of furniture, shooting only one look back at Ru before I made it to the break room door. "Need someone to come keep an eye on my witness," I said, and a local cop hurried to oblige me as I entered the swinging doors.

Every cabinet in the room had been opened since last I'd left through the giant hole in the wall that didn't look even a little Sienna-shaped. A variety of papers had been dumped out, and a lock box sat on the battered table in the middle of the room. It had been pried open, its contents dumped out across the surface.

And that...that caught my eye immediately.

Because in addition to a pile of US twenty-dollar bills that easily added up to a hundred K or more, there were dozens of red passports sitting on the table.

I sauntered up to the pile as Agent Santos handed me a pair

of latex gloves and I snapped them on, then picked up a handful of passports to leaf through.

"Well, here's Ru's," I muttered as I thumbed through the third in the stack. When I hit the fifth, I found a familiar face.

It was Firebeetle Bailey. "'Cheng Yu,'" I said, reading his name, and putting it off to the side.

Then I opened the next passport in the stack and got a rude surprise.

It was another one with "Cheng Yu," except here his name was listed as "Xue Wu." The next was for him as well, under another name. The next three were for someone else – one of the perps dead out in Virginia, I thought – and the rest of the pile was the same story. I'd hit a singleton from what I suspected was a store employee, like Ru, a captive of the store owner, then three with the same pictures – an operative like Firebeetle Bailey and the other kidnappers.

And every single passport was from the People's Republic of China.

CHAPTER THIRTEEN

I was still looking around the scene an hour or so later when my phone rang. I had filed an initial report with my boss's assistant, so the call wasn't entirely out of the blue, but still, when my phone lit up with the Caller ID note of *Heather Chalke*, I always had to mentally brace myself before answering the call.

"Hey, boss," I said, steeling myself for what could either be a quick and formal or long and uncomfortable conversation. With Chalke, it was a coin flip as to which I'd get. "What's up?"

"Just paged through your report from the scene," Chalke said, sounding brusque, business-like, and to the point. "What's your read on this situation?"

I paused, composing my thoughts. "Um, well," I said, "it's still forming in my head, but I have a couple of thoughts, I guess."

"Go," she said, sounding like she was reading something as she listened, like I didn't warrant her full attention.

Go? I shook my head as I stood in the back room of the furniture store, looking around to make sure no one was listening in. The cops were all still poking around the break room and the front of the store, though I had a feeling they'd start turning over furniture back here in case someone had written a coded message on a packing invoice or something. Being thorough was rather important in our line of work, after all.

"My thinking goes along a couple lines," I said, trying to put into words the ideas I'd had bouncing around in my head for the last hour. "One, that these kidnappers came into town with multiple passports because they're part of a Chinese criminal enterprise like the Triads, and their corruption has allowed them to take over a passport office somewhere in the country with impunity, get all the passports they want."

"Mmhmm," Chalke said. I could picture her nodding along as she...I dunno, trimmed her fingernails or approved color swatches for her condo on the other side of the call.

"But that's questionable," I said. "Option two is that the passports are fake. I sent an inquiry to the State Department, though, to go through channels to the People's Republic to ask about them–"

"You should have consulted with me before doing that." There was a dangerous edge to her voice, and now she seemed focused on me.

"Uh...sorry?" I was more perplexed than apologetic.

The storm in her voice passed quickly, though. "Go on."

"Anyway, I just wanted to see if the passports were legit and if we had records of the multiple personalities for our kidnappers entering the country," I said. "Or if they were sticking to traveling on one passport and using the others as backups in case of emergency or being outed. Regardless, haven't heard anything from State yet about their authenticity."

"Fine, fine," she said, and mostly, she sounded like it was. Chalke was a little bit of a cipher, except when pissed. Then it was very obvious what she was thinking. "Any other thoughts?"

"One," I said, kind of hesitating to say it because of the political implications. "But it's uncomfortable."

There was a pause. "When has 'uncomfortable' ever stopped you before?"

"Fair enough," I said. "What if the passports are real? All of them."

Chalke didn't reply at first. "That seems improbable. Corruption happens in the People's Republic all the time. Just a few years ago they had a poisoned milk scandal–"

"Yeah, I know," I said, feeling the discomfort build. I was fully aware I was voicing an uncomfortable sentiment in Washington politics right now. The elephant in the room that a lot of people didn't want to discuss: China's bad behavior. "But what if this is a sanctioned activity?"

"What you're suggesting," Chalke said, drawing out her words, "is that the People's Republic of China sent a squad of kidnappers into the US to abduct a college professor in Northern Virginia?"

"I'm not suggesting it," I said, aware of the thin ice I seemed to be perpetually skating on with my boss – well, always. "I'm just trying to float all the possibilities."

"What's the motive?" Chalke asked. "Because the act – doing that – would be cause for a major diplomatic incident. Maybe even war."

"I know, I know," I said, tiptoeing more than I would have a few months ago, when I'd been in New York, reporting to Willis Shaw. Life had been simpler then, before I'd been force-moved to DC and put under the not-so-gentle auspices of Director Chalke. "I don't have a motive. Hell, I don't even have all the kidnappers. All I have is a pile of passports that defies explanation and what looks like a professional snatch and grab that went wrong only because of random chance. That, plus the involvement of a meta..." I shrugged. "It all adds up to something, but I need more data."

"Why does the involvement of a meta matter?" Chalke asked. There was a steely heat in her voice.

I kicked myself for throwing that in. It was a thought that had been percolating in my head, though, and now it had to come out because trying to hold it in seemed unwise right now. "This might have happened before you got cleared into metahuman affairs, but back during the war, as one of his opening moves, Sovereign destroyed the official government facility for training and housing metahumans in China." I paused, letting that sit for a second. "It was suspected to be a special unit where the PRC trained metas for government service and it resulted in the deaths of pretty much their entire meta population."

"Interesting." Chalke was taking all this in, I could tell, because her voice no longer held the aura of distraction.

"Metas are – or at least were – pretty tightly leashed over there," I said. "If that move cost them almost all their meta numbers, and this guy is, in fact, a Chinese national? The smart money is that they know he's a meta, and that he's roped in with the government somehow. Which leads me to believe–"

"Understood," Chalke said. She paused for a second, then cursed under her breath. "All right. Well, a good portion of this is already in the open thanks to you passing it along to State. Nothing to be done about that now." She stopped again, tapping her fingers loud enough I could hear them on the other side of the call. "Okay. I need you at 1600 Pennsylvania in an hour for a briefing."

It took me a second to decode that. "You mean the White House?"

"Yes."

I tried not to frown, tried not to sigh. Failed the former, not the latter, fortunately, since she couldn't see me but could damned sure hear me. "Why?"

"Because I just got an email formally requesting your presence," Chalke said, icily. "Which tells me someone at State has already taken your inquiry and passed it up the chain. So get your ass over there and try to help me clean up this mess."

CHAPTER FOURTEEN

Julie Blair
Old Executive Office Building
Washington, DC

The email from the Department of State had been a hell of a thing. Julie Blair had grown used to being overworked, and being roped into all manner of communications from various cabinet departments and trying to coordinate the low-level executive functions of government so that the White House didn't get blindsided by the FBI making some discovery of a diplomat's corpse in Montana and not hearing about it until the State Department got an official inquiry from Rwanda wondering where their ambassador was. Mostly, though, her job was to put eyes on the communications of a thousand departments and find the diamonds within, the real value-add areas where she could pass along info that looked good for the Gondry administration. Or find the bad stories and find a way to file the edges off them before they became dangerous.

Overworked, underpaid, underslept, undersexed – keenly feeling it, especially lately – and missing her kids, Julie Blair's job was all this and much more. It kept her glued to her email day and night, even on those increasingly rare days off.

This State Department email about the pile of passports discovered in the raid on a DC furniture store? This was something.

She'd forwarded it up the chain as soon as she got it, then moved on to some serious business involving the Department of the Interior. Once she'd done her best to clear that, though, she came right back to the email from State and reread it, not something she usually did.

A few things drew her attention to it. One, it involved Sienna Nealon, who was definitely a hot topic. One minute she was a force for good, raising their profile in the world in the best possible ways. The next she was standing too close to a scandal, and getting painted by the stupidity of an outside contractor who made an inflammatory social media post. Either way, Sienna was always news when her name came up, and this time was bound to be no exception.

Second, though, and more interesting to Julie, it involved a stack of passports from the People's Republic of China that seemed to be the genuine article. The story was secondhand, but it sounded like it involved some element of human trafficking/near wage slavery via the visa process, plus a planned, violent kidnapping. And metahuman involvement.

As a story, it had it all, and she'd forwarded it to her boss immediately.

Maybe, if she was lucky, this one would get her noticed. She could use some attention, some help – hell, even a day off. The Gondry administration seemed to be perpetually running in every direction rather than trying to push one agenda item at a time, the way President Harmon had. No, President Gondry was trying to do it all, and Julie was on board with that. The world needed a lot of help. Though, privately, she sometimes wished he would focus more on a single area of policy and get some gains in that area before moving to another.

Still, the work had to be done. Putting aside the passports email, Julie drew a deep breath. Hopefully this would all turn out well. She had a feeling she hadn't heard the last of it, but a huge pile of unread emails had crushed in within the last few minutes, and so, with only a bit of regret, she clicked off the State email and went on to the next thing.

CHAPTER FIFTEEN

Jaime Chapman

It's time to play!

"I gotta step out for a second," Jaime Chapman said, glancing at his phone, then smiling up at the board of directors. "Please, continue without me."

There wasn't any protest; they'd been listening to quarterly results from the various divisions in the company, and there weren't any big surprises. Jaime strode out of the sunlit boardroom, built into the side of the Socialite pyramid tower in Mountain View, California, and into the blue-carpeted and wood-paneled private hallway outside.

A half-dozen assistants waited on couches and chairs for their masters within. Chapman flicked a look at them and found them glancing at him nervously. All were engaged in their own work, or goofing off while looking like they were working.

Chapman headed into the private bathroom outside, making his way into a stall under the glowing energy-efficient fluorescent lights. Once he was locked in, he opened his phone and slipped into the Escapade app. Words were already starting to appear in the chat box.

CHALKE: So there's a thing with China. Nealon unearthed a bunch of Chinese passports tied to a kidnapping attempt in Northern VA this morning.

BILSON: Interesting.

What the hell? He was missing a board meeting for this? Who cared about some stupid passports, or some isolated incident in Virginia?

CHAPMAN: Maybe I'm dense, but why is this significant?

CHALKE: Nealon thinks – maybe correctly – the PRC government could have a hand in this. Kidnapping an American citizen on American soil.

Chapman rolled his eyes. Again, so what? But he let the others dig in and just watched.

JOHANNSEN: Whoa. That's got diplomatic implications, if true.

CHALKE: Yep.

BYRD: Huge news, guys. So huge.

CHALKE: You can leak this on background, but don't mention any names or agencies. It can't come from the FBI. In fact, if you can make it seem like it came out of the White House, that'd be better.

KORY: No problem. "White House aides said, off the record..."

JOHANNSEN: Yeah. Easy.

BYRD: Big scoop! I M live n thirty, I lead with it. U think there will B reaction from Gondry admin?

CHALKE: Who knows what that egghead will do?

BILSON: I got a call to come in to the White House for a meeting shortly. Think I'll be talking to the man himself. Will try to get his perspective and coach him down.

Chapman raised an eyebrow at all this, mind racing. Now they were getting into interesting territory, and he was trying to digest the full implications.

CHAPMAN: This isn't going to cause a diplomatic incident, is it? Because I don't need any ripples in my new deal with China.

CHALKE: Doubtful.

BILSON: Don't worry. We'll smooth it over. But it'll make a great stir for the press.

BYRD: U know what'd make an even bigger stir? War with China LOL

Chapman felt his heart skip a beat. That wasn't the sort of shit you just joked about. Of course war with China would be great for the press in their ranks. Right up until the nukes started landing on LA and San Francisco. He wasn't sure if China had the capability to fling them farther, but it wouldn't surprise him.

KORY: lol, but seriously, the clicks from that would be epic.

Chapman didn't find that particularly funny, and didn't bother to hide the fact.

CHAPMAN: War with China would seriously screw up everything. Including for you guys, in ways you maybe haven't considered. For instance, Chris, your network has distribution deals over there which are helping keep you guys afloat. And Johannsen, the Free Press has been taking so much in advertising dollars to circulate Chinese propaganda as addendums to your papers that I'm not sure you'd still be able to keep printing without them.

BILSON: Relax, all. We're in this together. We can balance ratings/clicks with not messing up the business world. Tension is good for entertainment and keeping people glued to social media/websites. War...not so much, in the long term.

Chapman had his doubts about these idiots in the press. Brinksmanship seemed to be their game. How could they follow up the tension to a built-up war, after all? He'd seen the traffic numbers going to their sites post-Revelen. They'd been gangbusters up until the so-called war ended. Then their traffic fell off a cliff and they had to rebuild with a new narrative to capture attention in a busy world. Dave Kory was probably the only one of the three press people in the Network that realized that, though. Johannsen was more of a straight news man and Byrd was just an empty talking head.

JOHANNSEN: Agreed.

BYRD: Totes. Don't want 2 C any 1 actually die, lol.

Chapman's eye twitched. Of course Byrd wanted to see someone die. It would mean ratings for him.

But war with China would be a serious obstacle for Chapman, so he sat there and seethed in the bathroom stall while everyone else logged off the chat. These idiots and their games.

Inviting press to the Network had seemed like a mistake to him, and it was one that appeared to be borne out in real time as he watched.

CHAPTER SIXTEEN

Sienna

Entering the White House as an FBI agent was probably easier than doing so as a member of the general populace, but it still wasn't what I'd call easy. I was subject to search, to body scan, though to my surprise they didn't bother to take a single one of my weapons, making me wonder what the hell the point of the body scan was.

Then they took my cell phone. And only my cell phone.

If I'd been running the US Secret Service, and Sienna Nealon had come to visit me at the residence of the president, I'd have done a full strip search, confiscated every weapon, dosed the subject (yeah, I'm talking about me) with suppressant, and then watched her like a hawk with ten agents ready to draw and fire.

Instead, I was waved through with only a lone agent for escort, still wearing my Kevlar vest, carrying two guns with backup mags, along with my spring-loaded knife and a couple other rainy day surprises for unarmed combat. But no cell phone.

To be fair, this wasn't the first time I'd been to the White House in the last year. It was, by my reckoning, the third; the first being when President Gondry had announced my new role with the FBI and the second coming after a mission I'd been tasked to with Warren Quincy (who I affectionately called the Terminator) and some Navy SEALs to rescue some kidnap victims in East Africa. That had been a feel-good mission, returning those girls to their parents.

I doubted I was meeting with the president this time, though. He'd been nice enough last round, pinning a special medal on me and shaking my (gloved) hand. Smiles and photo ops were one thing. This seemed like a dedicated briefing, though, super granular and detail-laden. Way below the president's attention.

So it was with great surprise that my Secret Service escort led me into the Oval Office and told me to wait, disappearing out into the reception area and leaving me alone.

In the freaking Oval Office.

I kept my hands firmly anchored behind my back so no one could accuse me of stealing shit. I took a look around, keeping very stiff, feeling like I might strain something if I came any more to attention. The *Resolute* desk was smaller than I would have anticipated, but still very stately and imbued with a sense of majesty somehow. It had to be in my head, and related to the history of the thing, because objectively it was just a piece of furniture.

A quick glance around at the busts that sat on various tables, the blue rug of the National seal, the flawless paint job that suggested that the wall behind the president's desk had not been torn through by a running, screaming Guy Friday a couple years back – all these caught my searching eyes. I tried to imagine Gerry Harmon sitting in that chair – or one like it, since every president's chair was custom molded and also bulletproof – as Jamie Barton dragged him out into the atmosphere.

I had a history with this room and its previous occupant, and I really tried not to show it as I bumbled around killing time, since I had no phone to dick around on.

The door to the Oval Office opened a moment later, and Heather Chalke sauntered in, pausing only a moment, eyes flicking over me in cool surprise, then making her way to the sitting area in the middle of the room and sitting down, flipping open a leather-bound notebook, pen white-knuckled in her grip. "Find the place all right?"

"Yeah," I said, pushing down all the sarcastic responses. There were so many.

"Good," she said, back to business. "I need you to soft-play this, you hear me?" She looked up at me very seriously. "You need to–"

Whatever other instructions she was going to give me got lost to the opening of the door as President Richard Gondry came bustling in with an entourage behind him. "...Make sure you schedule that call with Cam Wittman after lunch," Gondry said, speaking over his shoulder and past Secretary of State Lisa Ngo, who was following him in. Someone called an affirmative response to that, and the Secret Service agent on the door shut it behind them, leaving me, the FBI's former Number One with a Bullet on the Most Wanted List, alone in a room with the FBI Director, the Secretary of State...and the President of the United States.

CHAPTER SEVENTEEN

I tried not to act like the slightly mad lunatic that I was often accused of being as I took a deep breath of the heady atmosphere. I was in the Oval Office with the President of the United States, a Cabinet official, and my immediate boss, the FBI Director, after all. This was not a usual thing for me.

"Thank you ladies for coming," President Gondry said, taking a quick lap around behind his desk and looking at something there. He only lingered there for a moment, then made a hand gesture for all of us to sit.

I hesitated as SecState Ngo grabbed a spot on a couch opposite Chalke, and reluctantly slipped in next to my boss and sat on what was, to my surprise, one of the most mediocre couches I'd ever put my ass on. I bet it was expensive, too. What a waste of my tax dollars.

No one spoke as the president sat in a freestanding chair at the head of our respective couches. Chalke seemed to ignore my relative proximity; the couch wasn't so small I was on top of her, thankfully, and she'd seated herself to be closest to the president, which I'm sure was the sort of power game Chalke would have been into. Ngo had firmly claimed the entire couch opposite us, plopping right in the middle of it. Sure, it was big enough and she was small enough that I could have sat down on either side of her, but I admired her claiming that land entirely for her ass and sort of pushing me to be on Chalke's side or taking one of the independent chairs opposite the president.

I was on a side, whether I liked it or not, so I sat accordingly. Now I was just interested to see which symbolic side I'd landed on, and whether I'd stay there once this conversation got rolling.

"Talk to me," Gondry said, crossing his legs a little more tightly than I would have liked to see from the most powerful man on the planet. "I only heard of this an hour or so ago. Bring me up to speed."

"Not much to say so far," Chalke said, stealing a glance at me and putting some emphasis on her look.

Yeah, yeah, I got it. Don't say much. "Mr. President, we just started the investigation this morning," I said, trying to keep myself stiff and business-like. Professional, even. "There was a kidnapping attempt on a first-generation Chinese immigrant by what may be China-connected persons. How they're connected is a mystery." I tried not to look around nervously, but my gaze fell on SecState Ngo regardless.

She took up the glance, sparing me from going any further – yet. "I've directed my people to look through customs records. Near as we can tell, only the primary set of passports has been used, not any of the duplicates with other names. So..." She pulled out a paper, "...this Cheng Yu entered the United States through LAX about two weeks ago. He listed a hotel address in New York as where he was staying while in the country. Hotel has no record of his check-in." She smiled tightly. "Similar for the passports of the other accomplices." Her eyes slid down the page. "As to the passports of the furniture store workers, they all came in on work visas in the last twelve months to three years."

"Hmmm," Gondry said, head inclined thoughtfully. "Why would China want to grab a college professor from Northern Virginia?"

"Well," I said, as Chalke turned to watch me speak, giving me a very frosty look as she did so, "as I mentioned, the victim is the child of Chinese immigrants – dissidents, actually, they came over post-Tiananmen." Here I stole a glance at Ngo. "Have you heard anything about reprisals against dissidents carried out in the US?"

"Something like that happened in London last year, but through the local police, not direct Chinese action." Ngo's eyes got a little bigger. "You think they're looking for revenge, or to suppress these people thirty years after the event?"

"I have no idea," I said, watching Chalke's eyes get angrier and angrier, though only I could see them, "we're lost as to motive here. We can't even prove the PRC is responsible for this crime. It could be criminals who have access to their equivalent of the State Department's passport office supplying Triad agents for all we know." I tried to keep a straight face as I posited this.

Ngo gave me a near-pitying look. I was pretty sure she could see Chalke's *shut the hell up* expression, in spite of the director's attempts to hide it. "While there is plenty of corruption in the Chinese government, the most probable explanation is that these passports were made with the full cooperation of their intelligence agencies." She shrugged. "It's impossible to prove, though. I've sent out feelers, and I expect a strong denial and a flimsy, nonsensical explanation blaming dissidents for this outrage, along with a statement that they'll be taking firm action against the people responsible."

"Sounds like we're nowhere with this, then," Chalke said, shifting around so the president could see her. Her face had melded back to completely neutral. "The Chinese will deny any involvement, we won't be able to prove it. Case closed."

"Uh...no," I said, before I could clamp my stupid mouth shut. My face burned as I realized I'd just overridden my boss in front of the president. Already out on a limb, I finished my thought, hoping it would allow me to dig out of this hole I'd started. "There's still this Cheng Yu meta out there, prowling around on American soil. He tried to kidnap a US citizen."

Chalke's eyes blazed at me, but the fire died down as she turned to Gondry, smiling sweetly. "Of course we'll pursue every avenue available to us in tracking down this metahuman criminal. I only meant that in terms of wide-reaching diplomatic effects, the case is closed."

"I wouldn't be so sure," Ngo said. "The story had already leaked just before I stepped in here."

President Gondry's eyes lit up, and he thumped his fist

against the wooden arm of the chair. "Already? *DAMMIT!*" He was on his feet in a moment, behind his desk seconds later, and hitting the button on his phone. "Janice! Call the press secretary down here. Five – no – ten minutes." He clicked it off halfway through her affirmative reply.

The president drew up behind his desk, staring past all of us to the fireplace on the opposite wall. "Secretary of State Ngo...Director Chalke...thank you both for your briefing." He nodded to each of them in turn, and I took it as a clear sign of dismissal.

They did, too, gathering their crap together as they got up. I moved to follow them, figuring I was too much of a low-level peon to rate a GTFO announcement by name, and was halfway to the door when the president's voice caught up to me.

"Ms. Nealon...would you kindly wait a moment? Please?"

Chalke sent me a look that, being in full view of the president, was much more veiled than the ones she'd sent me earlier. She disappeared out the door a moment later, very casually.

The message got through anyway: *Shut up*.

Then the door shut, and I was left alone with the president.

CHAPTER EIGHTEEN

This wasn't how I'd envisioned my day going.

A kidnapping attempt and corpse inspections followed by a leisurely jog across the Virginia countryside in the morning. Fisticuffs with a Chinese meta who had beetle armor and fire eyes in the early afternoon. Lunchtime meeting with the President of the United States.

What the hell was I going to do for a follow-up? Tea with the Queen of England?

Nah. She was an ocean away and far too busy to deal with my dumb ass.

"Thank you for staying," the president said, coming out from behind his desk. I stayed frozen like a statue, part of me hoping that Gondry was as dense as Harmon had always said, and that maybe he'd just forget I was here. "Come." He pointed to the couch, as he returned to his earlier chair. "Sit."

"Yessir," I mumbled, doing so.

"I know you and I have had a tangled history," President Gondry said, taking this opportunity to pick at a loose thread on his pinstriped pants.

That was one way to put him sending every US government agency after me with everything they had. "Yes, sir," I said, and sounded a little strangled to my own ears.

"But I mean you no ill will," he said. "I can be stubborn at times. Too stubborn." He chuckled under his breath. "My late wife said as much, often. But I trust the evidence of my own eyes, and I saw for myself in that footage of what you did in Eden Prairie that – well, we were wrong about you. Your actions in Revelen further proved it. And when I dug into the record like a good academic – like I should have to begin with, instead of just trusting the yes men and women like your boss there," I glanced up to find him almost winking at me with a slight smile, "well, I found that you've done a lot of good, even when we were chasing you with everything we had."

"It takes, uh," I cleared my throat, "it takes a lot of guts to, uhm, say that. Thank you." My cheeks were redder than a second-year student of Marxist theory.

The president stared me down. "All that said...you know we're six months out from an election."

"It would hard to miss the non-stop campaigning and political news, yes, sir," I said, wishing that my meta powers extended to cheek redness control. "No matter how hard I try."

Gondry chuckled. "Are you one of those rare apolitical types, then? Rare in DC, I mean. Probably quite a bit more common outside the Beltway."

"I try to stay out of it," I said. "I've got my ideas. Principles, I guess. But I don't like politics. It's too..." I shrugged. "Pick an adjective, it probably fits."

Gondry nodded slowly. "I know what you mean. There are a lot of days, especially since I took this office, when I wish I'd stayed a lowly college professor. But I'm in it now, thanks to..." His eyes flicked up to me. "...Well, you, if it's true what they say about my predecessor."

I felt a choking sensation in my throat. "Uhm. Uh. Sir...?"

"He was powered, wasn't he?" Gondry said, watching me carefully.

I nodded slowly. "And powerful. But I didn't–"

He waved me off. "I don't want to hear about it. I've seen enough of the evidence with my own eyes to know that he was up to things that I would never want to be compelled to talk about. Best we leave Gerry Harmon missing forever, lest some very uncomfortable questions prompt a panic. And regardless...he left me in this office, and...I don't entirely hate it." He stared at the carpet, the great seal of the USA. "I mean, I do hate it, often. I know exactly what you mean by your disdain of politics. I had grand ideas about the good I could do in this office, but since I've inhabited it, I feel all I do is chase my own tail. Still...I want another bite at the apple." He looked up at me and his eyes were as resolute as...well, his desk, I guess. "This China business...it has the potential to jeopardize that."

I felt a deep twinge of discomfort in my belly. "Sir...are you asking me to shitcan this investigation?"

He looked down, unable to meet my gaze. "No. No, I wouldn't do that. You need to catch that dangerous meta, regardless of what he might say when you get ahold of him." Here he looked back at me. "But...if he resists you..."

I couldn't hide my cringe. "I'm sure I'll react in my usual, stunningly lethal fashion, sir."

"This conversation makes you uncomfortable?" the president asked. "Good. You still have a moral compass, then. So many in this town don't."

"Sir?"

"The realpolitik in this city is stunning," Gondry said, rising and returning to look out the windows by his desk. "The pageantry. Your boss, for instance? She cares more about seeing me re-elected than seeing your case get closed." He turned his head to me and smiled. "I like that you still care about the justice of the thing."

"It's...all I've got," I said quietly. "Sir."

"You should work on that," he said, still smiling. His phone buzzed. "Yes?"

"The guest you requested has arrived," his secretary said through the speaker.

"Send him in." The president came around the desk again. "I trust you'll do the right thing in this case, but I hope you don't mind if I try and manage the potential political fallout, given the circumstances."

I was still pretty stiff, and had risen to my feet as soon as the president had. "Uh...I can try, but political sensitivities are not exactly my forte."

President Gondry's smile turned quite knowing. "Oh, I'm well aware." The door to the Oval Office clicked open, and in walked a man in an expensive suit, whose every detail of his appearance was perfectly manicured, hair graying and slicked back. His smile went well beyond "knowing" and into the realm of "ungodly smug."

The worst part? I knew the bastard on sight, though we'd never actually met in person.

"Agent Nealon," President Gondry said, shaking the man's hand, "I'd like to introduce you to one of my advisors, and a man you'll be working very closely with on this."

"You don't have to," I said, making my way over and offering my hand to the bastard standing in front of him, smiling smugly at me. "I'm familiar with Mr. Bilson."

"So nice to finally meet in the flesh, though," Bilson said, taking my hand in his and giving me a quick shake, smile never once wavering. "I mean...I feel like I've known you forever."

CHAPTER NINETEEN

The president's message had been loud and clear before he'd dismissed us out of the Oval: "Do what you have to, but try and let Bilson here manage any fallout that comes from your pursuit of justice." His exact words.

Bilson let me know his interpretation as we walked out past the secretaries. "I can't tell you how pleased I am to be working with you on this project. I really feel like you'll be able to contribute significantly to this endeavor."

I raised an eyebrow but held my tongue as I scanned the area. Director Chalke was nowhere in sight, to my surprise. She must have considered me not worth waiting on. I was sure I'd hear from her later.

"I have to warn you, though," Bilson said, hanging onto my elbow like a parasite as I made my way through the halls, trying to find the exit from the West Wing. I had a pretty good memory, so I was fairly certain I was on the right track even though his blathering was a constant distraction. "This is my first FBI investigation, so forgive me if I'm not up on all the lingo."

"I'll brief you as much as I'm allowed," I said cautiously, "but I don't think we'll be 'working together' on this so much as you'll be batting cleanup if anything goes awry."

Bilson let out a friendly chuckle. "No."

I frowned. "'No' what?"

"I think you've misunderstood," Bilson said, stopping me by stopping himself in the middle of a surprisingly narrow corridor. It was like this place had been built for Lilliputians. It certainly didn't look as roomy and spacious as it had always appeared on TV. "My role in this...it's unlimited."

I raised an eyebrow. "Beg pardon?"

"I'm not your janitor," Bilson said, still smiling. Sonofabitch was unflappable. "I'm not going to be 'cleaning up' after you. I'm going to be a fully involved partner in both the decision-making process through every turn of the investigation and in the press aspects." He sidled closer. "The good news for both of us, is that this opportunity presents immense advantages."

I kept myself from backing away from him like he was toxic, but only by tapping deeply into that well of self-control that I was cultivating. "Oh?" was all I managed to get out. Because that well was not very deep, and I was squeezing my hands tightly behind me to keep from bitchslapping him.

"I have connections in DC," Bilson said, teeth just crying to be knocked out. "These are assets at your disposal. Need information about Chinese intelligence? I know a lady with experience. Want to know more about what your college professor victim's work life was like? I have contacts in Georgetown we can talk to in both administration and student affairs. By the same token, I have many connections with MPDC if you need some behind the scenes juice there."

He sidled just a little closer. Not too close, credit to him. "But this *has* to go my way, you see. Not only because your boss, when you ask her, is going to make explicit what the president couldn't in our meeting just now. But because the president is in the middle of a re-election campaign I'm up to my eyeballs in quarterbacking behind the scenes, and we cannot afford to throw any spanners in the works." He brightened. "You understand?"

I drew a deep breath through my nose, let it out through my mouth, and felt like a bull in a cartoon where you could see the wind blowing out. Chill. "I think so," I said, "but I will have to double check with Director Chalke."

"Of course," Bilson said. That smile. "Naturally." He inclined his head a little. "After you get things settled with her, come on up to my offices on K Street." He pulled a card out of his pocket and handed it to me.

I took it without cramming it up his nose, along with my fist. I didn't look at it, though. Because I was still envisioning my fist up his nose. "Thank you," I said, strangely flat.

"See you soon," he said, and disappeared past me as I stood there in the hallway, pondering how much, really, I was growing as a person these days.

CHAPTER TWENTY

To my complete lack of surprise, Director Chalke confirmed everything Bilson had told me and then some.

"You're at his disposal," she said, probably being shuttled back to the Hoover Building in the back of her chauffeured car while I sat behind the wheel of my agency SUV, staring out at the sunny sky and pondering the state of my life.

"Just so I'm clear," I said, closing my eyes as I prepared to eat the heaping gob of shit she was placing upon my plate, "you're putting an FBI agent under the command of a civilian authority?"

"No, you're under my authority," she said in a clipped tone. "But I'm telling you to answer to him because he's looking out for my boss. See how that chain of command works? The president to me to Bilson to you. Surely that's straightforward enough for you to follow, given what's at stake here."

I warred with myself for a long moment, keeping the silence between us. Chalke didn't break it, either, for whatever reason. "Understood," I said at last, with a voice probably so full of regret it oozed out of my pores.

"Glad we're clear," Chalke said, and as was her wont, hung up without another word.

I squeezed both hands on the SUV's steering wheel. I was

headed back to my office, and stuck in the rising tide of DC traffic.

The FBI's main offices in the Hoover building had been too crammed to allow for our scrappy little division to find a place to rest our keyboards, so the General Services Administration had procured a disused building that had once held offices of the Department of the Interior for our use. It was a ten thousand square foot office space and we used approximately a thousand square feet of it, which left the three of us – me, Holloway, and Hilton – rattling around like a BB in a tin can.

Furthermore, there was no motor pool, armory, or any other services available on our little campus, including a receptionist, so we leaned heavily on voicemail, our cell phones, and our own ingenuity, which was, in some of our cases (Hilton's), more limited than others.

"All hail the conquering hero," Xavier Holloway said as I passed through the little anteroom space into our sprawling, damned near empty offices. "How's the view from the White House, Ms. Elite?"

"Heavily obscured thanks to the Secret Service trying to cut down on sniping opportunities," I said, breezing in and tossing my jacket on the back of my cloth-upholstered desk chair. It was old and beaten, probably from the 90's, furniture that had been in some government storehouse until we'd come in here with a need for furnishings. I plopped down in it, observing that my blouse was speckled with sweat from the day's activities. "Anything happen while I was gone?" I looked around for Hilton, but didn't see her, which meant she was probably in the bathroom. Or already enjoying her suspension for the shooting investigation. Though she tended to take long breaks since we'd moved here, which I attributed to us not having an on-site boss. And also not much to do.

I assiduously avoided ever following Hilton into the bathroom, or even using it at the same time as her, because, being only two of us women in this office, she always used the opportunity for a girl-talk powwow of the sort I absolutely hated and felt I could only barely escape with my life. I'd even gone so far as to use the men's room when she was buried in the women's and I had made sure Holloway wasn't coming.

"We got a whole lot of nothing from locals and our own people on scene at Save Much," Holloway said. "Passports are bagged and being dusted for prints." He seemed to be looking down a checklist. "No reports of your fire-eyed beetle guy–"

"Firebeetle Bailey. That's my code name for him."

Holloway raised a slightly fuzzier-than-necessary eyebrow. Dude needed a pluck. "I feel like that's not your best work, but okay. Here's something: we sent out agents to the dealership where that van the kidnappers used was purchased. Salesman said they bought another vehicle at the same time. Late model Volvo. We're getting a warrant for the GPS, hoping to track it down."

"Excellent," I breathed, logging into my computer. "I love it when leads fall into my lap."

Holloway was quiet for a second. "How else might they present themselves? If not falling into your lap?"

"Kicking me in the ass, usually," I said, pulling up the FindIt search engine and typing in *Russ Bilson*.

A ton of news articles popped up. I'd read a few of them in the past, but I really had nothing else going and figured I'd do at least a little surface-level research before I popped over to Bilson's offices.

"You really think the government of China is behind this kidnapping?" Holloway asked, just as I was delving into a profile of Bilson titled "The King of Backstage Politics." It was just as hammy and overwrought as the title might have suggested, filled with lines like, "He slides behind his desk like a shark fin through black, night waters." I checked to see which site I'd landed on and had a moment's revulsion: Flashforce.net, my least favorite address on the whole web.

"What?" I looked up from my browser window, feeling dirty that I'd clicked on a Flashforce link. If there was any site that had tried harder to destroy me during my exile than Flashforce, I didn't know of it. "China? I have no idea. It's possible."

Holloway took this as a sign I was willing to have a chat,

because he plopped down on my desk. "They do some dirty things, the PRC government."

"You're getting hemorrhoid cream smell on my desk."

He made a grunt of frustration and stood back up, crossing his arms. It was a mark of how much I'd needled Holloway over the seven months or so we'd been working together that he didn't retreat from that shot, just ignored it and went on. "You know what I mean?" he asked.

"Why don't you enlighten me?" I asked, stealing a glance back at the Flashforce story on Bilson.

"You heard of the Xinjiang region? In Western China?" he asked, taking no notice of me desperately trying to get back to what I was interested in, rather than his preferred topic of discussion. "They've got literal concentration camps there. They've imprisoned an ethnic and religious minority, the Uighur Muslims. No trial. No crimes. Women and children. Listen to how bad this is." He stopped, grabbed Hilton's chair and slid it over, plopping down on it.

"Now you're ass-creaming her chair."

"What do you care?" Holloway asked. "So these Muslims – they're being imprisoned just because of their religion. Because the PRC doesn't allow religion, so they have to 're-educate' it out of them, so they can be good comrades. Worse than that, the Chinese government has started doing DNA profiles on the people they're interning. But really, they're using them for a couple things. First, to identify any of the Uighurs that might have slipped the net. And also..." Holloway looked around, like he was afraid we'd be overheard. "...They built hospitals right in that area."

I glanced at him. "For...treating the sick in the camps?"

Holloway shook his head. "Everywhere else in the world, if you need an organ transplant, the wait time is a year, two years. If you take a flight to Xinjiang, though, and have an organ transplant done in the hospitals done by the camps..." His face twisted. "...The wait time is a week."

It took a second for the cold chills to run entirely down my arms and body and for the heebie jeebies to make me sit up and shiver. "No. No, they wouldn't–"

"Oh, yeah," Holloway said. "A Chinese hospital worker who got assigned there escaped. Told the whole ugly story. They harvest them alive, even conscious."

"That's some Third Reich level stuff right there," I said. "That's Unit 731 shit."

Holloway nodded slowly. "They learned well from the Japanese. Anyway, China's got people flying in from all over the world and paying cash money straight to the government for the privilege of getting transplants."

I suppressed a gag. "Leave it to the Commies to raise government cash by monetizing taking people apart for their organs."

Holloway raised both eyebrows at once. "Amen to that, sister. Now arguably, that's the worst they've done, but it's not anywhere close to the only dirty–"

My phone beeped. Holloway paused while I grabbed it out of my jacket and checked the text.

Come to my office. We need to go over some things.

It was from Bilson, apparently my new boss. Holloway took my sigh as a cue to ask what was up.

"Chalke has lend-leased my ass to that political consultant that's always on cable news," I said, nodding at my computer screen, where a picture of Bilson's smugly sneering face decorated the top of the write-up.

Holloway's crow's feet turned into canyons around his eyes. "What? Why?"

"China's a political concern," I said, "and it's an election year."

Holloway let out a sigh. "Walking on eggshells, are we?"

"That or broken glass," I said, logging out of my computer. Hilton or Holloway probably wouldn't mess around with it if I left it open, but there was no point in giving any more people access to it than necessary. I was already being electronically surveilled through it by the Network, I was fairly certain. "Anyway, she gave him carte blanche to boss me around. Maybe you guys, too, though she wasn't explicit about it."

"Oh, good, I'm glad to hear I'm still nominally working for the Bureau I signed up with," Holloway said acidly. "Because I don't remember transferring to the cheesedick school of political softbodies."

"Brief Hilton on this for me, willya?" I asked, swiping my coat and stowing my phone.

"Not sure I need to, she's heading for mandated suspension. You taking the car?" Holloway asked. We only had two SUVs for three people in the office, which meant someone was always getting screwed and having to rideshare.

I checked my watch. It was getting close to four o'clock. "I could probably take the Metro or Uber and make it faster." I shrugged. "Up to you."

"Yeah, if you don't mind," Holloway said, looking around. Once he knew Hilton wasn't lurking, he added, "Otherwise, Hilton'll ask me for a ride home and I'll get stuck with her jawing my ear off. In rush hour."

I watched his pitying look for a moment, then nodded. "I wouldn't wish that fate on anyone, even you, ass cream. Later." And I bailed as he stood there just shaking his head, smiling just a little, a man well accustomed to my blatant douchebaggery by this point in our working relationship.

CHAPTER TWENTY-ONE

Bilson's offices consumed an entire floor of a good-sized building on K Street, where most of the lobbyists and political organizations nested in DC. An even dozen political PAC and consulting groups had brass name plates slid into the sign outside their door, a familiar callback to the structure of these operations that I'd learned about from Bilson himself while investigating corruption in Louisiana politics last year. I took in the names with a glance, noting that he seemed to have his fingers in a lot of pies.

The receptionist showed me out of the lobby area with its water feature hanging on the wall, gently sluicing liquid down into a pot beneath and recirculating it back up. It was kind of cool, kind of soothing, and cost a lot of money, I would have guessed. Should it surprise me that Bilson furnished his business in opulent style?

No, I realized after being led through a warren of corridors and stepped into his office, I should not. Every surface was filled with pictures of the man himself with every conceivable political and social influencer in DC. He and the Louisiana operative I'd met, Mitchell Werner, were cut from the exact same cloth.

"Ah, good, you made it," Bilson said, rising to greet me with surprising enthusiasm.

"Well, I have a hard time refusing orders from the boss, you know," I said. He and Chalke had some connection, and I didn't need to ruin my post-Nashville streak of playing nice by having it get back to her that I was just posing.

"Have a seat," Bilson said, sliding in behind his computer. I noticed he had a Post-it note taped over his camera, like any sane person in his position would. He noticed me staring and said, with that grin, "Can't be too careful."

"Agreed."

"So," Bilson said, tapping at the keyboard for a moment, "let me start by asking you something: What do you think is your job here?"

I looked around his office, at the incredible display of back-scratching covering the walls, and tried to discern what my answer was supposed to be. "Seems like you've got 'photographer' covered, so...public relations?"

"Hah!" His laugh was not remotely sincere. "Good one. But seriously, guess."

"Based on my conversations with the director, the president, and yourself..." I put out there, a little tentatively, "...to make sure I don't blow something up that's going to cause political fallout. Like East LA."

He stopped typing and looked straight at me, eyebrows arched. "Wow. That was a lot more self-reflective than I would have expected. Yes, that's it exactly. We're going to steer your investigation through the minefield ahead of us. I'm going to help, not because I want to interfere, but because I want to make sure you don't blow any limbs off in your journey to justice." His grin widened, probably because of the alliteration. He was that kind of douche. "Given your history, I'm sure you can see the wisdom in this."

I tried to paper over my discomfort. "Yeah. I'm fully aware that I make messes others don't want to get covered in, or have to clean up. President Harmon made it extremely clear to me after the last election how much I helped his campaign, so...I get it. My actions have effects on the wider world. Furthermore, I get this is politically sensitive. That no one wants to see me stomp on China's junk in full view of the world."

Bilson cringed slightly. "Yes. No...junk-stepping."

"Here's my concern," I said, because this was the sort of thing Sienna Nealon would always raise, though generally in a more...adversarial...manner. "I'm afraid that my investigation might get compromised by the desire to play politics. If China is at the root of this, I mean."

"Can I be real with you?" Bilson asked, putting his elbows on his desk. The word *real*, in his mouth, sounded so wrong.

"Please. Be real, yo. And spectacular. Be Teri Hatcher's boobs." Yes, show me your authentic self, you smarmy ass.

Bilson's smile contracted, though whether it was because he sensed the sharklike intent behind my facade or felt the boobs remark was beyond the pale, he didn't say. What he said instead was, "Let's assume for a moment that your suspicions are true about China being behind all of this." He leaned back in his chair. "Let's say they tried to kidnap that college professor. Let's further assume you manage to collect incontrovertible evidence proving exactly that. So...what now?"

I looked for the verbal trap. I thought I saw it, but being that it wasn't an actual trap with lethal consequences at the end, I wandered in, mostly to feed his perception that I was a moron, because that, I deemed, would do nothing but help me. "We present the evidence to a grand jury. Capture the bad guys. Blow this thing wide open."

"Bring the truth to light," Bilson said in a strong voice, pumping his arm. "Enforce justice for all. And also...raise tensions with China, destroy our diplomatic and economic relations with them, resulting in the absolute crash of the American and Chinese economies, and possibly bringing us into a war with the largest standing army on the planet." Now he smiled again, smugly. I was so sick of that face and I'd only worked with him for an hour.

"You think that's the natural consequence of us bringing to light bad behavior on the part of the Chinese government?" I asked. "That it's so binary – trade war and actual war, diplomatic incident? No other possibilities in between?"

"China is not big on owning up to any *alleged* bad behavior on their part," Bilson said. "And alleged is all we get; it's not like there's a place to put their country's government on trial."

"What about the United Nations?" I asked, really trying to play the part of being naive about international politics.

Bilson laughed lightly. "The UN is like your high school."

"I didn't go to high school."

His smile vanished. "Regardless, I think you can understand the concept. It's a popularity contest. Nothing ever gets passed against China. They're too powerful, and becoming more so in the international community by the day. Their 'One Belt, One Road' initiative to try and create an economic hegemony around the world is spreading a lot of money around to countries who don't want it to stop. Which it would, if they took a stand against China in the UN."

"So nothing I'm doing here matters," I said. "That's what you're saying."

"No, I'm not saying that." Bilson waved his hand emphatically. "Let me put it another way – we're playing a game here. Chess, let's say. It's our board, but the king and a lot of the other big pieces aren't in positions where you could go after them. You can take all the pawns you want, within reason, but–"

"But if I try and go after the queen, I'm out of bounds," I said.

"Exactly. And you'll get called for it, and get in way more trouble than they will for what they did." His smile's wattage dimmed a bit. "My job is to help keep you in the bounds so you don't get in trouble."

"It's a real public service you're performing."

"I know it's not optimal," he said, coming around the desk and leaning against it. "I get that you want justice. That it drives you down to your very soul." He sounded so sincere, and his smile had disappeared. "That's noble. That's worthy of striving toward." He maintained the veneer of serious. "But it's also not how international relations work."

"See, and I thought international relations precluded the possibility of kidnapping people in other countries," I said, like a dog who just couldn't let go of that bone.

"It does. Generally," Bilson added hastily. "But China's not big on playing by the rules. And they're also big enough that no one player could push any negative actions on them. If you'd asked me yesterday, I would have said this thing that you suspect? That it was too hot even for China to consider." Bilson looked at the pictures to his right. "But you've got some decent evidence that they've not only considered it, they've sallied right past what I would have thought impossible thresholds for crazy action. But they're getting bolder and more confrontational."

"Look, I know I'm just a dumb agent in this," I said, looking down, "but in my experience, when someone gets boldly confrontational, punching them squarely in the nose is the only formula for settling them back down."

Bilson's smile came back, but strained. "That's not a perfect analogy for the world of diplomacy for a few reasons, not the least of which is that nobody can afford to punch China."

"Because they're too big. And too popular."

"Too connected," Bilson said. "Too many powerful people make a lot of money off China. Too many countries are beholden to them, tied to them, including America. They hold over a trillion dollars of our national debt. We do over half a trillion a year in trade with them. Every major American corporation has a presence in China or desperately wants one, and without exception those corporations donate to politicians on both sides of the aisle.

"Contrast that with the stakes in your investigation – one lowly Georgetown college professor who didn't even get kidnapped," he went on. "China will deny having anything to do with it, the press is not going to report it more than a day or so, and then the story will vanish because guess what? They're all either in China with reporters of their own, or trying to get into China, or actively taking money from the Chinese government to circulate their propaganda."

I couldn't stop the frown. "Wait, what?"

"The *Washington Post* has taken Chinese propaganda straight from state-owned *China Daily* and inserted it into their paper editions." Bilson's smile turned sympathetic. "It's called *China Watch*, and it's owned and approved by the Communist Party – state media propaganda, placed into the major Western newspapers. Their circulation is down, which means revenue is down and naturally, profits are down. They could really use the money, so..." He shrugged. "Absent that, every major press outlet lives under the threat that they'll have their China bureaus shut down if they get on the wrong side of the PRC government. They still cover some of the dirty things China does, but it's markedly less dogged. And who can blame them?"

Me, I didn't say. "Basically what I'm hearing from you is that even if I managed to implicate China, there's no justice."

"Not on the international scene," Bilson said. "Which is why I'm trying to work with you. Laying this out ahead of time, so you don't get your expectations out of whack. This guy you fought earlier? Him we can get. One way or another," Bilson said, and I caught a hint of what the president had suggested before, about Firebeetle Bailey not surviving to see trial – and thus not humiliating China, if he ended up talking.

I lapsed into silence, all these thoughts swirling around in my head. From my perspective, China was looking like a big bad guy, but one that no one had the guts to cross. I voiced none of these thoughts, instead saying, "All right, I get it. We play it cool, and do what we can do."

"Exactly," Bilson said. The smile had returned. "Pragmatism, see? And if we handle it right, there's going to be a lot of reward at the end of the rainbow. Enough for all of us – you, me, and Director Chalke."

Oh, yay. But I kept my internal dissent to myself. I had a feeling I'd be doing a lot of that in the course of this investigation. I just let him think I'd submitted quietly. It was becoming something of a habit. "Sounds good. Where do you want to start?"

"With something invaluable that I've learned in the course of my years in DC," Bilson said. "Any time you don't feel you know enough about a subject, it's time to borrow expertise from someone wiser than yourself." His intercom beeped, and he reached over to hit it. "Yes?"

"Mr. Bilson?" The receptionist's voice pierced through. "Professor Chu of the George Mason University Confucius Institute is here for your dinner."

Bilson smiled at me. “We'll be right out, Jean.” And he stood. “Shall we?”

“We're...having dinner?” I checked my phone. It was about that time, I supposed.

“With an expert,” Bilson said. He was smiling. Again. “Come on.” He waved for me to join him. “Let's brush up on China.”

CHAPTER TWENTY-TWO

I knew for a fact that Professor Chu was on the Chinese government payroll somehow within three minutes of meeting him. He was a delightful man, don't get me wrong, with lively, intelligent eyes and a sense of humor that seemed particularly clever. He was dark-haired with the first vestiges of a retreating hairline that suggested he might have had a widow's peak at one point that was now reduced to a widow's foothill. It had also climbed up his head some distance.

We walked a few doors down to a restaurant that was a half step down from street level. It had a glass front and we were seated with a perfect view of the street. I knew from passing earlier that the glass was tempered to keep pedestrians from looking in nosily at the diners. Silently, I approved.

What I didn't approve of? The prices on the menu I was handed. There wasn't an appetizer on it for less than $19.99, and a good many tipped the scale at $29.99, with some sort of seafood sampler bearing the letters *MKT* next to them, as though I could somehow guess the market price. The only guess I made was that if you had to ask the price, you probably couldn't afford it. I certainly couldn't on my government salary.

"I find China is severely misunderstood in Western circles," Professor Chu said. "For instance, they take a very long-ranging view of planning, issuing five-year plans at regular intervals." His smile broke a little wider. "Washington can barely pass a budget for six months. That level of uncertainty is not conducive to the stable running of a society."

Bilson nodded along, pausing to order wine as the server came to the table. He looked sidelong at me, and I was forced to say, "Just water for me, thanks," as he and Chu agreed to partake. Whatever, that was fine. At least he hadn't assumed I was drinking. It did suggest that he was well-informed. About me.

"Let me ask you this," Bilson said, with a pensive look, the smile gone as he contemplated deeply all the party-line bullshit and platitudes that Chu had thus far laid down for us. "What is the long-term goal for the Chinese government?"

"China wishes to be a part of the global order," Chu said as the server poured out a glass of red for him. He swished it around and tasted it, nodding his approval. "They are the second largest economy on the planet, and growing. There's plenty of room at the table for China to take their rightful place. And a strong China is good for the international community. Some of the responsibility that America has shouldered all these years can be shared." He looked to me. "For instance, your mission to Africa with the US Special Forces?"

I thought I saw where he was going with this but let on like I didn't. "The Navy SEALs? What about it?"

"In the event you had any difficulties during the execution, China had a task force from their support base in Djibouti ready to intercede to assist you," Chu said. "These sort of goodwill missions don't need to be solely the responsibility of America any longer. With China's rise, there is another voice, another pair of hands in the international community that could be of assistance in keeping order." He took another sip of wine and smacked his lips together. "Excuse me for a moment." He scrunched up his napkin and left it on the table in his place. Our server swooped in a moment later, folded it, and left it where his plate would sit, then disappeared.

I kept my voice to a whisper. "This guy works for the Chinese government, doesn't he?"

"Absolutely," Bilson said, taking a sip of his wine. "They've been funding specialized groups on college campuses called

Confucius Institutes. They're operating on over a hundred campuses right now, usually under the aegis of being explainers of Chinese language and culture to the world at large. But the professors aren't in the employ of the university – they're paid by China directly, a direct line to Chinese propaganda and talking points." He looked at me. "That's why I wanted you to meet him. Best you see all the sides of this, hm?"

"If I wanted a press conference with the Chinese envoy, I would have gone to their embassy," I said under my breath. "Also, I don't know what anything is on this menu."

Bilson almost snorted his wine. "It's Asian fusion."

"Thanks. That clears things up not at all."

Chu returned just then, folding his napkin back into his lap. "You didn't order without me, I hope?"

"Wouldn't dream of it," Bilson said.

"Couldn't do it with you here, so there's really no reason to do so without you," I said.

Chu frowned a little, but it passed as Bilson tossed him an uncomfortable question: "Tell me something. Can you conceive of a reason why the Chinese government might stage a kidnapping of an American citizen on US soil?"

The professor's response was completely calm, though whether it was because he legitimately had no knowledge of the events in question or he was playing it supercool, I couldn't tell. "They wouldn't," he said, very simply, then said nothing else, as if that was the end of discussion.

Bilson's eyes swept to me, as if watching to see if I'd push back on that. If he was looking for it, I didn't aim to appease him in that regard. I let it pass, sipping my water quietly.

Apparently Professor Chu had a question of his own. "Ms. Nealon...what do you think of China?"

"As dishes go, it's a little formal for me," I said, putting down my water. "You know, we millennials, we're not much for formality. Or things that cost money, because we don't have any."

Chu forced a laugh, but it was painful. Bilson mimed a chuckle. "But seriously," Chu said.

"I haven't had much in the way of dealings with them," I said.

"Other than reading 'Made in China' on who knows how many daily household items."

That lit up Chu's eyes. "Exactly. You see? China intersects with your life in countless ways. We have many opportunities to enrich each other."

I tried to avoid throwing up in my mouth from the cloying, saccharine sentiment he voiced. As if trying to save me, my phone beeped. "Excuse me," I said, and checked it. Honestly it could have said there was a slap fight going on at Logan Circle and I'd have been on my way. It didn't though. Instead:

Warrant approved for GPS trace of 2016 Volvo purchased in conjunction with the kidnapper van.

The file was attached, and up came a map with one terminus at the same dealership as the van.

I traced the series of blue lines and ended up with what I figured was the current position of the Volvo. It was in Baltimore.

"Sorry," I said, getting up. "I have to go. Call of duty." I waved my phone without daring to turn it in the direction of Chu, and I was out of the restaurant moments later, happy to be leaving Chinese propaganda behind for the real work of my case.

CHAPTER TWENTY-THREE

I had just about plugged the current location of the Volvo into my rideshare app when Bilson popped out the door of the restaurant, moving fast and with a purpose. "Come on," he said, brushing past me. I had been watching him with curiosity; apparently he had an idea.

"Uh, I have to go check on a lead," I said, waving my phone like a magic wand.

"Exactly," Bilson said. "We can ride together." He was walking back down the street toward his office building.

I really struggled for a second, trying to decide how to respond. Argument seemed right out; Chalke's orders were clear. Left with no alternative, I followed him, though at a slightly slower pace, pocketing my phone after cancelling my ride.

"You better not have a Prius," I muttered as Bilson led me into the parking garage next to his offices. Up three flights of stairs and we popped out into a field of cars that did not include any Priuses.

"I don't," Bilson said, stopping next to a bright red Maserati. He paused, brushing his hand against the handle. The car locks disengaged by his mere touch. His chest puffed in pride. "What are you thinking? Don't be shy."

"Well," I said, looking it over, "I'm wondering if I'm going to experience a mid-life crisis at 40, the way you have, or if it'll be more like at age 2,000, at my actual mid-life. And if so, what form it will take, because buying a Maserati seems unlikely. Will I end up nailing hot dudes in their twenties to prove I've still got it, all cougar-like, or–"

His eyes widened, threatening to pop out of his head. "Wait. Your lifespan is 4,000 years?"

"I hear it can be up to 5,000," I said, giving the Maserati a lazy once over. "Say, since we're talking about it...can I have your Maserati after you die?" I kept a straight face. "I mean, I can wait 50, 60 years, no problem, obvs."

Bilson sagged, waving at the car. "Get in."

He didn't drive like a total maniac, to his credit. Not that you could in DC traffic at this time of day. He hit New York Avenue and headed east on the Baltimore-Washington parkway. My GPS suggested we were a good hour plus away, which didn't surprise me given it was bumper to bumper, Bilson's Maserati totally wasted as it traveled at an average of 15 miles per hour behind a Ford Tempo from the 90's.

None of this seemed to bother Bilson, who made occasional attempts at conversation. I let him talk his way through opera, the TV show *Scandal*, and even the ins and outs of Socialite, none of which I had more than a passing familiarity with.

"...the other nice thing about Socialite," he said, not boring but not exactly tailoring the conversation to involve me, "they've made real improvements so that influencers like yourself don't necessarily have to deal with heavy amounts of negative feedback." He looked over, maybe to make sure I was still listening. "You know. From the average joes out there."

"I'm not allowed to have social media accounts," I said, shrugging. "Bureau policy. And obviously a very smart one."

Bilson puckered his lips. "But it's a vital communication tool for building your brand."

"My brand is pretty much destroying shit and killing people, and I think my calling cards are visible even if I don't post pics from the scene of my latest...uh...whatever. I doubt the FBI wants to remind people of that."

"See, and this is where I totally disagree with Director Chalke." Bilson shook his head subtly, diverting his attention from the slow-moving traffic to drive home his point. "You're known worldwide, you're respected or feared, sure, but if they want to rehab your image to maximum effect, they've got to put you out there, not hide you. Take that flap back in December with that contractor, where he posted those things on Socialite and tagged you into them? That could have been handled much smoother if you'd had an online presence. It's a direct line to the proles."

"Yeah, well," I said, looking out the window at a shining Lexus SUV next to us, "I guess Director Chalke doesn't want me communicating to the people. Which seems wise given my history."

"It's a missed opportunity," Bilson said, still shaking his head. "If you want, I can intercede on your behalf. I bet I could convince her to loosen that requirement. Give you a chance to gain back some of that popularity you had when you were first unveiled to the public."

I took a long breath, staring out the window. "Nah. I'd probably just screw it up again. Like with the Gail Roth thing, or when I punched that reporter in Minneapolis."

"Have you ever considered," Bilson said, "taking a little coaching in that regard?" His smile got toothy, but only the top teeth. "This is what I do. I wouldn't just get you on Socialite and turn you loose. We could manage your account for you." He snapped his fingers. "In fact, I'm going to do that. Even if you don't want to deal with it, I'm sure we could work something out with Chalke. It'd go a long way to helping you rebuild your public image."

What was there to say to that? *Leave me the hell alone and don't try to help me with that talking to people on the internet bullshit* didn't seem appropriate, though it was probably at the top of my thoughts. "Thanks," I opted for instead.

"You're very welcome," Bilson said, and lapsed into a silence for a spell. Probably planning my future as a social media maven. We rode quietly onward, and I wondered how the hell I'd gone from catching the world's most dangerous criminals to being paired with a political weenie who was more interested in saving reputations than saving people.

CHAPTER TWENTY-FOUR

Chapman

Time to Play!

Chapman sighed. He was right in the middle of something, so of course it was time for another of these increasingly annoying meetings. Was it his imagination or were several of the members of this group just using the opportunity to flex and show how great they were to each other?

Regardless, he opened the Escapade app and found...well, something.

BILSON: Was just having a long talk with Nealon. Must say, I find her much more pliable than you have, Chalke.

CHALKE: If you want to run her from now on, she's all yours. I'd love to cave her skull in, personally, and leave her for the rats to devour. I've met rabid cats that are less obnoxious.

BILSON: See, I think you two just got off to a bad start. She's been entirely reasonable with me.

CHALKE: Where are you?

BILSON: Baltimore. Investigating some lead. Stolen car or something. It's all very exciting.

Chapman rolled his eyes. They couldn't just text each other and spare the rest of the Network this bullshit?

Then...it got interesting.

BILSON: Did you know her lifespan is 5,000 or more years?

CHALKE: I doubt it, at the rate she pisses people off.

Chapman tapped furiously.

CHAPMAN: Sorry, did you say 5,000?

BILSON: Yes. I specifically asked. 5,000 years. Can you believe it?

Chapman settled back in his seat.

Five.

Thousand.

Years?

In the back of his head, Chapman knew that metahumans, in general, lived longer than normal humans. 5,000 years seemed...

Well, unbelievable.

CHAPMAN: You sure about that? She's not yanking your chain?

CHALKE: Her great-grandfather Hades was still alive last year, and he has roots that stretch back into the BC era, so it's not impossible that she could live that long.

Chapman settled back in his seat, the rest of the stupid, insipid conversation scrolling by without his involvement. Let the rest of these idiots prattle and network. Finally, being in this group had paid a solid dividend in the form of this information.

Now the question was...how the hell best to use it?

CHAPTER TWENTY-FIVE

Sienna

Bilson was dicking around on his phone almost as soon as we got to the scene, texting someone or another. The scene, in this case, being an abandoned street in East Baltimore. Rows of decaying brick row homes gave way to yards filled with trash. A rotting stink of dumped garbage hung heavy in the air, and red and blue police lights painted the scene.

There, waiting on the side of a nearly abandoned road, was our wayward Volvo.

The local police had taped off the area, and forensics crews were already giving it a good once-over. Their plastic suits caught the light of the too-few working street lamps. Night had fallen, and particularly hard on this neighborhood. Most of the houses in this row looked to be abandoned. One even had a tree growing out of its front windows and roof.

The smell of garbage was heavy and out of place. I'd been to the Charm City once or twice before. There were nice parts of it, like the Inner Harbor. That was a pleasant, touristy destination. I'd taken in an Orioles game at Camden Yards during the early part of the season, trying to get a feel for DC and its surrounding areas. Also, to get out of my apartment during the long, lonely weekends.

So I knew this neighborhood wasn't the only scenery of Baltimore. It was, however, quite distinctive. I wondered if there were any actual residents nearby. There certainly didn't seem to be any on this street.

"You from the FBI?" a plainclothes cop asked, sauntering up to me.

"Yeah," I said brusquely, because it didn't bear hammering the guy with a sarcastic reply. "What have we got here?"

"I'm Brockton. Baltimore PD." He shrugged. "You called, we came. Got a perimeter set, some officers door knocking, but..." He gave the place a look. "Not a lot of doors you're gonna get an answer on, at least on this street."

I nodded. The farther from the parked Volvo we moved, the less likely we were going to be to find a witness who'd seen anything. "This thing's been parked here for a few hours. I notice it still has its hubcaps."

"Yeah, no windows broken, either," Brockton said. "My guess? Nobody saw it. Or at least nobody who wanted to take it apart, because otherwise it would already be chopped. Or sitting on blocks."

"Unless it's protected?" I asked, fishing.

Brockton shook his head. "There was no one watching out for it. You'd know if it was protected. Someone would be standing sentinel to make sure it didn't get messed with."

"I figured, but thought I'd ask." I took a look over my shoulder. Bilson was still playing with his phone. Probably texting his mommy to tell her he was playing police officer today. "I'm gonna have a look at the car," I said.

"Help yourself," Brockton said. "The techs on it are all your people." He made a show of checking his watch. "Any idea how long we're going to be out here?"

"You can go, if you want," I said, talking over my shoulder as I headed for the Volvo. "Just leave the uniforms and the perimeter. This car's most likely abandoned. It was used by perps for a kidnapping in Northern Virginia this morning."

Brockton had a small smile that I could see in the faint glow of the street light behind him. "You're really getting around today, huh?"

I gave him a little wave over my shoulder in reply. It had been a long day.

The Volvo looked to be in perfectly fine shape. The techs were crawling over it in their plastic suits, swabs, magnifiers, and plastic bags in hand. No one acknowledged me as I came up, so I didn't bother to say anything.

They'd activated the accessory power, so the dashboard was all lit up. So was the dome light, but they had klieg lights operating on a generator sitting nearby, the rumble and scent of burning gasoline heavy in the air, covering over the stink of rotting garbage.

I ducked my head into the front seat. The Volvo had a little over 24,000 miles on the odometer. Must have been used when they bought it, which was unsurprising. The upholstery looked to be in good condition, no obvious stains or—

My nose wrinkled involuntarily as my meta sense of smell caught something. Something familiar.

There was an oily scent in the car, one that hung in the air like bad body odor.

I realized after a moment's consideration that it was, in fact, body odor. It was the smell I'd caught on Firebeetle Bailey back at the Save Much store when we'd fought in the back room. Heavy, probably natural, maybe something to do with his fire eye powers or that armor that sprouted from him. I stood up, almost bumping my head on the car roof I did it so fast.

"You guys smell that?" I asked. The forensic techs answer was a collective shrug. I sniffed, trying to isolate it.

The smell persisted now that I was out of the car, and I wandered away, a little experimentally. The generator nearby was putting off a diesel scent of its own, but it was different.

I walked down the sidewalk ten feet, then twenty. The smell was still here. Stepping off into the cracked street, it got weaker.

Looking around, I saw a couple of the techs watching my bloodhound act. Well, who could blame them? At least if I didn't get down on all fours and sniff the sidewalk, I might not add too much weirdness to my legend today.

Now that the sun was down, it was getting a little cooler. I thrust my hands into the pocket of my jacket, feeling fortunate I had it now, and shuffled after the oily smell, wondering how far it would lead me.

CHAPTER TWENTY-SIX

I had made it a block and just crossed the yellow crime scene tape when heavy footfalls on the sidewalk behind me made me stop and turn, hand tensed over my gun.

"Wait up!" Bilson puffed, jogging the last hundred feet or so to me. He had his cell phone clutched firmly in hand, suit jacket open and his tie askew. He caught up to me where I waited, then stopped. To his credit, he didn't put his hands on his knees and puff openly. Just looked me in the eye and asked, "Where you going?"

"I...caught a scent," I said, reddening a little as I was forced to speak that aloud. "A smell I got from the perp in the furniture store earlier." I raised my phone and pulled up the GPS map from the Volvo. "Based on the time stamp, I'm guessing he hid out in the woods behind the store until he had a clear shot, then came and grabbed the Volvo to make his escape." It had probably been easy, too, he'd just waited until Hilton and I had retreated back inside to wait for the local cops, then took it and bailed. I hadn't really registered it during my scouting of the parking lot, focusing instead on that Ford Taurus.

"Wow, this is so interesting," Bilson said, looking at my phone and the map on it of the Volvo's path for the last couple days. "What now?" He looked up at me, expectantly.

"Well, I'm gonna...follow my nose," I said lamely. "See where it goes."

He nodded. "Great. Lead on." He paused there for a second, then said, "I was thinking about your situation, and I came up with more that I think can help you. You know, besides the social media bit. Sort of a hundred-point restoration for your public image."

I stared at him blankly. "Uh...like what?"

"There's a lot of things you could do to improve your public perception." He started ticking them off on his fingers. "Be more public with your face. Do a PSA for kids on some white-hot issue, like vaping. Smooth out your interactions with others by paying attention to the general rules of sociability–"

"Wait, what?" I had a feeling I knew what was coming here, but I couldn't just stop him.

He paused, giving it a thought. "You know, develop charisma, both in person and with the camera."

"How...how do I do that?" Trying to focus on both the oily smell and Bilson's advice was not easy, and the advice was winning the war for my attention.

"It's a process," he said jovially. "The biggest thing you can do? Smile more."

I took a slow breath. "Hey, uh, can we put a pin in this until later? Also, can you stand back? This guy's smell is distinctive, but your cologne..."

Bilson paused, looked down at himself. "Oh. Yes. Sorry. We'll talk more later. I think this could really help you, though."

"I'm sure it could." Also to his credit, Bilson didn't spray himself in his cologne, unlike some guys I'd met. It seemed he dabbed, and not in the Millennial/Gen-Z way. I could still smell him, but now the oily scent was primary in my nose, and I began walking along the sidewalk, the row homes standing dark and empty to my left.

We crossed an abandoned street, and ahead I could see at least two of the houses on the next block were lit. I wasn't sure whether to take that as a good sign or a bad one, but I hoped it was good. Maybe a hint that the neighborhood – and our fortunes – were improving.

Old, rickety fences separated the overgrown yards from the street. A lot of garbage had been dumped here, and I wondered who would do such a thing. Did they just decide that they needed to get rid of trash, and any old place would work? Because there were bags of the stuff, like someone had just decided to make some of these yards their personal landfill.

I supposed that garbage collection services of the sort at my apartment cost money, and if you were down on your luck, it was a lot cheaper to just haul your crap to an abandoned neighborhood and give it the old heave ho into an overgrown yard. Still, that sensibility offended my desire for cleanliness and order. I shook it off, trying to ignore the smell of the waste in favor of the oily scent, drifting down the cracked sidewalk past one of the lit houses as I continued to make like Toucan Sam and follow my nose.

"How far do you suppose it is?" Bilson whispered, probably twenty feet behind me. It was another mark in his favor that he didn't yell it, but even a whisper was like a normal voice to a meta. If Firebeetle Bailey happened to be nearby, he'd probably heard it. Of course, he could have just dumped the Volvo and grabbed an Uber out of here, hoping the car would be picked apart by the time we found it. Or just not cared if we found it, because he'd cleaned it up first.

I shrugged, then held a finger to my lips to hush him. I doubted my foe was just hanging out, but weirder things had occurred in my criminal-hunting life. As I glanced back at Bilson, I realized we'd come a long way from the police cordon. Probably a couple hundred yards. Peering into the darkness, I noticed a couple uniformed Baltimore cops about halfway back to the yellow tape. They were heading this way, shadows in the dark.

Torn between waiting for them to catch up and proceeding in my search, I split the difference and kept walking and sniffing. I'd made it about thirty, forty more yards when suddenly the scent faded. I stopped, sniffing.

Bilson's footsteps stopped behind me as well. He said nothing, though.

I took a few steps back. The scent grew stronger. I was

playing the hot/cold game, and was getting warmer. This is where the trail moved off the sidewalk, I realized, and turned.

A dark row home stood empty and looming in front of me, windows all broken out. It was a two-story building, sandwiched between similar ones on either side. Two doors down was the lit house, and as the Baltimore cops caught up to us, I gestured for them to be quiet and come closer.

"Hobbs," one of them introduced himself, then pointed to his partner, "and McGee." Both were African-American, one I guessed to be in his twenties, the other in his early thirties, at most. Young guns.

"You know my name?" I asked, and caught the *Duh!* look from both.

"Saw you moving away," Hobbs said. "Thought maybe you might need some backup."

"Yeah, I'm following a trail," I said. "I'm going to take a look in this house, but I need someone to knock on that door." I pointed at the lit house two doors down. "Ask them if they've seen anything. But I need you to be quiet. Metas can hear for miles around them." A slight exaggeration, but it'd get the point across.

"You think your suspect is in there?" McGee spoke up. His voice was a little higher than I would have expected, a nice falsetto that would probably sound great in a choir.

"I doubt it," I said, "more likely he decided to cut through to the next street after coming across an inhabited building." That seemed plausible. If Firebeetle Bailey was out here to dump his car, he probably hadn't wanted to leave a clear and easy trail to follow. "I'm going to take a look, though."

Hobbs nodded, then looked at McGee. Without saying a word, they launched into a game of Rock, Paper, Scissors. McGee deployed paper against Hobbs's rock, then pumped his fist in victory. Hobbs, looking a little dispirited, started heading toward the lit-up house, presumably to knock on the door.

I watched the whole thing with barely-veiled disbelief. First, that McGee was excited to hang with me, and secondly:

"I have never understood how paper can beat a rock," I said, shaking my head. "Doesn't it seem like you could just drop a rock through a sheet of paper?"

McGee nodded sagely. "But it doesn't work unless something can beat rock. Otherwise it's like a nuclear weapon."

Bilson was shaking his head in either dismay or disbelief at our conversation. "Keep an eye on the civilian here, McGee," I said, lightly jumping over the gate and heading up the cracked concrete path to the house's front door.

"Roger that," McGee whispered, and I heard his hand brush against his duty weapon. Apparently I wasn't the only one feeling nervous in a dark and abandoned neighborhood.

I carefully minded my footsteps as I picked my way up the path to the front door. Whoever had been using this neighborhood as a dumping ground had done their chucking all willy nilly, and as a result the trash was strewn everywhere. This forced me to be very careful where I stepped, lest I turn an ankle on something or crush a discarded Coke can loudly and warn whoever was in the area I was coming.

Of course, all the whispering going on between me, Bilson and the cops might have already given us away, but I lived in hope that some element of surprise remained on my side. Mostly because thus far, Firebeetle Bailey had proven to be a tough fight.

I steered around a big black trash bag that had burst, leaving soiled diapers, a jug caked with rotten milk and a bunch of empty cans strewn across my path. I was trying to follow my nose, but now the stink of rot was beginning to interfere. I caught a whiff of the diapers and nearly gagged, soldiering on and trying to keep my nose focused on the oily undertones.

The smell seemed to lead to the front door, and I reached it shortly, catching a huge whiff of the oily smell coming off it. It was ajar, and had me wondering how long it had been this way. Pressing my nose right up to the crack, I sniffed within.

Yep. He'd gone into the house.

With a quick glance back at Bilson and McGee, I signaled that I was entering the house. Hopefully Firebeetle had moved through and gone out the back door, but I was well aware that he could be squatting within, though it was hard to imagine an agent of Chinese Intelligence – if that's what he was – deciding to use an abandoned house in Baltimore as a crash pad.

I ran through the options quickly – wait for backup, surround the place, try and contain him with the cops. Who didn't really have a hope of penetrating his shell, even with their guns.

Or, I could just cowgirl up and do what I always did.

I split the difference. “McGee...call for backup,” I whispered. He nodded, and went for his radio. As soon as I heard him radioing dispatch for additional units, I took a deep breath of trash-filled air and shouldered my way into the house.

CHAPTER TWENTY-SEVEN

I wished I had a flashlight as soon as I entered the abandoned house. My metahuman eyesight was good, but even it didn't operate in total blackness, and that was just about what I was dealing with. Distant light from one of the few functional street lamps outside cast faint illumination that seeped through the front window and painted a picture of despair.

The walls had been bashed open, pipes stripped for their copper, pieces of drywall and plaster caking the floor. Water damage marred the ceiling, chunks of which had collapsed into the corner to my right. More fallen ceiling pieces lay in a pile to my left, next to what had once been a kitchen. The staircase lay to my left, but I put aside searching that, at least for now.

I was pretty sure the first floor would be where my perp would be hiding anyway. His scent seemed to veer to the left, toward a hallway just past the kitchen. I could only hope he'd decided to go through, thus limiting my time spent in this place to a minimum. I felt a chill pass down my spine, and it wasn't from the cool night air.

The floorboards creaked with every step I took. I debated drawing my gun, given that I was now out of sight and Chalke wouldn't be able to crawl up my ass for drawing my weapon in sight of the public (apparently it panics people to see a crazy lady with a gun out, the wusses). But my gun wouldn't really do much against Firebeetle Bailey.

So I pulled my knife instead.

It was a CobraTec Spartan with a 3.75 inch blade. I held it behind my back to muffle the noise as I slid my thumb along the button on the side. The blade shot out, spring-loaded, making a hard, metallic popping noise. I gripped it for proper stabbing and advanced toward the hallway, listening.

Nothing except the faint sounds of McGee talking into his radio permeated the house. That and the occasional protests of the floorboards at bearing my weight. I stopped, concentrated on being quieter, and went forward again, a little slower.

The hallway wasn't very long and had two shadowy doorways on either side. It turned left about ten feet ahead, looking like it ran into a back door where it opened out into the yard. I sniffed, hoping that was where I was heading.

I reached the first doorway and paused, not even daring to breathe. Someone had taken the door off this room. It was a small bedroom. I leaned in and scanned the blind corners quickly, knife at the ready. No one was hiding in here.

Onward. I moved toward the next door. The smell was tightly confined here, and seemed like it was getting stronger.

Shit. I didn't dare curse under my breath, but I could feel the pressure mounting. My heart was thudding under my ribs, loud enough I worried that my foe could hear it.

An itch presented itself right in the middle of my shoulder blades, but there was nothing I could do about it. I wanted to jerk, to reach back with my knife and give it a good – but gentle – scratching.

No time for that now. The oily smell was so strong here, it felt like it might overwhelm me the way the diapers outside had. And I hadn't even drawn a breath in thirty seconds or so now.

Pieces of plaster had been chipped out of the walls to pull out the pipes, and they hung there, at arm level. I didn't dare put my back to the wall or stack up like I normally would have when charging a room for fear I'd dislodge one and have it make a noise as it dropped.

The next door was shut, or nearly so, a crack of light making its way out from the street lamp that must have been visible in the back yard. I held in place for just a beat, then pushed the door open–

It made a fearsome squeak, long and loud and terrifying to someone trying to be quiet. I took advantage of its noisiness to take a breath, then stuck my head in to check the corners–

Nothing.

I heard the creak of a floorboard behind me and started to turn–

Something slammed into me before I got all the way around. It hit me in the rib cage and I tumbled back, crashing through the wall. Ribs broke, something else broke, and pain lanced through both my sides – in one direction high, on the shoulder, where I'd led crashing through the wall.

On the other side, low, where I'd been slammed into by what felt like a speeding truck.

Crashing through the darkness, I could see only one thing.

Fiery eyes in the dark.

I'd found my enemy.

Or rather, he'd found me.

CHAPTER TWENTY-EIGHT

I crashed into the ground in a cloud of dust and plaster, feeling the dozen scrapes of skin and the cry of bones roundly abused. Common things that one feels when tackled through a wall. The flaming eyes of Firebeetle (no Bailey at this point, because he just wasn't jaunty enough to justify the appellation) stared remorselessly and inhumanly down at me.

Then he punched me in the busted ribs, and I thought I was going to explode.

All my breath left me, and I turtled up, curling into a ball. No thought went into it, pure instinct contracting my muscles to protect me from further injury. The level of pain was agonizing, even to someone who seemed to accumulate injuries for a living.

Firebeetle said something, but it was hard to hear over the rush of blood in my ears. The oily smell was lost, too, under the coppery taste of blood welling up in my mouth. The sharp pain in my tongue told me I'd bitten it on my trip through the wall. That seemed the least of my problems, though.

A dark whisper permeated my consciousness as Firebeetle said something else. Not in English, though, or at least not in English I could understand. He planted a kick in my side and I almost passed out, the ribs encircling my entire chest spiking pain like someone had laced them with C4 and pushed the detonator.

The world blurred into darkness and shadow around me, and I spat blood as I tried to draw a breath. I'd been a hit a lot. Even been battered through walls from time to time.

I couldn't recall a time where someone had smashed into me below my guard at forty miles an hour, shattering my lower ribs, then crashed me through at least one wall. I was pretty sure I'd broken my shoulder on the way through, though it was complaining much less than my ribs about the whole experience. If the ribs were a ten, the shoulder was maybe a soft six.

But the net result was that my instincts had me curling up and not moving. Everything in my brain was shut down, screaming at me to *PROTECT PROTECT PROTECT*, freezing me in the fetal position against a foe with superhuman strength and free rein to beat me to death.

Fighting against that instinct was hard, maybe impossible. Firebeetle moved as a shadow just beyond my range of perception, which was narrowed around me like I was stuffed back in the box. My sense of smell and taste were all blood and gasping for breath around it. All I could feel was pain, pain, pain, around my midsection and back, my ears were awash in the sound of my veins pumping past them like river rapids.

And all I could see was about a foot around me. Anything past that was like a projection shown on a screen. My brain had entered a primal state, seeking the predator hunting me but assuming it was close, choking me.

I gasped for breath, seething, stabbing pain hitting me in the lungs. Every breath was a fight that I lost, that resulted in what felt like another knife being plunged into my side. Having been stabbed my fair share of times, I was not exaggerating.

Like a shadow moving on a distant wall, Firebeetle and his glowing eyes looked down on me piteously. He said something else that I didn't understand, harsh and low, and I couldn't do anything but prepare myself for the end.

CHAPTER TWENTY-NINE

The pain had overwhelmed my system, curling me into a ball of helplessness. All these broken bones, my entire chest felt like it had been placed into a crusher at a junkyard, rendering my ability to save myself almost moot. I couldn't even concentrate–

Breathe.

It hurt to breathe.

Hold on.

I wasn't holding anything except myself.

Concentrate.

Yeah, that wasn't going to happen. Not at this level of agony. Firebeetle nudged me and it felt like a kick. I hadn't even seen him coming, and I didn't notice him again except to see that he'd receded beyond point blank range, my vision narrowed to inches in front of my face.

The blood rushing through my ears was punctuated by distant shouting. Officer McGee was calling for backup, but I couldn't tell how far away he was, if he was requesting urgently because he'd heard what was going on in here, or if something else had prompted it.

I'd lost my knife. Didn't even know when, but it was gone. I had a gun – two guns, in fact – but couldn't reach them because it would require letting go of my body. It occurred to me that all this pain I was feeling was in spite of the Kevlar vest that wrapped my ribs. It had done little to protect me against the devastating attack, and now seemed to be pushing my broken ribs into my very lungs, sparking a feeling of flaming combustion in my chest.

I took a couple of bloody breaths, the coppery liquid spraying out of my lips and sliding down my chin. Firebeetle moved just beyond my vision, like a shadow. He paused, like he was lining up a kick, and I knew he was about to finish me–

Something almost pure white crashed into him, bolting out of the shadows. It sprang at Firebeetle, almost melding into him. There was movement, his pure darkness against the strange, unearthly moon-glow color.

I blinked, trying to ignore the pain. I thought I saw...

The white thing had him in powerful jaws, shaking him, the flaming eyes blurring into motion like a lantern in the distance being shaken by an ungainly walk.

There was a moment's pause, then Firebeetle was flung through the wall, and the thing – the giant, white thing – turned and stared at me with pale blue eyes.

It...

It was...

It only looked at me for a moment, then sprang through the hole that Firebeetle had left in the wall. I wanted to get up and give chase, but there was roughly no chance in hell I could catch it or Firebeetle. Not now. Not in this state.

"You all right?" someone shouted from behind me. I looked up, and McGee's face blurred in, eyes deep with concern, pistol in his hand and pointed at the giant hole in the wall.

"No," I said, grunting out my answer. Hobbs was just behind him. "Did you see...?"

"We didn't *see* anything," Hobbs said, taking up station covering the hole, and the door behind him, as McGee dropped to a knee to administer first aid to me. "But we did hear what sounded like a bulldozer rolling through here. Came as quick as we could." He took one look at me, then quickly averted his eyes back to his watch. "Paramedics are on the way. Backup, too. You want us to stay or–"

"Do not go after that thing," I said as McGee gently pried my hands from my side so he could lift my shirt and assess the wound. The horrified look on his face told me everything about what he saw. "I don't think bullets would do much against it." I took a pained breath. "Against either of them."

"You find the perp?" Hobbs asked as McGee just sat there, looking at my rib cage, clearly unsure what the hell to do.

"Oh, yeah," I said. "I found him." I thought about the thing I'd seen. "And...something else." The thing that saved me.

The thing that no one would believe me about if I told them. Because hell, as beat up as I was, I half-believed I'd just seen a damned impossible ghost.

But...I did see it.

A white tiger. In the middle of a Baltimore slum.

And it had saved my life.

CHAPTER THIRTY

"You're concussed, you've got at least four broken ribs, maybe up to seven," the paramedic, an excessively tall lady with a copper nameplate that read *Stegenga*, was telling me. "That's not counting whatever's wrong with your shoulder."

"Yeah, yeah," I said, flat on my back on a stretcher. "Just...park me here and give me a sec."

They'd rolled me outside of the row house, which was now at least thirty percent more trashed than when I'd walked in the door of the place. I was unsure how that could decrease the property values. Maybe it didn't. Maybe my impromptu demo work would actually raise the valuation.

"You need to go to the hospital," Stegenga said, parking me on the sidewalk. "You need–"

"There's nothing a hospital is going to do for me that my body won't do on its own in the next few hours," I said, waving her off. I could tell by the sullen, resentful-bordering-on-furious look she was giving me that I was stepping on a big mood.

I didn't care. There was no point in me going to a hospital to roll around in agony in one of their beds when I could go home and do the same in my own.

Bilson edged up to the stretcher. "Ouch," he said, looking me over, his tie loosened as his lone concession to hanging out in the worst part of Baltimore. Otherwise he looked like he'd just stepped out of a board meeting downtown. "I was beginning to worry. You're going to be okay, right? You can heal from this?"

"Yeah. Tomorrow morning I'll be right as rain." I gave him a look, tasting the blood that now infused every drop of my saliva. "Still think I should smile more?" I forced a mirthless grin.

Bilson paled, almost stumbling away from me. I could imagine how I looked; crimson was coating my front teeth, seeping between each of them. "Maybe not...right now." He chucked a thumb over his shoulder. "I got a thing that popped up that I need to deal with back in Washington. You got this?" He started to back away.

"Yeah, I'm good," I said, dismissing him with a wave of the hand. I settled back on the stretcher like it was a Barcalounger poolside in the Caribbean. "You go deal with your thing. Whatever it is."

"Great, see you tomorrow," he said, "also, if you're not going to the hospital, you should probably go back inside. Or get out of sight. Because this is not a good look, and the press is starting to show up."

"What?" I lifted my head up, but he was already gone by the time I'd fully processed what he said. "Oh."

Very slowly, I rolled to my least injured side. My right shoulder did feel like hell, but a lower-grade hell, like maybe the second or third circle of Dante's Inferno.

The ribs, though...whew, boy. Those felt like absolute crap put in a bag, smashed with a broom handle, then lit on fire. If I keep describing them in comparison to fire, it's because the pain was the burning type that felt like it would never go out, no matter how much water I poured on it. Though a hot shower did sound like a great idea.

"So you just going to sit here on my stretcher all night?" Stegenga asked.

"Oh, don't be so sore about me not wanting to ride with you to the hospital," I said, bracing myself on my side, trying not to bump the shoulder. "It's nothing personal, I just don't see the point."

"The point is you're wounded," she said with steadily rising outrage. "This is what we do with wounded people: they call us, we treat them, then we take them to the hospital where doctors fix them."

"I have no interest in arguing with your outdated paradigm," I said. "I'll heal on my own, like I always do. No doctor necessary. Give me a second and I'll get off your gurney and you can go on about your night."

"Fantastic," she said acidly, and wandered off out of my field of vision. "Stubborn ass," I heard her mutter, not too far behind me. Clearly still watching in case I crashed.

I didn't bother to point out that I could hear her. All my energy was into getting upright, which I succeeded in doing on the third or fourth try, and after about ten minutes of steady effort. Another ten and I was able to drop to the ground. I even managed to stay on my feet at that point, in spite of the excruciating agony.

Picking up my vest from where they'd put it beneath my head on the gurney, I hung it over my chest and then pulled my jacket back on over it. They'd cut my shirt off to check my ribs and chest, but arranging myself thus at least made me look...I don't know. Tactical chic, presumably, with my black vest acting like a tank top and my jacket covering the shoulders and my sides.

McGee had found my knife in the rubble and returned it to me. I hadn't lost either gun, fortunately, which meant that tonight's casualties were limited to my blouse and my pride, since I'd gotten my ass kicked and had to be wheeled out on a stretcher in full view of the Baltimore PD, the forensic FBI agents on the scene, and–

"Sienna!" someone shouted as a flash popped in my peripheral vision. I turned to look and sure enough, Bilson was right. The press had arrived, albeit in limited fashion. I counted two local TV stations complete with their cameras, as well as two photographers and a couple guys with cell phones filming. One of them was doing the shouting. "What are you up to, Sienna?" he shouted to me when he realized he had gotten my attention.

"Back on my usual bullshit," I called back to him, heading in the opposite direction of the press. The street was cordoned off on either side, and they'd all filtered in on this one. Looking in the opposite direction, I saw a few gawkers but no cameras, which made it infinitely better for my egress.

Then I remembered, about thirty feet from the cordon: Bilson had been my ride to Baltimore.

I was stuck here.

"Shit," I mumbled, fishing in the pocket of my jacket. It was covered in white plaster dust, and as I reached in with my fingers, which were slightly numb at the tips, I felt my stray hopes vanish as I brushed against two major pieces of plastic that were perpendicular to each other in the pocket.

Yeah, Firebeetle had smashed my phone in two when he'd collided with me. Examining the fragments as I stood in the middle of the darkened street, I groaned. No ride, no way to get one. I was going to have to prevail on one of the local FBI agents to give me a ride back to DC–

"Hey, Sienna!" Another shout, this one from the direction I'd been going before I'd stopped to find my phone had been annihilated. So there was press in that direction, too. And me stuck without a ride. "Remember me?" the voice asked.

I turned my head to look, and caught a glimpse of a woman standing there, dark hair and yoga pants the only things standing out as I stared at her. A closer look revealed a small smirk on her lips, and as I hobbled closer I realized that yeah, I did remember her, even down to her voice.

"If it isn't Michelle Cheong," I said as I limped my way over to her. "My favorite yoga-pants-wearing Triad boss."

"Pfft," she said, tossing her jet hair over her shoulder with excessive theatricality. "Like you know a lot of those."

"Only you, actually," I said, limping a little closer. "What the hell are you doing in DC?"

"Isn't it obvious?" Her playful smile vanished in an instant, and she glanced around. There were only a couple other spectators – a homeless guy pushing a cart filled with crap, and a dude who looked like he'd stopped off while walking his dog, judging by the pretty little Labrador on a leash next to him. Once she was satisfied none of the professional press was listening in, she leaned closer to me, dropping her voice to a whisper. "I'm here looking for you."

CHAPTER THIRTY-ONE

"How'd you find me in Baltimore?" I asked, leaning against the seat of Michelle's rental car. She'd offered to give me a ride and, being more a beggar and less a chooser, I'd rolled with it. Ordering a rideshare without a phone, or asking the agents on scene to give me a lift was more humiliating, somehow, than taking one from New Orleans's premiere Triad boss.

She lifted her phone and wagged it. "Police scanner app. My flight got in this afternoon, but I didn't have a lead on where you were until I started getting the traffic out of Baltimore an hour or so ago. Anything about you tends to stand out."

"Lucky me, being all notable," I said, trying not to get blood on the seats of her rental car. "Well, now you've found me. Want to tell me why you came all this way?"

She looked me over. "Not right now. You look terrible. I don't imagine you'd absorb much of what I had to say."

"Having my looks insulted by a lady whose fashion sense extends no higher than athleisure wear seems like it would really hurt," I said. "Too bad for you I'm already laboring under several broken ribs and a busted-up shoulder. Your insult just fades into the background noise of that particular agony. Whoosh."

"Yeah, anyway," Michelle said. "Doesn't look like you've changed much since last we crossed paths."

"I'm a slow learner on the whole changing thing," I said.

"Usually takes me a few months, maybe a year to really add or subtract something from my character."

"And a lot of pain to speed the process along, I'd wager." She seemed totally calm, neatly riposting anything I threw at her.

"Well, you're not wrong," I said. "So...any chance you want to discuss the tiger in the room?"

Michelle's eyes moved back and forth, and her lips split slightly as she frowned. "I think the expression is 'elephant in the room.'"

"Yes," I said, "that is the expression. But I am referring to the enormous white tiger that just saved my ass from getting pounded into jelly by a Chinese intelligence operative that I am currently referring to by the codename 'Firebeetle'–"

"That's cute."

"He's not, I assure you," I said. "Anyway...the tiger. The white tiger."

She turned her head to look at me, blankly, then shrugged. "I know nothing about this. Sorry."

"So it's a coincidence this tiger shows up at my crime scene," I said, trying to marshal my thoughts together to make logical sense, "where no one knows I am, saves me, and then thirty minutes later you arrive? Total coincidence, y'think?"

"Well, it certainly sounds lucky for you about this tiger," Michelle said, "but no, I don't know anything about it. You might be thinking too little of yourself if you believe I was the only one who could figure out you were at that particular crime scene, though." Without looking down, she unlocked her phone and thumbed an app, then thrust it at me.

I took it and looked it over. It was a transcribed readout of police radio. I scrolled down through a patter of traffic that was familiar to me from my time in law enforcement. Countless calls for traffic stops, requests for backup, all the usual stuff that came through in the course of police doing their jobs on an average night.

It didn't take long to figure out, yep, my name was all over this thing. Spelled wrong in some cases by whatever autotranscription process had been applied, but there I was, "See in a kneel on," which would be hard to deny was me, in spite of the autocorrect-on-meth nature of the spelling.

"All right, so maybe my movement wasn't so secret," I said. "That's very disappointing to me and my mystique."

"You're wearing a bulletproof vest and a bra under your jacket and that's it," Michelle said, "Your mystique is long gone."

"All right, so, question, possibly unrelated," I said, "but is it a coincidence that you, Triad boss–"

"*Former* Triad boss."

"Oh, well, excuse me, *former* Triad boss, which is, to my understanding, Chinese mafia–"

"That's an oversimplification."

"Whatever, okay? Chinese organized crime. You were *of* them, yes?"

"Allegedly," Michelle said. "Yes."

"And you come looking for me on the day a big case with Chinese ties lands on my desk," I said, watching her carefully. She wasn't much for showing reactions. I doubted you could be at the top of the New Orleans Triad and do so, especially as a woman in a historically dude-dominated field. "I'm not a believer in coincidence, even leaving aside the white tiger thing."

Michelle kept a tight grip on the wheel, but finally nodded, slowly. "I don't know about the tiger, but as to the other...no, it's not a coincidence." She looked right at me, and here, I did see a very slight reaction, unmistakable, and shining through under the glint of the freeway lights passing overhead.

Pain.

"Because I heard about your case on the news, and I'm here to talk to you about other missing persons," Michelle said, and she paused to bite her bottom lip. "And like your case, mine has the fingerprints of the Chinese government all over it."

CHAPTER THIRTY-TWO

No matter how much I prodded and pressed, Michelle shut me down after that little revelation, promising, "We'll talk about it tomorrow, when you're not looking quite as much like you just got scraped off the freeway." I argued with her about this (not the fact that I looked like I'd been scraped off the freeway; that much was inarguable).

She left me at my apartment building, a five-story hipster and yuppie infested block in a refurbished part of town. There was no doorman, and I left a little blood on the elevator as I rode up to the top floor. Neither the building, the apartment, nor even this area of town had been my choice. Chalke's minions had found the place and rented it for me, committing me to a yearlong lease and forwarding me the bill. I would have thanked them (or given them a middle finger for the numerous deficiencies in all three of those criteria) but it seemed pointless, so I just started paying rent and unpacking my crap. The place was, to my way of thinking, not much better or worse than my apartment in New York. But at least it had the virtue of being bigger than that broom closet, though not by much.

Fortunately, my clash with Firebeetle hadn't destroyed my keys. I unlocked the door and hobbled in, trying not to stretch my injured side in the process. Locking the door, I dropped my keys on the table in the entryway, along with my wallet and knife, then started shedding shoes and clothes.

Blood had seeped into my boots, and not for the first time. They'd need to be laundered, and fortunately, I favored a brand that did well in the washing machine. There was not a chance in hell I was going to bend over in my current condition, though, so I just lifted each foot up behind me and untied them before kicking them loose in front of my laundry closet to deal with tomorrow.

The pants came off next. Once I was free of those, I figured out where the boot blood had come from. There was a huge cut along my shin that no one, not even me, had noticed. It had already crusted over, but it looked like it had done its fair share of bleeding before doing so. The back of my opposite calf had a similar wound that looked smaller but deeper. It was still nickel sized, a scab that suggested I'd caught a big splinter in my flight through the walls of that house.

Shucking off my jacket was easy, but getting out of the vest proved slightly harder. The shoulder was still crying out to be loved, loved, "Why don't you looooooove me, Siennna?" like I'd been ignoring it in favor of the younger, sexier, rib injury. Fortunately the vest could be unbuckled at the sides with a little effort, and I did so, managing to sort of slip it over my head with the uninjured arm. I was playing a dangerous game there, though, because that was the side that had all the broken ribs.

When I finally got in front of my bathroom mirror, I got a good idea of why Officer McGee had made his horrified face when he lifted up my shirt, and it wasn't because my bra was tan and the panties sticking out of my waistband were purple.

No, it was because I literally had broken ribs sticking out of the skin. I didn't know how medical professionals numbered these things, but there were splinters of bone the length of my pinkie finger halfway to the first knuckle, peeking out of my side. Two of them, just hanging out there beneath the bottom of my bra.

I swore under my breath. Maybe EMT Stegenga had been right, because having a doctor set these would be a huge help to proper healing. Still, there was nothing for it but to do it, so I took a deep breath, sat down in front of my full-length mirror, grabbed the nearly used roll of toilet paper off the dispenser and shoved it in my mouth, biting down hard.

Then I took two fingers and pressed on the first errant bone until I got it back under the skin.

I screamed a lot in the days, weeks, years that it seemed to take. Once it was back where it belonged, I sat drooling bloody saliva into the toilet paper roll clutched between my teeth. I might even have blacked out for a few minutes. But when I came to, I had another rib to fix, and I got right down to it.

When I woke again, cheek pressed to the cold bathroom floor, bloody toilet paper roll shredded and disintegrating in my mouth, I felt surprisingly better, a real shock given the injuries I'd had. After a few more moments, I managed to stand and take a look in the mirror. No more bones peaked out of my torso, or anywhere else, which left me with a couple oozing wounds and a whole lot of bruising and crusted blood.

The solution to that was obvious.

I sat in the tub as hot water cascaded down on me, my mind dulling under the heat and given sweet release in this confined space. There was something freeing for me about being in a tight spot. Some people had claustrophobia; I had claustrophilia, if that was a thing. I could almost sleep better in a coffin than an open bed, though I didn't sleep in tight quarters very often.

Tonight, I did, falling asleep in the tub, drifting off to the steady patter of the water on my skin, like rain on the roof, warming and lulling me into sweet unconsciousness behind the familiar shower curtain that kept me closed in this tight space, where I felt safe.

CHAPTER THIRTY-THREE

I woke to cold, drizzling liquid pouring down on me and just knew my water bill was going to suck this month. After toweling off, I crashed into bed without checking the state of my wounds, and didn't wake until a terrible honking sound drove me out of a deep slumber the next morning.

It took me a few minutes to identify the noise as my doorbell, a further few to work my way to the box in the living room and answer it with a mumbled salutation that landed somewhere between, "Hello?" and "Omgeffoff."

"Hey," came the sunny voice through the speaker, "it's Bilson."

I rolled my eyes like I'd just been called on by the teacher in my least favorite class. "What are you doing here?"

"I brought donuts," he said, like that explained everything. "Can you buzz me up?"

No, I wanted to answer, but instead I buzzed him up and went to get some clothes on. Passing in front of my bedroom mirror, I saw that other than a couple faint discolorations where the ribs had protruded from the skin, I was healed. Pushing against the spot where they'd popped out, I felt nothing but the pressure of my fingers.

Bilson knocked on the door just as I was buttoning my blouse, and I hopped on one foot answering it while trying to pull on a sock. I always had to be careful, because with meta strength, it was easy to rip a sock if I yanked too hard.

When I opened the door, I found Bilson in perfect order, box of donuts in his hand, smiling at me. I'd already strapped my duty pistol to my side before answering the door, of course. Just in case. "I come bearing gifts!" he announced.

"Like a proper Greek," I said, leaving the door open for him as I went to find my other sock. And my jacket. It was at about this point that I realized my boots were still filled with blood, parked in front of my washing machine, but luckily I had three pairs. It had become a necessity in my line of work. "Put them in the kitchen."

He didn't even have to ask where the kitchen was, nor did he make a show of having to guess. Which I found unsurprising. My apartment was not that big, but still, he showed a familiarity with the design, not having to look around much to find it, nor showing much interest in his surroundings.

"Feeling better this morning?" I could hear him munching on a donut and smell the chocolate from inside the bedroom.

"Yes, it's a wonder what a good night's sleep – and metahuman healing powers – will do for you when you've gotten positively curb stomped," I said, putting on the jacket that went with these pants. It neatly covered both guns, and I clipped the knife onto the back of my belt again.

"You had a rough night," Bilson said as I stepped into the bathroom to try and do something with my hair. It was getting a ponytail today, no two ways about it. The clock informed me it was already 8:46, something I would have known if I'd had my phone, given that my alarm always went off at 6. "I don't know that I've ever seen a person that badly beaten." He chuckled lightly. "I mean, I've seen some brutal debate performances and takedowns in the political world, but..."

"Doesn't really compare to watching the blood drip out of someone's mouth, does it?" I asked, snapping my hair binder in place and stepping out into the main room. Metahuman speed made everything quicker, even a ponytail.

"No," Bilson said, looking a little pained. This was not a man who'd seen real violence in his life. Which was fortunate for him, because he was the kind of soft sister a real predator could eat alive. "So...I suppose you're wondering why I'm here."

"I thought you were following me around until this thing is solved?" I picked up a glazed donut. There was a dearth of them in favor of the chocolate, which told me Bilson had terrible, chocolatey donut preferences. The bastard. How could you ignore the glory of glazed?

"Well, I will be working *with* you on this," Bilson said, shifting back and forth on his feet. "Not necessarily following you around. I can drive today."

"You've certainly got the car for it, though I might recommend not parking it in an abandoned Baltimore neighborhood if there's no police cordon present."

He cringed, then moved on. "I really am aiming to be of help to you in this." He brightened slightly. "To that end, I've scheduled a meeting for this morning." He must have seen me react in some unfavorable way, because he quickly amended, "Consider it a counterpoint to yesterday's, uh...discussion...with Professor Chu."

"Oh?"

His eyes widened as I sped my chewing up to meta speed in order to get the whole donut down without talking with my mouth full. "Her name is Bridget Schultz," he said, shaking off my odd display. I considered going in for another, just to weird him out, but I was trying to calorically limit myself these days and spite seemed a poor reason to pack on extra pounds. Besides, the donuts were mediocre. "She's an attaché to the State Department. Served half a dozen years in our embassies in China, knows the culture inside and out. In addition, she's more bearish on China, unlike Chu."

"So she'll talk the real shit, that's what you're saying," I said, still eyeing the donuts. Self-control was a terrible bitch.

"Yes," he said, "and I set up a meeting with her for this morning at her house." He fidgeted. "She's a bit under the weather, but she agreed to meet with us." He fiddled with the square of cloth in his breast pocket. "I hope it's not contagious. She sounded a bit...spacey, but I'm sure we can get the 'lay of the land' as she sees it."

"Great," I said. "I had an informant contact me last night to tell me they might have another missing persons case with Chinese government connections."

Bilson's eyes went wide. "What?"

"Yeah," I said, leaning against my counter.

"When?" Bilson asked, and his smile evaporated. "Where?"

"I don't have the details yet. My source was...cagey."

I could see his mind racing. "Well...then it didn't happen," he finally decided, and boy was he firm about it for a guy who hadn't actually heard the evidence (if any existed) of this particular crime.

"I know you're new to this field," I said, "but gathering evidence generally comes before we draw our conclusions."

"This person hasn't made a report to the police?" Bilson asked. He waited for me to shake my head, though I wasn't a hundred percent sure. Michelle wasn't really the "Go to the cops" type. "If there's no police report, then it's probably nothing. I mean, who knows if it even happened?"

I raised an eyebrow at Bilson's emotional commitment to denying a second case existed. I vacillated for a moment on whether to argue with him, and ultimately shrugged. "I guess we'll see."

His face flushed red, and he took a second to answer, seeming to really struggle. "I guess we will," he finally managed.

CHAPTER THIRTY-FOUR

A quick-ish stop at a cell phone place later and we were back in Bilson's car, moving through post-rush hour Washington, which differed from rush hour Washington by 20% +/- in traffic volume, in my guesstimation.

"How far to this meeting?" I asked, fiddling with my phone. The cloud hadn't dumped all my contacts in yet, but my cell service was active. I was an old pro at setting up new phones by this point.

"In this mess?" Bilson asked, surveying the stopped cars in front of us. "Maybe ten minutes? A little more, probably."

"I'm going to check with the office," I said, pretty sure my voicemail wasn't going to be online yet. "See if forensics at any of the scenes yesterday has come up with anything."

"Rock on," he said, tapping the wheel of the Maserati, the horsepower under the hood completely wasted in this city.

Holloway answered on the third ring, "FBI, Office of–"

"Idiots, morons, and the exiled," I finished for him.

"Sounds about right," Holloway said. "How'd your night go? I heard you ended up in East Baltimore."

"The answer to your question was in the question." I paused. "I mean, you already know I ended up in East Baltimore, so..."

"Yeah, say no more," Holloway said. "Forensics called from

the Baltimore field office. Early this morning, too, so you must have had them working all night, huh?"

"I'm a real job creator that way," I said. "All about giving the working man some overtime. Any other messages?"

"Yeah, we got some preliminaries from both the scene in Virginia and the furniture store. Which do you want first?"

"Chronological. Virginia first."

"You're like a three-state bandit here, Nealon. Hitting all those places yesterday, I mean."

"Beats when I was a bandit in all fifty states plus the territories. Virginia?"

"Yeah," he said, shuffling papers. "There was a bullet found in the victim's car. The one that shot out the tire. .22 caliber. Might have been subsonic."

"That'd keep it quiet," I said. "Definitely suggests the attempt was planned in advance, given they had to post a sniper along her route to bust her tire. Okay, that's good. Confirms the suspicion I had."

"Yep. Furniture store...not a lot there. They've got a shit ton of hair and fibers. Lab says not to expect anything from that, at least not anytime soon. Though they did find one thing after you left."

"What?"

"A bolt action .22 rifle. Forensics is working to match it with the bullet from Virginia. Better still? The shell casing was in the chamber."

"That'll help us tie a perp to the scene. Probably one of the corpses Hilton left at the furniture store, if I had to guess."

Holloway sighed. "Yeah. Lucky dog. She got to shoot someone and she's got some days off now." His chair squeaked as he spun, and I could imagine him in the empty office, twirling in his seat.

"Think of it this way: now no one's going to notice if *you* don't show up for work the next few days."

"You'd notice," Holloway said.

"But I won't care, so enjoy your time off."

Holloway laughed. "You'd notice when you didn't get your forensic reports." He sighed. "Nah, I'll stick around and play secretary. I don't know anyone in DC anyway, really, and the drinks here are stupid expensive, just like New York."

"I admire your willingness to sacrifice for your job. What about the Baltimore results?"

More paper shuffling, then Holloway grunted. "Huh, yeah, so, this one's interesting. Nothing from the Volvo."

"Not a huge surprise. These guys are pros, they know how to scrub a car before ditching it."

"Right," Holloway said. "They pulled something out of the house that may be nothing, but after I read your statement...well..."

"What?" I asked. Bilson shot me a look from the driver's side, like he was waiting expectantly for some bombshell.

"They found what looked like animal hair." He paused, and I couldn't tell if he was trying to be dramatic or it was just a rather dramatic pronouncement. "It was pure white."

I didn't show it on my face, because I didn't need Bilson jumping to any conclusions, but I did feel a brief surge of reassurance.

I hadn't been delusional.

The white tiger was real.

CHAPTER THIRTY-FIVE

Bilson's China contact lived in a third-floor walk-up not far from Dupont Circle, in a brick building that looked like it had been around since shortly after the Revolutionary War. For all I knew, it had.

The sun was already getting up there in the sky, pushing the mercury into the mid-eighties at 9:30 a.m. It was going to be a scorcher unless rain intervened on behalf of us poor, pale-skinned Minnesotans, and I didn't see that happening. Hell, even if it did, the humidity in the air post-rain tended to make it feel like I was sweating while standing still and not even exerting myself. Such was life in the swamp of DC.

"Nice place," Bilson said, making me roll my eyes. Where he couldn't see them, obviously, because I was well past the point of wanting to inspire trouble with my boss or her proxies like Bilson. This year of working for the FBI in New York and DC had convinced me of one thing: I was not a city dweller, and would never be comfortable being surrounded by this many people.

Oh, sure, I could work in the city on a case for a few days, but I always felt the pressure of souls around me, hemming me in in a way that physical confines didn't bother me. Stick me in a ventilation duct for six hours and I was fine; put me in a crowded subway car for five minutes and I wanted to rip the souls out of everybody in the place after thirty seconds just so I could breathe again.

I was clearly not normal, but was pretty okay with it.

Bilson chattered as we went up the stairs. I dutifully listened with one ear but mostly tuned him out, because he was going on about the Washington Nationals. "Gonna be a good season, I think," he said, and I just grunted in reply.

He stopped a few steps shy of the landing. "Not a sports fan, huh?"

I shrugged. "Not really, no."

"This is one of those things you could learn from," Bilson said, looking at me with all seriousness. "I don't care about sports either, but I pay nominal attention to it because it's a great way to connect with people."

I warred with myself for all of a second before my instinctive reply burst out. "What if I don't want to connect with people?"

Bilson chuckled patiently. "That's understandable, but short-sighted. Regardless of what business you're in, connections are vital to your success. Look at your field: you and Chalke butted heads for the longest time, always wrong-footing each other. I'd argue that's more her fault than yours–"

"Thanks, I think?"

"–because she's the boss, and the Director of the FBI. It's more her job than yours to deal well with her people. And she's not very good at it, to be quite frank," he said, lowering his voice to a whisper. "But this is where you can take up the slack, and I think you have, judging from my conversations with her since you've come to Washington. The tenor changed a little, am I right?"

I weighed how much I wanted to engage in a discussion with this guy about my boss. He was, at least, a political operator who I'd been warned about by Harmon before his death. If he was as tightly bound to Chalke as I thought, it seemed likely he was also part of this Network that had been on my back for years now.

Still, honesty was the best policy. "Yeah, she and I butted heads for the longest time. But I can only fight the power for so long before I have to choose whether I'm going to do it inside or outside the system. If that means I have to put up with Chalke's bullshit, I'll roll my eyes and get on with it. But don't expect me to smile while doing so. It's transactional, purely. She feeds me cases, I minimize the headaches I give her."

"That's a very mature approach given your mutual antipathy," Bilson said, nodding along. "I've met people like that before. Ones that just...they grate on me, you know?"

Of course I knew. But to this, I just nodded.

"What if there was a way for you to do your job but not have to answer to Chalke?" Bilson asked. He wasn't smiling, but he had a twinkle in his eyes. "Maybe you could work for someone who could give you a little more freedom to maneuver?"

"I think she tried that with Willis Shaw up in New York," I said, shaking my head. "Probably didn't work out the way she intended, thus our new arrangement."

"See, I think Director Chalke has been mishandling you," Bilson said. "You are a valuable member of the government team. The natural leader for any metahuman response. Vital to the national security effort." There went that gleam in his eye again. "I think you're wasted in the FBI. Once we get out of this, maybe we can talk to the president about finding a way to make your working life easier and more comfortable."

Easier and more comfortable? "Well, I wouldn't say no to that."

"All right, cool, we'll talk more later," he said, and turned to climb the last steps to the next floor. "Remember, her name is Bridget Schultz. Been in the State Department for her whole career, basically."

"Okay," I said, my forehead wrinkling as we came up to her door, which was just off the open staircase. The front of my head had started to ache, a slow, radiating pain starting from just behind my eyes. I put a finger to my temple and rubbed; the skin was tense on my scalp, and I started to wonder if I'd cinched my ponytail too tight with my meta strength.

"Coming," came a muffled voice from inside, then thudding, irregular footsteps. Someone bumped into the wall within, then hit the door. I frowned through the headache, because it sounded a little like Bridget Schultz was...well, drunk.

After fumbling with the deadbolt twice she finally got the door open. The thunking of the bolt both times told me she'd left it unlocked, and clearly didn't realize that it was. When she opened the door, we were treated to the visage of a person who was clearly in the throes of some illness. Her blond hair was dyed, showing hints of gray at the roots. Her eyes were blank, floating over my face without a hint of recognition, then to Bilson's where they lit dimly. "Oh. Hello, Russell," she said, in a very airy, distant voice.

"Hello, Bridget," he said, and leaned in to give her a hug in which he definitely kept his body as distant and rigid as possible. Whether this was because he feared a sexual harassment allegation from pressing against her red silken bathrobe or because of her illness was unclear, but I was banking on the latter by 60/40 or so. "How are you feeling?"

She brushed a pale, spider-veined hand over her forehead as though mopping off sweat with her silken sleeve. She looked a little young to be developing obvious spider veins, but I supposed they occurred in all sorts of people. "Fine. I'm...fine." She seemed like she lost her train of thought mid-reply.

"Can we come in?" Bilson asked.

Bridget blinked a couple times. "Oh. Did I invite you over today?" Her eyes were distant, scanning the horizons of her memory for something she'd forgotten.

"Uh, yes," Bilson said. "We came to talk to you about this China situation?"

"Oh, well, come in, then," she said, leaving the door wide and wandering back, thumping off a wall as she walked on unsteady legs.

I looked at Bilson, he looked at me. I could tell by his querying, quasi-apologetic look that he had his doubts this was going to go anywhere, given the state of her, but he led and I followed him in, shutting the door behind me. As I closed the door, my skull started to throb.

"Would you like some...some tea?" she asked, thumping into a countertop in the kitchen. The apartment was in bad shape; dishes were piled in the sink, some broken. I saw a sharp edge of what seemed to have once been a lovely dinner plate dotted with blood and piled in the stack. She turned, eyes not quite focused on either of us. Her pupils were dilated, lending credence to the idea she was on something, drug-wise. Charitably, I thought it could be to counter her current illness.

"No, that's fine, Bridget," Bilson said, and let an awkward chuckle be his shield as he launched into an uncomfortable topic. "I feel a little bad that I asked you for this meeting today. I had no idea you were so...under the weather."

"It's been...months of this," Bridget said, head drifting side to side as if she were on a sailboat being buffeted by winds. "Doctors keep saying...they don't know what's wrong." She let out a dry, pained laugh. "Not cancer, they say. But other than that," she just shook her head, face going blank like she'd just done a factory reset. "What was I saying?"

"Jesus," Bilson muttered under his breath.

Just then, I felt the pressure in my head go up a step, and I bowed my head forward, fingers against my face. I took a large breath, a huge intake of air sucked in through my nose to counter the – well, it felt a little like a brain freeze, really – and caught a whiff of something in the process.

Blood.

Ignoring the rapidly developing Category 5 headache spreading through my skull, I lifted my face. The overhead lights were off, but a window on the wall had a crack between the curtains that was letting in some light. It felt like someone was shining a searchlight on my face.

"Something is wrong here," I said to Bilson, the pain in my skull getting worse by the minute.

"Yeah, she's suffering from early onset dementia," Bilson said out of the corner of his mouth, not looking at me.

"No," I said, loudly, "there is something really wrong in this apartment."

He turned to look at me, and did a double take. "What...what is it?"

I shuffled across the kitchen to Bridget, stopping just in front of her. She weaved unsteadily, almost falling over on the counter from my proximity. I took a long sniff–

Yep. I didn't even need to get closer.

"Call 911," I said, narrowing it down as best I could around my splitting headache. "She needs to go to the hospital now."

"What is it?" Bilson asked, but cheers to him, he already had his phone and was dialing before he did so.

I didn't bother to answer. I was prowling out of the kitchen now, following my skull rather than my nose this morning. It felt like someone had stuck an air hose in my ear canal and was adding pressure by the second. I ducked into a spare bedroom, shut the door, and felt a moment's relief.

Opening it back up, I was assailed again, head back to splitting with pressure. It was like someone was chopping wood on the crown of my head now, that my eyeballs were being inflated and threatening to blow back into my skull.

I shut myself in Bridget's bedroom and again, felt relief. I was having trouble thinking while I was out in the main area, but each time I went into a bedroom – boom. Pressure off, at least a little, like taking the tea kettle off the fire.

Braving the main area again, I realized there was a bathroom. I closed the door without entering, felt nothing change, my head still threatening to blow off my shoulders. Old Faithful had clearly been placed in my neck by some magic I didn't understand. No, worse – Vesuvius. Mt. Saint Helens. The Yellowstone supervolcano. All three, maybe. My skull was suffering from the buildup of pressure, and if I didn't let it loose soon, maybe by running my head into the wall, I was sure I was going to die.

But no. That wasn't it. Something here was the problem.

I bumbled by an air vent, listening to Bilson in the distance talking to someone on the phone about sending an ambulance – no, two of them, now Now *NOW!* And felt the curious sensation of someone driving a railroad spike into my left ear.

The one closest to the wall.

To the vent.

I turned, and my whole head was assailed by pain, rapiers in both ears. I closed my eyes. Felt pain in darkness.

My fingers crept into the slats of the air vent, tightened. I ripped it free–

And was confronted, when I opened my eyes, by psychedelic

colors. And a dark duct that led two or three feet before disappearing in a turn.

I looked down. There, on the duct floor, before it dropped down, out of sight, was a little black...something.

Seizing it, I felt the pain, the pressure in my head threaten to explode everything. I turned it over in my fingers, cringing from it even as I forced my eyes open, looking for–

Hey, a switch.

I tried to flick it and failed. Four times. My fine motor skills were so pathetically enfeebled that I couldn't do shit.

"Bilson," I said, mouth full of cotton. "Bilth-on." It was getting worse by the second.

He was a distant blur of shadow, and I locked onto him, toddling to him on legs as unsteady as Bridget's by now. I held the little black blur on my palm out like an offering to a god. "Swish," I said, pushing toward him. "Swish...switch...it...off..."

I tumbled over at his feet, face going straight into the soft-pile carpeting. I cupped my hand by instinct, warring against dropping the black blur that was trying to kill me. Once I was safely ensconced in the carpeting, I opened my hand again, my face drooling into the soft pile.

"Swish..." I said. My mind hurt, but was nearly blank. "Swish it..."

A soft pressure on my hand released as he pulled the black thing from it. "Switch?" he asked, but he sounded like he was miles away, underwater, maybe.

Then...like a sunny day coming as all the clouds blew away...the pain stopped.

I enjoyed the pleasant sensation of the removal of the spikes from my ears for only a moment before my brain decided it had enough of this shit for today, and blessedly let me pass out.

CHAPTER THIRTY-SIX

"What is this thing?" Bilson asked. The black "blur" as I'd thought of it was in fact a piece of electronic equipment no bigger than half a standard business card. It was sitting on the counter in Bridget Schultz's apartment between us as the paramedics chattered somewhere in the periphery of my (still) clouded consciousness, working to treat the occupant of this inadvertently murderous hellhole.

I was not quite my best, but at least I was back on my feet, drool dried off my face and a couple dots of blood blotted out of my ear canals. "A sonic weapon." I rubbed my forehead. "I think."

Bilson stared at it as though doing so might make it combust. "Well...why is it here?"

Still rubbing my forehead, it took me a second to let his question permeate my melon, and another before I conjured an answer. "I have a guess, but I'd like to wait a minute before sharing."

"Why?" Bilson asked.

A knock on the apartment door frame heralded the arrival of someone else. It was a nerdy guy in a suit, with a plastic case in his hand. "Agent Nealon? I'm Speer. Electronics division. You called?"

"And you came, lickety-split," I said wearily, pushing myself off the counter and to full upright position, like a grownup, functional human being. Which I did not feel like, presently. "Two things. First, we found this." I nodded to the black device on the counter. "I think it's a sonic weapon."

Speer made a face. "That's not a thing we run into, really."

"Well, I'm not common," I said, and tilted my head to indicate Bridget, who was being strapped to a gurney by paramedics. "And this woman worked for the State Department. Chinese division."

Speer's face went from funny to panicked in a heartbeat. "Oh. Okay. Well." And he sidled over to me, snapping on a glove and pulling an evidence bag from his pocket as he came. Picking the device up gingerly, he bagged it, then labeled it with a black Sharpie. That done, he turned to me. "You're...you're sure it's a sonic device?"

"Pretty sure," I said, looking at Bridget again. "Based on her level of neurological deterioration."

"No, I want to stay here," Bridget said to the paramedic, sounding like a child arguing with an unfair parent. "I don't want to go. Not out there. It's so...*bright*," she whined the last part.

Speer's face switched to near-panic, eyes widening and face paling. "Oh boy."

"Yeah," I said, rubbing my face again. It didn't help make me feel any better.

"Why the weirdness, guys?" Bilson asked.

"I need this apartment swept for bugs," I said to Speer, snapping my fingers. "That's the second thing. Took a minute to remember."

Speer gave me a look of concern. "How long were you exposed to this device?"

"Less than five minutes," Bilson said, thankfully answering for me. My perception of the passage of time while in the mouth of hell that was the sonic weapon had been all twisted up.

I shrugged, nodded. "I'll be fine. Meta healing will take care of me. Worry about her." I looked again at Bridget, who was now being wheeled out and crying softly, bound to the gurney. "And sweep this place, please. Any bugs, I want them documented, and the listening source found. Okay?"

Speer nodded, opened his case, pulled out a weird-looking bug sweeper, and went to work on the kitchen while we were standing there. He finished that area in about a minute, then walked through the front door hallway before returning to us. "This section's clear. I'll get the living area next. Bedrooms last?"

"Sounds good," I said, and as soon as he was clear, I pulled Bilson toward the front door with a beckoning motion. He followed me, broad face full of curiosity.

Once we were in the hallway, and out of the range of any undiscovered listening devices, I gently took his collar and pulled his head to me. He acceded without fighting the motion, and once my lips were by his ear, I whispered the answer to his question. "Sonic weapons have never been used on US soil before, and we only know of two cases where they've been employed at all. The first was at our embassy in Cuba." I swallowed heavily. "The other was against a US diplomat...in Guangzhou, China."

CHAPTER THIRTY-SEVEN

"So are we out of leads for the moment?" Bilson asked, at the wheel of his Maserati.

"Yep," I said, resting my head against the wonderful leather seats, just enjoying the smoothness of the ride. "Until someone from forensics gives me something, or Speer gets me a clue from the device, I think we're tapped out...for the moment."

"You need to get back to your office?"

I started to shake my head, but it still hurt, so I said, "No. There's nothing I can really do there. I'd rather go home and rest."

"That sonic thing really took it out of you, huh?" Bilson asked, voice laden with concern.

"Felt like someone was trepanning my head," I said, not opening my eyes. The brightness of the world was a hell of a bother.

"There's a conference room at my offices with comfortable chairs," Bilson said. "You could chill there while I get some other business taken care of. I can have lunch brought in for you." He quieted for a moment. "I'm just not sure you should be alone right now. There's still blood in your ears."

I dabbed my left ear, and it came away wet. "Okay. Fine. Whatever." I didn't open my eyes. Didn't feel like arguing.

We made it to his offices, and I followed him to the elevator.

I didn't even remember walking into the conference room, or collapsing in a comfy leather chair. But I woke up in the chair, with the towel, a couple spots of scarlet suggesting whoever had put it there was a genius, because it kept it off the leather.

Checking my phone, I discovered that I had no messages and that it was now after 1 p.m. My head still ached, but it was more a stuffy kind of ache, the remnant of a worse headache now gone rather than the fresh, my-eyeballs-want-to-bleed pain I'd experienced at Bridget's.

Opening the door to the conference room, I found the offices bustling outside. I couldn't even remember what day of the week it was, but clearly it was a weekday because Bilson's political operation was in full swing. Rows of cubicles sat occupied, people working at computers or on the phones. I caught something about "donors," and I doubted they were talking about organs, the way Holloway had.

"How are you feeling?" Bilson's secretary intercepted me no more than ten steps out of the conference room.

"Muzzy," I said, and it felt right, though hell if I could remember what exactly that word meant. If it was a word at all.

She smiled, her face blurred under these bright lights. "Mr. Bilson left me instructions to show you right in to him when you woke up. Unless you need to use the ladies' room first?"

"No, I'm fine," I said, following after her. "Probably a little dehydrated, though." I smacked my lips together and yeah, they were dry.

"What would you like to drink?" she asked with great vivacity. "Coffee? Tea? Cola? Water?"

"Water's fine," I said as she opened Bilson's door. I walked in and she shut it behind me.

Bilson was on a call, little wireless earbuds in both ears. He smiled and held up a single finger to me, then gestured to the chairs in front of his desk. I plopped down in one as he nodded, looking down, clearly immersed in his call.

"Yes, Jonah, exactly. That's what we're looking for. Write the piece, send it to me, and I'll see you get paid handsomely for it." He reached down and touched the screen, looked up at me and smiled. "Rough couple days, huh? Feeling better?"

"Than when I was bleeding from the ears? Yeah." I looked around his office, trying to note the various politicians he was posed with, and in what settings. Most seemed to be at formal events, Bilson in a tux or suit, the other players dressed likewise. A few were in other venues, though; fishing boats and golf courses seemed to be a popular choice.

"Admiring the lifestyle photos?" Bilson followed my gaze to one of his pictures. "Ah."

My attention had caught on a photo of Bilson, looking a little younger, and posed, grinning, next to former President Gerry Harmon.

Bilson moved out from behind his desk, easing slowly to the picture. He glanced at me, and his usual smile turned a little sad. "Do you miss him?"

I froze. "I wasn't a huge fan when he was in office, and Gondry seems nice enough, so–"

"No," Bilson said, looking straight at me. He raised a finger to his temple. "I meant do you miss having him...in here."

Now I was starting to feel the discomfort. Two times in two days people had referenced knowing that I'd had a former president in my head, yet they seemed to know he was gone, too. Which was interesting, since that wasn't a story I'd been spreading around.

Bilson must have sensed my discomfort, because he took the pressure off. "Everyone knows."

"Can I ask *what* they 'know?'" I looked at him. "Because if what you just said about me is true, I'm guilty of...well, a lot."

"You want to know the official Washington rumor?" Bilson fiddled with his jacket buttons. "Gerry Harmon was a metahuman with telepathic powers, who had a plan to use that special serum that magnifies powers to take us all over. Mentally, I mean." His smile returned, but less smarmy. "Confirm or deny?"

"That was true," I said. "He got really close, too."

Bilson didn't show much reaction to that. "You stopped him. Nearing the last minute."

"I would have done it sooner but I was kinda on the run from the law at the time." I kept my eyes on the picture, but Bilson reacted, just a little, in my peripheral vision.

"Like I told you outside Bridget's apartment, you're a perfect guardian angel, and after Revelen, the world sees it," Bilson said. "We should be proclaiming your every victory loudly to the rooftops."

"Look, I'm not trying to fight with you," I said, finally turning and facing him, "but I watched cable news while I was on the run. I caught you magnifying my every fault the last couple years every chance you got. Why the change of heart?"

"I could ask you the same thing," Bilson said, and his smile faded. "But...fair enough. You're right. I did you wrong. Very wrong. I can admit it. I knew you killed Harmon. The rumor mill was loud and clear about that–"

"Oh, well, if the rumor mill said it, it must be true."

Bilson let out a mirthless chuckle. "You have a point. But there was peripheral evidence. I'm not looking for you to confirm your involvement, but Harmon did a great job covering his tracks in framing you."

I let that stand, though I was growing more and more suspicious Bilson was a cog in the Network that had done the actual job for Harmon, because that didn't seem like the sort of thing I could just get him to admit. "He did indeed," I said. "Because I was the only one he perceived could stop him."

"And you did," Bilson said. "Marvelously. With only an entire wall of the Oval Office as a casualty, which is impressive considering everything he threw at you. The entire military. Law enforcement. Your own friends."

"Yeah, it was a rough couple months," I said, feeling the discomfort pulsate through my veins. "Fine. You made a mistake backing Harmon. But what changed your mind about me?"

"The problem with people in this world," Bilson said, "is they get settled in their ways of thinking. You know, like, uh–"

"'Sienna Nealon is an evil monster we should hunt to the ends of the earth?'"

"Exactly," Bilson's eyes lit up. "We get caught up in our own point of view. The human is an emotional creature. You can't argue a person out of their position. We make our decisions, and then we will move heaven and earth to defend them, throwing out increasingly erratic statements to cover for them, even as the iceberg melts beneath us. You will nearly never change someone's mind unless they are open to it. And that's the way it was with me, I'm not too proud to say."

I searched his face for hints of lying. He was good, I'd give him that. "Well, I'm glad you came around," I said lamely, looking for a way out for both of us.

"I'm glad I did, too," Bilson said, smile fading. "But you never did answer my original question."

"Hm?"

"Do you miss having him up here?" Bilson pointed to his head again.

I took a deep breath, looking back at the photo of Harmon. "It's certainly a lot quieter up here these days. I miss the powers, that's for sure." Harmon was wearing a plastered-on smile. It looked totally sincere, but having had the benefit of knowing the man, knowing his thoughts, I knew it was fake.

"I can hardly imagine what it would have been like," Bilson said, voice laced with quiet awe. "Harmon was the single greatest political operator of our time. He was a man who could shift a person's paradigm in real time, while you watched. You know, as he talked to voters?"

"Because he was reading their mind and changing it for them," I said, giving Bilson the side-eye.

"I know that, now," Bilson said, a little defensively. "But watching him when he started his first national campaigns, you know, as a VP candidate, it was like watching a master work. Sure, we know he was 'cheating' at this point, but the awe that he inspired...well, it's hard to just erase that. Kind of like if we found out a sports legend was metahuman. Yes, I'd distantly think a little less of them, but it'd be tough to bring my brain around to completely disassociate their achievements from them given the new information." He looked over at me. "What...what was he like?"

How to answer that? Carefully, I decided, and quickly. "He was about what you'd expect. Quick-witted, intelligent. Dangerously intelligent. I'm not sure if it was entirely based on his mind-reading, but he was amazing at picking the weaknesses in people."

"I knew him a little," Bilson said, and gave me a hopeful look. "Did he ever mention that?"

Boy, had he. Not wanting to share Harmon's rather dim opinion of Bilson, though, I said, "Maybe in passing? He talked a lot. I didn't always listen."

Bilson slowly shook his head. "Such a loss. It was the Scotland succubus, then? The one who nearly took over their country?" He seemed to search his memory. "Rose Steward?"

I couldn't help the seething look that came over me, causing my eyes to twitch at the corners at the mere mention of her name. Even still. "Yeah. That was her."

"Such a terrible loss," Bilson said quietly. "A terrible waste."

He seemed to be voicing genuine remorse for my loss, which was strange, to say the least. I hadn't done a formal survey, but I had to believe your average person on the street probably considered it good that I'd lost the accumulation of abilities that pushed me closer to godlike powers than was comfortable for most people. At least those with a brain.

After a moment, Bilson seemed to switch tacks. "So...if you could paint a canvas of your ideal life–"

"I wouldn't. I'm terrible at the arts."

Bilson chuckled. "Metaphorically. If you could design your ideal life, what would it look like?"

"Well, there wouldn't be any painting."

"No, I meant–"

"I really hate paint. It smells terrible. Get a little on your hand and it sticks there, possibly forever–"

"But–"

"You have to use acetone to get it off, and that's even worse smelling than the paint."

"Okay, forget painting, forget I said anything about paint." Bilson drew a breath, let it out slow. "What would your ideal life look like?"

I surveyed his office, probably not-so-subtly looking for an escape route. "I don't know."

"Well, what are you into in your spare time?" He smiled. "Not sports, we know that much. Though, I must say, you might enjoy taking in a game in person. There's a different energy to being there versus watching on TV. It's fun. An event."

"I've gone," I said. "You're right, there is. The amount of people is disquieting. Also, I gotta be careful."

He raised an eyebrow. "Oh? How so?"

"Well," I said dryly, "think about it. You know the Kiss Cam?"

"Yeah...?"

"With me, it'd become a snuff film."

He chuckled. "I suppose it would. But seriously..." His amusement faded. "...What do you want?"

To be left alone, I didn't say. Wanted to. Didn't.

"To do my job," I said.

"No, no, no." Bilson made a sad little clucking noise, then shook his head. "Here, let me give you an example. My name is Russ Bilson, and I want to be the National Security Advisor."

I blinked my surprise. "Wait. You do?"

Bilson shrugged, a hint of defensiveness to his posture. "Well...yes."

"But it's a government job," I said, looking around his office, which was way nicer than anything I'd seen in government service. "You have this whole lobbying and consulting thing going on that's gotta pay way more than that."

"Definitely," Bilson said. "But money's not everything. There's real utility to having access to the policymaking apparatus at that level. Long-term experience, insight that would make me better at this job after spending a few years learning."

I let out a sound that was somewhere between a cow's bleat and a gag. "I'm not gonna lie, Washington, to me, looks a lot like a bunch of insiders switching seats on their way up the pyramid. There's a lot of gladhanding going on. It's an incestuous company town, where everyone's just slowly making their way up toward the top as best they can. Everybody at the top knows each other, they're all patting each other on the back–"

"Or stabbing each other in the back," Bilson said darkly. "There's stabbing, too. Trust me."

"It just feels very..." I made a face, then mimed the heebie-jeebie motion of shakes.

"I don't think it's that bad," Bilson said. "It's power, and access to power. There's a game element to it. There's a fair amount of networking going on. But that's life in any society. It's how we organize ourselves, right? There's always a ladder, and always someone above you, until you get to President Gondry's position."

"Maybe it's because I've been kicked down the ladder a few times," I said, "but I don't like people having power over me. And I don't particularly like exercising mine on others, which is why I generally reserve it for when they've done bad things."

"Well," Bilson said, his smile drawing tightly across his face, "I suppose it's a matter of perspec–"

"What did Bridget know?" I asked, the idea just hitting me like a stray lightning bolt.

Bilson took a moment for his brain to shift gears. "Uh...what?"

"What did she know?" I asked. "What motivated China to put a sonic device in her apartment?"

All the emotion left Bilson's face. "I don't think we can lay this at China's feet. We have no idea where that device came from, and making accusations like that given the dearth of evidence–"

"I'm not going on the news and shouting, 'China is hurting our diplomats!' while wearing a sandwich board," I said. "I'm investigating, and part of that means coming up with a working theory that you try and prove as you go. I realize the evidence is thin, and as soon as some starts to show up to contradict my theory, I'm fine with abandoning it. But for now, it looks to me like China has sent in agents to kidnap at least one, possibly more American citizens, and that they've planted at least one sonic device in a State Department employee's home."

"That could have been someone else," Bilson said with growing annoyance.

"Yeah, but probably not, given that these aren't commercially available products," I said. "Someone researched and built this, they didn't buy it at the local Walmart. Money was put behind its development. Ergo, a state actor is probably behind it, because they've got money, time and interest. Thus, China. But leave that aside for a second – what's the motive for rendering Bridget a barely-coherent radish?"

"I don't know," Bilson said, looking like he was about a second from interrupting me to argue again.

"Nor do I," I said, pulling out my phone, "but I want to find out."

CHAPTER THIRTY-EIGHT

"I cannot just get you a meeting with SecState Ngo," Chalke said over the fuzzing phone, "she's a cabinet level officer."

Bilson just looked at me coolly. He'd predicted this would be the response. He also hadn't offered to set up such a meeting himself, which told me either he didn't have the juice or was seriously uncurious about what Bridget might have known that resulted in her incapacitation by, presumably, the Chinese government.

"I know she's a busy lady," I said, "but I need to talk to someone at State about this employee. There was a device in her apartment that was causing her brain damage."

Chalke was quiet for a moment. "Was it a television?"

I ignored her facile attempt at a joke. "It was a dedicated sonic device designed to cause long-term brain damage."

Chalke went dormant again; I wondered if she was edging toward exploding at me.

But she didn't. "I might be able to get you a call back from her, but not right now. Later today, at best."

"That's perfect," I said. "Just give her my number and the employee's name. I don't even need to talk to her, necessarily, just someone who's known Bridget for a while and is aware of her work history."

Chalke made a noncommittal grunt, then asked, "Anything else?"

"Just waiting on a heap of forensic evidence," I said.

"Is she playing nice, Russ?" Chalke asked.

"So far she's fine," Bilson said, seeming to let go of the 2 by 4 I'd planted up his ass with my refusal to let go of accusing China of being involved in this. "I'll keep you in the loop."

"Sounds good," Chalke said, and hung up.

"You guys sound chummy," I observed, but Bilson turned away. Interesting.

"You need to keep any accusations about China to yourself," Bilson said, circling back around his desk, all business. "You understand?"

I debated being old Sienna and throwing some retort at him. I swallowed my pride instead. "I'm just pursuing possibilities. I'll keep it all to myself, if you want. I won't mention it again, in fact, unless some new evidence comes to light."

His face softened. "I don't mean to suggest you can't say it around *me*. I just don't want this theory of yours to go public. China, as a country...well, saving face is very important to them. It's cultural. So any accusation of this kind, especially from a leading light in American law enforcement, well...it could have implications."

"What kind of implications?"

"Bad ones," Bilson said. "Economic. Diplomatic. Military, even."

"I'll keep my theories to myself, then," I said, smiling tightly. "Hey, I should probably get out of your hair. I need to check in at the office anyway."

Bilson nodded, seemingly pulled toward his desk like an object trapped in a gravity well. "I do have a few things I need to catch up on myself," he said distractedly. He snapped his eyes up at me. "Let me know if you get any leads?"

"Will do," I said, edging toward the door. "You'll be the first to know."

And out I went, off to pursue a lead I wanted Bilson to know absolutely nothing about.

CHAPTER THIRTY-NINE

It didn't take long to find what I was looking for. It was a nondescript rental car parked just down the street from my special FBI office. A slate gray sedan, only a year or two old, with Colorado plates. I spotted it from the end of the street, where I had my Uber driver drop me.

Sneaking down a street in broad daylight is a bad idea, so I just walked casually, consciously keeping myself out of the arc of the sedan's rearview mirrors. This involved walking on the opposite side of the street until I was about twenty yards from the car, then crossing the road in the driver's blind spot.

And there was a driver. I could see her dark hair through the window, a little heat distortion at the car's tailpipe, the engine humming quietly as it idled. Based on the humidity collecting at the base of my spine (boy, did my back love to sweat in the DC summer), I thought keeping the car running was a pretty smart move.

I crept the last few yards and knocked on the window, causing the driver to freak the eff out beautifully. She tossed her phone as her whole body seized up in surprise. She jerked her head around and looked right at me, pure terror pasted on her face.

Whoooooooops.

"Sorry, sorry," I said, looking into the face of a black-haired woman I'd never seen before. From the side and back, she looked like Michelle Cheong. The hairstyle was exact. "I thought you were someone else," I mouthed as she flipped me the bird then bent to fish for her phone.

"That's some mighty fine policing you're doing there," someone called from just down the street. I turned my head to find Michelle chuckling at me from a little alcove built into the building across the street from my office. "What's next, harassing kids drawing on the sidewalk with chalk for defacement?"

"Ha ha," I said, crossing the street back toward her. "I was looking for you, you know."

Michelle's eyes were alight with amusement. "Oh, I know. Which is what makes it even funnier. You tried to get the drop on me and made an ass of yourself." She looked to the skies. "This is such a gift, really."

"Yeah, yeah," I said, slipping across the quiet sidewalk to stand next to her in the alcove. It was a function of the building's design; Roman columns extending out from the facade left a space that was perfect for someone to stand in, sheltered from the wind. Not that you'd want to be sheltered from the wind on a day like that, but it also perfectly protected her from observation at either end of the street, yet she could slip up and look in either direction any time she wanted. A nice little hidey-hole, and it was almost exactly across from my office. "You're like that cat that always lands on her feet. So?"

Michelle was smiling, but it faded the closer I got. "So." She lapsed into silence.

I looked around; no one could see us unless they walked by or glanced out one of the windows of my office across the way. Which was unlikely, because the offices directly across from where we stood were in the disused part of the building. The sidewalks had been pretty empty, too, but I suppose you can never be too careful. "What?" I asked. "Do we need to talk elsewhere?"

"No, this is fine." Michelle shook her head. "Besides, I don't know any of the local restaurants and I doubt any are as good as the Bon Ton Cafe. Just...trying to get my thoughts together before I launch into this." She lapsed into another silence. "You know I hire and bring in people from China to work in my businesses, right?"

"Uh, yeah," I said. "I remember well chasing after that Chinese grandma when you sent her down Bourbon Street and told her to wait for me." Also, that the rest of her work force was cut from similar cloth, in terms of ethnicity.

Michelle nodded slowly. "Right. Well." She stalled there again.

"Was one of them kidnapped?" I asked, tired of waiting. I kinda needed to pee, and all this cloak and dagger wasn't getting me closer to a bathroom.

"Well...they definitely disappeared," Michelle said. "And it wasn't *one* of them." She bit her lip. "It was three of them."

I frowned. "What?" Three?

She nodded. "Two sisters, and a guy that was a distant cousin of theirs. They lived separately – well, the cousin did. The sisters lived in the same apartment with some other people."

"Did someone come crashing into the apartment and drag them out?" I asked.

She shook her head again. "No. They just...disappeared. Didn't answer phone calls – phones are shut off, actually. Didn't show up for work. And when I checked in, the sisters hadn't come home the night before. Same with the cousin." She shrugged. "They're all just...gone."

Time for the tough questions. "Are you sure they didn't just...run off?" I asked.

"That does happen sometimes," Michelle said slowly. "And the fact that they're a family unit makes it more likely. But..." She hesitated, checking the street. Presumably there was no one out there, because she turned and meandered back to me, but lowered her voice. "These people worked in the legitimate part of the business."

I gave her a wary eye. "I thought it was all legitimate now."

"I'm working on it," she said, and a little fire lit in her eyes, giving her more pep than she'd had in our whole conversation thus far. Color me shocked that Michelle hadn't completely extricated herself from criminal activity. "But the point is – I'm not the only person who imports Chinese labor for massage parlors and other enterprises in this country."

"Ah, yes, the famed Sino Illegal Activities Guild and Yoga Club. You must be a charter member with those pants."

"Hah," she said mirthlessly. "I talked to a few of my peers. I'm not the only who's had disappearances. And they're not all labor, and not all first generation."

I blinked, thinking that one through. "How many are we talking here?"

"I don't know," she said, going quiet and sullen. "Near as I can tell, at least fifty. In my little neck of the woods."

I sagged forward, my eyes widening dramatically. *"Fifty?"* I took a step closer to her. "You're telling me fifty people of Chinese origin have gone missing from this pool of immigrants and no one's noticed but you?"

"Of course people have noticed," she snapped. "But think about who you're dealing with here. Most of these people came to the US looking for a better life. Lots come from rural China. A few from the cities. They're brought over for labor – cheap, labor, okay? Usually for jobs people don't want to do, like massaging the grubby feet of elderly tourists from Florida or giving handjobs to octogenarians or–"

"Selling furniture to residents of DC," I said, filling in the blanks from my own recent experience.

"Yeah, politicians and their staffers are generally awful people," Michelle said. "I might prefer putting a hand on an octogenarian to that. Anyway – they're not plugged into the American system, let's say. They're cloistered off by their employers. Kept in apartments with lots of fellow workers. They're either here on an employer-sponsored visa that can be revoked at any time the employer chooses–"

"Ah, helotage. The more things change..."

"–Or they're here illegally," she said. "Either way, they're less likely to call the cops if people start going missing, you know what I'm saying?"

"So they go unnoticed," I said as a pigeon flapped on a ledge above me. "Your buddies in the underworld – they're not going to report them missing, I take it?"

She shook her head. "Can't. It would lead to uncomfortable questions about how they got here, what they're doing, working conditions...also, they probably don't have the standing in some cases to file a missing persons report, even if they wanted to. Local cops would just say–"

"They ran away," I said. "But you're sure this is happening. It's a thing, Chinese nationals–"

"And some American citizens of Chinese descent. Like your case."

"Yeah," I said, shaking my head. "And...seriously, fifty?"

She nodded slowly. "That I know of."

"My God," I whispered. That damned pigeon flapped again above me, and I cast it a dirty look. Pigeons were the bane of my existence. Other than superpowered people with lawbreaking tendencies, I mean. Damned sky rats.

"What are you going to do?" Michelle asked, rubbing her arms and hugging herself lightly.

I started to walk away, because I sensed our conversation had reached its natural end. "I don't know. Go poking around, probably. How do I reach you if I need to?"

She gave me a sly look. "Why would you need to reach me?"

"Because I don't have a reliable source of information on China," I said, pausing at the street.

She stepped out to the edge of the alcove and looked left, then right. "That's kind of racist, assuming I know anything about China just because I'm Asian."

"I didn't assume it because you were Asian. I assumed it because you're the Triad boss of New Orleans, which, last I checked, was a *Chinese* organized crime syndicate–"

"Yeah, yeah." She waved me off, then stepped up to me, proffering a white business card.

I took it. All that was on it was a phone number and nothing else. "Oh, I get it. You're a criminal, so you give this to cops and they have to investigate their way to you. Clever. Very meta, joke-wise."

"A necessary precaution in my line of work," she said. "You don't want your name and address and whatnot out there, especially if you're talking to a cop."

"And you do so often enough to need a blank business card printed up," I said, waving it, smiling at her. "For yoga mom play-dates, I assume? I'll be in touch, Blankwoman."

"Don't call me if you can avoid it," she called out as I crossed the street. "I don't need to be subpoenaed to testify in some court about this."

"Yes, I know," I said, looking back at her as I went. "You're just doing it out of the goodness of your heart. Or something." I caught her frown before I left her behind, but somehow I knew, in spite of her denial, that Michelle hadn't put all this together and traveled to Washington for solely professional concerns.

She really did care, somehow. Who she cared about...well, that was still an open question.

CHAPTER FORTY

"I thought I gave you the week off?" I asked as I walked into the FBI office. Holloway was there, hanging out at his computer, checking sports scores. Baseball, it looked like.

He closed the window just as I got close enough to read them. "You're not my boss," he said, spinning around in his chair. "And also...since Hilton's on paid leave pending the investigation..."

"Peace and quiet for you, time off for her," I said, slipping off my jacket and draping it over my chair. "Sounds like a win/win."

"I feel like I'm the real winner here," Holloway said. "I know I'm a fossilized misogynist pig and all, but the shit she tells me about from her personal life–"

"I know, right? Who wants to hear about her latest Tinder date's foot fetish in action?"

Holloway blinked. "Actually, I could stand to hear about that. She only overshares *feelings* with me." He did a full body shake. "Like I want to talk about my feelings with anyone, let alone my co-worker who got out of the neonatal care unit around the time I lost my virginity."

"I bet that was a special time for both of you," I said. "It's something you have in common: both on the breast at the same time and all that."

Holloway chuckled. He really was a pig, but I'd dealt with

worse. Since that time he'd gotten out of line with me in New Orleans, he hadn't put one toe over it since. "You didn't ask about news."

"The news is always bad, unless it's the Huey Lewis variety, in which case it's always *amazing.*"

He just shook his head in response to my lame joke. "It's really not hip to be square." Then he lifted a Post-it note. "Also, there's this."

I squinted at the note. Tough to read at this distance, mostly because the handwriting was doctor-on-a-prescription-pad level bad. "'Spock's...ballin'?'"

He flashed a look at the writing, then rolled his eyes. "The Glocks carried by the guys at the kidnapping yesterday morning and the furniture store after that? Stolen. Forensics matched the serial numbers to an entry in the database."

"A stolen gun being used to commit a crime?" I asked, filling my voice with the requisite sarcasm. "Why, I am so, so very shocked. You could knock me over with a feather right now."

"That's not the interesting part," Holloway said. "The interesting part is that they were stolen, all together, down in Northern Virginia. Fairfax, actually." He dangled the Post-it in front of me. "Also stolen? A .22 rifle, among a few other firearms."

I snatched the Post-it out of his fingers before he even realized it was gone, leaving him looking at his fingers with blank eyes for a second after I'd grabbed it. There was more on the back, almost as illegible. "Is this a number for a local cop?"

"Yeah, and I called him," Holloway said. "Let me save you the trouble of reaching him by giving you the bullet point answer – he said the whole thing was fishy as hell. Thought the burglary or theft or whatever was staged."

"Where were they stolen?" I asked, trying to make sense of Holloway's writing. Hopefully no one ever asked him to pen a will by hand, because if so, the entire estate was going to probate forever as they tried to decipher his chicken scratch.

"HKKCME, Inc. company security force," he said. "Guy in charge said they disappeared out of a storage locker, but our officer taking the report says the guy was nervous, twitchy, and generally full of shit."

"Is there an address for this place on here?" I asked, scouring the note. "Because I really want to talk to this suspicious character who lost the guns that ended up being pointed at me yesterday. Also, that name is suspiciously like another company I've run across in this. Bunch of garbled or random letters."

"No address," Holloway said, getting up. He pulled his coat off the back of his chair. "But I know where it is."

"What, you want to drive me?" I asked, picking up my own coat.

"I'd really just like to not be a desk jockey for a while," Holloway said. He seemed a little stuck in place, like he was waiting for me to veto his ability to come. I didn't have that power, but it was my investigation, and he was standing there like a hopeful puppy.

"Come on, little dog," I said, inclining my head toward the door. "I'll even let you ride with your head out the window."

"Oh, gee, thanks," he said, but he did come along. Tail wagging, almost.

CHAPTER FORTY-ONE

HKKCME, Inc. was located in an industrial/office park in Fairfax, Virginia, a scenic suburb half an hour outside DC. We hit Interstate 66 and were there pretty quickly. Fairfax was a burgeoning suburb that looked like so many I'd seen across America: big box stores, lots of greenery between the commerce zones, and a section of office parks a little off the beaten path from the aforementioned stores.

As Holloway cruised us into the parking lot of HKKCME, Inc.'s office, he nodded at the security checkpoint. "This looks vaguely serious."

"Really?" I asked, scoping the booth, which had a tollbooth barrier keeping us from entering. A white-shirted security guard with a tie and a baseball cap with HKKCME written across it started over to us. "Because it looks to me like a cheesedick operation that funneled guns to a Chinese kidnap team." I slapped my hand over my mouth. "Oops. *Allegedly*, I mean."

Holloway gave me a weird look, but the security guy was at the window so I didn't have time to explain the heat that Bilson had put on me about implicating the Chinese. The guy at the window was a basic white dude with glasses who looked about two missed meals from being a ninety-eight-pound weakling. So he was probably a hundred-pound weakling. He held a clipboard in his hand and peered in at us. "Can I help you?"

"FBI," I said, flashing my ID because Holloway's hands were on the wheel. "I need to talk to your head of security."

He looked in at me, and I caught a flash of recognition. He played it cool, though, and just nodded. "Uh huh." Coming up with a walkie-talkie a minute later, he radioed ahead. "Hey, this Brett...we got a couple FBI agents here to talk to Leif."

"What do they want?" the answer crackled back.

"To talk to Leif," I said, using my RBF game to my full advantage.

"Uhm," Brett said, stealing worried looks at me through his glasses. Poor guy was sweating. "I'm gonna send them through. Let Leif know they're coming up."

"Thanks, Brett," I said sweetly, and he hustled back to the booth to lift the barrier arm.

It swung up, Holloway drove through, then shot me an amused look. "Do you ever get tired of playing the bitch?"

"Do you?" I shot back, smiling.

He grinned as he pulled up in front of the HKKCME building, parking in the fire lane. I popped out as a guy in a suit came bustling out the front door. He was clearly on his way to intercept us, which I thought was hilarious. He was still fastening the bottom button of his suit when he got to us, talking to himself as he walked. I caught a snatch of it:

"...Can't believe he'd just let them in here like...didn't even call for an appointment...right in the middle of lunch, didn't even get to take my afternoon shit yet..."

"Hey," Holloway said as he got close. This time he flashed his ID. "Holloway and Nealon. FBI."

Leif wandered up, forcing a smile and looking at Holloway. "Yes, well. Leif Wallis."

He turned to me to shake my hand, and I let him, smiling from beneath my black glasses. "Sorry to interrupt your lunch before you could get your afternoon dump in, Leif," he paled, "but this is kinda important. See, it turns out those guns you Barney Fife wannabes lost? They got used in a kidnapping case yesterday. Also, to shoot at a federal agent."

"Oh, uh, well, ah..." He made a choking noise deep in his throat, "...see, uh, ahm, they were...stolen."

"Were they?" I asked, and watched Leif fade whiter. "Because I gotta tell you something..." I came up next to him, draped an arm over his shoulder like we were old chums, and started walking him toward the front door, "...the federal agent that was on the barrel end of your lost weapons? That was me. And I don't like being shot at, Leif. It's right up on my list between having to listen to Taylor Swift putting to music her terrible choices in men and getting my toenails pulled out during a light torture sesh. Capisce?"

"Yeah, I, arrrr..." Leif's voice failed him and he sailed straight into pirate vocalization territory. I'd never heard anyone do that before.

"So I need you to tell me something," I said, pushing into the office complex. "I need to know wh – what the hell?"

Leif's gulp was epic. He had a good reason to gulp, too – he had probably thought he could bullshit us out on the curb and keep us from walking him in the front door. Too bad for him I was the type to do whatever I wanted and ask for permission *never*.

The office building for HKKCME was absolutely empty. By which I mean the only damned thing in there was the metal pillars that framed in the basic outline of where offices should be.

There were no desks.

There were no people.

Hell, there were no *walls*.

There was a chair, however, and a card table, and a guilty-looking guy in a security uniform just like Brett from out at the gate, staring at us with half a turkey hoagie in his hand.

"I...I..." Leif was now stuck in broken record mode.

"Well, this is interesting," Holloway said, looking around. "Where did these guns get stolen from, exactly?"

"We, uh, up on the second floor we have a...lockbox," Mr. Hoagie managed to get out.

"What are you protecting against?" I asked, looking around. "There aren't even any copper wires to steal." I directed my gaze at Leif. "Where the hell were you going to take a shit? In the woods out back?"

Leif pointed, wordlessly, at the ceiling, which, to be fair, was present. There was a staircase in the far corner of the building that looked fully constructed.

"Show us what's up there," I said, giving Leif a light shove in that direction. Light for me, I mean. He still nearly went sprawling with its force.

Leif steadied himself and started in that direction, stiff-legged, like he needed to take that dump very badly. He turned and started to say something, but my face must have dissuaded him. He made his way, shaking and pale, toward the staircase.

"You come with us, peckerwood," Holloway said to the other guard. "I don't need you on my flank."

"What?" the guy sputtered.

"I don't trust you at my back," Holloway said, spelling it out for him, slow and derisively.

I trusted Holloway watching mine, though, so I followed after Leif as he reached the stairs and started to climb. We made it to the top and voila, here was a functional, built-out office building.

That was still completely empty.

"Well, you at least have the walls here," I said, looking the place over. It had a glue smell that presumably came from installing carpet. "No desks or people, but walls. It's progress."

Leif just shrugged, mouth and brain not exactly working in concert to provide me...well, anything.

"Is there anyone here?" I asked. I was standing in an open reception area. Ahead the room gave way to corridors, walls and offices. An empty elevator shaft lay to my left, just a gaping and swift path back to the first floor for anyone dumb enough to step into it.

"I don't think so," Leif whispered.

Holloway had made it up to us just then, the other guard a pace in front of him. "How do you not know? There's one entrance and you're guarding it, aren't you?"

"Sometimes," Leif said under his breath. "But we take breaks and leave, and sometimes...people...come in while we're gone. Also...we're not allowed on the second floor."

"Do you abandon the security gate?" I asked. "Leave it open?"

"No!" Leif said. "That has to stay manned. During the day, at least."

I exchanged a look with Holloway. "Rough luck for Brett. He has to hang here while you guys head to the local bar, huh? When was your last excursion?"

Leif looked helpless, but the other guard answered for him. "We got our sandwiches over at Jersey Mike's."

"How long were you gone?" I asked, keeping a very close eye on him.

Leif sagged; the other guard got a guilty look. "Uh...an hour or so?"

"This is a really sweet gig, guys," I said, looking around the white walls of the empty office. "You're security guards who don't actually have to do much in the way of guarding. Why, you could drink on the job, shoot heroin, have strippers over–" I caught a stiffening movement in Leif's posture. "–You've done that, haven't you? Wow." They both reddened visibly. "I guess the only downside to working here is that you've occasionally got to file a fraudulent stolen weapons report."

They both went quiet, and I knew I'd hit my mark.

"Where did the guns go?" Holloway asked. "Really, this time."

"We went out," Leif said, finally finding his voice. "When we came back...they were gone."

"And...?" I asked, just knowing there was something more to it, and that we were close on this one.

"We were told when to leave, and what to leave in the lockbox," Leif's shoulders slumped. He looked on the verge of tears.

"Dude, no," the other guard said, doing some sagging of his own. "You should have talked with a lawyer first."

"Well, I've got good news and bad news for you boys," I said, taking Leif by the arms and snapping on the cuffs. "Filing a report for stolen weapons you allowed to be stolen? Under federal firearms laws, that's illegal." Holloway was cuffing the other guard. "The good news is that our prosecutors and judges don't really take these laws seriously, even for twats like yourselves who traffic in guns, so you're probably going to get off with a slap on the wrist."

"You have the right to remain silent," Holloway said, by rote, as his eyes swept the far end of the room. There was a whole floor up here that we hadn't cleared, after all. "Anything you say can and will be used against you in the court of law. You have the right to an attorney. If you cannot afford an attorney, one will be appointed for you." He shifted his attention to me. "How you want to handle this?"

"The sweep?" I asked, gently(ish) taking Leif's legs out from beneath him and lowering him onto his face on the carpet. "You guard these yahoos, I take a look around while you call in backup?"

"Uh, why don't we call in backup first?" Holloway asked, lowering the other guard – much more gently – into facedown position. Having seen my move with Leif, the other guard was eagerly cooperating.

"Because I'm all about efficiency," I said, drawing my pistol and starting for the nearest hallway. "Make the call, will you?"

Holloway sighed, but pulled out his phone and started dialing. "This is Holloway, Metahuman section. I need forensics at..."

I tuned him out as I stepped into a hallway darkened save for the exposure it received from the windows in the open room and shafts of light beaming out of open office doors to my right. Motes of dust hung in the air in those beams, and it made me wonder how long ago this place had been constructed. And why hadn't they bothered building out the bottom floor, too? If you're going to set up a *maskirovka*, as Gavrikov used to say, do it right.

Listening as I walked, I stuck my head – briefly – into each office. They were – no surprise – empty. The ones on the left side of the hall were dark, because they backed to other offices in a similar corridor on the back of the building. The ones on the right were sun-soaked, though. Also empty, with only the occasional carpet scraps left behind or unfinished wiring sticking out of the wall.

"Find anything?" Holloway called after me. His voice echoed a little.

"Other than some substandard construction? No," I said, ducking my head into the next office. Ahead, I could see the end of this corridor – or at least a spot where it took a left turn, presumably horseshoeing around to eventually rejoin the lobby. Follow this grey carpet road and I'd end up right back where I started. Not exactly the most imaginative office design, but then, who used imagination in designing suburban office buildings?

As I turned back, something sent the hairs on the back of my neck to prickling. I slowed, started to react–

But I didn't have enough time.

The wall ahead of me exploded and something launched out of it, a dark shadow flying at me–

With glowing, fiery red eyes.

CHAPTER FORTY-TWO

I had about a second to react to Firebeetle flinging himself through a wall at me. My gun wasn't up, and I definitely wasn't expecting my opponent to crash through a wall and attack me when I hadn't heard a single sound to indicate he was even up here.

Didn't matter. Reflexes won out.

I managed to get a hand off my gun and throw a weak palm-heel strike, slamming the meat of my hand into the jaw of my opponent. If he'd been upright and on his feet, charging me on churning, metahuman-powered legs, it would have done jackety-squat.

But Firebeetle had flung himself through the air, counting on his strength on the initial lunge to carry him through his attack. Even now he was reaching out to do me harm, ready to wrap his armored arms around me, getting me in a bear hug. Or beetle hug, as the case might have been.

My palm-heel caught him in midair, on the downside of his jump, and snapped his head back.

It also arrested his momentum and sent him flying sideways, outreached arms denied a chance to wrap around me in a hug I neither wanted nor needed. From him, at least.

"What the hell is going on back there?" Holloway shouted from down the hall.

"Contact!" I shouted back as Firebeetle crashed into the wall to my left. Not very hard; his legs went into the drywall but his upper body stayed out, and he was left suspended there, getting his bearings. Every inch of him was dark, shell-like armor. "It's our guy!"

"Shit!" Holloway said. "HQ, we have hostile metahuman contact, request immediate backup." He blurted the address after that, along with a few choice expletives. "You! Stay right there! Either of you run, I will shoot you dead, you hear me?"

The weak replies of Leif and the other guard followed, but I only barely heard them over Firebeetle extracting himself from the wall.

I fired a couple rounds at him – okay, maybe five, maybe ten – but they were ineffective, so I holstered my pistol. Then I drew my Cobra-tec knife and flipped the switch.

The blade sprung out, and Firebeetle stared at it with those glowing eyes. He made a hissing noise deep in his throat, and now I could see his mandible had undergone some sort of change in development as well. It really matched that roach theme he had going on.

"Gonna squash you like the thing you look like," I muttered as he came at me. His fingers had changed, too; now he had two of them, wider and fatter, plus a bigger thumb. He balled them into fists, ready to throw some hurt my way.

Not knowing his capabilities made me uncomfortable. I tossed a look over my shoulder; Holloway was covering me with his pistol, watching this unfold. I cursed. Having him watch was worse than just brawling it out with Firebeetle.

The beetle came at me with a hard punch, and I stepped back, lowering my knife in a hard, hacking slice, like I was cutting through some underbrush with a machete. I caught him across the wrist and cleaved into the armored shell that he'd sprouted over him. He hissed and jerked back. The knife with meta power behind it wounded him where a gun couldn't.

Good. Maybe I could slide this thing between the plates that girded his abdomen and gut this roach.

"Bet that hurt," I said, taking a step back, dancing on the tips of my toes. "I wouldn't worry too much about it, though. Where you're going, you'll only need those hands for scooping food, fighting off other inmates, and maybe masturbating." I pretended to give it some thought. "Actually, I guess you'll really need 'em. Hope you're a righty, for your sake."

He feinted at me, then sagged back to a neutral stance, scanning me for weaknesses. I didn't know how much I'd hurt him with my knife thrust, but I had to guess it wasn't insignificant. A little whitish-gray liquid was welling out of the wound.

No response, though. Either he was incapable of speech in this mode, or he didn't want to dignify my insults with a response. If the latter was the case, he was way more dignified or restrained than 99% of the criminals I dealt with, who always seemed to rise to my bullshit provocations.

Firebeetle, too, danced back and forth on his feet like a boxer. He had martial arts experience, I could tell by his stance. Now that he'd failed to fully get the drop on me, though – unlike the furniture store and in the row house – he was wary. Or lulling me. Either way, I wanted him to make the next move.

He did, finally. Lunging at me with reckless abandon, he apparently decided to go all-in on his attack. He charged – a bit less aggressively than last time – but led with his head and fists.

I'd been bull-charged by the best of them, though, and saw him coming a mile off. I took a slight step to my right and let him go by, pincering him with a knee to the gut – typical response to this sort of attack, and did nothing but ding my knee with pain at striking his shell – and then I brought my knife down into his exposed back.

The tip of the blade slammed home in his heavy, dome-like shell. It thudded in, and then stopped about an inch in. Stabbing him like that was a reflexive response, and I realized about a second too late where I'd screwed up.

He looked at me with those flame eyes, burning in triumph.

The bastard had just disarmed me.

CHAPTER FORTY-THREE

Gulp.

Firebeetle had just tricked me into burying my knife in his back, then stood up and slipped right out of range of me, neatly ripping my only effective weapon out of my reach.

He knew it, too, dancing just outside arm's length, biding his time, contemplating his victory. Motes of dust flashed in front of me from his smashing into and through various walls during his ambush and my response. Light flooded in through those same holes, giving me a perfect look at his beetled carapace.

His was a visage that was not going to be fronting any kissing booths anytime soon. He really did look like a cross between a demon and a cockroach, taking the worst attributes of both for his own. I started to vocalize this in hopes I could hurt him with my one remaining weapon – my assholery.

But he interrupted by lunging at me again, roach arms extended, grasping. Each three-fingered appendage gave me the heebie jeebies, and I lashed out with a standing kick that greeted his jaw as he rushed in at me.

My kick plowed him off his feet, reversing his momentum and booting him through the air with metahuman force. His red eyes widened in surprise, and he blasted through the glass window and down, down to the ground below.

"Did you get him?" Holloway called down the hall at me.

"I kicked him, yes," I said, "did I defeat him? No."

"Well, get on that, will you?" Holloway asked. "I'm not excited to be standing around here with these two yahoos while a meta battle is going on down the hall."

"Imagine how I feel being in the middle of it," I said, staying frozen in place. "Did you see him shrug off those bullets?"

"Yeah," Holloway said. "Any chance you think the armorer at the Hoover Building would let you check out another Gatling gun?"

"I kinda doubt it given what happened last time, but remind me to make a visit and plead my case, cuz..." I closed my eyes, just for a second. "Aw, shit."

"What? What is i–"

But he must have found out before I could answer him, because Firebeetle smashed into the facade of the building below, hitting at least one load-bearing column in the process. The ground shook beneath my feet, then gave way–

A ten-by-ten foot segment of the floor suddenly dropped beneath my feet, leaving me plunging down a sudden slope. I landed roughly, and managed to roll out of it, coming to my feet on the grass outside, stumbling a little.

"For the sake of f–" I started to say, but got pounced on by a certain Firebeetle who came flying out a window about twenty feet away, spraying toward me in a flurry of sparkling glass mixed with an enormous roach.

Chalk it up to blinking from being hit in the eyes by the flying glass, or just slow reflexes from my fall, but this time I failed to react to Firebeetle in time, and he crashed into me in a tackle with some martial arts pizzazz attached.

He pummeled me with a couple tenderizing blows to the torso (ow), then got me a good one in the kidney (double ow), and finally wrapped his arms around me in a giant roach hug, lifting me off the ground as he came down in a perfect landing.

"Urgh," I muttered, his arms trapping mine, my feet off the ground by several feet, all my leverage gone. He squeezed me tightly, and my ribs – still tender after yesterday's ambush – protested the strain. "...Crushed...by a damned cockroach..." I groaned. "...what an...ironic...reversal...of roles..."

I tried to squirm out of his grasp, but he had me solidly. Jerking left, then right, throwing myself against his arms, it didn't even unsteady him. I caught a little chuckle under his breath as the pressure increased on my ribs and my breath left me.

He was braced against side to side motion, I realized, giving up after one last flail to the left. But...

Was he braced against forward and backward motion?

I flung all my weight forward, keeping my head about me as I lost my breath under his pressure squeeze. I tried to remember my training, which was a little something I'd picked up from Navy SEALs I'd worked with a couple months ago. Trying to keep your wits when you're drowning was paramount. Being oxygen deprived activated that instinct, and I needed a cool head to prevail now.

Firebeetle took a staggering step, but managed to keep my feet off the ground at my maneuver. Points to him; I was flinging every bit of my weight behind that move.

But now I had him at least a step off balance, so I followed up and flung myself back, doing the pendulum swing with the weight of my head and upper body, driving it backward.

That got him. Firebeetle went tumbling over backward, arms still wrapped around me.

My body weight landing on him shouldn't have done much. Not with that armor plating. But...

The smart guy had gone and appropriated my weapon...in his back.

When the two of us landed on the ground, our combined body weight hitting the ground, the knife absorbed all of it first.

Firebeetle let out a bizarre scream, and I realized what happened when he jerked his arms off me and automatically redirected them toward the thing causing him pain. Unfortunately, his carapace really restricted his mobility, and he couldn't get at the knife.

While I was enjoying my newly rediscovered ability to breathe, I was still in almost full control of myself. Following up on my minor victory, I rammed an elbow into his armored side. My arm went numb from the forearm down, but Firebeetle, driven into the ground once more, let out another screech of pain as I drove the knife a little farther into him.

I sprang to my feet and spun, delivering a stomping blow to his midsection that almost sprained my ankle, but made him writhe even more wildly. Adjusting my kick, I prepared to strike again–

Some small noise behind me tipped me off that trouble was coming even before Holloway shouted, "Watch out!" from the giant hole in the upper floor.

I didn't even look. I threw myself out of the way on Holloway's warning alone.

Something swept past in a blur of white, just missing where I'd been standing a moment earlier. It took my brain a moment to make the identification:

A tiger.

A *white* tiger.

"What the hell?" Holloway offered his opinion from the upper floor. "Did you go make friends at the zoo or something?"

The tiger was ripping into Firebeetle with a fury that looked like something out of Animal Planet. Firebeetle was making that screeching noise, being jerked around by the leg as the tiger tore at him.

I watched, uncertain of what to do for a nice, long moment, and then–

Firebeetle lashed out with flames from his eyes, blasting the tiger and sending it mewling away. It staggered, on fire, rolling in the grass–

I stared, unsure what to do. Firebeetle was my collar, and I needed to arrest him, but this fire eyes thing? That was new. Or at least new to me, and it added an element of uncertainty to an already uncertain battle.

Firebeetle must have sensed my hesitation, because he stared at me, bleeding that whitish fluid from his leg, then flared his eyes at me before entering a hobbling sprint. He plunged into the nearest window, and I heard him running through the empty office building before hurling himself out the other side.

"What do we do?" Holloway called.

I turned back to the tiger, trying to gather my senses and

answer that question for myself. "You – stop," I said to the albino predator.

The tiger looked at me for about a second, with eyes of bright blue.

Then it turned into a hawk and swept off, ignoring me completely. It flew up and over the office building at incredible speed, disappearing before I could even get a bead on it with my pistol. Which was not exactly designed for bird hunting.

"What the shit was all that?" Holloway called. We'd gone from one meta in combat to two to none in ten, fifteen seconds by my reckoning.

"I have no idea," I said, plopping squarely onto my ass. My sides hurt, and I was in no condition to run down Firebeetle on foot, let alone try and hunt the damned hawk that had just flown off. But it seemed clear to me now that not only did I have one problem, in the form of Firebeetle and his Chinese-linked kidnap syndicate, but also a new mystery:

Who the hell was that shifter? And what did they want?

CHAPTER FORTY-FOUR

Shortly after my bad guy and the shifter escaped, the scene was teeming with local cops crawling over the partially destroyed office building. It was a mess of uniforms, various jurisdictions trying to assert their authority over the scene: local PD, some state agency, and of course me and my little FBI division. More like a micro-division now that Hilton was on leave. I tried to defer to the locals while getting leeway for my forensic team to crawl the battle site, but I had about as much interest in an internecine pissing contest as I did in a real one. Control of the scene went to the locals.

Which is why it shouldn't have surprised me when someone very definitely not in law enforcement appeared, touring the ruin of the building, trailed by a police officer. It all looked very aboveboard, and I tried not to jump to any conclusions when I looked up from filling out my small mountain of paperwork and saw them poking around my scene.

It was kinda hard to miss, though. Because one of them was Bilson, and the other was a random Asian guy in a nice suit.

"What the hell kind of circus is this?" I muttered under my breath, putting down my clipboard on the back of a police pickup truck.

"Well, you already had the tiger, so a pretty decent one,"

Holloway answered back from where he'd been filling out his own incident report.

I ignored him and crossed the distance between the truck and the collapsed facade of the building, where Bilson was standing, just talking with the Asian man. I tried not to come in hot, but I was curious why he would show up here with a not-cleared civilian. Hopefully he was someone connected to the US government and not someone related to the People's Republic of China (I didn't want to leap to a conclusion here).

"Ah, there you are," Bilson said sunnily as I approached.

"Here I am, where the trouble is," I said, looking theatrically at the collapsed floor. "It's the first place you should check whenever you lose me."

Bilson chuckled, then, gentleman that he was, immediately turned to his companion. "Sienna Nealon, this is Gang Liao. He's an aide to the Chinese ambassador."

I should have jumped to that conclusion like Evel Knievel over the Grand Canyon, apparently. I tried to control my reaction, but my eyebrows probably climbed into my hairline. "Nice to meet you," I said in a way that probably indicated I was in no way pleased to meet him, at least not at this time nor this place. "Can I ask why you brought the aide to the Chinese ambassador to my crime scene?"

"This building is owned by a Chinese citizen," Gang Liao answered, in flawless English. "I was having a conversation with Mr. Bilson about other matters when the calls came in to both of us. In his case, informing him of your unfortunate incident here. In my case, from the owner of the building, who is currently in Shenzen, managing other businesses."

Now I was only raising one eyebrow. "Oh, you're talking about the owner of HKKCME?"

Liao chuckled. "No. I'm referring to Mr. Huang, who owns this property. The company that leases it is unrelated to him or his businesses save for the leasing transaction."

"I'll just bet," I said. "Any idea how Mr. Huang ended up with this particular piece of property?"

Liao wore a small smile. "Chinese businessmen have made many investments in America, from real estate to the bond market. I couldn't say why he would pick this particular parcel. Only that he owns it, and was concerned enough to ask that I take a look at how things have turned out for him here."

"Well, this place certainly hasn't suffered what I'd call 'Maximum Sienna,'" I said, "but it's obviously not good."

"Indeed not." Liao's smile faded. "Still, the damage could have been considerably more." He pulled out his cell phone and snapped a couple pictures of the facade. "If you'll excuse me, Ms. Nealon, Mr. Bilson." He raised the phone. "I'd like to send these to Mr. Huang immediately."

"Hey, if the local cops don't want to stop you from taking pictures in my active crime scene, far be it from me to object," I said, catching a warning look from Bilson.

Liao chuckled, inclined his head at me, then wandered away, texting.

The moment he was out of earshot, Bilson leaned in toward me. "That was a little antagonistic."

"Be thankful it wasn't a lot antagonistic, cuz I'm doing my best here," I said, drawing a barely-controlled breath. "I know you're new to this law enforcement thing, but you cannot bring a civilian into a crime scene until it's been sifted. It's an ironclad thing in our field. Civilians have this tendency to trample on evidence."

"Understood," Bilson said, but went on in a way that suggested he clearly did not heed. "But this came from the president. Huang, the owner of this place? He's a big wheel in China, and holds a lot of sway in the US, too."

"He's the one who just got that big deal with Jaime Chapman, right?" I asked, watching Liao mess with his cell phone.

Bilson cocked his head at me in mild surprise. "Yes. How did you know about that?"

I gave Bilson a look. You can imagine what kind. "I know I'm just a blunt instrument to you, but I do read the paper every now and again. Or at least the internet. Chapman's China deal was not small news."

"Right, sorry," Bilson said, shaking his head. "Didn't mean to suggest you were stupid. It's a little outside your field is all."

"I'm a multi-dimensional person," I said. "I have outside interests."

This caused him to raise an eyebrow. "Okay, I'll bite. Such as?"

I felt my breath catch in my throat. "Finding new and creative ways to cause maiming harm to lawbreakers, for one. Did he just make a less-than-subtle reference to how China is buying up US Treasury bonds?"

Bilson smirked. "You caught that, huh? You're right, it wasn't subtle, at least for those who follow the Chinese model of communication. It was a little for Americans, though. We're so blunt, comparatively."

"And me more than most," I agreed. "Why would he bring that up now?"

"Could have just been him poking at you in a way he thought you wouldn't notice," Bilson said with a shrug. "It didn't seem all that serious."

"Why is it a poke at me but not at you?" I asked. "Aren't you an American?"

Bilson shrugged again. "I guess I just don't care about that particular bait. They're buying our debt. Good. Someone should."

That raised my eyebrow again. "Maybe it's just my inherent paranoia, but most people associate money with power."

Bilson let out a little chuckle. "'The borrower is slave to the lender?' That kind of thing?"

"Exactly."

"Or, alternatively," Bilson said, "the Chinese could be investing in the stablest currency in the world because they recognize the return is thus stable. Because it's backed by the full faith and credit of the United States."

"Yeah, but strategically, they're trying to supplant us," I said, causing Bilson to raise another eyebrow. "They literally have a fifty-year plan to outpace the United States economically and in a global security sense."

"Well, the longest Treasury bond is thirty years, so..." Bilson's smile was so annoyingly effervescent, and I could tell he wasn't taking my pronouncement very seriously. "...By that logic, they'll be well clear of the investment in US debt before they overtake us. Where did you hear about this 'plan,' anyway?"

"I read it on the back of a cereal box," I said, trying not to snap at him but failing. He was being a little condescending.

"Just curious," Bilson said, voice losing not an ounce of his usual friendliness. "I was wondering the source to see if it was something easily refuted."

I started to open my mouth to throw out a response, one which was not designed to be patient nor nice, when a forensics monkey in the full suit came walking over to me. "Ma'am?" she asked, a clear plastic bag in hand, piece of paper secured inside it, her pale blue eyes all I could see behind the mask. "We found this in the office where you were ambushed."

"Oh?" I took the bag from her and peered at the paper within. It was a single printed page, written in English but...it had an awful lot of names of Chinese origin. It was a list, I realized while scanning it. Most of the names were crossed out with a pen. But not all. "Who are these people?"

Then I got to name number five, which was not crossed out, and part of the question got answered for me. "Shit," I muttered.

"What?" Bilson asked.

I turned it around and flashed it at him. Gave him a moment for it to sink in.

"Names," Bilson said, scanning it. "What about them? Could be a client list. Or workers. Or–"

"It's not," I said, feeling an ominous prickling. "Look at the fifth name."

"'Cathy Jang-Peters,'" Bilson read. "What about her?"

"That's the name of our first victim," I said, "her name uncrossed, but so many of the others aren't?" I could see the slow comprehension dawning on Bilson, but I could also tell he didn't want to admit what this was. So I said it for him. "This...

"It's a list of kidnap targets."

CHAPTER FORTY-FIVE

"Impossible," Bilson said as I snapped a picture of the list with my cell phone. He was looking a little pale, and it wasn't because of the Virginia sunshine, which was bright and hot, glaring down at us. "That's...there have to be forty, fifty names there!"

"Yep," I said, sending the picture to Holloway and Chalke. I wrote: *Evidence recovered from most recent conflict with kidnapper suspect. Original kidnap victim Cathy Jang-Peters is on list. Suspected list of kidnap victims. Need to track these people down.* Then I sent it.

"Look, you said before that maybe there were more victims," Bilson was still talking, but his voice had dropped to a pleading tone. "You didn't say anything about there being fifty people missing."

"The case just took a hard turn, yes," I said, plowing my way toward Holloway, who'd just picked up his cell phone and was frowning at – presumably – my message.

"Wait, hold on." Bilson seized my arm.

I spun on him. Not violently, just in a hurry. "What?"

"You cannot possibly believe these kidnappers got...*fifty people?*" Bilson laughed weakly, the desperate laughter of a man who didn't want to believe what he'd just heard.

"Why is that a problem for you?" I asked calmly.

Bilson paled further, looking around, presumably for Liao,

who was nowhere in sight. "Because kidnapping fifty people is not a small undertaking."

A very tiny smile may have made its way across my lips. "You mean it's an operation large enough it would require, say...a government to be involved?"

The deathly twitch of Bilson's eye told me that yes, this was exactly his fear. He didn't say it, though. Didn't need to. If you were going to kidnap one person in the US, you needed a team.

If you were going to kidnap fifty...

That was a whole 'nother organizational ballgame. Kidnap one person and you could stuff them in a trailer in the backwoods, keep them tied up or prisoner by very easy conventional means.

Kidnap fifty and you needed a warehouse, ways to feed them, places they could relieve themselves. That would require a compound of some sort. You had a serious chain of logistical difficulties to deal with. That wasn't a game for one person, or a small crew of criminals.

That was a conspiracy. That required resources, planning, scale of a sort that some small gang couldn't manage.

But a nation could.

"You don't know that a state actor is behind this," Bilson said, just this side of panicking. "Or that it's this specific state actor."

"No, I don't," I said airily. "But I am going to find out." My phone lit up with a call. Chalke, of course. I figured when I sent the text I'd hear from her in mere minutes. Seconds, if she wasn't too busy. "Excuse me." And I answered the call.

"What the hell is this?" Chalke asked.

"Don't know for sure," I said, "but I think it's a list of kidnap targets. I'm going to have to run them down, see if any of them have been approached, or snatched like Jang-Peters."

There was a pause. "I'm getting you that call with SecState Ngo," she said. "But this..." She let out a not-mild expletive under her breath, which of course I heard. "Do your checking, but it goes nowhere past your team and me, you hear?"

"You might want to loop the president in on this," I said. Bilson was watching me, and shook his head.

"No," Chalke said.

"...No?" I asked. "You want to cut him out of this?"

"Until we know these people are definitely taken, yes," Chalke said. "If it is what you think it is, we'll brief him. But you need to prove it first. Until we know they're gone, it's nothing more than a list of names. Got it?"

"You got it, boss," I said. It was not a ridiculously unreasonable request, though my preference would have been to be more communicative with the president rather than less, but he was probably experiencing a firehose of information on any given day, so keeping this back until we were sure didn't strike me as grossly negligent or conspiracy-ish. A little overcautious, maybe, but not malign – yet.

"Get on it, then," Chalke said. "Ngo will be calling you within the hour."

"Roger that." And she hung up.

"The president doesn't need to worry about this yet," Bilson said. "Prove it's something and then–"

"Yeah, I got it," I said, heading for Holloway again. "He's a busy man, this is just a thread so far."

"Yes," Bilson said, sounding a little taken aback. "Exactly. That's very...reasonable."

I shot him a playful smile. "Were you given to understand I'm unreasonable?"

Bilson chuckled. "Well, this is DC. Rumors circulate."

"I've had some bad bosses," I said. "We've butted heads. I'm probably at least half the problem, but..." I took a breath, really aimed for seeming contrite. "...Well, I'm trying to do better."

"Good for you," Bilson said sincerely. "So...what next?"

"Need to talk to Holloway," I said, nodding in the man's direction. He was still waiting for me at the pickup truck where I'd left him, watching my progress but staying patient. "We're going to have to do the leg work of trying to find these people. Chalke said I have to compartmentalize this info, which means it's on us, I guess. So that's phone calls and scut work, beating the bushes to find these folks with just a name and nothing else to go on."

Bilson nodded. "I might be able to help with that. Let me prevail on Chalke, see what we can come up with."

"I'm all for getting help with chasing down names," I said, "but she was pretty firm about not letting this list out, so..."

He nodded sympathetically. "I'll work on her." And off he went, fiddling with his phone.

"You seem to have made some new friends," Holloway said when I drew close to him. "And dug up some new trouble. This kidnap list legit?"

"That's what you and I have to figure out," I said. "Come on. Screw the incident report; we need to get on this."

"Ah, the glorious life of an FBI agent," Holloway said, tucking the clipboard with his report under his arm. It was the report for the local PD. His FBI report would come later, and be typed up rather than written. "Screwing the locals and running down leads on the phone like a damned telemarketer."

"I could do with a little of that kind of glory right now," I said, taking one last look at the collapsed facade of the office building. "Besides, we bagged a couple of security guards committing firearms felonies and trashed a building. What more could you ask for?" Holloway's sour look told me the answer – a lot more.

CHAPTER FORTY-SIX

Julie Blair

The email came across her desk shortly before normal quitting time, and Julie Blair was tired. Not only because she'd been up late the last few nights, not only because she hadn't seen her kids in the daylight in two weeks (and seldom awake, at that), but because she knew that at best, her workday would not end for three or four more hours.

And she'd started at six this morning.

Bleary-eyed, she pounded down a cold coffee as she read the missive for the third time, trying to fully comprehend it.

Ms. Blair,

My name is Marta Hale, and I am one of President Gondry's donors. We met at his fundraiser at Marian Cain's apartment in New York last year, and you and I talked about balancing work and motherhood, and the tensions that those twin poles of responsibility create, especially in high-powered careers. I have been holding onto your card since then, preferring not to prevail on you or the White House for any favors and quietly cheering for the president to make the policy changes that you and I discussed.

However, I write to you now with a heavy heart. My children's nanny, Zhen, has disappeared as of five days ago. Local police have not seen her, and after (sensitively) interviewing the people she shares an apartment with, they have not had any luck in identifying a culprit, nor finding her. It is as though she has disappeared without a trace.

This is very unlike Zhen. She is the most upright, responsible person I have ever met, and she has made our lives richer by her presence. It is not an exaggeration to say that my life as an attorney or my wife's as a news producer would not be possible without her aid. Her loss has been felt most keenly, and we are deeply concerned both for her and picturing our lives going forward without her.

Yesterday I heard on the news about the case in which Sienna Nealon was involved, the one with the Chinese kidnapping victim? Zhen, too, was from China, and I wondered if this disappearance might be related? I wanted to bring this to your attention in hopes that, perhaps, you might be able to pass it along to the FBI. I spoke with the local authorities but they made only vague promises to look into the matter, essentially concluding that Zhen probably just ran away, and informing me that they saw no reason to pass along this information to the FBI or Sienna Nealon.

Please, Julie – help me. I beg you. For Zhen. Our little Kaden misses his nanny dearly.

Sincerely,

Marta

Julie peered at the screen. If she'd been well rested, she probably would have known what to do after only one read. But on her third, she made a decision, and forwarded the email up the chain to her boss, with a "Is this something?" written above the body of the forwarded email.

Because she really didn't know if it was something or not. Maybe it was just a runaway nanny. Or maybe it really was something deeper.

Whatever it was, it was above her pay grade.

After she hit forward, she didn't think about it again, already on to the next email.

CHAPTER FORTY-SEVEN

Jaime Chapman

Jaime was rocking the treadmill desk today, on his tenth mile and still going, knocking things off his action items list and lining things up for tomorrow. He missed walking outside on days like this, but hey, the compromise was that he got to look out over his kingdom from the top of his glass and steel pyramid, and man, did the world seem small from up here.

He was about ready to cross off another task when his phone started ringing. This was the private line, the one he kept for the most important people. Top echelon only. Hell, he was debating even booting the stupid Escapade app off of it, just so he could have a phone to himself that wasn't constantly dinging with notifications for dumb shit.

Wu Huang, it read. That was an instant pickup.

"Wu," Jaime said, hitting the stop button on the treadmill. "How's it going?" Grabbing the towel off the corner of his desk, Jaime hit the ground, his Vibram Five-Fingers absorbing the impact across the whole foot. Marvelous shoes. It was like walking barefoot, but without as much risk of random tetanus.

"Not so good, Jaime," Wu said.

Jaime mopped his forehead, frowning. "Sure. Talk to me. What's on your mind?"

"My government is becoming concerned," Wu said. "With some issues surrounding our merger, and with America's current stance in general."

That ratcheted the tightness of Jaime's forehead lines even further. Damn, he might need a Botox later just to loosen things up. This deal was vital; nothing could stand in its way. "Who's screwing up what? Tell me. Maybe I can do something."

Wu laughed lightly. "I doubt this is in your purview, my friend. As you know, we are a bit tighter with our government over here than your own is with you. It allows for more continuity of control, you know?"

"I've always admired that cohesiveness about the Chinese system," Jaime said. "You guys have amazing vision. It's one of the reasons I want to be in business with you."

"I know, my friend, I know," Wu said. "But I doubt there's anything you can do. I just needed to let you know that I have been informed – in light of recent events – we are going to experience what you might refer to as 'regulatory headwinds.'"

What the hell? "I thought this deal with the government was as good as done," Jaime said, keeping a very even keel on his voice, even while his stomach dropped from beneath him. He needed this deal. The stock price's recent rise was predicated on it.

"Let us just say...they are concerned in Beijing," Wu said. "There have been some accusations floating around in your own government about this silly kidnapping business. Have you heard of it?"

"A little," Jaime said. Who cared about a local kidnapping story? In DC? "I don't really pay much attention to minor things going on across the country, you know?"

"Well, China does," Wu said, sounding quieter than Jaime could recall hearing him in the past. "The rumors are swirling in your government that they want to implicate China in this somehow."

"Well, that's stupid," Jaime said. Then, realizing how what he said might be misinterpreted. “I mean, it's utterly ridiculous to blame your government for some local crime in the US.”

“I agree,” Wu said, “but it seems the police officer on the case has named our government several times to various sources.”

Jaime felt a cold shiver run down his spine. “This is Sienna Nealon, isn't it? Her case?”

“Yes. She's high profile.” Wu was still being quiet, which was concerning. “Her words carry weight. All the way to Beijing, even.”

“She's just a silly little...” Jaime searched for a word that fit. “...well, bitch, really. No one who's met her, who knows her background, would take her seriously, Wu. She's an idiot. No college education. Didn't even graduate high school, for crying out loud. Her claim to fame is that she supposedly saved the world from some guy that no one ever heard of, and she's been milking that fame ever since. Guess what? Her fifteen minutes are long ago up. If it weren't for some stupid screwup in the handling of that Revelen business a year ago, she wouldn't even be high profile right now.”

“I agree with your assessment,” Wu said, “but it is built on a foundation of 'should' when 'is' reigns. She has credibility with your government, and she is saying things – harmful things – about China. It worries our officials that someone with that level of status is bringing her credibility to bear against us. We have long been misunderstood in your country, in spite of being one of your largest trading partners.”

“I know this, Wu, and I agree,” Jaime said, thrusting a hand in front of his face like a knife chop. Like he could cut through Wu's argument and make him see that blowing up this deal because of Sienna effing Nealon was the worst idea and most terrible waste possible. “I want to make people understand that China is a fantastic country. That you guys are the future. There's a lot to love and to learn about the way you do things. Which is why I'm in this deal with you in the first place. If any of the big dogs – Gates, Ellison, Zuckerberg – in America came to me with your deal, there's no reason I'd want to sell a piece of my company to them. I chose you because together we can build an outpost of this empire in the Middle Kingdom that will make China stronger on the world stage. Less misunderstood. And, just to be honest, we're both in a great position to increase our portfolios by orders of magnitude. Let's not incinerate that because of some dumb cop in Washington."

"I don't want to put things off," Wu said, "especially for that reason. But Sienna Nealon...she's a problem. She needs to keep her ideas to herself. Our officials are nervous that this could precipitate real consequences in our economy and in our other dealings with America. She had a meeting, alone, with the president yesterday. Did you know that?"

"No," Chapman said. "I didn't."

"Think how much damage someone with that kind of ax to grind against China could do. With her powers? She could mind control him. You know?"

Chapman's mouth felt a little dry. "Yeah...that'd be..."

"Disastrous," Wu said. "For all of us. You can see why my government might be concerned. Because it seems to them that she's carrying around 20th century prejudices against our people."

"Yeah, no, that – I'm with you, a hundred percent," Chapman said, mind whirling. "Maybe I can – I mean, I've got some influence. I could maybe help block her. Push back."

"Could you?" Wu asked. "I didn't think law enforcement was your area of specialty."

Jaime laughed lightly. "I've donated so much money to the president and the party that I could go in and lecture Gondry on cloud formations at this point. Leave it with me, Wu. If this is what your government needs – Sienna Nealon shut out? Her words to fall on deaf ears? I can deliver that. That's easy."

"Is it? Really?" Wu sounded skeptical.

"Money talks over here," Chapman said. "Absolutely, I can do this. For us. Not a problem."

"That would go a long way toward getting our officials' concerns assuaged about the danger she presents," Wu said. "If she's just a lone voice, that's a lot less threatening to us than a mind controller having private meetings with your president."

"Yeah, that'd concern anyone," Chapman said, nodding along. Did Sienna Nealon really have mind control abilities? Was that something a succubus could do? Wu might know better than the US government. Her ability to steal memories and souls was well documented. Messing with the mind while doing so was in the realm of possibility, though it didn't matter for his purposes. He just needed to shut her out of the White House and get this deal back on track. "I'll take care of it, Wu."

"That would be fantastic," Wu said. "Let me know when you do, so I can talk to the people responsible for approving our plans in China. It will certainly buy us some goodwill."

"I'll get right on it," Chapman said, nodding furiously in his empty office. "Say, we should probably have a talk, too, about some of the co-projects going on right now between us? You know, with Socialite and Lineage and the rest."

"Absolutely," Wu said. "I'm on a tour of a facility in Shenzen right now, but we can set that up for next week sometime, when I'm back in Beijing. Have your assistant call my secretary. Got to go, Jaime. Thank you for your diligence in this matter. It will not go unrewarded."

"You're welcome," Jaime said to the dead phone. Wu had already hung up, leaving Jaime to plot his next move and figure out how to get Sienna Nealon's dumb, uneducated ass the hell out of this situation.

CHAPTER FORTY-EIGHT

Sienna

"Hey next time you want to set us an impossible task," Holloway said, a phone handset pinched against his ear, a bored, bordering-on-angry look on his face, "why not make it something fun, like drinking a hundred beers an hour?"

"I'm sure that'd be really good for my sobriety," I said, listening to the phone ringing fruitlessly on the other end of my own waiting phone call. "But I could probably take a hundred beers in an hour." I popped myself lightly in the mid-section. "Meta liver constantly heals itself, after all."

Holloway slammed the phone down. "We're trying to track down people by name that – we don't even know they're the right people." He pushed fingers back through his hair, strands falling through them. He'd probably been good looking in his youth, but a few too many miles on the odometer left him looking like a tired lawman who'd seen too many cases go to shit. "We can't get help from above, laterally, or from the State Department, INS – hell, I'd take an assist from Health and Human Services at this point." He shook his head and picked up the phone to dial again.

All we were working from was the list recovered at the office site, which presumably had been dropped by Firebeetle before he'd fled. I was willing to work from that assumption, at least for now, until I could either prove or disprove it. Hard to say which would come first, given how little we still knew after pounding the phones for an hour with no luck.

"When are we going to talk about the albino tiger?" Holloway asked. He had one foot up on his desk, leaning back in his chair, the phone cord stretching dangerously taut.

"Not a lot to talk about," I said, dialing my next number. We'd pulled these out of a database, but whether they actually synched up with any of the names in the list was questionable. We'd gotten few answers in any case; most were probably cell phones, and who wanted to answer an unknown caller? The real crime was that almost nobody had set up their voicemail, which meant we couldn't even leave a message asking for a callback.

Of course, if these were the phones of people who'd been kidnapped, they weren't likely to return a call, but still...it was a frustrating feeling, trying to chase down this stupid lead by dialing the phone over and over and getting nothing for it.

"It was a damned tiger," Holloway said, staring at me in disbelief. "And white. And it came dropping down out of nowhere to save your ass from getting killed."

"Yeah," I said, hanging up the phone. "Saved me in Baltimore, too. It's an animal shifter."

Holloway just stared at me. "So it couldn't become, like...this phone, for instance?" He held up the handset just away from his ear.

"Not as far as I know."

"You known any of this kind of meta before?"

"I knew one," I said.

Holloway just stared at me. "You gonna share a story, or do I have to fill in the blanks in my own head?"

I rolled my eyes, picked up the phone and dialed again. "Glen Parks."

Holloway squinted at me. "I know that name from somewhere." He thought about it a second, then snapped his fingers at me. "You killed that guy."

"That's really an evergreen statement. But yeah." I listened to the trill of another unanswered phone ringing over my handset. "He was my training officer at the Directorate."

"Guess you guys weren't too close if you ended up killing him."

"He was one of the best mentors I ever had," I said without emotion. At least, none in my inflection. "And he told me I was his best student."

"Shit." Holloway hung up the phone. "If you were his best, what the hell did his worst do to him?"

I chuckled. "You'd have liked Parks. He was old school military. A gunnery sergeant type, y'know?"

"Squared his shit away," Holloway said with a stiff nod. "Yeah, I like that." He sat bolt upright. "Hello? Yes?" He bent to look at his copy of the list. "I'm sorry, I'm looking for...Niu?"

Without any answer on my call, I hung up again, and waited, listening and watching Holloway's own. It was strange to try and pick out what was happening solely by how he was reacting. His face was pinched for a second as he concentrated on the answers he was getting; the voice on the other end was far too quiet for me to discern what they were saying from here, so I got up and moved closer.

"And you haven't seen her since two days ago?" Holloway stood before I could cross the couple steps between our cubicles. "Have you filed a missing persons report?" He was concentrating heavily, listening, ignoring me as I eased closer to listen. "Okay. No, you should. Definitely should. Can you give me your address? I can send – what? No. Well, look, I'm with the FBI and we're trying to locate–"

I heard the click of the person hanging up very distinctly. Holloway pulled the handset away from his ear and looked at it as though puzzled by what had just happened.

"We have one missing person confirmed?" I asked.

"I guess," Holloway said, hanging up the phone and circling the name Niu Chang. "I'd prefer an actual missing persons report to confirm it, but the lady sounded like she was one step from hanging up on me through the whole conversation."

"Lends credence to this back-channel informant I've got," I

said, sitting back down. "Says that most of these kidnappings are people below the margins. Chinese citizens either trapped in a work visa or here illegally and don't want to get tossed."

"So they're willing to let their own family members disappear before calling the cops?" Holloway gave me a distinctly disbelieving look.

How the hell did one answer that? I didn't get a chance, though, because my cell phone rang with an unknown number with a DC area code, and I hurriedly picked it up. "Hello?"

"Hold for Secretary of State Ngo," came a cool, female voice at the other end of the line.

"Sure," I said, and a moment later, I was connected.

"Sienna?" SecState Ngo's voice came on the line.

"Yes, ma'am," I said. "Did Director Chalke inform you what I wanted to talk to you about?"

"Not entirely." Ngo sounded a little distracted, like she was signing something even now. "Something to do with your current case, though, right?"

"You could say that. This morning I met with a State Department employee by the name of Bridget Schultz. She was suffering from the effects of a sonic device planted in her apartment–"

"Wait," Ngo said, "you were the one who found that?"

"Yeah," I said. "Damned thing felt like it was going to pop my head off my shoulders when I got close to it, but I did. Anyway, I was supposed to take a meeting with her to talk China–"

"Interesting," Ngo muttered under her breath. "You think this was done to keep her from talking to you?"

"No, ma'am," I said. "I suspect the device has been there for some time. My understanding of this technology is that it causes its damage via long-term exposure. Bridget had clearly been suffering from it before there even was a case. Which is why I wanted to talk to you – do you know why someone – some government, maybe – would target her?"

Ngo made a small, noncommittal grunt on the other end of the phone. "Bridget had worked in the China section in DC for a while, spent years in the country before that. She's a solid expert."

"But?" I asked, fishing.

When Ngo continued, her voice bore the hallmark signs of discomfort. "She's on the outs with the policymaking establishment. At least in regards to China. Thank you, Mark. That'll be all for now." Someone shuffled around in the background and I heard a door shut before she spoke again. "Which is to say..."

"She didn't like the Chinese government," I said.

"Correct," Ngo said. "Don't get me wrong, she loved the country, the culture, the people. Everything except the government – the PRC, the Communist Party. The majority of our China Natsec policy apparatus is called, colloquially–"

"'Panda huggers', right?" I asked.

Ngo's voice registered surprise, but it vanished quickly. "Yes. Well, Bridget was no panda hugger. Quite the opposite, in fact. Her assessments lined up with the more hawkish folks at places like the Pentagon, who view the People's Republic as a bona fide threat. You're asking why I could see her become a potential target?" Ngo hesitated. "There was no more vocal critic in the State Department's China section than her. She didn't trust their government, didn't think they operated anywhere close to aboveboard, and she didn't hesitate to spread that opinion...oh, everywhere, anytime she could. Which is why I'm able to parrot it to you now with complete ease."

"Do you think China would do that, though?" I asked.

Here, Ngo started to sound wary. "I wouldn't accuse them of it, no. Not only because it's a diplomatic atom bomb, but because I'm assuming you have zero evidence to link it to anyone. Correct?"

"Results from dissecting the device aren't in yet, but even if it said 'Made in China' we'd probably struggle to connect it to the government."

Ngo laughed lightly. "You're right about that. And I can predict their response – they'd accuse us of anti-Chinese bigotry."

"They've learned to play our favorite games," I said. "I could almost tear up with pride."

Ngo laughed again. "There's a very smart and capable cabal running the show over there, and they understand the West very well. Over here, if asked, most people know that the People's Republic is not a democracy. Very few realize exactly how much of an oligarchy it is, though. Especially after their current premier solidified power over the last few years. He's got an iron grip on it, and probably won't ever be 'voted' out. You add that to the level of planning they already engage in...they know what they're doing. Especially in regards to how far they can push us. As I'm sure he told you, the president doesn't need trouble from them. Especially not this year."

"You ever get the feeling that politics is getting in the way of doing what's right?" I asked, then realized I'd just blurted it out without thinking. *Brain, filter, mouth?* Nahhhh. I went straight to *Brain, mouth, whoops!*

Ngo laughed again, though. "This is Washington, Ms. Nealon. Better get used to it. Did you need anything else?"

"Unless you have a report from your underlings on those passports we sent over, I think that covers it," I said. "Thanks for the candor."

"I'll have my people get in touch if there's anything else on those passports," Ngo said. "But we got the denial from China. I wouldn't count on anything else."

My turn to chuckle. "They didn't even bother coming up with a reasonably legit-sounding excuse?"

"Why would they need to?" Ngo asked. "Who's going to call them on it? Especially for a small issue like this." When she spoke again, I could almost hear the tight smile through the connection. "Good luck on this. I don't envy you, but I'm sure you'll do your best. Reach out if you think anyone else at State can be of help."

"Thanks," I said, and listened to the click as she ended the call. Pretty words were nice, but a break in the case would have been a hell of a lot better.

CHAPTER FORTY-NINE

Chapman

W*HAT THE HELL IS YOUR GIRL UP TO?* Chapman typed furiously into the Escapade app. He didn't usually go all caps, but the occasion certainly warranted it, and he went with it.

Chalke came in with the first response. Of course. Bitch had nothing going on but this stupid chat screen and managing her pathetic, dying federal bureaucracy. Which was messing up his life.

CHALKE: Was this supposed to be a text to one of your boyz?

FLANAGAN: I was thinking the same thing lol

Figured Flanagan's dumb ass would weigh in here. Could barely be bothered to weigh in most of the time, but here he was with the funny when Chapman's multi-billion-dollar China deal was going down in flames thanks to Sienna Nealon.

CHAPMAN: No, it was not a wrong text. What the hell is Sienna Nealon doing messing up our relations with China?

Long pause. Good. Let these morons reflect on that bombshell. Bad relations with China had to resonate in Washington if the reverberations were hitting him in California.

BILSON: I'm sorry, I guess I'm late to the party on this one. What do you mean?

Chapman just fumed. Late to the party, indeed.

CHAPMAN: My deal with Wu Huang just blew up in regulatory approval over in Beijing because they're hearing that Sienna Nealon is trying to pin her current case on China. That she's had meetings with the president. That she has his ear and she's spewing this noxious, anti-Chinese venom in every direction. Concerned about a chilling of relations, they put my deal on hold.

JOHANNSEN: Ouch.

Chapman started to type, *That's not for publication, Johannsen. Or you, Kory*. But he stopped himself.

What was the downside if word got out Sienna Nealon was sinking relations with China? None to him; Kory and Johannsen knew well to attribute anything he said to "a Silicon Valley source," which would keep him in a deniable position.

No, this was all upside. Let the word get out; no one wanted a war with China, trade or otherwise. America did too much business with them, all across the board. Everyone would feel that pain, at nearly every level of American society. People who bought, well, anything, would see prices go up, probably considerably. People like him who did business in China would be hurt, probably worse, but they could better afford the hit.

The stock price, though...it would crater.

BILSON: I've been watching Nealon closely this entire case. Whatever opinions she may have of China, she's not talking to the press, they're not leaking out in public, and she's had one meeting with the president, and a brief one, at that. So there's not much room for her to spray "venom," as you put it.

CHAPMAN: Then why is Beijing telling me my deal is off?

God, he was just fuming. This idiot girl had been toxic to them from the word go. Chalke had called it, and nobody had listened, not even him. He felt a twinge of annoyance; her 5,000-year lifespan was interesting and all, and had its possible uses, but for now all he could think was how long she'd be a pain in his ass.

CHAPMAN: Chalke was right. We never should have tried to bring her under our control when things went sour after Revelen. She should have died somewhere off the public stage: alcohol poisoning, a bullet to the back of the head, anything, really, to get her out of the damned way. We got cute, and she's done nothing but bite us in the ass ever since.

Yeah, that was pretty much how he felt in the moment. Had she ever produced a net good for them? He couldn't think of one. Even the blowup in San Francisco with that hard-skinned meta could have been resolved with much less trouble if she hadn't shown up. The damned thing would have just taken what it wanted – which it did, anyway, in spite of her – and moved on to do whatever scheme it had in mind. Something about an EMP that wasn't even real, right? It had all faded into the background of his mind once it was resolved, because he didn't sweat about the little things.

Instead, she'd blown that up into a huge deal, made a mess of herself on social media to the point where even he was being asked for comment. Coupled with involving herself in the governor of Louisiana's downfall and suicide, and he just couldn't see any advantage to having her "on board." Whatever the hell that meant. If she was sabotaging relations with China to the point where he lost his deal, it seemed like it meant she was actively sinking their ship.

BILSON: Actually, I've found her to be bright, engaged, and willing to own up to her mistakes. She has copped to bad behavior with Chalke, made no bones about it, and seems open to learning and changing. In my conversations with the president, I don't believe she's had any influence at all. Gondry is very aware of the minefield that he's walking through during this re-election campaign, and he's not looking to rock the boat with you, Jaime. If this China thing is real, it's happening almost entirely on their side as an overreaction to Nealon's investigation. Which is producing some adverse evidence against them, I have to admit.

Of course he added to his bullshit. Covering his ass, Chapman thought in disgust.

BILSON: (Rather unfortunately and against my interest. I believe good diplomatic and trade relations with China to be absolutely key to moderating their regime's excesses, so I have no more interest than you in seeing things tank with them.)

FLANAGAN: Gotta be honest, I'm not as deep on this China busi-

ness as the rest of you, but I'm perfectly capable of reading a paper and I have to ask: We've been dealing with them for, what? Fifty years? How much "moderation" have you seen in that time? I mean, I'm all about eschewing war in favor of diplomacy, but they don't seem to be getting better. In fact, in spite of favorable treatment from almost every corner of American/Western cultural powers, it looks to me like their human rights abuses are worse than ever.

Chapman saw red. His fingers moved automatically.

CHAPMAN: How are you going to influence that to change without any relations with them, Tyrus? I mean, really. You want to try and box them in? Cut off all trade? Impose sanctions? That'll go great, I'm sure.

FLANAGAN: I think a Chinese version of the Magnitsky Act might be just the medicine to bring about some change over there. They've got an oligarchy. Let's hit those guys (because they're pretty much all guys, as I understand it).

You know nothing, Chapman seethed. But he had regained enough control of himself not to type that.

CHALKE: Look, I'm not sure what the problem with Nealon is this time, and you know I have zero issue with calling out her excesses. But like Bilson, I'm not seeing it. Not saying it's not there, that she's not making a shitstorm (she's really good at those), but I'm just not seeing it. Yet.

CHAPMAN: It's there. Trust me. If I'm losing a multi-billion-dollar deal with China, it's not for no reason. She's doing something.

BILSON: We're watching her.

WATCH HER CLOSER! Chapman wanted to scream. But then, he had the full ability to watch her himself – that was the idea, anyway. He tapped the button on his desk for his assistants. "Send Devin Fuller up here ASAP. Thanks."

Instead of venting any of that, instead, he moderated himself.

CHAPMAN: I hope so. This is having serious consequences on our relations, business and diplomatic. I know none of us want that.

Though some of them clearly had less skin in the game than others. Like him.

CHAPMAN: But this is another critical situation in which we're reliant on someone who has proven herself less than reliable. I don't like *it. I haven't liked it since we embarked on this project post-Revelen. I had hopes it could work out, but it's not doing so thus far. We need more assets on our balance sheet if we're going to be effective in shaping policy and changing things to our liking, the way the world *should* change. If she continues to be a liability, we need to start discussing how to exit her off the books.*

There. That was a modest proposal, not too suggestive, but enough so that everyone would get the implication.

CHALKE: Trust me. If she needs to be dispensed with, I'll be the first to agree to it. We're not quite there yet, I don't think. Whatever she's doing is probably just spooking Beijing. Probably because they're behind the shit she's investigating.

CHAPMAN: WHO CARES? This is so stupid! So they tried to kidnap some college professor in bumfuck Virginia? She's a nobody in the scheme of things! She's an ink stain on the path of progress.

Privately, he would have handed her over to the damned Chinese himself if it meant salvaging this deal. This was going to change the course of the world. What the hell was she going to do that was on that level? Nothing, that was what. He was busy orchestrating a deal to bring information and news to all of China and she was...well, who cared? She'd teach some people, maybe, and that was it. In the great book of the universe, she'd end up a zero, Jaime Chapman reflected.

CHALKE: I agree she's a no one, but the Bureau has to at least look like we care, even when presented with cases that we know we'll never get to the bottom of. It's our job. But it'll be fine, Bilson and I are managing the political ramifications of this. Stay tuned. Even if China was involved, no one is going to hold them to account.

BILSON: Because how can we, really? No one wants war. No one wants sanctions. It'll all work out. You'll see. China's just hitting you because they know you have influence. We'll smooth it out. Don't worry.

Chapman bit his lip. It would be hard to not worry, with billions on the line. In fact, he'd have liked to see Chalke or Bilson take that cool attitude if they were watching that money burn in front of their eyes. He doubted they'd be quite as chill if that was the case.

But, it was a benefit of being master of his own destiny that he didn't just have to wait and let things play out. No, indeed, Jaime Chapman was not a "sit on the sidelines" type. If Sienna Nealon was going to push her way into messing up his deal, he'd have to insert himself in the process and push right back. And for one of the richest and most powerful men in the world, which he totally was, that would be an easy thing to do.

CHAPTER FIFTY

Sienna

"So that's four confirmed," I said as Holloway finished hanging up the phone. "Five if you want to count that weak one that hung up on you."

The office was quiet as always, the sound of Holloway's pen scratching along on his list the only sound other than his breathing, which was steady and rhythmic. Slightly elevated, because we were making some progress after hours of pounding the phones and getting little for our trouble.

Still, four kidnappings confirmed out of a list of fifty names wasn't nothing. And we were down to the last five or so each.

"I want more," Holloway said, eyes fixed on the list. "Every one of these doesn't feel concrete enough." He looked up at me. "I mean, just what we've discovered about the ones we've confirmed – easy prey, all in the shadows," he said, sitting back in his chair. "Except your patient zero." He tapped the list with his finger. "College professor. Why her?"

I did a lean back of my own. "Why any of them? I mean, that's where I break down on this. Why is China – if it is the

PRC government – reaching out and conducting a stupid, high-risk kidnapping op in America? And this close to DC, no less?"

Holloway shook his head. "They got a billion people over there. Why do they need fifty more from us?"

That made me wrinkle my nose. "Good question. Their motives aren't usually that murky, are they? I mean, it's not like they move in indecipherable ways."

He nodded along. "Right. They want to assert themselves in the South China Sea, they built out atolls to function as strike bases to cover the area."

"They use everything they have at their disposal to block weapons sales to Taiwan," I said, "because it's a strategic enemy just across the Formosa Strait. Because they think it should be part of them, a rebel province they can't get their hands on."

"Tibet pisses them off, they send in troops to crush them," Holloway said. "Xinjiang Muslims make them mad? Stick 'em in concentration camps and sell their damned organs. Dissident pisses you off? Jail them and order their execution with a bullet to the back of the head. Then bill their family for the cost of the bullet. They've even grabbed people off the street in Hong Kong, and that was before they tried to make it formal with that extradition bill." He rubbed the bridge of his nose. "Yeah, it's pretty straightforward stuff. Brutal, in some cases...but straightforward."

"This was a little more sly," I said, staring at the list. "It was calculated, even. Grabbing these people." I held the list in front of me. "Who were these people to China? Jang-Peters's parents were dissidents. They were at Tiananmen Square and came over afterward to avoid the reprisals. Which were significant, I believe."

"You think all the rest of them were dissidents, too?"

"I don't know," I said. "This whole thing is a black box to me. Totally opaque. Is it revenge? If they are dissidents or dissident-linked, it starts to make sense. Motive-wise, I mean." I shook my head. "But I can't help but feel there's something else at play here. They've always cracked down on their own citizenry, sure. But look at Hong Kong; they've flinched from doing the big, nasty things, the violent things that would bring widespread condemnation, outside their own borders. They have a public image to maintain. It's not that they care nothing for world opinion. And masterminding an overseas kidnapping scheme?" I let out a low whistle. "That's not something that's liable to raise their Dun and Bradstreet in the international community, if you know what I mean."

"Right, right," Holloway said, face scrunched in thought. "Which is why I'm struggling with this whole thing. Could it be a Chinese businessman masterminding it, maybe? Instead of the government."

"Maybe," I said. "Less likely given the scale of the op, but not impossible. The thing that makes me doubt it? There was an aide to the Chinese ambassador that came to the scene with Bilson."

"Which scene? The one we were just at?"

"Yeah," I said. "Came over and talked to me while you were filling out the report. Said he was taking a look on behalf of the owner of the building, a Chinese citizen."

"Wait." Holloway sat forward now. "There's a corporation linked to our China investigation in the building, and another Chinese businessman *owns* the building? You get his name?"

"Yeah," I said, and Holloway spun around to his computer, ready to type. "Wu Huang. That billionaire who just jumped into bed with Socialite. Or, with Jaime Chapman and his associated companies."

"Hummm," Holloway said, tapping the keys. "I'm going to send an email to a friend of mine in the fraud division. He's good at linking corporate ownership and finding out what else this Huang guy might have in terms of properties in the neighborhood. Gonna include that front company HKK-whatever, too." He finished typing it out and hit send. "I'll text him to let him know it's coming. He's generally pretty quick to do a favor, especially if he sees some value in it for himself."

"What kind of value is in it for him?" I asked, because I didn't see it.

"A bottle of real quality scotch," Holloway said, and stuck his hand out. "So fork over fifty bucks."

"To quote what I'm sure is you, talking to a long line of

women in your past, 'I'm not paying shit until I get some satisfaction,'" I said.

Holloway laughed. "That does have a familiar ring to it."

"Here's another thing," I said. "That ambassador's aide? Liao, I think his name was? You can't tell me the average Chinese citizen gets that kind of on-the-spot, personal service like Huang did."

"Huang's probably part of their ruling junta or something," Holloway said, giving himself a single spin around in his chair. "I hear it's like a cartel over there at the top."

"Maybe," I said. "If so, he's got some real sway with the government, and to me that makes this smell even more suspicious, given that this HKKCME corp is tied to our case. It's a little too much China to be a coincidence, right?"

"It's suspicious, yeah," Holloway said, "but devil's advocate? It could be a coincidence. Long odds, but not impossible."

"This Liao, though...him showing up suggests to me that whatever Huang's relationship with the situation, it's got the imprimatur of the government's hand on it. One way or the other, they're involved somehow. Either in the scheme all along, or at least the cover-up. The circumstantial evidence alone is starting to make quite a pile."

"Lay it out for me," Holloway said. "Like a prosecutor. Convince me."

"Okay," I said, and drew a deep breath. "Stolen guns linked to this company are used in a kidnapping attempt to take an American citizen, the daughter of Chinese dissidents, a professor of Chinese culture. I track them back to this furniture store, tangle with a meta and accomplices who have multiple Chinese passports–"

"Which China says are fraudulent," Holloway interrupted. I must have given him a look, because he quickly added, "Devil's advocate."

"You want to advocate for the devil, don't be surprised if you go to hell later," I said, doing a little tapping of my own at the keyboard. "Anyway, Chinese passports, either real and generated by their government or intel agencies, or fraudulently obtained. Again, circumstantial evidence. Add it to the pile. Chinese nationals, acting as thugs and kidnappers. Actual ID and connections to China – unknown. Though we should get autopsies from them, and maybe something will turn up. Anyway, we tie the guns to this HKKCME, which is renting an office space from Huang, a Chinese billionaire with indeterminate ties to the government."

"'Indeterminate' is a big word," Holloway said, "and a big stumbling block for a case."

"Fine, more circumstantial evidence, but it's becoming a mountain, like Rushmore, except instead of faces it's a bunch of stone fingers pointing at China, China, China–"

"That's the worst metaphor I've ever heard."

"Then there's that State Department employee," I said, "Bridget Schultz, which is unrelated to our case – I think – but who just so happens to be suffering from a sonic weapons attack, and the Secretary of State suggests–"

"She's a China opponent," Holloway finished. "But like you said, probably unrelated, because her condition was in motion long before you took this case."

I picked up the list of targets we'd been working. "Yes, but maybe not before our *kidnappers* started working this case."

Holloway stared at me blankly, then he got it. "I'm willing to accept some of the circumstantial stuff – outside of my devilry advocation – but that one's a bridge too far for me. I think you can mark her down as independent of this, unless you find some compelling reason they'd want to take her off the board at the same time they're engaging in this kidnapping case."

"Maybe you're right," I said, nodding along with his chain of logic. "But to me it speaks to the pattern – China is engaging in increasingly bad and hostile behavior. Aggressively so."

"Could be," Holloway conceded. "It certainly fits. But you're lacking a smoking gun, which means...there's no case here. You've got crimes. I even agree with your chain of reasoning on these suppositions. But in terms of an actual case? You're nowhere. No prosecutor worth their salt would bring anything except the charges against the guy you call Firebeetle. China'd be free and clear in our courts. Not that we have any influence over them anyway."

"Okay, Mr. Devilry Advocate," I said, "what's the flip side of this?" He gave me a funny look. "If you were looking to make the case that I was not only wrong about China, but spectacularly wrong, what would you say all this means?"

"Well..." Holloway started to take a deep breath, gathering his thoughts. I couldn't wait to hear what he had to say.

CHAPTER FIFTY-ONE

Chapman

"Well..."

They were in.

Devin had been as good as promised, logging into the trojans that Chalke had made sure were implanted in Nealon's FBI team's computers, their cell phones, even Nealon's TV and laptop at home. Chapman's best engineers had designed them, and now...

They had everything on her. Full audio anywhere she carried her phone, full video from the camera, even her computer.

Some of that had been Chalke's idea, when they moved her to Washington. Traditional FBI bugging had been one avenue, but Chalke had gotten kind of skittish about that. Its traceability bothered her.

Chapman had her covered, though. And now they had Nealon covered. He'd had a small team sifting through the video and audio files live, watching and listening to them, reporting on her moves. He got a neat report at the end of each day, which he'd been disregarding.

Until now.

Now...he needed to take a more active hand in the situation, clearly.

Which was why he was staring at the video feed from Nealon's computer camera, looking at her dull face as she looked at her partner, a washed-up FBI agent who looked like he'd pulled himself out of a dirty clothes basket. Thank God the surveillance didn't have an olfactory component, because Chapman sniffed just looking at him.

"...If I were going to make the case against Chinese involvement," the male partner said, "I'd start with you. Personally."

"Me?" Nealon's voice was a little higher than usual in her reply.

"You're the weakest link, dumbass," Chapman muttered under his breath.

"You need anything else, sir?" Devin asked, waiting across the desk from Chapman.

"What's this idiot's name? The one she's talking to?" He didn't care, he just wanted a name to go with the face so he didn't have to mentally tag him "schlubby loser" while watching this shit play out.

"Agent Holloway, sir."

"Great, perfect, get out." Agent Holloway's face was moving, his mouth opening, he was about to pour forth his utter lack of wisdom, Chapman sensed.

"You're a soft target for dedicated political operatives," Holloway said. "You ought to know that. It's not like they haven't hit you before."

"Thank you for acknowledging that," Nealon said softly. "Most people just think I accidentally fell into being a fugitive from the law."

"Naw, I've seen political ops play out before," Holloway said. "And that was an op. But regardless, you've left enough bodies and been hit enough times that there's plenty of fertile ground to blast you on. If I were China, looking to do some damage to your case – yeah, I'd take aim at you first."

"Awesome," she said with clear sarcasm. Clear to Chapman, anyway. Maybe the moron Holloway missed it.

"You know all the evidence is weak," Holloway said. "That's

the problem with circumstantial. You tie enough of it together, you can paint a picture – if you can get it admitted. But regardless, how do you put China on trial?"

Chapman's pulse quickened. Here it was. How the hell could Chalke and Bilson have missed this? It was right there; he'd been watching her for two minutes. Idiots. Even in the Network, competence was at a premium. It was a constant frustration for Chapman, and he considered himself lucky that Socialite was one of the best companies to work for in the world. It allowed him to skim the cream of talent and keep these relative morons out of personal contact with him. Except for now, when he was unfortunately forced to watch these stupid normies have their dumbass, idiotic conversations, because they were shaking up his neatly constructed world.

"Okay," Nealon said, appearing to take a long breath to compose herself. Not too bright. Fast fists, slow mind. Not a total moron, but extremely average in Chapman's estimation. "How would you do it?"

"You want me to spell it out for you?" Holloway asked. He seemed wary. Maybe of pissing her off. "Fine," he decided. "They'll go after every weak point they can find. The big one: the number of people you've killed. Because it's a lot."

"I'm just going to defend myself here by saying almost all of them had it coming."

Chapman chuckled. "That'll play well in the media." It was an obvious weakness, one that had been exploited before. No matter how much the average Joe Sixpack might respect Sienna Nealon as a hero, show them video of her burning someone to death and she immediately lost favorability points with suburban housewives. Or so Bilson had said. Chapman hadn't cared until now.

"Maybe," Holloway said. "But you pair a good attack campaign with some of that ubiquitous video that's out there..." He shrugged. Maybe he wasn't a total idiot. But nearly.

"What else?" she asked, posture tightening. She was getting defensive. Good.

"Everything you can imagine," Holloway said. "Attacking the witness on every avenue possible is a time-honored tradition.

The media are on-call for Beijing. Every single network and major agency has a bureau there. They get most – not all, but most – of their stories from China hand-fed to them by the Chinese government. Write an unfavorable story, and they hear about it straight from the top. The threat of bureau closure there is persistent. Get too critical, you get cut out of the loop." He shrugged. "So what do most western media with a stake in things do?"

"Feed straight from Beijing's waiting nipples, I assume."

Holloway laughed, but behind his monitor, Chapman cringed at the crude assessment. Disgusting.

"You gotta admit," Holloway said, "it's an elegant way to control them. They decide to write a few articles about you...these major outlets dig up a few 'golden oldies' from your exile period..."

"Isn't all this...violence stuff about me...kinda baked in at this point?" she asked. "Everyone knows what I've done. What is rehashing it going to do for them?"

"Muddy the waters, I assume," Holloway said, "but if you think that's bad, that's just their first line of attack. The one the press used on you before. They've got other ones, new ones. Your alcoholism–"

"Dirty."

"–your sex life–"

"Hey that's...extremely boring, especially lately."

"You can absorb a soul during the act. I don't care how boring it is in actuality, I was shocked last time they didn't play that up for titillating effect. It's tailor-made for catching the attention, especially of men, who think of little else. Any man who knows what a succubus was – prior to you – had that one damned thought on their mind when you came along."

"Ewwww! You're telling me the male population of America–"

"Probably the world."

"–That they've thought about me like–"

"Yeah. Probably."

Chapman let out a chuckle under his breath. That was a wonderful smear idea. Hard to believe it came from an idiot. He made a mental note to press that particular button first if need be.

"This is not the first time I've thought of my power as a sort of disability," Nealon said, doing a full-body shiver, "but it is the grossest time I've thought of it as such, if that's what's going on in guys heads' when they think about me. Yuck."

"Sorry to be the bearer of bad news vis-a-vis your position in the sexual fantasies of men worldwide."

"I hate this. I hate knowing this. And right now, I hate you."

It was Holloway's turn to chortle. "You're going to hit me with some sort of subtle, femme mind-fuck later to make up for this aren't you?"

Nealon's face curtained, losing all emotion. "I strike you as the subtle type?"

Holloway laughed, but it died quickly, giving way to seriousness laced with discomfort. "No. You're more the sort that would set my car on fire. With me in it."

Nealon winked, snapping a pointed finger at him. "Your insight into people is super keen. What else would China do?"

"Run the PR playbook. Drag out old lovers, people who hate you for a variety of reasons. Anyone you've failed to save – you know all this."

"No, I suspected it. But you're giving me new avenues of paranoia."

"They'd put surveillance on you. Tails. Bug your place. Hit you with one of those sonic devices, maybe–"

"Huh." Nealon sat back in her chair. "You know, I would not have thought they'd go that far, given I'm an FBI agent, but now that we've seen some of the things they've done..." She nodded slowly. "Yeah. I need to watch my back."

"PerSec is going to be an issue if you're right about this," Holloway said. "And–" He stopped, an electronic dinging ringing out over the speaker.

"What?" Nealon asked, sitting forward in her chair.

"Already got an email back from my guy," Holloway said. Now Chapman was watching him through the camera on his own computer, reading the screen, eyes scrolling.

A couple taps, and Chapman could see what he was reading. It looked dull, boring procedural stuff, then–

Oh.

Suddenly it wasn't so dull anymore.

"What the f–" Chapman breathed.

"This is something," Holloway said on the monitor. Well, duh. The dumbass.

"What is it?" Nealon asked, leaning forward over Holloway's idiotic, old-school, Marlboro man shoulder, framing her slightly doughy face in frame with his like the most puke-worthy selfie Chapman could imagine. And as the chief of the world's largest social media site, he'd seen his fair share.

"This HKKCME company that lost those guns? Whose offices we–"

"I know who they are. What did your guy find?" Nealon said, looking like she was about a half second from shoving him aside to read for herself. She really did have a hair trigger and the violence was always ready to manifest. Chapman had seen it in her eyes when she'd been here, in his office. Just below the surface, ready to blow up like a dormant volcano.

"They've got exactly one other asset on their books," Holloway said, face bearing a trace of a smile. "A lease on a pier at the Port of Baltimore."

CHAPTER FIFTY-TWO

Sienna

The ride to the Port of Baltimore came at rush hour, of course. Holloway rode shotgun while I drove, spending his time on the phone with our FBI lawyer. They had a warrant from a judge for us to search the pier by the time we reached the halfway point, but we were stuck in traffic moving a solid fifteen miles an hour, so I knew it was going to take a while.

"So about this whole China thing," Holloway said, breaking the silence he'd punctuated with news of our warrant procurement. "What *is* the motive here? There's got to be something. Even if we go from the assumption that China's getting too big for their britches, there has to be a reason to snatch these folks. They're not just doing it for kicks."

"I agree," I said, white knuckling the wheel as some tool in a Prius (but I repeat myself, because all Prius owners are tools at heart) with little regard for their own life angled in front of my big SUV, cutting in. I toyed with flipping on the lights and siren just to get them out of the way (and maybe give them a well-deserved heart attack), but this wasn't an emergency and I didn't have the power to write traffic tickets. Though sometimes I wanted that power. "It's either a shift to a more aggressive strategy for stifling dissidents – if that's what those people are – or there's something else going. Something we're missing."

"But how's the tiger fit in?" Holloway asked. He looked about a second away from propping his feet up on the dashboard. "That's what I want to know."

"We figure out who the Firebeetle is," I said, "we'll get a better idea of who the tiger is. They're linked somehow. The tiger keeps showing up at the same places as Firebeetle. That can't be a coincidence. There's a death match going on there."

"What if that's not it?" Holloway asked, looking very pensive, so unlike him. "What if the connection is you?"

I was pretty sure I made a face. Then had to tap my brakes because the Prius stopped for no reason. Seriously, he had miles between him and the car in front of him. "Asshole!"

Holloway swayed forward and back with the motion of my braking. "Whew."

"What?" I asked.

"For a second there I thought you were talking to me. Just relieved is all."

"Yeah, I haven't forgotten your little revelation that the men of America have contemplated what it'd be like to have me take their souls, and 'asshole' definitely still applies to you. But in this case..." I frowned. "...You may have a point. He does keep showing up and saving my bacon. The tiger, I mean." I shook my head. "Ugh. This one's too tightly wrapped. So many threads to keep track of. Something needs to start making sense soon or I'm gonna lose it."

Holloway kept his silence for a five count, at most. "Like...more or less than when I told you that thing about American men's contemplations of what a succubus–"

"Dick." I thumped the wheel lightly. "There's too much in play here. Nobody I'm talking to is unraveling the nuttiness."

"I'm sure a break is coming," Holloway said.

"Good," I said, "because so far we're getting a ton of evidence piled up. Warehouses full, even. But none of it's adding together in a coherent way. Stolen guns. Kidnapping. Sonic weapons used against State Department employees. Reams of fake/real

Chinese passports. Workers being held in country by Chinese corporate interests. A meta with demon eyes who keeps fighting me but didn't turn loose his fire powers on me. All these crimes, all these little mysteries intersecting. It's the ultimate Turkish carpet of bullshit, and it's got to form a pattern." I kept tapping my fingers against the wheel.

"It'll make sense soon," Holloway said. "You can't trip across this many crimes without discerning the pattern. We're just missing a couple key breakthroughs. Hell, maybe even just one." He wore a partial smile and I found it weirdly reassuring. "Who knows? Maybe it's even at the Port of Baltimore."

"We should be so lucky," I muttered, wondering when the traffic – and this damned case – would break.

CHAPTER FIFTY-THREE

Chapman

It took him a while to get through to Wu, but when he finally did, Huang sounded like he'd been shaken out of a deep sleep. "Wu, it's me," Chapman said, then wanted to kick himself for his lameness of speech. Whatever, though; he looked out the window of the Socialite glass pyramid over the grassy, sparsely wooded campus, breathing like he was in meditation.

"Yes?" Huang's voice was all grog, a little edge seeping in, as though his patience were waning. Chapman hadn't done the calculus on what time it was in China, but it was probably very early morning.

"I've taken some steps toward curbing the Sienna Nealon problem we discussed earlier," Chapman said. "And I've learned a few things about her investigation I figure I should pass on."

"Oh?" Huang's voice suddenly got clearer. Good. The offer of a quid pro quo cut through the fog of sleep.

Chapman launched right into it. "She's currently on her way to the Port of Baltimore with a search warrant for a dock facility that's linked to a company called HKKCME." There was no point in not blurting it out; if it came to whose side Chapman was on in this, it damned sure wasn't Sienna Nealon's. Get her out of the way and a deal that would reshape the world would recommence. Let her win and...what? Shit would fall apart, that's what. His deal, diplomatic relations with China, who knew what else? The last thing they needed was World War III, especially with Gondry going into re-election. He'd looked strong after Revelen. Things falling apart with China would undo all the victory that came from that conflict.

"That's interesting," Huang said, a catch in his voice. It was more than interesting, Chapman judged. "But what are you doing about keeping her from making her poisonous and fruitless accusations? These are of far greater concern to us than whatever she's doing on a moment by moment basis."

"I've talked to some people," Chapman said. "People close to the president. She has little influence with him, and she'll be boxed out of any further meetings with him." He could hardly promise that, but Bilson and Chalke didn't seem inclined to put her in a position to talk to Gondry. Really...why would the president want to talk to that moron anyway? The perspective of a corn-fed Midwestern dullard could be had from a much prettier face or brighter mind.

"Our officials fear that the damage may already be done," Huang said.

"I'll work to undo it," Chapman said. "I have PR firms on the payroll. Lobbyists. Lawyers. Even reporters who eat out of the palm of my hand." A small bead of sweat dripped down his temple. "I can marshal them all and turn them against her. I know the people the president listens to." Here he thought of that knucklehead Chris Byrd, newly added to the Network. "I can get them to say anything you want about her to keep her out of the Oval Office."

Huang was quiet for so long that Chapman was almost afraid he'd lost the man. He was on the verge of asking when Huang chimed back in.

"That...might just work," Huang finally said, and Chapman let out a long breath he hadn't even known his was holding.

They were back in business, and he was going to save this deal yet. No matter what.

CHAPTER FIFTY-FOUR

Sienna

Getting out of the car at the Port of Baltimore, I was suddenly struck by the feeling that I'd forgotten something. Seagulls cawed in the distance, and a quick look overhead revealed birds circling – or at least a pigeon or twelve.

I snapped my fingers, realizing what I'd "forgotten." "Shit," I said under my breath as Holloway slammed his door.

"What?" he asked.

"I gotta make a call real quick," I said, pulling out my phone and dialing Bilson. I'd headed to Baltimore without checking in with him like I'd promised. Whether I'd wanted it or not, Chalke had assigned me to him, and if I was going to try and make nice with her – even for my own reasons – I needed to at least pretend to jump through the hoops in front of me.

"Yeah, cool, I'll just sit over here and look at the warehouses," Holloway said under his breath. "And sweat. A lot, actually."

He wasn't wrong about that. Even with sundown coming, it was sweltering out here. The sea breeze might have been the only saving grace, and even that wasn't doing much.

Bilson picked up on the fifth ring. "Hello!" So chipper.

"Hey, got a lead," I said, launching right past the pleasantries. "The company that we checked out earlier? They have a lease on a pier down at the Port of Baltimore. Judge approved a search warrant, so we're about to take a peek."

There was a subtle change in the timbre of his voice. "Right now?"

"Yeah, sorry for the late notice," I said. "It's potentially dangerous, though, given the company connections to stolen guns, so you should probably stay back from this one."

"I'll be there shortly," Bilson said, and then he hung up, leaving me staring at my phone.

"Not in rush hour, you won't," I said under my breath, pocketing the phone.

"How'd that go?" Holloway asked.

"Marvelous. We'll see our civilian observer as soon as traffic permits, I reckon."

"Oh, good, I love oversight," Holloway groused. "How'd you get saddled with him, anyway?"

"He's not bad," I said. "Chalke insisted. I think she's afraid I'm too much trouble if left without adult supervision."

"What the hell am I?" Holloway asked as we crossed the steaming pavement toward the pier in question. "Chopped liver?"

"A problem drinker, at least," I said, "and also – not in charge of me. Thank God."

His shoulders sagged slightly, then he shrugged. "You got a point there. Maybe a couple of them, actually."

I caught a sly hint of a smile from him. "Did you just make a boob reference?"

Holloway blinked innocently, and I knew that bastard had, figuring he could just slide it past me. "What? Me? Noooo."

"Do you ever live your life out of the gutter?" I asked. "Even for a moment? I mean, I thought my head could go to some dirty places, but then I met you, and *Sokath, her eyes were uncovered*."

"It's the Army," Holloway said. "It's a full perversion mentorship program."

The pier was ahead, a jutting concrete structure that extended hundreds of feet into the dirty beginnings of the

Chesapeake Bay. No ships were parked alongside at the moment, but a multi-story heavy-loading crane waited at the end, and stacks of corrugated metal cargo containers lined the edges. A warehouse lay to our left, and the activity level out here was nonexistent. Because it was after quitting time for the longshoremen, I presumed.

"What did the email say the company rented?" I asked, peering at the cargo containers all stacked in multicolor piles.

"This one," Holloway said, looking around. "I think it might have listed a warehouse, too, but I don't see any clear, identifying marks on these warehouses."

"Neither do I." A little tingle went up the tiny hairs on the back of my neck. "Hey, you getting a feeling like–"

"Yeah," Holloway said, slipping his jacket back so he could draw his pistol off his hip easier. "I am."

I had to wonder what kind of Spider-sense we were sharing when both of us were picking up an ambush vibe at a random dock in Baltimore. Not so random, though, I suppose, given I'd already been bushwhacked by Firebeetle at one location under this company's aegis. I, too, slipped my jacket back and put my hand on my service Glock. It wasn't my favorite gun, but it was what the bureau offered, and it definitely shot straight, working under some adverse conditions.

"You know what to do if we get ambushed, right?" Holloway asked. He'd slowed his walk and was scanning everywhere, mostly for the closest cover. It was about ten yards away, a cargo container to his left. My closest cover was fifteen yards off, and to my right, because we were split with a gulf of about ten yards between us.

"Attack into the teeth of it, right?" I asked, trying to decide if keeping the split between us was smarter than bunching up. "That's Army doctrine?"

"Yep," Holloway said, and I could see the meat of his hand digging up against his own Glock's grip. The urge to draw was getting to him, too, but we couldn't do that just for a feeling. No matter how solid or shared that sense was. "Attack in the direction of the ambush and knock their damned teeth out."

"The Army philosophy strangely mirrors my own."

"You know a good battle tactic when you hear one," Holloway said. We were both creeping closer to our respective covers; splitting up had seemed a better idea, giving our potential ambushers more targets to shoot at.

"I think I saw movement ahead," I said, trying to figure out exactly what I'd seen. We were heading toward a valley of cargo containers, a box canyon of a very literal sort, stacked two and three high and walling us off from the water surrounding the pier on either side. I couldn't tell if I'd seen a bird or just the interplay of colors between two differently shaded containers. Hell, it could have been a shadow, given that sundown was well underway and half the containers were colored with the orange glow of the setting sun.

"Me too," Holloway said, now whispering and easing toward his container. "I say we break for cover and call for backup from the locals. Hang here until they show."

A younger, bolder, maybe stupider me would have made a joke about him being a chicken. Current me's alarm bells were all ringing, though, and I matched his move, heading for my own container. "Agreed," I said, just loud enough he could hear me. "I'm all about the cavalry on this one, and I'm getting a feeling that–"

The abrupt clang of metal stopped me before I could finish my thought. Two of the shipping containers ahead burst open, their doors springing wide and disgorging men with guns, laden with tactical gear.

Staccato bursts of gunfire echoed in the Baltimore dusk and rang through the stacks of shipping containers as Holloway and I both bailed for our respective sides, finally drawing our pistols as we raced for cover.

CHAPTER FIFTY-FIVE

Chapman

"...Request immediate backup!" Holloway's voice rang tinny over his speaker as Chapman watched. The FBI agent had his phone to the side of his face, cradling it there while he fired his gun with his other hand. It wasn't a great view, given how both the cell phone's cameras were positioned; one was giving Chapman an up-close visual of the shipping container the agent was squatting behind, the other an extreme close-up of Holloway's face as he made his emergency call. The man stuck his gun out and fired a couple times before ducking back under cover and proceeding with his phone call. "Agents under fire, repeat, agents under fire! Port of Baltimore. Request immediate assistance, all units!"

"What a chicken," Chapman said, watching him slightly angle his pistol's barrel around the shipping container, firing a couple times, then pulling the gun back. He wasn't even looking where he was aiming, let alone sticking his gun out far enough that he could hit anybody. "This view is for shit, man. Come on. Look out there. Lemme see."

Nealon's phone was buried in her pocket, and he had it

muted since all it was giving off was echoing gunshots. Their opponents in this little fracas were firing like mad. Probably had some of those assault weapons that seemed so ubiquitous in middle America. Crazy.

"I want to see what's going on," Chapman moaned. He was getting pretty tired of watching Holloway's face during this exchange. Was there a nearby camera bank he could seize control of, maybe? Sure, that'd be slightly illegal, but if he couldn't do a little hacking and cover his tracks, pretty much nobody on the planet could.

Chapman messed with his VPN settings; better if this looked like it came from somewhere external. Revelen seemed a good choice, so he went with it. That done, he went to work. Someone had managed a ransomware attack on the whole city of Baltimore last year; surely it wouldn't be too difficult to get into the camera systems...

CHAPTER FIFTY-SIX

Sienna

"...Repeat, we are under heavy fire!" Holloway was screaming into his phone. I couldn't blame him; I'd seen what we were up against, and a combat vet like him had to know we were absolutely borked the way things currently stood.

Our enemy numbered at least twenty, and were moving and covering, layering their fire and chipping away at our shipping containers. Mine had about two hundred holes already punched into the edge I had sheltered behind. If I moved up to shoot, I'd get a hail of bullets for my trouble. Holloway was experiencing a similar fate; his container looked like seriously aged Swiss cheese at the edge where he'd been firing only a moment earlier. He'd stopped and moved back, wisely.

I scanned the area around me. The situation was dire. Our cover options beyond our current containers were dismal. The next nearest to me was over twenty yards of open ground. Holloway's next alternate was maybe a little closer but not much. And toward the enemy, which was unfavorable. Twenty yards of open ground was a hell of a lot given we had twenty-plus hostiles with fully automatic weapons unloading on us. I hadn't gotten a great look before I'd been forced to jump behind my container, but they looked like they might have been in the AK family of rifles. AK-47 or AK-74, I couldn't tell.

The constant thundering of the guns, and the occasional shouts in some foreign language I wasn't well acquainted with, both suggested a plan to me. I was pretty sure the shouts were these guys calling out that they were reloading, a verbal cue to let someone else know to pick up their own volume of fire. They were pounding us in shifts, not letting up.

And getting closer, I had to guess. Advancing.

We couldn't fire back without getting annihilated, either, which meant when they got close enough to turn the corner on us, if we weren't ready...

Well, it'd be game over.

"Holloway!" I shouted, waving to get his attention. He looked over, in the middle of loading a fresh mag in his pistol, and met my eyes.

I telegraphed my plan with one hand while keeping my pistol pointed at the end of the container with the other.

Holloway's eyes went wide as he took it in, then nodded after the shock wore off.

"One for the money," I said, taking a breath and steeling myself for what I was about to have to do. It was not going to be pleasant. "Two for the show."

I turned around, facing toward the far end of the container. They hadn't started spraying it with suppressing fire yet, which told me they hadn't quite made it to the no man's land of their own part of the container maze, at which point they'd have a clear field of fire at it.

These were my last moments to act before they had me penned in.

Breaking into a sprint, I ran for the far end of the container, dashing out of cover–

A guy in all black tac gear was coming around the next nearest container just as I rounded the curve. He raised his gun at me–

Too late. I shot, stitching him with 9mm bullets as I ran. Two in the chest, one in the head that made it in just under his tactical helmet. It made a mess but held in the pink mist, and I was already behind cover, then leaping before he fell.

My feet left the ground as I reached the edge of the pier, hard concrete footing gone from beneath me as I took a deep breath and plunged twenty feet down and into the chill waters of the Chesapeake Bay.

CHAPTER FIFTY-SEVEN

Chapman

"What the hell are you people doing?" Chapman wondered. Nealon's camera had registered the splash, and now was dark. It had taken him a couple seconds to work it out, then – duh! They were on a pier, there was a splash, ergo...

He was almost into the Port of Baltimore camera feeds. They were amateur hour, really, and lucky for him, because he only had so much time and bandwidth to dedicate to this little side project.

Muting the cell phone cameras was almost an afterthought, he was so deep into the process. Coding was second nature to him; hacking, slightly less so. He'd done his fair share in college, mostly harmless stuff, for the lulz. This, though, was more than for the lulz, though not that serious.

"Who sells these municipalities their encryption?" he scoffed, bringing up access to a couple of servers. Run his program on them, remotely access and–

Chapman let out a small chuckle of victory. This was the problem with being quantum leaps ahead of everyone else in the country, tech-wise. "Can't stand up to the best," he muttered under his breath. Now where had Nealon gone...?

Ah. There she was, swimming along the side of the concrete pier. Chapman had wondered if maybe she'd try to hide beneath it, like they did in the movies, but it was solid concrete all the way through. She was swimming along the side, though, and quite rapidly, all the way to the end. What was she going to do once she got there? Swim out to sea?

Finding himself inextricably drawn into the drama of her stupid little life, he settled down to watch. Should he have one of his assistants bring him some organic popcorn...?

CHAPTER FIFTY-EIGHT

Sienna

I swam to the end of the pier as though my life depended upon it, because it did. The gunfire did not stop while I was swimming, either, in fact, I was pretty sure it increased in volume once they heard and saw me take out one of their boys. It reverberated through the water as I swam, cold chill all over my skin, my hair falling in line behind me.

That was fine. I wanted them to keep shooting at the shipping containers. Hell, they could burn through all the ammo they wanted. By now they were firing in the wrong direction. I held my breath, lungs starting to complain as I windmilled my arms in a meta-speed breast stroke.

Reaching the end of the pier, a little shiver running over my lip, I surveyed the concrete structure in front of me through the rippling surface of the water.

It was ten feet back up to the decking. Safety ladders had been placed along the side, and the nearest was just a few feet away.

I scaled the ladder in two good leaps, not wasting my time climbing safely. I shook my Glock a couple times to get the preponderance of the water out, then drew my backup Sig and did the same. The Glock had definitely passed underwater fire tests, but I wasn't sure about the Sig. It'd probably work, but the sooner I swapped these out for one of those rifles the better off I would be, no doubt.

Even without the incredible volume of fire blasting away at us, Holloway and I had been outmatched. Rifle ranges were measured in miles, their accuracy so much better than a pistol. Longer barrels meant better accuracy, which meant our attackers could have pinned us down with lethally accurate fire at a much greater distance. Add to that the fact they were loaded for bear with ballistic vests and reload magazines that held thirty-plus rounds while Holloway and I had maybe – maybe thirty-five rounds each, total, and we were outgunned by a factor of a hundred. The guy I'd shot? I'd counted six, seven mags visible in just the two seconds I had to observe him. He could have had more behind him. That was two hundred rounds just on him. And a much more rapid rate of fire.

Contrast that with Holloway and I with our seventy bullets, all snubby little 9mm pistol rounds. They might penetrate the ballistic vests these guys were wearing, but it wasn't a clear-cut, definite thing I'd want to bank my life on. Which is why I ran when I had the chance.

Now I was in their rear, and it was time to turn the tables.

The key to springing an ambush is making sure your enemy doesn't see it coming until they can't stop it. To that end, I had to be fast, lethal, and quiet. At least two of those were my favorite things. Not so much on quiet, but we all have our flaws.

The pier ahead was much less of a maze than it had been at the entry. I had my suspicions that someone had moved the containers around to obscure the ambush from view until it was almost too late. Poor planning had led them to forget to remove the blocking containers before they sprang it, though, leaving us with a bare amount of cover to exploit. That little whoopsie worked to our advantage, though they'd done their damnedest to offset it by turning the shipping containers to Swiss cheese with us behind them.

It was hard to believe they didn't conceive of us jumping off the sides, though. I'd gone deep, out of view from the surface, but the splash might have been audible. Maybe not, though, given the volume of gunfire.

Either way, I was poised to find trouble – meaning sentries – guarding their rear. These guys looked like pros, moved like pros. It was unbelievable to me that they could have failed to watch their flank.

Huddling next to a shipping container, pistol at ready, dripping like crazy, I stripped off my clinging jacket one arm at a time. My ears were ringing from the constant, thunderous gunfire. That done, I slipped up to the edge of the container and peered around.

Ahead, down the aisle between shipping container piles, I could see one of the black-suited bad guys. They had the feel, the look of mercs, a species of loathsome I was well acquainted with at this point. Who hired them? Hell if I knew. I caught snatches of shouts in a foreign language, but not one I could identify, especially not with water still dripping out of my ears and the sound of gunfire covering everything like a steady jackhammer in the background.

I snuck between the containers, heading for the dude in question. He was alone, a little lost sheep away from the flock.

Time to be the wolf.

He had his gun nominally pointed in my direction, but his head was turned, derelicting his duty in favor of the interesting sounds of hammering gunfire coming from behind him. I crept up on him, light on my toes.

When I reached him, I grabbed the barrel of his gun and yanked it sideways, twisting it and catching his finger in the trigger guard. He let out a yell that ceased when I hit him in the throat with the butt of my gun, crushing his larynx. He let out a gagging noise and sounded like he was drowning. I kicked his feet from beneath him and knocked him unconscious to let him choke to death quietly. Ish. At least this way he wouldn't be trouble at my six o'clock.

I stripped his vest off his limp, twitching form, slinging the rifle over my shoulder when done. This one was different than the rest, but definitely in the AK-47 family. I couldn't be sure, but it looked like an Eastern European edition of the famous weapon. A terrorist favorite, this particular gun was common as dirt, though not in the US, where it was illegal. A quick chamber check confirmed it held the larger 7.62 bullet, which meant I had a better chance of punching through the body armor these yahoos were wearing now. Worlds better than with just my pistol, that was for sure.

I continued my prowl, sweeping up the next aisle and taking cover behind one of the containers. The gunfire had slowed; clearly our pursuers had realized Holloway and I had jumped ship. Military trained, they'd begin a search pattern. It'd be careful, thorough, and would probably catch us in the next two minutes since it'd be obvious we hadn't swam back toward the car. I'd written that idea off because it was too exposed. They'd have seen us going across the water and would have had a clear line of sight to shoot us down getting out of the water. Sticking close to the pier had let us move under the cover of the containers stacked at the sides, invisible to any watchers high above.

Speaking of...

I looked up and behind me. My back was firmly planted against a shipping container. The unloading crane stretched a few stories skyward, and I peered into its confusing depths. It was a series of steel supports and a frame designed to slide back and forth. I had a suspicion...

There. A sniper, nesting up in the heights. A few more seconds of searching revealed another. Smart. Also, probably soon to be deadly for our backup when they showed. Those guys could cover the entire approach to the pier from up there, using the steel supports as cover against fire from below. Mostly.

I raised my AK knockoff to my shoulder and took careful aim. I picked the one closest to me first, because I had the clearest shot at him. A stroke of the trigger and three bullets blew out of the barrel. I controlled the rise of the sight picture, keeping it on target as the stock reverberated the recoil through my shoulder.

My bullets hit home and the sniper sagged, his weapon falling. It caught against the sling and hung there, a rifle swaying gently back and forth a hundred feet off the ground.

Switching targets, I saw the second sniper had taken notice of his buddy's sudden death. He was scanning frantically, looking for me–

I drilled him with three and watched him jerk. He'd been scooting to the side, trying to use the girder he was lying prone on for cover. Not having a lot of room to maneuver, he'd partially moved off of it. My bullets helped complete the move, and he rolled into space, dropping to the ground behind one of the containers, headfirst. A perfect swan dive, except he was already limp when he made it. If the bullets hadn't already done the job, the fall would definitely kill him.

A whisper to my left and down the container row broke through my preoccupation with dealing with the snipers and I spun, planting my AK barrel against the side of the shipping container and easing around until I had a tac-geared target in my sights. I let it rip and beat him to the draw. Whatever surprise he might have had at seeing a rifle barrel appear around the side of the container I was covering behind was gone with his brains as I blew them all out the back of his head with a controlled three-shot burst.

Continuing my sweep, I managed to land my sight picture on his wingman. I squeezed off three shots, but he was already reacting to his buddy's sudden death before his eyes–

Bullets sprayed the container where I was covering, whizzing past my face. Shards of metal peppered my forehead as the 7.62 rounds ripped through the metal, forcing me to retreat before I got perforated. I heard my attacker grunt; at least some of my shots had found their target.

He shouted in pain, and it was loud. Loud enough that I was under no illusions; my position was blown. Darting to the other side of the container, I swept the aisle–

Shit. Two more coming this way. Seeing the silhouette of my head popping out from behind the container, they raised their guns–

I sprinted for it, spraying with one hand and no hope of hitting anything. It was suppressing fire, designed to get them to duck away so I had time to cross between the container rows, getting my ass to cover that wasn't being flanked on both sides by hostiles.

They fired at me, and I felt a hard sting against my left shoulder, like a horsefly. Another whipped across my side, like someone had blown a puff of air there.

I entered the cover of the container across the aisle and found myself faced with a view of the Chesapeake Bay once more. I'd reached the end of the pier, nothing but an empty aisle to my left and right past this container.

Gunshots continued behind me; holes were being punched in the corner of my container, my foes advancing unchallenged. Leaning out to slow them down was almost certain to result in me catching a bullet or three.

With a glance to my right out the aisle separating me from the water, I found a team of three moving up and I realized I had no choice – again. They opened fire as I committed to my maneuver, and leapt once more over the edge of the pier, slinging my rifle as I went, plunging back into the cold water of the bay.

CHAPTER FIFTY-NINE

Chapman

Now Chapman was glad he'd decided to go for the popcorn. It was organic, with just a drizzle of fresh, whipped butter, locally sourced, of course. Watching this crazy gunfight unfold almost three thousand miles away provided just a hint of danger – it was actually happening! Right now! – but far enough away that it held an element of unreality, too. Authentic entertainment, no actual danger.

This was great. He was recording the whole thing, and if it weren't counter to his aims – i.e., it kinda made Sienna Nealon look cool – putting it up on Socialite would be awesome. Guaranteed virality. Not that he needed that boost. But it was the kind of content people loved.

He switched to a different view once she plunged back into the water. There were about ten guys in black vests and pants with their funny little helmets moving up to the water's edge. They were forming a firing line, which was interesting. They'd be shooting down into the open water, and Chapman was hard-pressed to see how Nealon was going to get out of this one...

CHAPTER SIXTY

Sienna

Getting dropped in the water again for the second time in five minutes was not my idea of heaven, even on a hot day like this. I had a bad feeling about the water quality of the Chesapeake Bay, especially in this area, and so I did my best to keep my mouth shut and not let any ooze into my sinuses. It was probably a lost cause, and I was immune to most diseases, but I still had a healthy germaphobia for some reason, which was why I always used the toilet liners provided in public restrooms.

I could see the bottom of the murky bay, about twenty feet down, and it was a trash heap of decades of discarded crap that had gone overboard, never to be recovered. Ahead lay the concrete pier, and I beelined for it, knowing they'd be setting up a firing line above me shortly. I needed to act quick.

Reaching the side of the pier, I floated on the surface, raising a fist. I had a very short time to do what I was going to do here. I needed a distraction, something to put these assholes on guard. Left unchecked, they'd fire indiscriminately into the water, raining bullets on me until I was dead. I needed to put them on the defensive.

My guns had been plopped in the water with me. Shooting them now *might* work, but the ballistics could be iffy and, in my estimation, wouldn't produce the desired effect. I couldn't shoot and swim; they'd know when I was firing and when I wasn't, and act accordingly.

I needed something silent. Something lethal. Something that would make them keep their heads down.

Something...horrifying.

I punched the concrete pier, shattering the surface in one blow. Bracing myself, I hit it again, cratering a foot of concrete by giving it everything I had. Pieces of gray, wet detritus fell away as I swept the debris away with a bloody hand.

Bingo.

My strikes had unearthed a piece of rebar, and I seized it with wet, crimson-covered fingers. Bracing both feet against the pier, I shoved off, ripping out a section about two to three feet in length.

The shouts of the men above me were echoing over the quiet waters. The gunfire had ceased, and I hoped Holloway had gotten clear of these assholes.

A couple of frantic shouts tipped me off that one of them could see me. I locked eyes with him; all I could see was his head framed in black in front of the red corrugated steel container behind him. I lay in the shadow of the pier; he moved to bring up his gun high enough so he could fire down at me.

He didn't get the chance.

I raised that piece of rebar like Zeus's own lightning bolt and fired it overhand, javelin-style.

He saw it coming, but his eyes only had a moment to widen before it landed like a cruise missile in the middle of his forehead.

I didn't wait for him to drop. My distraction done, I plunged back under the water and swam down, diving rapidly to get below the darkening surface so that hopefully they wouldn't be able to see me.

Executing a sprint-swim, I went meta-speed down the length of the pier, rounding the squared edge before I came up for air.

When I did, it wasn't until I saw one of the convenient ladders leading up the side.

I sprang up the ladder blindingly fast, turning my AK to let the water drain out of the barrel. Hopefully I wouldn't need it, but I damned sure didn't want to need it and find it inoperable, or worse, ready to blow due to water obstructing the barrel.

The crane stood over me, a mammoth empty frame soaring stories above. I ran through the empty middle, AK in hand, sweeping for hostiles as I plunged back into the maze of containers. I had a plan, a purpose, and I could still hear sporadic fire from the line of mercs that I'd just left behind.

Sweeping through the maze at high speed, I relied on my instincts and reflexes to keep me alive. I encountered no one, none, not one hostile, which made sense, because they'd all been lined up at the water's edge to pump rounds into me.

There – the cargo container that I'd been backed against. I could tell it by the holes in the corner where the bad guys had shredded it trying to shoot me. I could hear them talking, distantly, behind it as I darted into cover past the holey corner. Drawing a quick breath and scanning around me, one last time, to confirm no hostiles were sneaking up, I spun, planted my back foot, and lifted my front–

I gave that container an almighty kick, putting all my martial arts training and meta strength behind it. It jumped across the pavement, skittering and screeching as it blew into a wild skid across the pavement toward the pier's edge–

Screams, crunching bones, splashes; these were the sounds that followed as the container skipped along the ground some six feet toward the edge. It hit the solid half-step that surrounded the pier, a barrier designed to keep containers and other such objects from toppling into the water. The metal rang like a bell, and it started to tilt, momentum still with it, threatening to tip over into the bay. It stopped at about forty-five degrees, though, then settled back to the ground with a slam of metal against concrete.

I hustled over behind it, ignoring the crimson stains, drag marks the container had left behind when it had, uh...hit and...well, dragged a few of the mercs beneath it like a rogue snowplow. A quick leap up the short step and I was pointing my gun along the pier's ledge–

No one was there. No one alive, at least. A couple bodies were floating in the water, but none were moving. If they hadn't gotten crushed beneath the skidding container hitting them at automobile speeds, they'd been thrown into the water, apparently unconscious.

"Ew," I said, not enjoying my own handiwork. I got blinded by the guts and gore just a moment too long, though–

A gunshot rang out and I felt a surge of pain in the back of my right shoulder. I'd been grazed the last couple times; this felt like a real gunshot, though, a bloody through-and-through that left another wound on the front of my rotator cuff.

I collapsed, because the surge of pain knocked the wind right out of me. I came down hard, catching my rifle beneath my hands, trapping it under my body. I turned around to look, and saw a single merc in black advancing on me, skin beneath his ski mask pale, eyes a bright blue.

"Shit," I said, writhing, trying to free my AK to shoot back. It wasn't happening, though. He had me dead to rights, and was lining up his fatal shot–

Boom.

Red mist exploded out of his neck, his gun barrel rising and letting off a staccato burst like an angry animal. He sagged to his knees, muscle control gone, and fell onto his face, already dead.

Behind him, advancing, pistol drawn, was Holloway.

"Oh, hey," I said, rolling to my back and freeing up my weapon. "Good timing."

"Yeah," Holloway said, sweeping in and kicking the merc's AK out of his grip, then picking it up for himself. "I think we got 'em all."

I raised an eyebrow at him. "Oh, did *we*? How many did you get?"

"Just the one," he said, checking the chamber of the weapon. "You?"

"All the rest, I damned well hope," I said, taking his offered hand and letting him pull me up. Sirens echoed in the distance over the ringing in my ears. Help was on the way. A little late, but still...on the way.

CHAPTER SIXTY-ONE

Chapman

"That was some high quality violence," Chapman said, putting aside his popcorn. Man, he wanted to package this up and release it. It wouldn't be hard to come up with a dummy Socialite account from behind his VPN. It wasn't like it was difficult to open an account, obviously. They hadn't become number one on the planet by making it difficult to surrender your personal information. No, it was painfully easy, and it was right there if he just–

But no. That may have been his main mission when he'd started the company, facilitating that transfer of personal information and connection, but that wasn't his mission anymore. Well, it sort of was – but his eye was on the ball with this China thing. A hint of disappointment coursed through him. As much fun as it would have been to watch this spread through the net like wildfire, it'd hurt his current cause to play Sienna Nealon up as a hero.

"Damn," he muttered, though. It was so disappointing making these adult choices.

Whatever. The cops were on the scene now, which meant

hopefully things would calm down over the next few minutes. Which was good, because Chapman really had to pee.

Still, he carried his laptop with him as he went, watching the split screens between the overhead cams and Nealon's and Holloway's phones, hoping something cool would happen to give him just a fraction of the thrill he'd had when the gunfight had unfolded.

CHAPTER SIXTY-TWO

Sienna

I shook my phone and water flicked off the screen. It was supposedly waterproof, and when I lifted it up and pushed the button to activate it, it lit up like nothing was wrong. Which was good, because replacing phones was such a drag. I probably needed to just switch to a never-ending series of burners, honestly. That'd be a huge timesaver.

"What the hell happened here?" Bilson wandered up, clearly allowed past the police line, where Baltimore PD had already set up. He sounded more amazed than disappointed, which was a good reaction in my view. I'd gotten tired of having my putative bosses greet my activities with disappointment. If my mother hadn't been able to guilt me with it when I was a pain-in-the-ass defiant child, their likelihood of success now that I was a pain-in-the-ass defiant adult seemed low.

"Crime-fighting," I said without missing a beat. I had my boots off and my socks drying in the last light of day as I sat on the hood of the FBI SUV. An AR-15 was just sitting in the lockbox in the back of the vehicle. Too bad it had been parked here, some hundred yards away from where it would have been useful an hour ago. "What's up with you?"

"I expected to find some questioning going on," Bilson said as an EMT rolled a stretcher past, the body on it covered with a white sheet. "But it doesn't look like you left anyone alive to question."

"Well, they decided to resist arrest," I said, touching my socks to see if they'd dried yet. They hadn't. Big surprise. They'd been soaked and the temperature was dropping. Sundown was over. Likelihood they'd dry out here? So very low. Looked like I'd be wearing wet socks in my boots again soon.

"Did you get shot?" Bilson's eyes widened as he saw the bloody compress resting on my shoulder.

I glanced down, as if unsure. Duh. Of course I'd been shot. "Barely," I said, though, playing it cool. I pulled the compress away, and the bullet hole already looked much reduced, maybe half the size of a pencil. Still stung, though.

"What...what was this?" Bilson asked, sidling over to me. His eyes were on the scene, which was swarming with Baltimore PD and FBI. They'd started to dicker over the mess, with divers from the locals working on body recovery and the limited FBI presence picking over the pier for clues. Mostly they'd just found bullet shells so far, though apparently there was some form of written orders – in another language, naturally – left behind by the mercs in one of the containers they'd been waiting in to spring their ambush.

None of the mercs were Asian. I was unclear how a group of Eurotrash mercenaries had gotten roped into my Chinese case, but here they were, and not a one left alive for me to ask. Alas.

"Any idea–"

"No," I said, pre-empting him.

He made a face. "I didn't even finish."

I sighed. "Doesn't matter. I have no idea who they were, what their connection to this case was, other than they appear to have been hired by this HKKCME, since they were guarding the company's pier. I don't know why they tried to bushwhack me, especially here. I mean, they came at us hard–"

"'Us?'"

"Yeah, Agent Holloway was here, too," I said, waving into the distance. "He's off managing the FBI guys."

Bilson blinked a couple times. "Why?"

"Because he didn't get shot, barely or otherwise," I said, tossing aside the bloody compress. It had done its job, and now there was adequate scabbing to keep me from bleeding all over the place. "I tell you – this case is a head-scratcher. Or headache inducer. I am so baffled. So very, very baffled. All I have are extraneous pieces that don't fit together, like an eighties hair band but without the unifying theme of the hair, y'know? Like an eighties hair band where one is bald, the next has pigtails, another has a mullet–"

"Please stop," Bilson said, looking pained. "This visual is traumatizing."

"Sorry. But seriously – tell me you have a clue."

Bilson shrugged expansively. "Nothing to add, no. I came out here to see what you were going to find. Official Washington has nothing on this, not even rumors. Or at least not good rumors. There are always rumors, of course–"

"Give me the bad rumors," I said, grasping at whatever straw I could get my hand on. "I don't even care at this point. Pure lies probably make more sense than whatever I'm digging at the edges of here. I mean, from my gap-brained vantage point it's basically, Step 1: commit kidnappings. Step 2: ????? Step 3: Profit!"

Bilson chuckled. "*South Park* fan?"

"Early seasons, yeah. I dropped out after about five, I think." I settled my face in my hands. "Come on, Bilson, give me a rumor. Give me something. Hell, distract me for a minute, because this is seriously gonna blow my pea brain out if I get one disparate, nonsensical piece of information added to my clues list right now."

He seemed to take that on board. "Well, there was one interesting rumor, I suppose. That Chinese dissidents decided to make some moves that would shame their government."

I sagged a little. "That's depressingly mundane. Dissidents are responsible for this, and framing the PRC? Bleh. Pure Chinese propaganda."

Bilson let out another chuckle, but softer this time. "It does sound like the party line, doesn't it? I imagine considering it further won't help your brain."

"You're right," I said. Another car was pulling into the scene, a big government SUV like my own. The driver was flashing FBI ID to the cop manning the line, and he dutifully lifted the tape so they could drive on in. "Oh, look, here comes my boss. The real one, not this week's edition. By which I mean you."

"Heh." Bilson turned as the big SUV drove right next to my vehicle and stopped. The driver popped out and opened the back door, and sure enough, out came Chalke a moment later. "Hey, Heather."

"Russ," Chalke said formally. There was a hint of understanding between them, something beneath the surface that I didn't quite get. Chalke made her way over to me, eyeing the exposed shoulder wound and the blood that had darkened my blouse. "You all right?"

"Mostly," I said. "Holloway and I came here to execute a warrant to look around and got bumrushed by mercs with automatic weapons. It got a little dicey."

"I heard," Chalke said coolly. "Glad to see you're okay."

"Thanks," I said, not really sure how to take that. I assumed it was sincere, because assuming otherwise would have opened the door to mad sarcasm, yo. "You didn't have to come out here just for me, though. I would have given you a report...once we had something to report other than 'Shots fired!'"

"I'd like to have known before the shots were fired," Chalke said primly. Not quite as arch as she had been after I'd made other ridiculous, stick-the-neck-out first moves, but not happily, either.

"I called Bilson when I was on the way," I said, "but you're right. I should have called first. We had a break and I ran with it."

Her lips moved as though her tongue were battling for something to say. Finally, "Well, lucky you weren't injured." She eyed my shoulder. "Seriously, at least. But this might have been prevented with a little more warning."

"True," I said, because I didn't feel like arguing.

"What do you have so far?" she asked, settling back on her heels, arms folded over her blazer.

"Dead bodies," I said, "automatic weapons. The guys looked and moved like mercs. None appear to be Chinese–"

Chalke got a pained look. "That's a bit accusatory. Let's tread lighter, shall we?"

I paused. "Uh, okay. None appeared to be of East Asian extraction...?"

She considered this for a moment. "Better."

"I think they were Eastern European," I said. "At least the ones I fought. Dressed in full tactical gear, like one of our Spec Ops teams. No camo, just black. Popped out of a container in ambush, filled the air with lead, and didn't quit until they died. Forensics is trawling now, but I'm guessing they'll come up with little. We have written orders. Maybe the guns will lead us somewhere. If any of the guys have tattoos, we might get a nationality."

Chalke nodded. "Dental records?"

I felt a very slight flush. "There might be a possibility of using that on a few of them, yeah. The majority, though, uhm..." I mimed moving my hand across a horizontal plane. "Splat."

Chalke peered at the docks, gaze alighting on the containers. The scene wasn't much of a puzzle, the container I'd kicked absolutely covered in blood spatters. "I see."

"Like I said, it got ugly." I shrugged. Bilson was paling just looking at the bloodied container.

"Hey Nealon!" Holloway's shout reached me, causing me to turn my head around swiftly. He was all the way over by the pier, waving at me. "C'mere!"

"My partner appears to have discovered something urgent," I said. Chalke raised an eyebrow; presumably because I'd called Holloway my partner on this when she'd clearly designated Bilson as my wingman. Bilson showed no interest in standing up for himself, though, and Chalke's ire was quiet and passed in moments.

"Anything else I should be aware of?" Chalke asked as we strode toward the pier entrance.

"Nothing since my last report," I said. "I've just been working that list since."

She looked at me sidelong. "And?"

"Tough to say anything for certain. Seems like there might have been some additional kidnappings, but they weren't the sort to file missing persons reports."

Chalke's eyes were narrowed in thought. "But the first target was a college professor. You're saying the purported others...?"

"Were kinda like those witnesses we ended up with at the furniture store," I said. "People dependent on a work visa or outright smuggled in."

Chalke nodded. The water lapped at the concrete edge, loudly, like waves against the shore. The cawing of gulls was in the background, mildly annoying. Damned flying rats. "This is a confusing one. Are you sure there's something here?"

I thought about answering with a reflex, "Duh! Yes, dumbass!" but didn't. And not only because I was trying to play nicer with Chalke, but because at this point in the case, I *honestly didn't know*. If there was a larger conspiracy here, I was at a loss to explain the how or the why.

"Hey," Holloway called. He'd moved back down the pier fifty or so feet from where he'd initially shouted out to me. "Think we might have something. We're busting open containers."

"What's in 'em?" I asked.

"Electronics," he said. "Consumer goods. All from China, so far."

"Stolen?" I asked. Because if they weren't, I was hard pressed to see how this implicated HKKCME in anything criminal, barring the written orders having the issuer's name on them.

"Dunno," Holloway said, "but one of these containers started making noise." He raised his eyebrows significantly.

"Like how?" I asked, holding out an arm to keep Chalke back. "Like a ticking bomb?" Because if so, we didn't need to expose the FBI director to that.

He shook his head. "Scratching at the metal."

I made a face. "Could be that white tiger."

Holloway chuckled. "Interesting your mind goes to that."

"You should wait here, Director," I said. Chalke had been

giving my arm, which was across her chest just south of her collarbones, a mildly irritated look. "If this is some sort of radiological or biological weapon–"

"No sign of radiation," Holloway said. "At least from outside."

"I'm taking a look," Chalke said, ducking around my arm. I didn't stop her, though I could have. Far be it from me to keep my boss from doing something stupid.

A small mob of local PD and FBI agents was gathered around the container in question. I could hear the faint scratching now, though I was hard pressed to quantify it. It sounded a little like a cat picking at a door, and I approached the entry just as an FBI agent cut the lock off with a bolt cutter. Two others threw open the latches keeping it closed, and pulled the doors wide–

We were all nearly bowled over by the wave of stink coming out of the thing. It was ripe, rank, smelled like an outhouse I'd visited once in rural Kentucky. I pulled my blouse top up over my nose, but it did almost nothing.

Chalke retched behind me, and she was not alone.

I didn't take my eyes off the prize, though, and boy...was it a hell of a prize.

Because the container was filled with people.

Asian people, to be specific.

Chinese people, if I was forced to guess and absolved of racism if I guessed wrong.

"Holy hell," Holloway muttered. I couldn't tell whether he was taken aback by the smell or the sight of them; they looked utterly wretched. Dirty, bedraggled, bloody in some cases. They stared out into the deepening dusk around us like we were aliens come to take them to another planet.

A thought occurred to me, and I blurted it out before I could stop myself. "What do you bet..." I looked at Holloway, and I could see he'd already come to the same conclusion as I had, "...these are the people from our list of kidnapped?"

CHAPTER SIXTY-THREE

They were the kidnap victims.

It took almost an hour, and the work of Chinese translators of various stripes (because China has many languages, not just Mandarin), but we confirmed it. The people in the container matched the list that Holloway and I had gotten to a T.

Perfectly.

"How do you like that?" Holloway asked me. We were watching at a distance as the kidnappees were being interviewed. We were both sidelined due to being in officer-involved shootings, at least temporarily. I had a feeling that wouldn't stick, though, given our entire division was now sidelined from shooting people. Holloway, at least, deserved a reprieve, having only shot one person in the last few days. Hilton was at two, and I was at...hell if I even knew. Though I was technically guilty of agent-involved squishing, I'd also drilled a couple snipers and at least a couple mercs on the ground. Sad that I couldn't keep track of these things, I suppose, but killing mercs was so passe for Sienna Nealon at this point.

I looked to Holloway. "You mean how do I like our case busting wide open right before our eyes?" Chalke was talking to Bilson a short distance away, but I couldn't overhear them with all the background noise. "I find it very convenient."

"Me too," Holloway said. "The exact list? I mean other than your college professor? That's..."

"An orgy of evidence?" I asked. "A beautiful coincidence?"

"I mean, it's probably great for these people who they get to go home now," Holloway said. "Assuming they're just released without complication, which is probably far from certain. But..." He shook his head. "I don't like it. Too easy."

"I've long said I could really go for things being easy on me, for once," I said, fighting back a nagging feeling. "But I didn't for a minute believe it'd actually happen. Especially not like this." I settled back against the cargo container we were both resting against. We'd gotten the basic story out of the translators, having been kept at a least a little in the loop given it was our case. "There's still the question of who could execute this many kidnappings? This is full-on human smuggling activity. You can't tell me this HKKCME just evaporates as a paper trail from here."

"Right," Holloway nodded. "These mercs weren't the source of this. They were hired muscle. I bet they didn't even do the kidnappings; they seem like after-the-fact accessories. They're nothing like that crew that tried to snatch your professor."

"That's another thing," I said, "where's Firebeetle? He's been a persistent thorn in my side, showing up everywhere – the original kidnapping, the furniture store, the Baltimore slum, even that office complex. Where is he?" I folded my arms in front of me. "This is a huge break, presumably the focal point of their plan, and he's nowhere to be found? My poor head."

Someone walked up to Chalke and Bilson, and I almost fell over.

It was Yan Liao, the Chinese attaché. Behind the tape on an FBI crime scene. Again.

"Who's that?" Holloway asked. "Looks familiar."

"He was at the office complex, remember?" I asked. "Works for the Chinese government. Diplomat, aide...spy, maybe."

He raised an eyebrow. "What's he doing at our crime scene?"

"Showing himself around, apparently," I said. He shook hands with Bilson, then Chalke waved over an FBI agent, who escorted Liao toward the rescues. He immediately engaged in conversation with a bedraggled woman, touching her shoulder sympathetically. There was a Chinese translator standing next to him, nodding all the while, and Liao's posture was all sympathy. I watched the woman's eyes. They were the kind you'd see on a traumatized person, all fear, adrenaline long since blown through and leaving her weary.

I was familiar with that feeling, having experienced it a time or two in my own life. Still, suspicion settled over me.

"You ever seen human trafficking before?" Holloway asked.

I shot him a confused look. "What, you didn't hear about my adventure in Nashville?" He stared at me blankly. "I took out a whole house of sex traffickers."

"Good for you, Nealon," Holloway said with genuine enthusiasm. "Man, I always miss the fun."

"Well, maybe if you hadn't been swimming while I was wiping out these mercenaries, you'd have had more fun today."

"Is that any way to treat the man who saved your life at the buzzer?"

"Probably not," I said as Bilson broke away from Chalke and trotted off, heading back toward his car. Chalke lingered for a second, watching operations, then headed our way. "But it's how I treat you nonetheless, regardless of whatever you've done on any given day."

"I appreciate the evenness. Sort of." Then he hushed up, because he, too, saw the boss coming.

"This was some good work," Chalke said, moseying up to us.

"We just followed the leads," I said. Not really being modest.

"It was well done, though," Chalke said, a little stiffly. "I'm glad we can put this behind us."

Holloway and I exchanged a look. "Ma'am," he said, "we haven't caught the metahuman kidnapper yet. And there's still a lot of loose ends here."

"I know," Chalke said, nodding along, taking in roughly none of what we'd just said – or maybe just ignoring it. "But this is a big deal. You broke open a huge kidnapping and smuggling ring tonight." She glanced around, gaze settling on the bloody cargo container I'd used to pulp the balance of the mercs. "The ringleader is probably under there, and it's unfortunate that we may never get the full story, but it is what it is." She was speaking so confidently, so definitely.

There was a rising alarm – or maybe irritation – present in Holloway's eyes. He started to speak up, and I put an arm out in front of him. "Thank you, ma'am," I said, cutting him off.

Holloway looked apoplectic, but he kept his mouth shut. Good.

Chalke gave us each a nod, then a smile. "I hope you each have something nice to wear. You'll be getting a commendation straight from the top on this one."

And with that, she walked away, her bit said, and all right in her world.

"What the hell was that?" Holloway hissed as soon as she was out of earshot.

"The answer that was wanted, I think." I watched her go, pretty sure that one way or another, we were done here. Maybe not just at the scene, but period, with this investigation.

CHAPTER SIXTY-FOUR

Chapman

He'd nodded off watching the crime scene footage and listening to the muffled conversations caught by Nealon's and Holloway's phones. Nothing had been nearly as interesting as the shootouts, and soon enough, Jaime had found himself dozing behind his desk.

He was awakened with a kiss, to find an impishly smiling face looking down at him. Her black hair was in a bob now, and the diamond piercing in her nostril glittered in his office's dim light.

Gwen.

"Hey," he said sleepily, feeling a smile creep across his face inadvertently. "What are you doing here?"

"Security gets kinda lax after about nine," Gwen said. She leaned forward and brushed her lips against his again. "Only one of your assistants was out there, and it's the one who likes me, so..."

"I told them all to let you in," Jaime said, feeling the smile plaster slowly across his face, spreading. He looked at the darkness outside the windows. "What time is it?"

"I don't know." She brushed her lips against his forehead, and he shuddered. "Late."

Jaime moved in his chair. He felt surprisingly good given that he'd fallen asleep sitting upright. His eyes fell to the monitors–

The activity on the screens had settled down. Sure, there was still a hum of busy-ness going on around the Port of Baltimore, but the phones were both dark. He reached past Gwen and clicked the sound up on both; the first registered soft breathing, the sound of someone asleep. The other had a hum of conversation. Conversations, actually. And music.

Jaime frowned, unable to quite decipher what he was hearing.

"What is that?" Gwen asked.

Chapman listened too. "I don't know," he said after a moment, nose wrinkled. It was a low din, the sound an irritating buzz, broken by the occasional peal of laughter. Low music played in the background.

"No, I meant what are you watching?" Gwen asked, leaning down to stare at the video. "Whoa, that's a lot of cop cars."

"Oh, it's a scene for a...thing...that happened earlier," Chapman said casually. Gwen watched him intently. She wasn't going to let him off with no answer, and his cheeks began to redden. "Yeah. Well. So...it's kind of a project I'm working on. That's a crime scene that Sienna Nealon got tied up in earlier."

"Uh huh," Gwen said, that casually dangerous look on her face telling him that she not only wasn't buying his cool playing of this thing she'd caught him in, but her brain was moving very swiftly to its own conclusions. Better to head those off before they became...unpleasant.

"I'm using my mad skills to surveil her for her boss," Chapman said, letting that go in a rush. Felt good, man.

Gwen just looked at him for a moment, and he could feel the weight of judgment in her eyes. "Was that so hard?" she asked, finally, and back impishly. "Scoot over."

He moved over a little and she sat on the arm of his chair, causing it to squeak. She was slight enough that it didn't mess with it too much, though, and he kind of liked having her next to him like this. "It's just for this project thing."

"Uh huh." She didn't believe him, not a bit. He could tell. "What's with the pocket view? Did you RAT her phone?"

"Yeah," Chapman said, not looking straight at her. She kind of chuckled, and that gave him a dash of relief. "And her partner's."

"Oh, so that's what this one is." She pointed at the one that was slightly less dark, concentrating. It was also the one the buzzing, humming, crowd noise. "He's at a bar," she finally said.

"Ohhhh," Chapman said, nodding along. That made sense.

"Couldn't you have just pulsed the GPS to figure it out instantly?" Gwen turned, smiling slyly at him.

"Didn't think of that," Chapman grunted. "I haven't really used RATs before."

"Get better at your job, slacker." She slapped him lightly on the arm. "I mean, if you're going to use your tech skills to spy on people, don't half ass it. You should be dumping their GPS data regularly if you're going to monitor them. Also..." She leaned over the keyboard and pulled up the interface for the Remote Access Trojan.

"What?" Chapman leaned forward to see what she was doing.

"Just checking what other apps they've got on their phones." She let out a laugh. "The partner's got Tinder. That's hilarious. Let's see his profile." She pulled it up, then cringed. "Ooh. Old guy."

Chapman let a laugh of his own. "He does look like he's due for a hardware upgrade."

"He's at the age where he's probably experiencing 'firmware' problems." Gwen shot him a look out of the corner of her eye and then casually landed a hand on Jaime's crotch.

"Oh!" Jaime jumped slightly. Was not expecting that, at least not after she caught him spying on people.

"You should get all their app data, too," Gwen said, finishing up on the computer with a couple more keystrokes. "If you're going to invade someone's privacy, do the thing right, man." She gave him a pitying look. "You never were much of a hacker, were you?"

"I was more of a coder, programmer," he said. Her hand was

still...there. “Parlayed that into business pretty early. I did a little hacking. It was barely black hat, though. Like...gray hat, kind of.”

“Not a bad boy?” Gwen made pouty lips at him. She stood and spun his chair around, then sat back down, straddling him.

Jaime felt himself having trouble breathing for a second. Gwen ran a hand over his face, and it was electric. It was like all the weariness of the day washed away as his heart started to beat much faster than it had been a moment before.

“Hey, Mr. CEO,” Gwen said playfully, “do I have your full attention now?”

“Yes. Yes, you do.”

“Good,” she said, and leaned in to kiss him, “because I don't want you having any 'firmware' difficulties, okay?”

Chapman smiled and she kissed him long and slow. When they broke, he said, “I don't think that's going to be a problem.” And it wasn't.

CHAPTER SIXTY-FIVE

Julie Blair

"Hey," Dominic Blair said sleepily as his wife slipped into bed next to him. "How was your day?"

"Busy as ever," Julie said. She'd had her last cup of coffee around seven p.m., and the drive home had felt like forever. Now she was strangely wired, a caffeinated edge overlaying the ragged exhaustion she felt beneath, a facade to cover over the fact she hadn't had a full, decent night of sleep in what felt like years.

"Oh, yeah?" he murmured. She slipped in closer to him, felt his warmth beside her. She'd checked on the kids; they were all fine. Little Paige still had her hair in lopsided bows. Daddy wasn't very good at those, but with Julie gone before sunup every morning, he did the best he could. And Julie could admire the cuteness it inspired.

"Yeah," Julie said, snuggling closer. Dom was a big bear, and it felt like she rarely ever got to just be close to him like this anymore. He worked short hours so that he could get home in time to meet the kids coming off the school bus, then watched them all night. It had to be a little rough on him – hell, she knew it was – but he'd done so well at it. Hardly complained at all, at least until recently. But that was understandable; work had gotten more intense for her. "This China thing is spinning off into some interesting directions."

"I thought it was over?" Dom mumbled.

"Maybe," Julie said. She'd heard the news, but when she checked the email she'd gotten from that donor and compared it to the list that Sienna Nealon had recovered earlier in the evening, that nanny – Zhen – her name hadn't been on it. She'd forwarded that note up the chain to her boss, and replied with this detail to the donor, figuring it would be good to give her an update so she didn't get her hopes up. "But I don't think so."

Dom just grunted in his sleep. Julie snuggled a little closer, letting her fingers run over his skin. It had been a while; she felt this little thrill of hope that maybe tonight they could...

A bleary snore from Dom shattered that hope instantly. He wasn't even really awake. "Aw, come on," Julie muttered under her breath. But Dom didn't stir, and so she cuddled up to him, burying her disappointment. He'd have to be up early with the kids, so it was probably better to just let him sleep.

This wouldn't last forever, after all. Soon, maybe, she'd be recognized for her work and move up. And President Gondry wouldn't be in the White House forever, either. A few years, and she could even move into the private sector. K Street, maybe. Julie chuckled. More like E Street, for easy. Because after working in the high pressure environment of the White House communications office, doing some PR/lobbying work would have to be a change of pace. On that note she settled in next to the warm, lightly snoring form of her husband, but couldn't get to sleep for hours.

CHAPTER SIXTY-SIX

Sienna

I woke the next day feeling vaguely grimy. I'd gotten home so late that showering hadn't really been an option; I'd fallen into bed and conked out, leaving my sheets stinking of the Chesapeake Bay and my boots in desperate need of a wash. When I got up, it was before dawn, and I had completed a load of laundry and washed both my filthy pairs of boots before I went for my morning run.

Back at my apartment before sunrise, I showered and ate a quick breakfast, mind churning the whole time. I'd been handed a big break last night, and recovering all those trafficked Chinese folk felt good – for a minute.

But there were too many nagging questions to put my mind at ease. I was still fully in this case, mentally, even though I knew my boss wanted me to rubber stamp it and call it good. She'd been clear enough the night before.

I resolved, staring at my morning bagel, covered in a light spread of cream cheese, that no, I couldn't let it go yet. But I needed to at least do whatever came next off the radar, because I wanted blowback from Chalke like I wanted a bomb to go off under my bed the next time I lay down on it.

Michelle Cheong was waiting in the alcove across the street from my work when I strolled up, just before nine. I crossed the street and sidled over to her. She was scrolling her phone and greeted me with a, "Hey," when I walked up.

"You hear about last night?" I asked, trying to look casual about standing next to her in the little carveout in the building's facade. I'd done more natural-looking things in my life, like turning into a dragon and shredding a human being in my teeth, probably. Looking casual while lingering on a street? Not the easiest look.

"I have cable in my hotel, a phone with news alerts, and ears attached to my head, so yes," she said, not looking up from her phone. She flashed a look at me, or appeared to, at least, under those dark sunglasses. "They didn't release a list, though."

I looked out on the street, again violating casual behavior principles. At least we were out of the view of the cameras mounted up and down the street. I unlocked my phone, pulled up the list, and thrust it in her face. "See anyone you know?"

She stared at it, then scrolled a couple times to the bottom before shaking her head. "No. None of the people I tracked down are on here."

I cursed under my breath, a very unladylike thing that made Michelle smile for some reason. "Is it possible they're on here under a different name?"

Her eyebrow inclined slightly, rising above the top edge of her sunglasses. "No."

"That was pretty definite."

She just shook her head. "These people haven't changed their names just because it's convenient for you not to have more victims to look for." She did a little glancing of her own; once more, the stupid pigeons were cawing above us. I could just see one crapping on me before I walked into work this morning, ruining my nice new blazer. "Want some more bad news?"

"Oh, yes, I'm just dying for it."

She didn't smile, plowing ahead. "I've been networking while in town. Talking to some locals in my field."

"How do gangsters meet, you know, socially? Is there a country club for human traffickers?"

"In the Triads, we mostly play Mahjong."

I blinked. "Seriously?"

God, she was inscrutable. "No, I'm totally fucking with you. There are others missing, locally. More than the number on your list."

I let out another beneath-the-breath curse. Not because I was averse to swearing, but I did try not to yell them in public places. Kids could be walking by, after all, and it'd be really embarrassing for them to tell their parents they learned that word from Sienna Nealon, of all people. "Great."

"Doesn't this help?" Michelle asked. "Isn't it useful to know the depth of your problem?"

"No," I said. "Because my boss is trying to declare this thing 'case closed' after last night's big break. Do you at least have something concrete for me? A list? Someone I can talk to? Verify identities? A missing persons report?"

Michelle shook her head. "No one's going on the record on this one. For their employers, it opens enough cans of worms to fish for a lifetime. Whoever's doing this, whether it's China's government or not, they chose their targets well." She frowned. "Except that college professor. I can't figure out why they did that. That was stupid."

"That's not the only thing I'm having trouble figuring out in all this," I said. "Do you have any idea why the Chinese government would go to all this trouble? This is a lot of shit to go through to recapture some...what? Dissidents?"

"Maybe," Michelle said, sounding skeptical all the way. "Don't get me wrong, the Chinese government is that kind of vengeful, especially if they thought they could get away with it. But it breaks my brain to think that all these people are dissidents." She paused, considering. "Actually, I know of at least one person in my organization who was a dissident, went to prison for it, got released, got on a boat and has agitated against them, loudly, from America, and is not kidnapped, so...no. I don't think that's the motive, or else why would she be able to keep being a pain in their ass?"

"Maybe they just haven't come for her yet." I shook my head. "I have no insight into why they're doing this. Can't even prove it's the PRC government."

"I'm pretty sure it's them," Michelle said. "Don't get me wrong, there's some sleaze in their billionaire class outside the official Communist party leadership that might do something this dickish if given a chance, but...just the whispers I'm getting suggest this is backed from the top of the government. Of course, that's nothing you can take to the bank..."

"I can't rely on the word of criminals? What is the world coming to?"

Michelle smiled. "So...boss wants you to quit. You know there's more to this. What are you going to do?"

I looked her right in the sunglasses, shook my head, and walked away. "Like you even had to ask," I muttered, just loud enough she could hear it.

"That's what I thought," she called after me. "Good luck."

"I don't need luck," I said, crossing the street during a break in traffic. "I need a damned break in my case," I said, this time, mostly to myself.

CHAPTER SIXTY-SEVEN

"Who's that you were talking with out there?" Holloway asked as I came in. He was already in his seat, and I could see the report from the previous night already pulled up in his word processor.

"Aren't you suspended for shooting someone?" I asked.

"Technically, yes," Holloway said, turning his attention back to the screen. "Aren't you?"

"I'm above such mortal concerns," I said. "Though technically, probably yes. But I, too, have reports to file."

Holloway snorted under his breath. "Which you could write from home, like your co-millennial."

"Uck," I said. "Don't compare me to Hilton. I have yet to drop an overshare on you, Holloway."

"I don't know, the constant jibes about my hemorrhoid cream seem like the very definition."

"Yeah, but you know you're wearing hemorrhoid cream, so I'm not really 'sharing' it with you."

"But a decent person would let me keep the appearance of my dignity."

"No one has accused me of being decent," I said, flipping on my computer. "At least not lately. Word of my character has spread to all corners of the earth, clearly."

"Yeah, well, it's certainly spread to 1600 Pennsylvania

Avenue," Holloway said. "Got a call from the White House offering congratulations from some functionary." When I looked at him blankly, he elaborated. "For solving the case."

"Which is not entirely solved yet," I said. "As to who I was talking to–"

"That mob boss from New Orleans!" Holloway snapped his fingers. "The one with the yoga pants that sent you on the chase down Bourbon Street after the Chinese grandma!"

"Yeah," I said. "Anyway, she says–"

"Wait, *she's* your CI on this?"

"Yes, and please keep up."

"I saw your feet after what she did to you," Holloway said, staring at me with barely veiled disbelief. "You really gonna trust anything she says after that?"

"She helped us nail Governor Warrington."

"Uh, no," Holloway said, "if you'll recall, he jumped out a window after we left town."

"Po-tay-toe, po-tah-toe. Justice was served."

Holloway let out a low peal of laughter. "Remember when you told me you joined the FBI to re-establish your sense of justice? Because I do. Seems like *you* might have forgotten, given you're now cool with people kersplatting on the street without trial..."

"Can we focus?" I asked. "What she told me? There are more people missing than were on our list."

"That list hasn't been released to the public yet," Holloway said, almost whispering. "You can't go showing it to–"

"Just pretend she's a CI," I said. "That's what I pretend when I have to justify shit to myself to get things done. There is more to this case than we've unveiled. It's not over."

Holloway just stared at me, shifting in his chair. "Tell me something I don't know. Except our boss disagrees."

"Yeah, I know," I said, folding my arms in front of me. "But I can't just...let it go. I mean, the people packed in that container..."

Holloway nodded slowly. "Pitiful sight, right?" He let out a long sigh. "I'm game if you are."

I stared at him. "You mean...for keeping this going? Even though Chalke says we're done?"

He nodded his head slowly. "Yeah. Where do we start?"

CHAPTER SIXTY-EIGHT

Chapman

He watched the scene of re-commitment between Nealon and Holloway play out in near-disbelief. It was morning; sunlight was shining through his windows. He felt a little sticky, but a kombucha was already dripping condensation on his desk, and he'd been ready to go.

Then the revelation played out. First from Nealon talking to the lady who he couldn't quite see. Then from the chat with Holloway.

"I thought this thing was over," Chapman moaned. His phone started to buzz and he looked down at it.

Shit. Huang.

Of course he had to answer, so he did. "Hey, Wu." Definitely some cringe to his voice, though.

"Good morning, my friend." Wu sounded pretty...uh, well...jacked, actually. "I have excellent news."

"Oh?" Chapman was bracing himself. He had a feeling good stuff was coming, only to be snuffed out as soon as Huang and the Chinese government got wind of the fact Nealon wasn't moving along with grace.

"Yes," Huang said. So chipper. For now. "I am assured by friends in Washington that everyone is putting this chapter behind them now that this mercenary company that was kidnapping people has been dispensed with."

"Yeah, I saw that," Chapman said. "Uh...I don't mean to be the bearer of bad news, but I should warn you – it's not over."

There was a forever pause before Huang spoke. "What do you mean?"

"I'm sure the government is letting it go, but Sienna Nealon..." Chapman paused for breath. Felt like he was falling. "...I don't know, Huang, she's a dog with a bone. She and her partner aren't letting it go."

Huang's voice rose a little, an edge of concern – panic, maybe even – undergirding it. "I was assured by my friends in Washington that it was over."

"Everyone sensible wants it to be," Chapman said. How could he placate Huang but still deliver the bad news? That would have been a question to have an answer for before he picked up the phone. "It's just Nealon. She's not quitting."

There was a very long pause before Huang responded again. "Interesting. I trust your sources are good on this?"

Chapman let out a small chuckle. "Wu...let's put it this way: I heard it straight from the horse's mouth."

"I appreciate your assistance in this matter," Huang said. "You have faithfully tried to help keep this deal on track in spite of the ups and downs. This new information is important to our interests. I will transmit it to those who would most be affected and try to make sure their gratitude to you for passing it along will not be marred by the message itself."

"Sounds good," Chapman said, feeling a little dry mouth set in. Needed some water. "I'll let you know if anything changes."

"Please do."

And that was that. Chapman pondered the conversation for a few minutes, wondering where it might go from here, but truthfully – he didn't want to think about it. And he had a full schedule today, so he put aside watching the monitors for a while and moved on, hoping that whatever and whoever Huang was going to talk to, they'd solve the problem for everyone.

CHAPTER SIXTY-NINE

Sienna

The hours passed like lead. I stared at my computer screen, in a mental fog after having checked the forensic records on everything, from the .22 bullet recovered at Cathy Jang-Peters's crime scene to rereading the witness statements from her and the guy who saved her. I combed through the reports on the van, the dead bodies of the kidnappers, the furniture store, the house in Baltimore, the abandoned car...

And so on, and so on. We had accumulated reams of evidence in this case. More forensic reports piled in by the hour.

None of it led anywhere. Except somehow, mysteriously, to a dock in the Port of Baltimore, where we'd found a shipping container filled with people of Chinese ancestry who'd been kidnapped for unknown purposes.

"Are you getting the feeling that this is a maze?" Holloway turned to me, and I could tell by his bleary eyes that he, too, was hitting a wall.

"It's amazing, all right," I said with a sigh. "I had a thought, though, sort of related to our last break."

"Oh, you mean the corporate search thing?" Holloway let out a yawn. "What about it?"

"Remember the guy that owned the building?" I asked. "Huang?"

"Yeah."

"I started to look into him – you know, when I got tired of going through the evidence that didn't contain anything actionable," I opened a tab I'd been fiddling with a while ago, "and boy, does this guy own a lot of stuff."

Holloway slid over. "You just did a search?"

"And started reading the results," I said. "Look at this. In addition to the huge share of Jaime Chapman's company, he owns dozens of holding companies in the US with stakes in an incredible number of industries. Petroleum, manufacturing, banking, real estate – if there's a sector of our markets that this guy doesn't have a piece of, I'm not seeing it."

"An expert on investing, are you?" Holloway asked, leaning forward.

"Well, I don't exactly have a huge portfolio to manage these days, so no," I said. "But I'm not economically illiterate."

Holloway nodded, grudgingly, as he read. "Hell, buying that piece of Chapman's company alone put him in several sectors. Look at what that guy has – social media, search engine, that company you see the ads for all the time–"

"If you're seeing them, I assume they're the ones related to erectile dysfunction."

"Hah hah," Holloway said, but his face fell. "No, I mean the ones where you send in the DNA swab and they match you with relatives you never knew about and will probably regret finding once they hit you up for a loan 'just til payday' a hundred times in a year."

I stared at him curiously. "I think your family experience is maybe a little different than mine."

"Yeah, your people have probably lived for a thousand years, during which they've developed that investment portfolio you're so keen to start." Holloway settled back in his seat. "I mean, if finding clues consists of sifting the dirt, seeking for gold, then this guy owns a mountain range. How could you even find anything to pull on his portfolio? It's not like that HKKCME company, with its tiny holdings. He owns pieces of thousands of companies."

I picked up a pen and tapped the end at the corner of my mouth. "Right, but he doesn't wholly own them. What if we looked at companies he owned a majority stake in, like this real estate company that leased to HKKCME? Because those would be the ones that he'd be able to have some influence over, if he's dirty."

"He could have influence over a lot of things, even if he's not a majority stakeholder," Holloway said. "Look at that Chapman douche. You know how much of his company he owns at this point? Fifteen percent."

My eyebrows went up. "Really?"

"Yeah, because he holds the majority of the voting stock, which is different than the common stock," Holloway said, staring at the screen. He must have sensed my surprised eyes holding on him, because he shifted his gaze to me. "What? I have a portfolio. It's about half the size it used to be thanks to my ex-wife, but still."

"Is there a way to find out who owns the voting rights in a company?" I asked, staring at the screen.

"Yeah, my buddy can do it," Holloway said, "but for a holding the size of what this Huang guy has? It goes way beyond a favor. And the fact we're officially without an investigation?" He shook his head. "This is too close to the line. We're supposed to investigate crimes, after all, not go trolling for possible lawbreakers like some local cop pulling over people for minor violations to see what majors they can haul down."

"So you're saying we won't get help on this?" I looked back to the partial list of Huang's business enterprises. It filled multiple computer screens. "Argh."

"Yeah," Holloway said with a sigh. "I know how to do a few things on this. Let me get started, then I can probably show you how to do – well, the second stage of it, which is combing through bullshit." He rubbed his weary eyes. "This could take a bit, though." He paused, and I saw a thought run over his face. "You know what I could really use right now?"

I let out a low, long grunt. "You're going to turn me into your coffee and lunch bitch, aren't you?"

Holloway flashed me a grin. "You said it, not me. But since you mentioned it...this is thirsty work. And hungry work. And there's that Chinese takeout place a couple blocks over..."

CHAPTER SEVENTY

I hit the street with a plan in mind: get the Chinese takeout order, hit the coffee place on the corner for a quick refuel, and head back to the office, where Holloway had damned sure better have something for me to work on to justify me being an errand girl for his sorry ass.

It wasn't that I objected to being sent to fetch food, coffee, elements of survival. It wasn't as though it was beneath me. I just didn't like being told what to do or made to feel like a servant for other peoples' quality of life.

Just ignore the fact that, really, that's what I was, in total. I stopped bad guys before they could wreck people's lives. How was that different than fetching coffee and lunch for a bureau colleague?

Well, it just was. Less bloody. Less violent. Less likelihood of dying. To me, these were all negatives.

The DC street was quietly abuzz. It was so much different than life in suburban-ish Minnesota. I'd lived in a quiet neighborhood – mostly. Just south of the city, with yards and fences and leafy trees in the front yard, when it wasn't all blanketed with snow.

This part of DC was busy, bustling, like my neighborhood in New York. People were everywhere, at all hours. In my Minnesota neighborhood, you could go out at three in the morning and not run into a soul. Hell, you could even potentially go out at three in the afternoon and not run into a soul.

Not a chance in DC, or New York. I missed that element of quiet, that increased space between people. I wasn't big on closing the personal distance unless I was going to pummel a person. Or...hug them, I suppose? Though the former was more common with me, especially lately.

I raked the street with my eyes. This was another element of the city I disliked. In a suburban neighborhood, it was harder to hide a threat. Sure, a SWAT team could come bursting out of a garage as you walked by, or a group of mercs could swarm you out of a panel van parked on the street, but those spaces were obvious. Panel vans weren't common; you could cross the street to avoid walking past one. Garages were a ways off the sidewalk, you'd have some warning before you got hit. Unless you got shot right from a window.

In DC, at least, the buildings didn't extend quite so far up as in New York. I had sniper fears, especially this last year, worrying that someone might take a potshot at me from above. I had a lot of non-fans out in the world, and it would be easy for someone on an eighth floor to blast my brains out from a hundred yards away without me even seeing the gun barrel extending out the window. Here, the limited rise of the buildings versus the skyscrapers of midtown provided a lower limit to the number of windows I had to scan as I walked the city.

And scan I did. The cars going by, the people passing on the sidewalk, the windows overhead. All of them got eyeballed from behind my tinted sunglasses, the things worthy of a second and third look mentally filed away for further checking. A van I passed three cars back: darkened windows up front, no windows in back. Who's hiding what there? The face I saw two floors up, one block down on the left: is it a kid watching the street? Or a hostile watching me?

Such was the life of Sienna Nealon, the world's most paranoid person. Having been thoroughly bushwhacked to the point of nearly losing my life on numerous occasions, my guard was forever up. I could be *in flagrante delicto* with Harry, and I'd shush him because a strange noise outside our door sounded like someone scraping metal against the lock, trying to pick it. (That actually happened. He explained to me that the neighbor across the hall was drunk and uncoordinated and we proceeded, my gratitude for having a precognitive boyfriend never more present than in that moment, maybe.)

Taking my time and doing all this observation, I didn't move as fast as I could have if I was determined to meta-speed it across town. I could be at my destination in minutes, and back in the same time. Brisk jog for me, car-like speeds for a normal person. It was all possible, but I didn't do it. Not here.

Making people feel safe meant not tooling down the side-walks at thirty miles an hour, blurring past as people wondered, worrying what crisis I was into. So I walked at the equivalent of a snail's pace – for me – and took it all in. The two businessmen arguing about politics as they exited the swanky new restaurant across the way. The hipster guy ironically wearing an old-timey railroad engineer's coveralls and a pork pie hat (God, let it be ironically). The Asian guy stepping out of the carpet cleaner's van parked just ahead of me–

I slowed my pace and stepped to the edge of the sidewalk. Maybe I was racially profiling, but I caught him looking at me as he got out. Nothing too heavy, just a glance in the rearview mirror, then another glance as he circled the vehicle to the back door and opened it–

No swarm of mercs came flooding out, which was a relief. There was equipment inside, equipment I couldn't quite make out. A door slammed down the block, behind me, and I chanced a look. Lady in a power suit, staring at her phone, heading across the street to the tax consultancy across the way.

I filed her under innocuous and prepared to cross the street, just in case the carpet cleaner wasn't on the level.

My boots clopped against the pavement, the warm, humid air causing me to perspire against my blouse and blazer combo. I looked right, then left, then right again, and started to cross. All clear.

A squeal of tires to my right drew my attention. A sedan had turned onto the street and was heading toward me, accelerating. It was fifty yards back, plenty of room for me to get off the road and onto the sidewalk before he collided with me. Hell, I could just leap over him, if I wanted to. I kept a watchful eye, looking to see what he did–

He sped up. Squealed his tires. Put pedal to metal.

That was cause for alarm. Not serious, because I was me, but still. You don't see a pedestrian in the street and gun it, at least not if you're normal human being. I set my feet, prepared to glare him down.

He continued to accelerate.

Now he was thirty yards away, speeding toward me, passing the FBI office. I wondered what the hell he was playing at as I reached for my pistol, sliding my jacket back to draw–

And suddenly I was wrenched by an agonizing – and very familiar – pain.

My brain pounded like it was going to explode, my ears filled with something like icepicks, stabbing in either canal in a simultaneous rhythm of murderous intensity. I went from ready to draw my pistol to wishing for death, swift and sure, just so it could be over. My legs turned to pure jelly and my head throbbed with the intensity of a metal concert turned up to 1,000 decibels behind my eyes.

I didn't even feel my knees hit the pavement. My eyes were squinted closed from the agony, the pure, brain-killing agony. It was like a telepathic attack, except not – it worked my brain like a double-barreled shotgun/machine gun combo firing straight into my skull with an infinite mag.

It was a sonic weapon. But not a little pussy sonic weapon like they'd used on Bridget over the course of weeks or months. No, that was a toy for babies and little birdies. This was the big boy, the nuclear version of it, and it was pointed on me, humming through my bones like I was standing next to the bass speaker at a concert.

Prying my eyes open, another sound broke in – barely – over the anguish of the weapon. It was an engine gunning, and I split my eyelids enough to see a grill coming at me–

Then the sedan smashed into me, my face, my body, and I went flying, limply, into darkness.

CHAPTER SEVENTY-ONE

Chapman

"...And I think that's our key takeaway so far on engagement on Instaphoto this month. More of that, amirite?"

The director of product development for Instaphoto was...hell, what was her name? Chapman couldn't remember, didn't really care. Instaphoto was an afterthought, an acquisition he'd picked up because photo sharing was hot, and because he could buy it and integrate it into his empire with ease, squashing it as a competitor before it got into Socialite's weight class.

"More of that, absolutely," Chapman said, forcing a smile. "I'm liking your targets, your growth curve is great." He glanced at her, trying to be sincere in his delivery. Instaphoto might not have been his passion but she was killing it on revenue targets. It was a cash cow, and had been since they'd taken it off the developers' hands and started properly milking it. If he had a gift, it was figuring out how to maximize the cashflow on a business that others couldn't quite figure out how to monetize. It was why he was on top of the heap, raking it in. Provide a service, find the money, go to town.

Chapman's intercom beeped, interrupting him in the midst

of composing the next stanza of his song of praise for this particular underling. "Just a sec," he said, and hit the button. "Yes?"

"Mr. Chapman, you have a call from Devin in special projects regarding that thing you handed off to them this morning."

Chapman raised an eyebrow. That "thing" he'd handed off was surveillance of Sienna Nealon, because he couldn't afford to sit around and watch her all day himself. "Perfect. Let them know I'll be online in a few minutes. And kindly reschedule this meeting with a little more time – say an hour on next Thursday? Uninterrupted? Once things calm down here." He hit the cutoff button without bothering to wait for acknowledgment. One of his assistants would see to it. "Really – truly proud of what you're doing here. Want to hear more about it next Thursday, okay?" He forced a smile. "Sorry for the reschedule."

"I know you're busy, thank you – I'll make sure that I bring something worthwhile to discuss in that extra time." She was flushed, pleased – good. She saw herself out, too, which made her better than most. Everyone wanted a piece of his time. And he had so few pieces he wanted to part with, really.

Once the door was shut, Jaime popped over to the multi-display and logged in, getting the VPN rolling and the RAT for Nealon's phone up.

It was black. Looked like there might have been a crack in the screen. Hm.

"What's going on here, Devin?" Chapman asked, picking up a mic and entering the special voice chat server they'd set aside for conferring on this project.

"I, uh, took a look at your work from last night," Devin's voice came on.

Chapman froze. "Oh?" The implication was hanging; had Devin seen that he'd hacked into Baltimore's camera system? Devin seemed pretty white hat, based on what Chapman knew of his resume. That could be awkward.

"Yeah," Devin said, and hit the screenshare to show Chapman what he was working on. "I took a liberty or two – behind some VPN protection." He sounded nervous. "The, uh, cameras outside that FBI office? The encryption is weak tea, boss."

Chapman looked at the screen; sure enough, there was a DC street in front of him. He'd seen surveillance pics, knew this was Nealon's office. "Okay," he said, still feeling a little nervous that Devin had caught on to what he was up to, hacking-wise. Not the end of the world, but it could be a pain if Devin decided to squeal.

"This was two minutes ago, let me speed it up for you."

The screen started to advance quickly. Ah – there. Nealon walked out the front door of the FBI office, head on a swivel like she was expecting hell to come rushing from every direction. What a savage.

She crossed the street, moving in fast motion, with the unnatural gait exaggeration fast-forward produced. Then the picture – and her gait – went to normal, just as she was about to cross the street about half a block from the office.

Then she stopped, halfway across.

Chapman watched, leaning in.

It didn't take long to see the source of her pause. A car racing at her.

"Move, dummy," Chapman said.

Then the air around her distorted, and she dropped, hitting her knees.

"Whoa–" Chapman started to say.

The car hit her before he could get it out.

Nealon went flying, flipping, really – and down she came on another screen, landing on a two-door coupe, crushing the top and shattering the window. She hung there, ass partially drooping through the smashed windshield, looking like she'd been folded up and thrown like a three-pointer. Watching her tumble, ragdoll style, through the air? It had been almost unreal.

"Holy shit," Chapman said, right into the mic.

"Yeah. But wait – it gets worse," Devin said.

Chapman's eyes widened. She looked like she was already dead; how the hell did you get worse from there? He settled back to watch and find out for himself.

CHAPTER SEVENTY-TWO

Sienna

I opened my eyes to a glaring sun, to pains beyond easy counting, to the taste of blood and at least three teeth scattered inside my mouth like stray corn kernels. Blood mingled with sweat in my eyes, which I could barely get open, and my ears rang like distant alarms, sounding through the streets of Washington DC.

My shoulder hurt; my back hurt. I was at an absurd angle, neck cast to the side. I could feel my toes, luckily. Everything north of them hurt, too. Shins, calves, knees – whatever. All of it. The shoulder, though, that was maybe the worst. Except for the chest. And the back.

Triage was out the window. I was broken, irreparably, at least in the short term. Couldn't even string two thoughts together other than:

I'm busted.

Because I was. I could barely even tell what position I was in, though I felt like it was akin to having some asshole leave the seat up and toppling in the toilet in the middle of the night. Whatever liquid I was feeling beneath my ass was too warm to be water, though. Blood was slipping down my body, pooling in whatever clothing could catch it.

Shadows moved just outside my vision. Like darkness dancing with the light around it.

I couldn't see them. Couldn't tell who they were. Couldn't tell if they were male, female, dogs or cats.

Well, I could kinda rule out quadrupeds, but only just. They were bipedal shadows.

With long black extensions on one hand, each. A strange pattern that even my messed-up head could pick up on, though it didn't render a verdict on what I was looking at immediately. That came moments later, from a different part of my brain, like a distant shout I could barely hear over the ringing.

Guns.

There was nothing for it; my arms didn't move. *I* couldn't move. Every attempt failed, because my mind was failing. I'd been battered beyond the ability to hold a thought together, too wrecked to make a sentence, too smashed to lift a hand.

They closed in, and in. The black weapons raised, becoming part of the main shadow.

They're taking aim.

So helpful, that. But I couldn't move, so it didn't matter.

My brain fuzzed; blackness seeped in.

Then, somewhere, over the sound of the ringing, the shooting started.

CHAPTER SEVENTY-THREE

Chapman

"She got *rekt*," Devin singsonged, quiet awe mixed with distinct amusement.

Chapman felt a little sick. The traffic cameras in this area were in HD; maybe Devin thought it was a videogame, but Chapman knew what was happening. Yeah, he really didn't like Nealon, but he didn't need to see her get wiped out.

Four guys in black hoods were advancing, long guns out. What kind? Hell if he knew. They all looked like AR-15's to him, every rifle did, really.

Executioners, he thought, a little poetically. But he turned his head away.

There was no sound, so he wasn't going to hear it, wasn't going to see it. He'd mention it in his next call with Wu, who'd undoubtedly be pleased to hear this loose end was so nicely tied off. For Jaime's part, he wasn't sure what to think about it, so he tried not to. It was just a thing that happened, far away from here and far, far, from his important deal with Huang. That there was a human being lying on top of a car about to catch a bunch of bullets thousands of miles away?

Well, that didn't bear thinking about, either.

"Whoa! Whoa!" Devin chimed in, and Jaime didn't dare open his eyes. "Who the – aww, man!"

Now Chapman looked; Devin had moved the screens so he got the full feed.

Holloway – that damned chimp – had come charging out the office door and thrown himself into it. Covering behind a car, he was firing like mad. No sound, but you could see the barrel flashes. Two of the black hoods were down. The other two...

They were each advancing in a different direction. Covering behind cars, one firing, the other moving up.

"Oh, damn, oh dayum..." Devin whispered. "They're coming for him..."

And they were. They looked well-armed; he watched one of them cover behind a car, drop a magazine, load a fresh one as his partner fired. Holloway was ducking, but the guy on the right was circling around him...

There was really nothing Holloway could do. Chapman watched until he didn't want to see it any more. The guy on the left was firing, the guy on the right was circling...

Chapman closed his eyes as Devin yelled, "Yes! Oh! Pinched that pig!"

He opened them again to see that, yeah, they got him all right. Both of the black-clads were moving now. Holloway was laid out on the sidewalk. Under the HD camera, Chapman could see what looked like brains on the pavement, and he squinted his eyes shut. "Can you...shift that? I didn't want to watch a snuff film today."

"Oh, yeah, yeah, sorry – this is just...wow. Intense, you know? Do we have to...turn this over to the FBI?"

"Let's not," Chapman said, opening his eyes. Devin had shifted camera views down the block, to Nealon, who was unmoving, on the car. Still. She twitched, stirred–

"Guess she's not dead yet," Devin said. "Oh. Nope. Here they come for her."

And they were. Both of the men in the hoods were walking up the street, guns at the ready, dropping old clips and cramming fresh ones in. They started to raise their guns as they approached her, and Chapman waited for the flash–

Something appeared behind the closest guy, something big and white like it was appearing almost out of thin air.

It was a tiger! A white one.

"Whoa!" Devin shouted. "What!"

The tiger ripped the gunman up as he started to spin. Didn't even get the gun around and he got shredded. Chapman squeezed his eyes closed again.

"Holy – it's going after the – ohhhhhhhHHHHHH!"

"What?" Chapman asked, not daring to peek. He'd seen a lot of blood just now. He didn't shrink at the sight of blood, exactly, but...come on, that was a lot. That guy had gotten eviscerated, he was pretty sure, though it was hard to tell from that angle. "What happened?"

"The tiger ripped up the other guy," Devin said in quiet awe. "Just tore him, like, in half. So brutal." He sounded pleased.

"Did you record any of this?" Chapman asked, reaching up and killing the screen share.

"Huh?" Devin sounded like he was coming out of a food coma. "Well, yeah, I mean–"

"Delete it," Chapman said. "Now. And change the VPN settings. We never log in via those IP addresses again. Hell, we never log in via that country again. Got it? I want that gone from our servers, no personal copies, Devin? You hear me?"

"Dude, but that vid needs to be online. It's–"

"Devin," Chapman said, voice in full boss mode. "We just watched someone murder an FBI agent. I don't need to be questioned about this, and neither do you. This company doesn't need it. Make that shit vanish from our servers. Let it be DC police's problem, you hear me?"

Devin sounded crestfallen. "Yeah. I gotcha. Makes sense."

"You know someone's going to leak something as choice as that," Chapman said, trying to adopt a conciliatory tone. "Give it a few days, you'll be able to search it. I just don't want it connected to us or Socialite. You get me?"

"I got you, boss," Devin said. "On it. In twenty minutes there'll be no sign left."

"Good," Chapman said, and turned off his mic and logged out of the chat server just as Devin cut the feed. Ugh. That had been properly disgusting. And Sienna Nealon was still alive. Talk about a rough morning.

Still, whatever Huang had done – and Chapman was pretty sure he was behind that little show – Jaime didn't want anything to connect to him. As long as he was clear of the fallout, Huang could play all the murder games he wanted.

That video, though...Chapman shuddered. He didn't need to see that – or anything like that, really – for the rest of his days. Trying to put it out of his mind, he marshaled his thoughts about his next meeting, though he found he couldn't fully get it out of his head, no matter how much he tried.

CHAPTER SEVENTY-FOUR

Sienna

I woke to the familiar beeping of hospital machines, and more. To shouts, to talking, to the bustle of people trying to save my life.

"Stop," I said, brushing off gloved hands that were working on me. My clothes had been cut off, and someone was probing my midsection. "Ow!"

"Prep for peritoneal lavage," someone said.

"Don't bother," I said, slapping away another hand so forcefully that the bearer took a step back from the gurney. "I'm healing as we speak. Any internal injuries will work themselves out on their own. You try and put me into..." I wavered for a second, consciousness threatening to fade, "...surgery and you'll just make it worse."

Pushing my eyes open – and past the blinding light above me – I could see a bunch of doctors and nurses with surgical scrubs on, gloved to the hilt. They were peering into my face.

"What?" I asked, raising a hand to brush at my upper lip. It was bloody beyond belief, and as I wiped it away, something hard and lumpy was waiting there. "Hey, is this a tooth?" I tried to pluck at it but some or maybe even most of my fingers were broken.

"Uh...yeah," one of the doctors said, but he sounded a little uncertain. "Listen, you need–"

"Dude, I don't need shit from you," I said, and slapped his hand lightly. He recoiled in pain. "Leave me alone. I'm going AMA here and I'll clear out as soon as I can walk. Save your treatments for people who can use them."

There was some muttering, which I caught. Mostly disbelief. Someone asked, "Can you believe her?" Someone – the voice of reason – mentioned my ability to heal in muted, though profane – terms.

When they'd all cleared out, I was left with one nurse, and the machinery still beeping.

"What happened?" I asked.

"You don't remember?" She sounded pretty calm about it. I peered at her for a moment, trying to figure out if, like last time I'd ended up in a hospital, she was a relative of mine.

She wasn't. She was African-American. My eyes were still blurry, but that much I could see. Also, I didn't recognize the voice. "I remember..." I thought back. I'd gotten hit by a sonic attack, then run over by a car. Plowed into, anyway. Then...

"There was a war zone on that street," she said. "Or so the paramedics told us. Dead people everywhere."

I brushed my head. "How...how many? And...how did they die?" My head felt like it was filled with cottony fuzz. Whether that was the product of the concussion that probably ensued post-car crash, or the sonic attack, I didn't know.

"Four dead," she said, then looked sideways at a pair of swinging doors. "And one..."

Someone banged through the doors as if on cue, grabbing a machine in my room and pulling it back through into the other trauma room. As the doors swung shut, I caught a flash of the patient, with tubes sticking out of his mouth and nose–

"Holloway," I whispered.

"Hey, stop!" the nurse leapt forward as I started to pull electrical leads off my skin. I ripped out my IV line and then crashed to the ground, unprepared to stand and walk yet.

"That's my partner in there," I said, trying to shove myself back to my feet. Pain shot through me, and a gnawing, nervous sensation chewed at my guts. I failed to stand.

Holloway was in the next room, dying.

I'd failed at a lot more than standing.

"Good luck getting to him in your current condition," she said dryly, making no move to help me up.

"Please," I said, turning my head to give her a beseeching look. "I just...I need to know if he's going to be all right."

Something in my voice must have sold her, because her eyes softened. She didn't say anything, but she did step over to the swinging doors and pulled one open, propping it with her body.

I couldn't hear very well, I realized. There was a faint ringing in my ears that muted conversations in a way that I normally didn't experience. I could hear rooms away under regular conditions; now that she had opened the door, I could hear the frantic talk in the trauma room, but only barely, and undergirded by the ringing all the while.

"Charge to 300," one of the doctors said.

My heart fell.

"Clear."

The sound of a defibrillator rang out, and the part of Holloway I could see from my perch on the floor, cheek pressed against the cool, dirty tile, leapt up an inch or two at the shock of electricity.

"No response."

"No, no, no," I muttered under my breath. My chest felt tight. His skin was so pale, even under the spray tan.

"Charging."

"Clear!"

They hit him again. He jerked languidly, then settled back.

A silence followed.

"Nothing."

"Charge to – aw, never mind. I'm calling it."

No. No.

The longest pause came after that, then:
"Time of death: 1432."
Holloway was dead.
Because of me.

CHAPTER SEVENTY-FIVE

Chapman

Jaime was on a late lunch when the call came through – urgent. Desperate. It wasn't phrased that way, but the way it came through made it clear.

"How did this get on the schedule today?" Jaime asked the assistant that was in with him. New guy. Jaime didn't learn their names anymore, because these people rotated often, thus memorizing a name was a waste of time.

"They called and got themselves added," the assistant said. "There was a concern – they're bringing a rep from legal, too. Something about exposure."

Chapman's face automatically crinkled. Anything that required lawyers to be present was not good. "And this is now?"

"Right now, yes, sir," the assistant said, just as the phone buzzed.

"Great, thanks for the warning." Chapman hit the button on the phone. "Send 'em in."

"Yes, sir."

Two men came in, one grim faced, in a suit – lawyer, he knew immediately – the other in a sweater-vest with slacks and skinny beyond healthy levels. Stick figure, Jaime thought of him, probably a little uncharitably. But whatever news they were bringing, he already knew it was not good. They introduced themselves – well, the lawyer did, anyway – and Jaime immediately forgot his name. The other, he knew, vaguely. It was Connor Lawsom, the acting CEO of Lineage.

"We have...some potential exposure," Connor said once the ten seconds Jaime had allotted to initial pleasantries passed.

Jaime looked at the lawyer. He revealed nothing, sitting there, staid, like a rock. "What kind?"

"As you know, at Lineage," Connor said, fiddling with his pants leg, crossing over his knee, "we handle DNA profiling. As well as–"

"I knew what you did when I bought the company," Jaime said, feeling his patience, like sands running through an hourglass, starting to wane. "How do we have exposure?"

Connor fiddled with his pants leg again. "Someone...accessed our DNA profile database."

Jaime blinked, then nodded. "A breach, then? Those are commonplace. We can explain it away. It's not as though we have immense amounts of credit card information or social security numbers in that business." He chuckled. "Exposure? This is just a cost of doing business."

"Yes, but..." Connor smoothed that pants leg again. Jaime wanted to hand him an iron so he could get on with fixing it. "That's not...exactly...the kind of exposure we're talking about. This was...internal."

Jaime straightened. "Internal?" He didn't need an answer to that, was merely verbalizing his surprise, and he disregarded their reactions and answers because he simply didn't care. "What kind of data?"

"The genetic data," Connor said. "The ancestry data. Family lines...and such."

"Wait, not even credit cards?" Jaime asked. A shake of the head from Connor. "Personal–"

"Some," Connor said. "Names and addresses, mostly. But the majority...it was the ancestral data."

Jaime took a deep breath. "And you're sure it wasn't an

external breach?" A nod. "Well, we need to start an investigation. This isn't as serious as other data breaches, without the financial component, but we need to take it seriously."

"We already know who did it," the lawyer said. "They didn't even try and cover their tracks."

Jaime chuckled. "Well, all right, then. That makes it simpler. Who was it?"

"Qiu Yeung," Connor said.

Jaime frowned. Why did that name sound familiar?

"I'm afraid that's one of the people Mr. Huang added to our team upon execution of the merger," Connor said. At least he'd stopped fiddling with his damned pants leg.

Jaime just sat there in silence. Huang had pushed for him to be added to Lineage.

"We believe he also downloaded the entire back end of the website," the lawyer said. "The interface, all the algorithms."

Jaime stared, disbelieving.

Huang had stolen the information right out of that company.

And it had to be Huang. Huang had put this guy in place, had gotten him right there – right where he could download everything. Then this Qiu did, and brought that information – the DNA and family ancestry database, along with their entire site – to...whom?

Huang? Maybe. But why? They were going to roll it out in China together, eventually. It wasn't exactly highest priority, this silly little DNA and genealogy site. It wasn't exactly the most lucrative part of the business. Hell, it wasn't lucrative at all, it was running at just above break-even. There were a lot more valuable things Huang could have stolen.

"I need you," Chapman said quietly, "to make inquiries. See if any other of Huang's people have done anything similar at our other subsidiaries." He pursed his lips. Huang didn't really have anyone in Socialite, Instaphoto, Cash-Fer, or FindIt, though some were slated to come in. He'd wanted to start small, hence the addition to Lineage, as well as a couple of the smaller companies. "Start preparing a report on this. We'll have to release it to the board, and..." He looked at the lawyer. "I'm assuming it's going to have to go public at some point."

The lawyer nodded. "As data breaches go, this one is not among the top tier. That said, I'm not in PR, but if you don't inform people that their data and genetic information has been stolen, your liability will be significant."

"Agreed, no, we'll make it public," Chapman said, nodding along. The problem was how transparent he wanted to be about it. Could he burn this Qiu without the blowback hitting Huang? "Make sure you center your investigation on Mr. Yeung, though. I want to know what he was up to. Hell, I want the cops to arrest him."

"That...would be difficult," Connor said, back to tugging on that damned pants leg. He really needed to find some wrinkle-free pants. He squirmed in his seat but finally blurted out, "He left to go back to China two weeks ago. We made some inquiries before bringing this to you and China's saying..." He squirmed. "...Well they're saying no such person from their country ever traveled here."

The lawyer nodded. "It's like he straight-up disappeared. Like he never even existed."

CHAPTER SEVENTY-SIX

Sienna

"Hey."

Bilson found me sitting in the waiting area of the ER wearing a hospital gown over my bloody jeans, the only article of clothing they hadn't cut off me by the time I'd woken and fought them off. My weapons must have been held by the investigators at the scene, because the only personal effects the nurse had handed me before sending me on my way was my cracked cell phone and my little wallet.

I looked up to find him staring down at me, eyes rimmed with concern beneath his wire-frame glasses. He kept a respectful distance, but looked like he wanted to reach over and put a hand on my shoulder. He didn't though. I was completely shut down, barely registering any surprise at him appearing out of the blue. Which was unexpected.

He must have taken the cue from me staring up at him, blinking, because he said, "I heard about what happened on the news. And when I checked with my local contacts, they said you were taken here."

I nodded slowly, then looked around. The ER waiting room

was a study in quiet despair, and I blended in perfectly. No one was even looking at me, nor daring to sit close to me. Probably because my hair was mussed beyond belief, my jeans were bloody, and the hospital gown was not a great look. I doubted it was doing a great job of covering my back, but who cared? Let the world see my shoulder blades if they wanted. They were probably caked in dried blood anyway.

"I know you're probably feeling pretty raw right now," Bilson said, offering a hand. "Let's get you out of here, huh?"

I stared at his hand for a moment, then nodded, and stood under my own power.

He smiled weakly, clearly pained for me, and waited for me to get my feet underneath me. It was a bit of a struggle. My legs were still uncomfortably weak, and I almost stumbled a couple times. I was pretty sure I had a break somewhere south of my knee, but there wasn't much I could do about it except stay off it until it healed. "You want me to get you a wheelchair?"

"I'll be fine," I said.

We made it out to the parking lot and Bilson's Maserati was there waiting. To his credit – again – he didn't fidget or fuss over me sitting my bloody jeans on his leather upholstery. He just held the door for me and offered help – which I didn't take – to get in. Then closed it gently behind me before getting in and starting the car.

"Are you hungry?" he asked.

"Yes," I whispered, thinking of how Holloway had asked me to get lunch and coffee hours ago. I had been wondering, for quite a while, if I'd been my usual stubborn asshole self and made him go, or ordered in, if this whole thing wouldn't have happened.

Basically, I wondered if I had gotten Holloway killed. But I was past that now. I was certain.

I'd definitely gotten him killed.

"I'm sure we can find a drive-thru," Bilson said. "Unless you want to get out and eat in a restaurant...?"

I looked down at my hospital gown. No self-respecting restaurant would want me as a patron in their dining room right now. "Drive-thru is fine. Or if you want to drop me at home, I can order delivery when I get there."

"No, I'll go with you. We'll get you something. What are you in the mood for? Burgers? Chicken? Tacos?"

"I don't care," I said numbly. Everything was numb for me right now. This was the second time since I'd joined the FBI that I'd had one of my partners die. But the first one I'd felt actually responsible for. Georgia West had been with me when we'd taken on Grendel, and that had just been a fight that was over my head at the time.

Holloway, though...

FBI investigators had caught up to me in the trauma room just after Holloway had died. They'd hit me with the questions. The same ones I'd have asked if it had been me. *What did you see? What happened? What do you remember?*

The answers, in order, were, *Not much, I don't exactly know*, and *Relatively little*.

I remembered the car coming at me, being ready to face it down. I remembered getting hit by the sonic weapon.

Then...

Boom. And that was it, other than four long shadows with rifles moving up to fire on me.

After that? Nada.

They had footage of the attack, they said, so they didn't push me too hard. I didn't even realize until later, when the nurse that was watching over me told me I had a white strip of skull peeking out from beneath my hairline the whole time they were talking to me. Which explained the effort they'd seemed to put into hiding their revulsion.

"I'm sorry about your partner," Bilson said softly. "I know he was with the bureau for quite some time."

"He was a prick sometimes," I said, drawing a sharp intake of breath from Bilson, "but he was a good agent."

Bilson seemed unsure of what to do with my mixed assessment. It shouldn't have surprised me that he was the sort that bought into the idea of canonizing the dead. To hell with that; Holloway was a man with deep flaws. Alcoholism he refused to take seriously, womanizing, grabby hands that he'd drunkenly applied to me once – and only once – before he learned his lesson. A soul-deep cynicism from seeing a little too much war and a little too much law enforcement. It had left him hobbled in his ability to believe there was good in people. I'd seen it in lots of long-service cops, the kind that forget that ordinary people aren't all criminals.

But dammit...when those bastards ambushed me on the street, he'd charged out into the middle of it and taken a half dozen rounds for the trouble.

"Did he have family?" Bilson asked.

"An ex-wife," I said. "Kids. The bureau's talking to them. They weren't...close." The last word was like a whisper, fading away, some stupid shit I'd probably be telling myself for years to console myself at his loss. *Hey, he died saving my life, but at least nobody's really going to miss him.*

I choked down a rancid hunk of feels, my eyes suddenly threatening to fill right there in Bilson's car, and felt generally terrible about myself and this state of affairs.

We stopped in at a Burger King and I ordered one of their vegetarian burgers because I wanted to feel worse. It worked.

Bilson drove me home and followed behind me as I limped up the stairs on my bum leg. I thudded against the wall next to my door, looking for my keys. I tried to remember if I had gotten them back at the hospital, then wondered if maybe they'd been lost either during the attack or after.

"I can call a locksmith if you'd like," Bilson said. So helpful.

"Don't bother," I said, and broke the guts of the lock out, then turned the knob and forced entry.

"Maybe I should get one anyway," he offered, standing outside in the hall. "Get that repaired for you."

I took a few hobbling steps and collapsed in the chair nearest the door. It was soft, well-worn, used furniture procured by the FBI when I moved in and never replaced by a tenant who just didn't give a damn about where she lived at this point.

Bilson seemed to wake up to this fact as he lingered at the door, looking around. He'd been here only yesterday, but now it seemed like he was finally realizing my apartment was an empty shell, like a set dressed for a film with only the barest effort put into it. "Do you...do you want me to–"

"You can come in," I said, leaning my head against the soft cloth. "No need to hang out in the hallway."

He eased inside and closed the door, messing with the busted lock like he didn't know quite what to do with it. Finally he got it closed enough and stopped fiddling. Then he looked around the darkened place, hesitated, and asked, "Do you want me to turn some lights on? Or...?"

"I don't care."

His voice was quiet when next he spoke. "You want me to leave you alone...?"

"They came after me because of the investigation, you know." I said it firmly. "I wasn't quitting it. After what we found yesterday. I know you wanted me to drop it. Chalke wanted me to drop it. Case closed, she said. I'm sure the White House wanted this over, but I just..." I shook my head.

Bilson was quiet for a minute. "You don't think it could have been something else?"

"No," I said. "No, I don't."

He nodded slowly. "I don't think so, either." He took a long, deep breath. "I think you're onto something here that has a lot of people scared."

I leaned my head against the chair, watching Bilson. "What is it that has them so scared?"

He seemed to think about this. "Forgive me for answering slowly. I'm not trying to put you off, it's just...there's a paradigm shift occurring. I'm changing my mind about something, and it's...painful, in its way. See, I've had this long assumption in my political dealings that China, for whatever faults they have, is a key partner for the future. I mean, a billion and a half people – it's not like you can just ignore them, right?" He laughed weakly. "Politicians. Business leaders. Industry analysts. We have an established 'Washington Consensus' about China. How to treat them. What to do with them."

Bilson pursed his lips, pale skin almost blue in the darkness of my apartment. "And I think we've been wrong all this time."

I waited for something more than that. "You finally seeing the PRC government for what they are? Because of this?"

He nodded slowly. "They have never done – to my knowledge – anything this bold before."

I chuckled quietly. "They've been doing things for a while."

"Allegedly. It was always impossible to prove."

"They break into State Department employees' homes and search them," I said, "in China. Our people, and they do this shit. To rattle them. Mess with their heads."

"So I've heard. Again, alleged."

"They–"

"I know there's a litany coming here," Bilson said, "and I agree. I get it now; the PRC government does some very, very bad things. But you have to understand – the consensus in this town is powerful. It's how policy gets made. Dissenting voices get pushed to the margins – like Bridget. Because the results of taking action would be too much to bear."

"Why?" I asked. "Why doesn't anyone have the balls to play Churchill with China? Why is everyone so damned eager to be Chamberlain?"

"Because there's no margin in it," Bilson said, "and I mean that in all the ways. You want a war with them?"

"No. But I don't think we have peace right now, exactly."

"Maybe not," he said, "but the alternative? We send carrier groups to their coast. Formosa, the South China Sea. Start hostilities? I've talked to the military guys. You know what they'd do?"

I nodded slowly. "They have a missile that can target our carriers. Sink them. They have islands in the South China Sea that they've built out as airbases to launch against anyone transiting that body that they don't like. They have nukes that can hit the homeland thanks to dirty dealing US companies. Satellites in orbit that can see everything the way we can."

"Our military guys say that even if it didn't go nuclear," Bilson said quietly, "it'd be potentially very ugly. High casualty. Make Iraq and Afghanistan look like a day at the beach. We'd face a military that has been preparing for conflict with America for decades...while we're more or less unprepared for them. So that's out, as a practical idea. Because as a worst case scenario...well, it's the worst. Business relations between us die. The economy takes a brutal hit. We lose people. Politics, business, military. A trifecta of losing." He sighed. "Or at least that's the perception. No one wants that."

"So what are we stuck with?" I asked, trying to sit upright in my chair. "Appeasement? With some of the worst people on earth, the assholes who lead that government? They oppress the shit out of the Chinese people. Literal concentration camps in Xinjiang. Social credit scores – I mean, you can't even buy a train ticket if you piss off the party."

Bilson nodded slowly. "What are you going to do?"

I sat and fumed, pondering his question. "I don't know."

"I only ask because–"

"I'm not going to start a war with the Chinese government," I said. "Much as I might like to. Much as my ego might call for it. The righteousness...it does burn."

"I understand completely." Bilson's voice was incredibly quiet. The smile, usually ever-present with him, had not made a solitary appearance since he'd picked me up. "I wish I had some words of solace. Some course of action to recommend." He started to slowly shuffle toward the door. "All I have is my condolences."

"What would you do?" I called after him. "If you were me, and that shit happened...well, it happened, but to you?"

Bilson seemed think about it. "I don't know." He put a hand up to his forehead, and for a second I thought he was wiping his eyes, but he was brushing his hair back. "I look at our policies this last however many years, and I see a China that is emboldened enough to undertake a brutal attack on our very shores. What is the point of diplomacy with that? Business relations with that? This is the equivalent of giving up your lunch money every day thinking that things will get better if you just meet the bully's demands. But it doesn't. Then the bully goes home and beats the hell out of his younger siblings unchecked. I see no answers. Only a worldview that's completely checkered in a way it wasn't before."

"At least you know where we stand," I said as Bilson shuffled for the door, looking like he was the one with the busted leg. "By the way...the ones we recovered? That wasn't all the people they kidnapped." He turned, looking back at me. "I think that's the ones they let us find, thinking we'd call it off if we thought it was over."

He just stared at me, and there was no mistaking the haunted look in his eyes. "The Washington consensus," he mumbled.

I nodded slowly. "They counted on it, you know. That no one would want to keep pulling on this thread."

He swallowed, very obviously. "I know now." And with that, he quietly left, leaving me alone in my darkened apartment with nothing but my thoughts and my guilt.

CHAPTER SEVENTY-SEVEN

Chapman

Some days, Chapman's Mountain View mansion didn't seem like much of a mansion anymore. It had when he'd moved in, sure. But Chapman was a child of privilege. Born in the suburbs of Seattle, he'd been raised into the culture of coding by schools that had computer science classes on the cutting edge paid for to service their clientele – the children of Microsoft and Amazon execs, with an expectation they'd know and learn the key skills by the time they exited grade school.

And he had. Chapman's parents had been upper middle class, his father a high-ranking officer in a tech company, his mother an executive in accounting. He'd been born into tech, and moving to Silicon Valley after his incubation period had been natural. Starting a company? Well, that had just been the next step in his evolution.

Now, though, his mansion didn't seem so big anymore. At least not the way it had when he'd moved in. Seven thousand square feet, polished, pristine – he'd felt like he could get lost in it when he'd first come here.

But tonight he was bouncing around like the ball in a game of pong, and it just didn't seem big enough to hold in his unquenchable rage.

He was marinating in his aggravation, pacing. Typing things out, deleting them. Couldn't get his thoughts straight. Watched the clock move to eleven, then midnight. He wondered if Gwen would turn up tonight. Probably not, if she hadn't shown up by now.

Dammit.

He sat in his favorite chair, spent by the emotional effort of the day. He wanted to rage more, but he needed to sit, at least for a minute. He stared up at the ceiling, and pretty soon he was waking to the sound of knocking at the glass back door.

"Hey," Gwen said when he opened it for her. She had an airy smell, like she'd been outdoors for a while. Her usual mischievous smile was missing, and for a moment he forgot his own problems and wondered about that.

It didn't last, though. Before she could even say anything, he unloaded. Because he had to. "You are not going to believe the shit that blew up on me today."

Gwen's smile did return, for a moment – flashing effervescent and impish. "Oh, I can't wait to hear this," she said, throwing herself onto the couch. "Hit me."

"You know the Chinese deal I've been on?" He paced as he spoke. It helped him gather his thoughts. "With Huang?"

She nodded slowly. "Mmhmm."

Chapman nodded furiously. "As part of the deal, we took in some of his people into the lesser subsidiaries. I figured no big deal, because he wasn't asking to plant anyone at Socialite, or FindIt, or Instaphoto–"

"So he wanted people in your non-critical companies," she said, thinking. "Interesting. Non-offensive."

"An easy ask," he said. "Innocuous enough. Well, today I find out he's done a data breach. Or at least one of his people did. Stole the entire website for Lineage, plus the DNA database, and all the family connections. Then poof, disappeared back to China where no one seems to have even heard of this guy."

Gwen's eyebrows went up. "Wow. You're saying this guy is just...like, gone?"

"They told me it's like he never existed," Chapman said, letting the rage vent. "They claim his passport, ID? All fake. My guys hired a PI over in China to check him out before they came to me. He's just gone."

Gwen nodded along, and he could see her thinking that through. "Wow. You think this was, like, a Chinese spy op?"

"I think so," Chapman said, nodding too. Then he stopped his pacing. "But if so...why Lineage? I mean, I would get if they wanted to clone Socialite. Or even Instaphoto. I don't like it, but it makes money. And FindIt is a cash cow. Lineage, though...it's a middling genealogy site that I bought on a whim because of the data. I mean, I thought I could integrate it into Socialite, but all the ideas my people proposed were stupid and messed with our core competencies...I just don't see why Huang would jeopardize this entire deal and write out a check that big over something so trivial as Lineage."

Gwen seemed deep in thought. "Maybe it wasn't trivial to him. Or the people behind him."

"He's a billionaire," Jaime said, smirking. "There's no one 'behind' him." Then he froze.

Gwen had beat him to it, smiling like a Cheshire cat in the dimness. "In America, in Europe, there might be no one behind a billionaire. In Communist China...there's always someone standing behind the billionaire, either granting them permission to do the things they do or directly guiding them."

"Shit." Chapman closed his eyes. "You're right."

"Waitaminute." She was beside him in a second. "Is this about that Sienna Nealon thing from last night? Because today–"

"I know," Chapman said, and man, his voice sounded down even to him. "I saw it happen." He looked up and found Gwen looking at him in complete calm. She even stroked his back. "I mean, I didn't have anything to do with it, or know it was coming, but...I heard her talking about something...and I told Huang about it."

Gwen's eyes widened. "And then she almost gets killed!" Her voice lowered to a whisper. "What did you tell him?"

"That she wasn't letting go of her investigation," Chapman

whispered. "That's it. I heard her say it to her partner this morning...and he called, and I told him. And then..."

"Whoa," Gwen said. "They tried to kill her for it. Your boy Huang and whoever was behind him."

Chapman let that hang for a minute. "Yeah. I think so." He didn't feel very comfortable with where this was going, now that he had to verbalize it to Gwen.

She kept her hand on his back for a few seconds, but didn't say anything. When he looked at her, she seemed deep in thought. She patted him a couple times, then went to the couch and sat back down.

Chapman followed, dropping to his knees next to her, and took her hand. "What are you thinking?" He stroked the back of it, feeling the smooth skin up to her wrist, where some tiny hairs started to pop up. "Right now?"

Gwen didn't answer for a second, and it made his heart skip a beat. Then it skipped again when she did.

"That you got screwed by this Huang guy," she said finally. "If he went to this much trouble to get the DNA info and whatnot out of Lineage, I'm thinking that's what he was after. Plus, you were a perfect conduit to tell him what was going on with Nealon. You even gave him access to your connections in the US, which I'm sure was great for him."

"At least I got a big check out of it," Jaime said, trying to smile.

"How did he pay you?" Gwen asked, frowning.

"Cash, mostly," Jaime said. "Yuan."

She nodded. "If he's backed by the PRC government...I'm no expert on currency exchange, but what do you bet they just printed that money right up in their treasury?"

Chapman felt a little prick of conscience. "I should probably cash out then. Quickly. Before the devaluation consequences of that one hit."

"That'd be smart." She was still deep in thought. "I'm still stuck on the why of this. Like, why would Huang do all this for what he got? Because he couldn't have planned on this Sienna Nealon thing, right? On having you be able to spy on her?"

"I don't think so," Chapman said. "It only even happened

because..." He looked around, as though someone was going to pop up in his living room. "...Well, because I'm part of this group that's...sort of...helping run Sienna Nealon at this point."

Gwen laughed. "'Run her?' Like a dog on a racetrack?"

"No!" Jaime said. "Like a...secret agent...kind of thing. Yeah, it all sounds lame now, but whatever. We were having her work for us, sort of."

"I thought she worked for the FBI?" Gwen's voice was thick with amusement.

"Yeah, well, the director's in my group," Chapman said.

She poked him in the side, smiling. "You have a secret club? How very grade school of you. Or maybe 'Skull and Bones.'"

"It's more like a network," Chapman said. "Of connected people, you know. Ones who have some power in their respective spheres. Press, government, law. We know people who know people. Can get things done."

Gwen's smile evaporated. "But Huang didn't know you were part of this."

"I don't see how he could," Chapman said. "No one knows. Except you."

"Well, the other people in your group have probably told at least one person in their own lives," Gwen said, and boy did that sound reasonable. "So...I agree with you in general. Huang probably didn't know about this. But he did know about your general connections, because you're kind of a big shot, guy." She patted him on the back again, but there was an air of mockery in it.

"Yeah, take some shots at the rich and powerful mover of people and industry. I can take it."

"I know you can, sweetums," Gwen said with that same mocking tone. "It's what I like about you. But seriously...if we eliminate all this other stuff? It looks to me like Huang got what he was after. The Lineage data. So...what the hell was of value there?"

"I have no idea," Chapman said, and really, they were at the root of it. "Algorithms on how to piece together family history? Silly, but I guess it's kinda specifically tailored for that sort of thing. Some user data – addresses and whatnot, most of which you could have gotten from a lot of other places. And the DNA stuff, which...I mean, I guess we had the most number of DNA tests done worldwide, but..." He shrugged. "What the hell would Huang want with any of that?"

Gwen didn't answer at first, and when she did, all the mockery was gone, replaced by a dead serious quiet. "I think the question is..." And she looked at him, a worried look in her eyes, "...What would China want with the DNA profiles of that many people?"

The way she asked it...the knowledge as it finally hit home. Hell, just the mystery itself, of what China could do with the DNA profiles of that many people? Well, that thought chilled Jaime right to the bone.

CHAPTER SEVENTY-EIGHT

Sienna

I woke from a sorry-ass, not even close to restful sleep, pain in my leg and shoulder radiating out madly from the places where I'd been blasted by a sedan.

Standing was easier than when I'd hobbled to bed hours ago, without even bothering to shower. My sheets were a disaster of sweat and peeled-off blood, which I'd deal with tomorrow.

A long, hot shower took some more of the sting out of things, physically.

The mental sting, I thought, was going to be with me for a long while yet.

Wandering my apartment in a robe at three in the morning didn't seem like a risky move, but then, neither had walking down the street yesterday. My paranoia in full flower, I went to the gun safe in my bedroom and opened it up, pulling out the AR-15 I'd checked out from the FBI armorer when I'd first hit town. Strapping it across my back as I brewed a cup of tea seemed like a reasonable precaution, with a couple extra mags resting in my robe pocket in case I needed them.

The fact that I hadn't seen Firebeetle lately, that he hadn't partaken in the hit attempt yesterday, suggested to me that China had probably already extracted him from the United States. Smart move on their part, given the level of heat that had come from this. He was the only direct link I had left to the case that was still breathing. He looked like a hard mofo, the kind that probably wouldn't break under questioning but still, better safe than sorry. Getting him out of the US was safe.

I was having trouble piecing together...well, the pieces. I'd gone over them in my head so many times they'd started to swirl. Now that I'd lost Holloway, I'd also lost my sounding board for all this craziness. Bilson seemed nice enough, sympathetic enough, but he was also not a cop. Whether I could trust him with the case details was irrelevant; he had access to them, thanks to Chalke's decree. Whether he was nosing into them, I doubted it, since I was his conduit for that.

Still, his change of heart last night meant something. I remembered how he'd acted during the opening moves of the case – cautious, but on the side of preserving relations with China. Sure, he'd set up a meet with Bridget, but that was about it in terms of sticking his nose out past the Washington consensus.

But if what he told me last night had been true...he was coming around.

A distant sound of a bird cooing broke me out of my thoughts. A second coo followed, and I couldn't help myself. I checked for my phone; it was still cracked across the face and resting in the charging station in the kitchen.

I threaded my way into the bedroom, closing the door behind me, and made my way to the window. Pulling the curtains back, I looked out.

There was no apartment across the way. Just a construction site where a building was going up, torn-down guts of the old no longer even remaining to mark the passage of that piece of old Washington giving way to new. A quick look to either side confirmed no action out there.

Except a lone pigeon staring in at me from my window sill. It – he – cooed again, and for the first time I noticed its eyes were bright, not black.

I opened the window wide; this was the only one in the apartment with no screen. "Shh," I said, holding up a finger to my lips as I looked at the pigeon, then again to either side. No activity anywhere on the street, not even in the cars below. There was no light behind me, and I watched for almost a minute in utter silence.

The pigeon watched, too, and didn't make a sound, nor took flight to get away from this shushing human hanging out her window inches from him.

When I was sure the coast was clear, I stepped back, leaving the window open, and beckoned him. "Hurry," I whispered.

He did, flapping in.

But he didn't stay a pigeon. Oh no, he did not.

He shifted in seconds, becoming a man, and a naked one at that, grabbing my sheets as his wings morphed to fingers. He wrapped the sheet around himself as he settled into a human form, wearing my dirty bedding as a toga. With one hand, he smoothly reached back and shut the window.

Leaving me alone, at last, with the meta who had been saving my life all this time.

CHAPTER SEVENTY-NINE

Being alone with a naked man in my bedroom felt a little weird, if only because we were strangers. And I wasn't the type to go for one-night stands with random guys.

It was maybe made a little worse by the fact that his chest was...bulging. His hair was perfect, a black faux hawk that looked strangely like his bird alter ego, but in a good way. And his face was...quite nice. Handsome. Indisputably Asian, too.

All in all, it made me feel awkward to be wearing just a bathrobe. And an AR-15.

When he started to speak, I pointed to the door, then my ear. "They're listening," I whispered, meta-low.

He nodded slowly, then lowered his own voice, which bore a trace of an accent. "I wasn't sure you'd know it was me. I had to talk to you after what happened before. On the street, I mean." He bowed his head. "I am sorry about your partner."

"Not your fault," I said back. We kept our voices in that same range, and I moved a little closer, in spite of our light amount of clothing. Definitely not because of it. "I didn't see the footage, but...you saved me, didn't you?" The agents who interviewed me had been pretty quiet about the end of the fight, other than asking me about the albino tiger swooping out of the sky. They had my earlier accounts of the battles with Firebeetle where he'd jumped in, so...

He nodded.

"And you've been following me?"

He nodded again.

"Why?"

There was a cloud of emotion on his face. "The man you have been fighting. The meta."

"I call him Firebeetle," I said, and realized, "Uh...I don't know your name."

"Jian," he said. "Jian Chen. You can me 'John' if it's too difficult to pronounce."

"Jian," I said, rolling the 'j' like he did. Probably not as well, but still. "It's not too hard."

He nodded, looking down at my substandard carpeting. Or his feet. Or his towel. I couldn't tell which, but he wasn't looking at me or my mom-style fuzzy bathrobe. "This Firebeetle...he is an agent of the Chinese government."

"I kinda suspected that."

"When I read about your fight with him in the paper," Jian said, "I knew who he was immediately. I came to DC right away. I had to." He paused, but his eyes were burning, emotion welling up in them.

"Why?" I asked. "What did he do to you?"

Jian took a hard, ragged breath. "He pursued me through all of China. I came across the Pacific eight years ago. I escaped from a compound in China...that you are probably familiar with."

It dawned on me at last. "You mean the Chinese meta facility. The one that was destroyed by Sovereign."

He nodded slowly. "I escaped just before that happened, but...yes. That is the place."

I blinked a couple times. "Wait...that place was a prison?"

"Part of it was," Jian said, a small, bitter smile graced his lips. "You didn't think it was all voluntary, did you? Every meta the Chinese government could find, all in one location?"

"I didn't really think about it," I said, "since the first time I heard of it was when it was destroyed. Did they...scoop you up out of your village or something? Kidnap you and stick you there?"

"No." Jian's face hardened, and a flicker of unmistakable hatred ran across it. "It was much worse than that."

CHAPTER EIGHTY

Jian Chen

I was born in a valley in Shanxi, a province in mountainous Northern China. My parents were overjoyed with my birth; they had been fearful that I would be a girl, and girls born during that period in China, well...

By the time of my birth, my parents had seen the worst that China had to offer. Shanxi was a very corrupt province, and was rocked by scandal related to that later, in my adulthood. At the time, little was said except in quietest whispers. Still, what was there to do? My parents kept their heads down, their mouths shut, and they worked to provide a future for me.

I grew up in the school system, learning to love the party, to love China. My parents didn't dare speak a word against the government. They'd seen how things went for those who did.

I didn't realize how bad things were until I got to what you would consider high school age. There was a girl in my school. She came from a family that was disgraced. Not treasonous, but undesirable. Her parents had committed some sin long before I was born. They were forever marked with that shame. They never did anything bad that I saw, but there was an undercurrent. Rumors about them abounded. Children threw rocks at her, called her...well, something terrible.

I...I threw rocks at her, too. It is a shame that will fill me to my dying day.

My powers manifested when I was a teenager. I had grown up, made it to college age. She had grown up, too. I noticed. I always noticed her. I didn't want to...my parents warned me to stay away, but...

I didn't know it, but she had been attending meetings with other...undesirables. I see you looking at me, wondering what that means. There's a religious movement in China called Falun Gong, an offshoot of Buddhism. At first they were embraced by the government. Then...they outlawed Falun Gong entirely, and began a campaign to eliminate it from China with every tool the state had at its disposal.

They came for her one day while I was walking through the village. Chinese police, moving in packs like dogs. They caught the practitioners – and her – after a meeting...worship...I don't really even know Falun Gong. They beat some of them. I saw blood dripping down the face of a man old enough to be my grandfather. They dragged away a woman unconscious.

When I saw her, she wasn't bloody or unconscious. She just looked...her eyes were a thousand miles away. Like she didn't even know what was happening to her, couldn't believe it. Or maybe she was resigned to it by now, after all the years of hatred directed at her from the village.

I saw her face, that look, that...resignation...and I couldn't stand by and watch her be led away.

I stuck my chest out at the police officers holding her. Blocked them. All I could think was how my parents would be so ashamed. And scared.

One of them tried to swipe at me, hit me with the butt of his gun.

I knocked it from his hands. Turned into a tiger for the first time in public.

And I pounced.

Oh, I didn't do it like I do it now. I didn't kill him. But I hurt him. Knocked him down, knocked down another, batted a third over. But there were so many, and so many guns.

I tried to hide in their ranks; low to the ground, moving between them. Faster, stronger. I got quite a few, but my unwillingness to kill – I was so young, so...innocent, I suppose.

They shot me. Many times.

I didn't die, of course. And you can see by looking at my chest, I don't even have any scars from it.

I totally was not looking at your chest! Really. For really real.

It's fine. You should hear all of this, though. Because when I woke up, I was in a Chinese prison in Qinghai. And that...was where things started to get really bad.

CHAPTER EIGHTY-ONE

Jian

I thought when I woke, naked, chained to a concrete floor, a hole in the ground for my toilet and a water spout above it for drinking – I thought things couldn't get any worse.

How very naïve I was.

I don't know how much you are aware of Chinese prisons, but most of them make American prisons look like palaces. Decaying buildings, poor plumbing. When my water spigot failed to work, I was expected to drink from the toilet hole, and no one thought anything of it.

Beatings. Brutal discipline. These were all parts of the service.

There's a thing they don't talk about much in the western press, and that's how dissidents are treated in China. Even for lesser infractions. A famous Chinese actress, Fan Bing Bing, was discovered to have worked for western movie companies. She was paid an amount more than she declared on her taxes, presumably pocketing the rest.

She disappeared. No one heard from her for months. The Chinese government did not even acknowledge having her.

When she finally reappeared, it was with a long, forced apology like one of your hostage videos, you know? Reading from the script: I have shamed myself, blah blah...however you would say it. I'm not native to American ways of speech.

I had no idea if anyone from my village, my family, even knew what happened to me.

As it turned out...this might have been fortunate for them.

One day the guards came for me. They took me to the prison clinic. Swabbed the inside of my mouth with one of those long, cotton-tipped swabs. Then they threw me back in my cell. I didn't think anything of it for weeks afterward. Just a strange incident in the course of brutal days, occasional beatings, and long stretches of confinement.

I considered trying to become a worm to crawl through the prison bricks. I worked on it. Becoming a worm, I mean. It's difficult because of the mass differential between worm and human forms. It takes practice.

Before I could, though...they came for me again. This time, they moved me to a different prison. Bag over my head, beatings before I left and along the way to keep my powers in check.

They took me out in a camp that was impressively better than the aging dung heap I left. It was new, down to the train line that carried me there. New roads, new buildings. A sleek, modern facility, with an airstrip of its own nearby.

Even my cell was new, with a functional water spigot and toilet straight out of modern times. I wondered what I'd done to deserve such paradise.

Then...I found out.

They came to me on a cold morning, frost on the edges of the cell window. I went with them, not wishing to chance a beating. My powers were ineffective against these guards, who had powers of their own. They took me across the compound to a building in the medical complex. Nurses and doctors in their sterile garb waited.

I was given a shot just before I entered the room. A little sting, numbing me, making me ready for...what followed.

I never really passed out, you see. I was awake the whole

time. I couldn't lift my hands; I fell down on a table, my limbs no longer responding to my commands.

"Get him on the gurney," a man in a medical gown said.

They did. Then they wheeled me into an operating theater.

I tried to scream but I couldn't. My vocal chords were as paralyzed as the rest of me.

It was a surgical team, I realized as they started.

They took...organs. Skin. Corneas. I can only assume they had donors waiting for most or all of it, I don't even know. I passed out repeatedly throughout the procedure. I don't even know how long I was on the table.

When it was done, they didn't even bother to stitch me up. I think they left my heart in me; one lung. Enough for me to survive.

Then they threw me back in my cell for a week, maybe two.

And the nightmare started over again as they came for me with a needle already prepared...and did it over...and over...again.

CHAPTER EIGHTY-TWO

Sienna

"My God."

My whisper was already meta-low, but there was a creeping, horrified sense of awe in hearing Jian's story. It hung in the air of the bedroom, bringing with it such fresh horror that I'd even allowed myself to forget we were both nearly naked standing here, the scars of his trauma written across his face in the emotions that played there.

"They took my organs...twenty...fifty...I don't even know how many times," Jian said, still looking at the floor. "Eventually, this new woman came to the prison. Her name was An. She yelled at the guards about how they treated me. She demanded my release, and they moved me to the meta compound in the north. Or she did, at least. Only her. No other guards were on the train. I was still young and foolish enough to believe she liberated me from the hell I'd gone through."

I was coming to some slow realizations in the midst of all this horror. "She worked for the government?"

"Of course," Jian said. "Everyone does. Or so it seemed to me at the time. She seduced me along the journey. It had...been a long time." His face fell with shame. "She took me to the compound that Sovereign destroyed. Told me 'these people are different.'" His face hardened, twisted in hatred. "They were the same. It was a re-education camp. They wanted me to learn to love the state again so that I'd work for them. She left me there. With them."

"But you ran?" I asked.

He nodded slowly. "Not at first. I played along, because I was afraid if I didn't, they'd send me back to the hospital prison and harvest me forever." He shuddered. "The screams in that place at night..."

"So you bided your time."

"And escaped when the moment presented itself," Jian said. "But this Firebeetle, as you call him? I knew him. He trained with me."

I blinked. "He was in the reeducation camp?"

Jian shook his head. "Just the meta training section. His loyalty was not in question like mine. He came straight out of the People's Liberation Army." Jian smiled, ghostly. "I came out of a prison where dissidents had their organs harvested for 'fun and profit' as you would say. When I escaped, I had to make my way across China, on foot, stealing and scraping until I snuck into Hong Kong. I managed to get on a ship, come to America, declare myself and request asylum." He let out a low breath. "I've been here ever since. And been fine...until I heard about your fight with this Firebeetle. Though I knew him as Cheng Yu."

Cheng Yu. Hadn't that been the name on one of his passports? "He's a pretty stoic fellow," I said. "I don't know that he's said much to me in our fights. Does he speak any English?"

"Definitely," Jian said. "We were all trained, in the compound." When he caught my surprise, Jian didn't hesitate to explain. "It was understood in our training that we were working so that we would be used against America."

"That's not subtle," I said.

He shook his head. "And now this man is kidnapping Chinese citizens over here. But that's not all."

I hung my head. "For crying out loud. Of course it's not. Nothing's ever easy, no matter how it's presented." A simple kidnapping and it had ballooned into a Chinese plot to snatch people from a foreign country.

"Do you know why they're kidnapping these people?" he asked.

I had a suspicion. "How many metas did China have left after Sovereign destroyed that compound?"

"Very few," Jian said. "Firebeetle – Cheng – only survived because he was chasing me at the time. And he redoubled his efforts once the compound was destroyed."

I nodded slowly. "Because metas are a valuable resource to China."

"A strategic and tactical advantage that is indelibly interwoven into their long-term planning," Jian said. "China has a fifty-year plan to become supreme over the world. How can they do that if they have no superpowered people?"

"You can't replace a population like that naturally, not in fifty years." I shook my head slowly. "The metahuman serum."

"That would be my guess," Jian said. "They need subjects to inject. Metahumans to become their new army."

"This is the part that is confusing to me," I said. "Why kidnap here? They have plenty of citizens back home they could dose, right? A billion people. Presumably more loyal than these people who have fled their country."

"I don't know," Jian said. "I have some Chinese connections I have made since arriving in America. People who talk with their family still in China. There is something going on in this vein. Outside the normal unexplained arrests that China makes."

"Then why expand the franchise to America?" I asked, pacing around my bed as I thought. "I mean, this sounds like some pretty evil shit. Like, maybe the most evil I've ever encountered, other than this one Scottish bitch who – sonofa!"

And the idea hit me like a lightning bolt.

I thought of Rose and her endless vials of serum in her secret room in Edinburgh. Of how she'd harvested thousands of people to accumulate the right collection of powers to crush me.

A Rakshasa for the power of illusion.

Wolfe for his rapid healing.

An Achilles for the invincibility.

"They've got a billion people back home," I said. "Lots of genetics to work from, but these powers...lots of them are uncommon." I looked at Jian. "What if they needed to trace down certain genetic lineages – family lines – in order to get certain important strategic powers – like telepathy for instance?"

Jian considered this. "That would be a good reason to take the risk of operating overseas."

"Yeah," I said. "They're not just randomly snatching people, though. They've gotten their DNA somehow, and that's the targeting vector they're using to determine who to grab." I clenched my fist. "That's why they're doing it. They're building an army. I don't see how this works, loyalty-wise, but they're rebuilding their meta army with these people."

Jian was quiet for a moment. "It may not be as simple as that."

"What do you mean?" I was already feeling a cold chill from these dark thoughts and plans, but something about the look on Jian's face made my blood temperature fall by another ten degrees.

"There was...something else that went on in that camp," Jian said, his eyes low. "Some of us, we were...intractable. Not me, I went along, kept my plans to myself, mouthed the pieties until I escaped. But some...didn't."

I waited, breath almost held. "And they were...what? Executed?"

He shook his head slowly. "Worse."

How the hell could it get worse than that? I wondered.

I didn't wonder long.

"Remember the woman who came to me at the hospital prison? An? Who...seduced me?" Jian asked. "They had others like her. Loyal agents. If the dissident – the meta that refused to be 're-educated' and loyalized – which did happen – if they were...powerful enough. I watched the same display that An staged to 'save me' from the hospital play out in the camp. These women would leave with him, for somewhere else." He swallowed heavily. "I heard later what they did, from a guard who got away, defected. We ran across each other through mutual contacts when he fled to California."

My eyes widened.

"It was a breeding program," Jian said. "They would act like An, and seduce the man, if they could. Retain the..." He shuddered. "...The genetic material. Produce...children."

I felt a near full-body spasm. "That's...terrible."

"It was worse even than that," Jian said, and his face seemed suddenly shrouded in darkness. "If the subject was female...or didn't cooperate." Now his mien became stone, anger seething behind his eyes. "They would take what they wanted surgically, extracting...whatever they had...and make as many children with loyal surrogates as the People's Republic wanted."

CHAPTER EIGHTY-THREE

"What the hell do I do with this information?" I wondered aloud, still stinging from Jian's last revelation. The possibilities for what the Chinese were up to were endless, but logical: kidnap these people with potentially valuable powers locked in their genetic code, loyalize them...

...Or harvest them for reproductive materials and have the child raised by the state. Loyalty just about guaranteed.

"There are many people missing now," Jian said. "Not just around DC."

"I know," I said, thinking of Michelle's warnings. "They've got to have grabbed...hundreds of people. Too many."

"But they have to get them back to China," Jian said, voice rising with urgency. "This doesn't work unless they do. That's the key point of their plans. Once these people reach China, they disappear forever behind the fortress walls of the People's Republic."

I looked up, staring at my ceiling, hoping for further inspiration. "Then we have to get them before then, which leads to rough possibilities – either wherever they're being held now, like that shipping container in the Port of Baltimore we recovered, or else as they're moved." I walked through it mentally. "Which has to be either by plane or by ship."

"Or submarine," Jian said.

"That's iffy," I said. "They can't dock a submarine at the Port of Los Angeles. And they'd need one specially modified to carry people, even in shitty conditions like that cargo container. I think subs are out."

Jian nodded. "The shipping container, though...that's preferred for smuggling people. It's how I came over."

"Holy shit," I breathed. "But would they really do that, after throwing us the bone of the container in the Port of Baltimore?"

"Think about it," Jian said. "Customs and Border Protection wasn't all over your find. Because it's not uncommon. There's no need for China to get creative here. Smuggling people in that way is the perfect cover, because it happens normally. Why break the mold to do something that might not work when you have something that does, and has, for years?"

"Then they're smuggling these people out of major US ports," I said. "Like Baltimore. And our Customs people are...what? Missing them?"

"Yes," Jian said. "Or are bribed to miss them."

I felt a pang again, in my head, and the same question came back to me: "What the hell am I supposed to do with this?"

As if in answer to my question, there came a knocking at my apartment door, and Jian and I stared at each other like we were caught, eyes locked, panicked, on each other.

CHAPTER EIGHTY-FOUR

Chapman

The worst thing about the Network in Chapman's estimation was the hours. These East Coast people had no respect for those operating on the West Coast. Couldn't they keep their bullshit to Pacific Daylight Time? The answer was apparently no, as reflected by the Escapade app squealing out at him at zero dark thirty.

"What time is it on the East Coast?" Chapman asked, fumbling for his phone. He looked around; Gwen was already gone. Figured. She was an early riser, and didn't seem much into the idea of sticking around after...well, after. He knew those days himself, though, as a CEO burning the candle at both ends. Show up way before your first employee, stay into the night until everyone else was heading home. In a way, he missed that crunch time feeling.

Unlocking his phone with a quick keying in of his passcode, because Chapman didn't trust facial recognition or fingerprint scans, he looked at the scroll already starting on his screen.

BILSON: Nice segment talking me up for National Security Advisor last night, Chris.

Was this what he got up for? If so, Chapman was going to barf in his own mouth. All this stupid flexing.

BYRD: Thx! I hear potus himself was listening. u deserve it after this kidnapping bizness. Scary times. We need a cool head at NatSec. This China thing cud get out of control if some1's not sitting in that seat with clear eyes about the bizness.

Chapman stared at that response. What the hell did Byrd even mean? Was he just tired or was Byrd as much a blockhead as he'd always suspected?

Well, there were no points for remaining in the dark so Chapman tapped out the question on his mind.

CHAPMAN: What's so tough about the current situation? Maybe China did this thing, maybe they didn't, but it looks to me like they're pretty much just grabbing their own nationals back. And there's no evidence. So who cares?

CHALKE: It's not a good look for China if they get implicated. The public has feelings about foreign countries operating kidnapping rings on American soil for some reason. They get kind of uppity about it, like it's part of our job to prevent that sort of thing.

Chapman rolled his eyes. He could hear Chalke's sarcasm like she'd spoken it straight to him. His impatience got the better of him.

CHAPMAN: Honestly, who gives a fuck what the people want? Not me. I run a company for my investors, okay? Not for the sheep in the pen, waiting to get sheared. And we run this country for the people who actually have the brains to understand what's going on. I don't give a flying crap if Joe Ordinary in BFE, Oklahoma, is pissed about a kidnapping ring in DC that will never touch anyone he knows. What the hell does he know? Nothing, that's what. Meanwhile, everything he buys at Walmart is made in China, which means if we escalate to a trade war, Joe's bullshit fishing rods go up 100% in price and Joe ends up whining about how his lures are costing him an arm and a leg. Because Joe's an idiot who has no idea how things work. So screw Joe. We'll keep his stupid fishing lures cheap, and all he has to do is sit down and shut up and let us take care of his stupid ass.

Jaime was seeing some red by the time he got done typing. But that didn't cover the whole thing, did it? He went on, of course.

CHAPMAN: And another thing about these idiots in the mob we call a country. In addition to being dumb, they eat out of the palm of our hands. What's the point of having Chris and Morris and Dave in this group if we're not writing the narrative that best suits our agenda? The public only gets mad about shit they're told. Downplay this crap and they'll save their rage for some other stupid story, like Kim Kardashian getting an ass reduction or something. That's all it takes. These people are pigs in a trough, we're the farmers, and we need to feed them an organic diet instead of letting someone else give them the slop that we don't want them to have. So let's shape the effing narrative and stop worrying about what anyone thinks. I've got the algorithms to make this happen, to drop some of this stupid shit off the grid, to shift the Overton window past any thoughts of war with China, trade or otherwise. Who's with me?

He settled back, still seething at his screen. Huang's betrayal had done a number on him, but he wasn't so burnt he'd suddenly decided pouring gasoline on this China thing was a good idea. Besides, maybe this Huang business would still work out. If the man lived up to the original arrangement and got him into China, forgiving the bullshit he pulled with Lineage would be easily done. Because it was such penny-ante crap.

BILSON: I'm not sure I agree with you on this. Not that I'm advocating war with China, at least not the conventional kind, but if they're kidnapping people on our soil...there should be some sort of response. Sanctions, something.

Chapman rolled his eyes. Dumb. When had Bilson gotten struck by a case of the stupids?

CHAPMAN: Seriously...who gives a shit? We're talking billions of dollars in trade with China. Why would you endanger that over them grabbing people who look to be mostly their own citizens anyway? Right? Am I right on that, Chalke?

CHALKE: Yes. They're mostly citizens of China, or asylum seekers.

KORY: Wait, so these people are refugees?

CHALKE: Not necessarily. The ones we recovered last night were almost entirely Chinese citizens with green cards in the US ranging from work visas (H-1B, H-2B) and student visas to some with asylum claims (religious persecution, etc.) mixed in.

CHAPMAN: See? They're pretty much just Chinese citizens. Who knows what they actually did in order to get the Chinese government after them? This looks like an internal matter, and it bothers me to the tune of none if they get dragged back home. Why would we get involved in that?

BILSON: Why would you get involved if your neighbor starts beating his wife in your living room?

Asshole. Chapman's vision went red. That was dirty, and it sent him into a rage immediately.

CHAPMAN: Not the same at all.

BILSON: Yes it is. How long are we going to sit back and pretend China doesn't run actual concentration camps? How long are we going to turn a blind eye to their constant abuse of human rights? And why? So we can feel good about getting our microprocessors for thirty percent cheaper than if they were made somewhere else that's a little less cruel to their own people? I'm not asking for miracles, but maybe we do business with countries that don't have legit concentration camps for their own citizens. With countries that don't organ-harvest their dissidents. It's a low bar, but I think we can clear it.

CHAPMAN: This is one of the largest countries in the world, and you want to scuttle our trade with them over this bullshit? Wreck our economy, wreck theirs?

CHALKE: I don't think any of us wants that. Let's just take a step back.

BILSON: I didn't say that, but this behavior they've engaged in ought to be beyond the pale. We should at least have the moral courage to say, "Not here. Not on our soil." We don't have to invade them, or sponsor a rebellion, we just have to say, "Not here. Not now. Not ever."

Chapman just shook his head. Where was this coming from?

CHAPMAN: "Moral courage?" Are you kidding with this shit?

He stopped, laughing out loud. Seriously?

CHAPMAN: I think you've been hanging around with that so-called superhero for a little too long. She's warping your brain with her stupid ideas. Cutting off diplomatic and trade relations with China now would be a direct provocation and do nothing to aid these people you supposedly care about, other than make their quality of life worse as you crash the Chinese economy (and ours). If you want to change China for the better, we need to keep trade open and modernize them/liberalize them that way.

"Let me get Socialite in there and watch things change,"

Chapman muttered. "Let me get FindIt in China and you'll see more change than you ever would by cutting the economic legs from beneath their ruling class now."

BILSON: We've tried that for almost fifty years. Hasn't worked. In fact, judging by this, China's only getting bolder and more willing to show their true face. They went from a "Hide your strength, bide your time," mantra under Deng Xiaoping to flexing for the world to see and not bothering to admit they're doing it. We do what we've done before, we get the same thing – more defiance, more ugliness. It's time for a change.

BYRD: This isn't clear-eyed. We need 2 b patient.

KORY: I like the idea of drama as much as anyone, but I'm pretty on board with not having an actual war with China.

JOHANNSEN: Agreed. The nukes almost hitting the homeland last year was plenty close enough for me for this lifetime. Like Dave said, I enjoy the drama and the clicks from the headlines, but there's an edge I don't want to fall over. This is it.

BILSON: It doesn't have to be war or nothing, guys. There's a middle ground where we call China on their bullshit without engaging in total war. (Which they don't want, either.) But someone needs to stand up to them and say, "This is enough." And now is the time.

CHALKE: Not sure I'm comfortable with a National Security Advisor that's this confrontational. Starting to wonder if Nealon is affecting your thinking.

Chapman smiled as he watched the consensus form. "How do you like that, Bilson, you little bitch?"

FLANAGAN: Agree with the others. Brinksmanship with nukes is a fad best left in the eighties. Our agenda is mostly toast if Gondry loses re-election and there's no quicker path to that than getting in any kind of a scuffle with China. I'm cool with the rage-clicks from our news brothers, but would rather not see things get out of control. This talk sounds like a big step in that direction, Russ. I'm not for it.

BILSON: Your purview is the courts, Flanagan. Chapman's is tech, Chalke's is law enforcement. The news guys = obvious. My background is Washington politics, and I'm telling you, you're all being short sighted here. If Gondry takes a hit because he looks weak on China, re-election is not happening. So...poof to the agenda then, too.

CHAPMAN: Seriously, guys...I'm all in on making this China busi-

ness disappear. I know you can't steer the ship from your three respective publications, but you can influence the direction, and I can mess with the algorithms to downrank anything negative on China in the search engine or even get flagged as a hoax story and banned from appearing on Socialite. Back when Inquest was the biggest search engine on the scene, I couldn't do that, but now...

Jaime smiled.

CHAPMAN: We can totally do it. I have 75% of the search engine traffic on any given day and growing. I have the largest two social networks and can influence opinion in my peer set.

KORY: My reporters are in Slack channels with their peers. We could put feelers out, see if we get any pushback. That'd tell you which sites were going to write anti-China articles.

CHAPMAN: And I can downrank them until they stop that bullshit. Their organic traffic will die overnight, and they'll be crying for a meeting to figure it out.

This was all in his power now. That was the dirty secret of the modern news media; they relied on social networks for their very lifeblood. Without those shares, they'd croak in short order.

JOHANNSEN: If you could give us a little boost, we can do a similar thing. Our reporters are in constant communication with their peer set as well. Downrank the competitors who don't toe the line and they could watch the info stop circulating.

CHAPMAN: Done.

Johannsen had to be smiling on the other end of his screen. This was like Christmas for the media people.

BYRD: I m so in!!! I hav the presidents ear and will def get the msg out u guys

CHAPMAN: Good. We need to be the adults in the room. Be more circumspect than the idiots out there.

Because we're better than them, Chapman didn't type. He knew it, though. Everyone knew it.

CHAPMAN: What do you say, Bilson?

He waited.

Everyone waited.

It took a long minute of creeping uncertainty before he – and everyone else – realized that wherever he was, whatever he was doing...

...Bilson didn't answer.

CHAPTER EIGHTY-FIVE

Sienna

"We need to talk," Bilson said, barging in as I opened my door. He took no notice of the fact I was standing there in a bathrobe with an AR-15 strapped to my back, nor that I was surprised to see him.

"Uh, okay," I said as he stalked past me, turning my head to follow his path.

He stopped in the middle of the living room and turned, looking around furiously. His eyes alighted on something in the kitchen, and he surged around the corner, disappearing behind the wall that separated my entryway from my kitchen.

"Uh...what are you doing?" I asked. I realized he'd whispered when he came in, something I hadn't noticed at the time given I'd just been having a conversation with Jian – who was still in the bedroom, door closed – at meta-low volumes. Whispers sounded like shouts by comparison to my most recent conversation.

I came around the corner to find Bilson unplugging my phone, holding it out from his body as far as he could, completely lateral so it was facing up toward the ceiling. Keeping it in that odd position, extended from him like it was about to explode, he walked it over to my fridge and opened the door. He cast it onto the (empty) top shelf, then pulled out his own and threw it in there as well before slamming the door shut.

Blinking at him, I started to ask, "What the f–"

He held up a hand urgently to his lips, and spun, scanning the apartment. When his eyes alighted on my laptop, sitting on my kitchen table, he snatched it up and then tossed it into the refrigerator after the phones. Apparently satisfied, he closed it again and looked around once more. "Do you have any other electronics like that? Tablet computer, other phones, wearables...?"

"Uh, no, I'm a luddite, so you've successfully fridged all my electronics." I stared at him, arms crossed over my fluffy robe. He hadn't even said anything about the AR-15 still slung over my shoulder, and I felt like on a normal night, that would have been the first thing a guy like Bilson would have commented on. Tonight, nada, though, which told me something about his state of mind. "Is there a reason for that, or do you just think my devices needed a time out to cool off?"

"You're being watched," he said, eyes animated as he stepped closer. "Constantly."

I rolled my eyes. "Duh. Tell me something I don't know."

His eyes got wider, more wild. "Chalke is behind it."

"Well, I kinda figured," I said. "She did give me my phone and laptop. I assumed they stuck something in my cloud downloads to bug me at work and play. Wouldn't want me to have a moment of joy or despair without seeing it."

Bilson sagged, looking flabbergasted. "You...knew?"

"I strongly suspected, yeah," I said. "I mean, come on – I got pushed into this gig. The whole game for Chalke has been to control me. You can't do that unless you have a baseline idea of what your target is up to."

Bilson's eyes flicked around; I could almost read his thoughts by the paranoia written on his face.

"There are no ordinary wiretaps, if that's what you're thinking," I said. When he registered surprise, I went on. "I made friends with the electronics guy in New York and he taught me how to sweep for bugs. I do it twice a day. Haven't found any yet, presumably because they consider me well-covered with the Remote Access Trojans in my electronics." Kinda arrogant on their part, but hey...that was who I was dealing with.

Bilson seemed to think about this for a moment. "I fear I've made a terrible mistake."

"Well, if it's just about bugging me, I forgive you," I said. "Like I said...I knew what I was getting into."

"How?" Bilson asked, straightening, his face beneath the glasses the most curiously surprised I could recall seeing him. "How could you possibly have known?"

"I know the 'Washington consensus' is that I'm stupid," I said, slowly, feeling a little heat in my face, "but, I mean...I investigate crimes for a living and a hobby. I know how these things work. I've put surveillance on people, I'm familiar with the methods. And I'm really, really paranoid." A slight lie buried in a lot of truths, but they didn't need to know about Harry.

Bilson stroked his face. He was sweating profusely. "This China thing...it's a mess."

"Maybe more than you know," I said. "But I guess I should ask – what do you mean?"

"There are powerful forces that want to bury this story," Bilson said, stepping closer to me. "They want it to just...disappear. Attribute the attack on you to random violence or a past grudge...they want to make the China angle vanish so they can get back to business as usual." He licked his lips. "So they can solidify the consensus and move on, unchallenged."

"What are they doing?" I asked.

"Doesn't matter." Bilson had looked like he wanted to say something for a moment, then broke off. "What's important is what we do about it."

"Why the sudden change of heart?" I asked. "I mean, don't get me wrong – I'm happy to have someone on my side for once, but...why?"

Bilson stared at the ground. "How can you look at what's happening here...and not see yourself in these stories?" He turned his head to look at me. "That professor at Georgetown...what did she do to deserve being almost kidnapped by the

Chinese government? I mean, what would they have done with her if they'd succeeded?" He swallowed visibly. "I've met her before, I'm pretty sure. At a party at Georgetown. She's smart. Educated. Like most of the people I've associated with. Not particularly well-connected, but that's hardly a sin worth vanquishing her to the stocks for."

"So you're saying," I said, "if it could happen to her...?"

"If they're that brassy," Bilson said, "to attempt an abduction of an American citizen in the middle of the morning without bothering to cover their tracks...what won't they do? What wouldn't they do to you, or me, if we stood up and said something against their agenda?" He looked me right in the eye. "Hell...they already showed us with you yesterday."

"Yes, they did," I said softly. "And I think they did it a whole lot more than with just that one container load." I chewed my lip, hesitating. "I think I've figured out *why* they're doing it."

I took a deep breath; I was ready to trust Bilson in this, at least. I wasn't going to call out for Jian to join us, but I needed to at least get this out to someone besides myself and him.

Bilson just watched me, head tilted slightly, waiting.

"I think China took its DNA profiling to the next level," I said. "They're already grabbing it from their citizens at regular doctors' appointments through their health system to identify their 'undesirables,' like the Uighur Muslims they're interning in camps. I think they escalated things, using the DNA they're collecting to establish a 'map' to people with genetic heritages ripe with certain latent metahuman powers."

Bilson's eyes narrowed. "'Latent?'"

"Most humans have the ability to develop metahuman powers," I said. "With the proper serum, they go from normal to meta – of some sort. But lots of meta powers are weak, bordering on useless. The really strong ones, like mine, or, say, a Gavrikov's? Those are the ones that a country could put to work for their army."

Bilson nodded slowly, the facts snapping into place like puzzle pieces in his head. "They're after these valuable powers."

"I think so," I said. "Their metahuman numbers were wiped out in the war. I think this kidnapping scheme is an attempt to restart that program, by hook or by crook, with some favorable powers that they maybe don't possess latently in enough numbers in the homeland."

"My God," Bilson breathed. "That's eugenics."

"Basically, yeah. It's probably even worse than it sounds when you get into their next steps," I said, not really wanting to delve into Jian's theories about how far China would go to produce loyal supersoldiers. "But at least now we know why they were willing to do this."

Bilson's eyes bulged. "This is monstrous. All this...they're doing all this...for a strategic advantage?"

"Think about what metahumans can do," I said. "Think about how that might matter to a country obsessed with becoming preeminent in the world. I know metas can't rule countries like they used to be able to, pre-World War I, but certain powers, like Harmon's..."

"They're invaluable," Bilson said, nodding slowly. "You could dominate your enemies with a clutch of loyal telepaths."

I thought of how Zollers had subverted Russia only last year by himself, and how Rose had quietly taken over Scotland on her own. "Yes. And with other powers you could ruin your biggest enemies, destroy their critical cities, sneak attack their armies. Imagine a Gavrikov stepping off a plane, riding into the middle of New York City and lighting off." I shrugged. "Completely deniable. Think about it – the Glass Blower wrecked a building in the middle of the city and they never caught him." I couldn't remember if Yvonne had ever been outed as a she. There certainly weren't any surveillance photos of her floating around in the case file, which I'd reviewed as part of my job.

Bilson paled. "Yes. The strategic possibilities are endless. We need to stop China."

"I'd like to," I said. "Really. I don't want to see innocent people forced into servitude under China's system of serfdom. But..." I shrugged. "My sway at the bureau is limited. I was at a near dead-end before this thing happened yesterday, poking at the edges of a guy named Wu Huang's affairs for clues–"

"Huang?" Bilson frowned. "The one that signed the deal with Jaime Chapman?"

"The very one," I said. "He's hooked into this, somehow."

Bilson stared into space over my shoulder. "Chapman...he owns that DNA registry company, Lineage."

"You think that's where this DNA map came from? Not a bad guess." And it wasn't. Bilson was no boob, that was a logical assumption.

"He's had access to your surveillance," Bilson said quietly. There was a desperation in his eyes that smelled like guilt to me.

I looked at the fridge. "Yeah. That figures." Looking back at Bilson, I asked, "If he's talking to his business partner Huang, and can monitor my every move, you think he...?" I didn't want to finish that sentence.

Bilson did it for me. "Orchestrated the hit on you yesterday?" His eyes found his shoes. "I wouldn't have wanted to believe it before, that Jaime Chapman could be that callous, that cold, but..." He stared into space, and when he spoke again, it was in a very brittle voice. "Yes. Wittingly or un, I think he had a part in what happened to you yesterday."

"I can't deal with that right now," I said, turning my back on Bilson. "Whatever Chapman has going on, with Chalke or whoever...I have to focus on this. Front and center needs to be the kidnapping, needs to be China." I spun back on Bilson. "There are other victims out there, unreported. China's got to move them, because there are limits to how long they can keep these people fed, watered and alive, especially in this heat. Unless they've got some kind of compound to hide them in on US soil."

"I can look into that," Bilson said, staring up at me with ghostly resolve. "One of my groups...we do oppo research on our political enemies. Their corporate connections. I can set my people to looking into this Huang. See what else he owns. What we can trace to him. Maybe, if he's the owner of this property where they're being held...or has a dock slip somewhere..."

"It could give us a clue," I said. "Which we desperately need right now."

Bilson nodded once, then hesitated. "Is this how it is for you? All the time?"

That one caught me off guard. "What do you mean?"

"There's this...clarity to what you do that I didn't anticipate," Bilson said, speaking quietly and slowly. "I thought the black hats and white hats idea...that it was passe. Product of a simpler time that was never really that simple." When his eyes found mine, he looked...haunted. "But there really are evil people doing evil things. It's not some remnant of the past, some overstatement of modern political disagreements. There are genuine...evil...people running China right now."

I nodded. "Yes. But we can stop them. At least in this."

He seemed to take heart from that. "And we will." Throwing open the fridge, he seized his phone and was dialing it almost before it was fully in his hand.

"While you do that I'm gonna...go change," I said, pointing a thumb at my bedroom door. He nodded, though distantly, his mind already on the conversation he was about to have.

I slipped into the bedroom and found Jian just behind the door. "You heard that?" I asked, meta-low.

He nodded. "Do you trust him?"

"To a point," I said. "But I need you to do something while he's chasing that lead. Do you remember the woman I met with outside my office yesterday?"

Jian looked about as abashed as a naked man could without having dropped his sheet. "The one in yoga pants?"

"Yeah," I said. "I need to talk to her, and I can't do it by phone or in any other way that can be electronically intercepted." Michelle had never contacted me by phone, come to think of it, at least not since she'd come to town. And a woman as connected as her surely could have rustled up – or asked for – my cell number if she'd been of a mind to.

"I...followed her after your talk," Jian said, embarrassment giving his cheeks a nice glow. "She's staying at a hotel off–"

"Find her," I said. "Tell her what you've told me. Tell her I'm under surveillance, but that I'm seeking an exit port that the Chinese kidnapping vics could have been shipped out of. She's got connections in the area, maybe they can help."

Jian nodded, and stepped back toward the window, opening it with one hand. Then he started to shift, sheet dropping as he flapped his way out into the night.

I shut it behind him, catching a breath of the warm, humid air of summer's dawn coming just over the horizon. Hopefully one of my leads would turn up something, and we could get these people rescued before the Chinese government made them vanish for good.

CHAPTER EIGHTY-SIX

Chapman

"Hey, Wu," Chapman said, a little cooler than he might have yesterday. He stared out the windows in back of his house, into the green, vibrant brush and trees back there. The early morning light wasn't even close to rising yet, but the stupid Network text he'd been on this morning had set his mind whirling long after everyone else had logged off.

And dumbass Bilson still hadn't replied. That was concerning. At least the rest of them were in agreement.

"I've got some good news regarding regulatory approval in Beijing," Wu said.

Chapman felt a flare of joy cut through his black mood. "They're coming around?"

"They are indeed," Wu said, and Chapman could hear the smile. "They see the value in what your company brings to the table for long-term communication. Provided we can put the appropriate safeguards in place to assuage worries that criminals or foreign actors won't be able to propagandize to the Chinese people, we have approval to move forward."

Chapman pumped his fist, a quick, cathartic jerk of emotion

expelling itself. "I'm glad to hear that, Wu. I know we've both had to jump through some hoops to make it happen, but this is a deal worth making some sacrifices for. And my commitment to making sure your government feels comfortable with what we do is absolute."

"I think they've seen that with your cooperation over the last days," Wu said. "I don't think things would have calmed down quite as much if you hadn't been steering us through this, Jaime. I might have to make a trip stateside in a few days. I'll have more news then. I'm not sure exactly when yet, but can we get together for dinner, if you're up for it?"

"We'll make it work," Chapman said, all smiles. "See you then, Wu."

Victory.

CHAPTER EIGHTY-SEVEN

Julie Blair

"Hey, Julie, come on in and have a seat," White House Communications Director Betsy Suffolk was smiling as she motioned Julie in.

"Thanks," Julie said, taking the proffered seat in the smallish office and pulling her chair closer to the desk. She smoothed out some wrinkles in her skirt; this was the boss, after all. This hadn't been a scheduled meeting, but rather one that had appeared on her calendar suddenly. Julie smiled nervously, waiting to see what would happen, for Betsy to speak first.

"I've been following that email you forwarded me yesterday with some interest," Betsy said, looking at her own computer. "The one from the donor in New York?"

"Yes," Julie said, still feeling a vague churn of nerves. As one did when called into the boss's office unexpectedly.

"It was a good call, pushing it up to me," Betsy said, glancing at the computer. She looked back at Julie and smiled. "I know you're getting cross traffic lately from a lot of different directions as we're moving toward the general election and the other guys are finishing up their primary. It's a tough gig, especially given how...aggressive the president has been in moving in different directions simultaneously, policy-wise."

Julie kept the smile pasted on her face. It was a joke among the rank and file that Gondry was a policy schizophrenic, trying to work on everything at once, from domestic to foreign, from healthcare to the judiciary to tax reform. It wasn't her place to critique her boss, though.

"But you folks are really soldering through," Betsy said, looking up from the screen again. If her inbox was anything like Julie's she'd probably gotten fifty emails while they were sitting here, forty-nine of them marked critical. "I just wanted to tell you 'good job' and attagirl.'" Betsy smiled.

"Oh. Well, thank you," Julie said.

"Keep up the great work," Betsy said. "I'll let you know what we find out about this missing nanny. I've sent it up the chain."

"Great," Julie said, almost falling over her chair as she left. She cleared it, though. Barely.

Well, this was an unexpected pleasure, Julie thought, a little more spring in her step as she walked back to her desk. Being recognized for her work. Heck, this was the best news she'd had all month.

CHAPTER EIGHTY-EIGHT

Sienna

"It's starting." Bilson's voice was quiet as he put down his phone, stuffing it under the seat cushion of my couch.

"What?" I asked. I'd dressed after sending Jian on his way and before rejoining Bilson, putting on my Kevlar vest, my sidearms, and slinging the AR-15 back over my clothing. He'd made some calls, presumably to his contacts, and had been reading his phone when I'd come back out, not saying a word. I hadn't broken the silence, instead fighting my tangled hair into a ponytail. Because I had a feeling I'd need it up for whatever was coming.

"Info ops," he mouthed, beckoning me toward the bedroom. "Four glowing stories on China dropped in major news outlets today." He must have sensed I wasn't quite sure what he was talking about, so he broke it down. Such a considerate teacher. "Reporters get their stories from sources. People like me feed them almost fully-formed stories these days. Sometimes they're even pre-written and the reporter just puts their name on them. That's what I'm seeing planted in the pages of papers and news sites – credible ones, too. It's what we call an 'info op,' where someone wants to change the narrative on something, form a new one by getting a chorus of reporters singing the same song in unison. In this case..."

"They want China to look good," I said. "Though you gotta tell me something – is there ever a time when the corporate media doesn't want China to look good? Because I feel like they go out of their way to make the PRC the heroes in stories, to not breathe a bad word about China in any Hollywood production, and they rarely get flak in the major papers."

"They've got a deeply vested interest in China," Bilson said, staring straight ahead. "I don't know if I'll be National Security Advisor or if I've scuttled my chances this morning, but either way I know this – China needs to answer for what they did here. In full view of the public, diplomatic relations be damned."

"A man with moral courage," I said quietly. "You're not going to make it long in Washington with an attitude like that, Mr. Smith."

Bilson chuckled. "Do I sound that naïve?"

"You don't sound as jaded," I said. "As when I first started talking to you, anyway."

He bowed his head. "I'm sorry for what I've done to you, talking you down the last few years. I've been part of a...group. One that's viewed you, the things you've done, as antithetical to our aims for progress. The level of violence you've brought to bear, the way you've blown up carefully-crafted discussions...and of course what you did to President Harmon...we viewed you as a threat, this group."

"Oh, it's a group?" I asked with a slight drip of sarcasm. I checked over my shoulder to make sure there was no phone nearby, and whispered, "I thought of it as more of a...Network."

Bilson blinked a few times. "You...know about us?"

"I'm not stupid," I said. "You think I didn't notice somebody was trying to run me into a ditch or under a bus? Whichever. Hell, both."

"But we were secret," Bilson hissed.

"You know what Ben Franklin said about secrets." I caught a blank look from him. "'Three may keep a secret, if two of them are dead.'"

Bilson's eyes widened. "That's dark."

"It's accurate," I said. "Your secret club isn't that secret. I know you've been running me for the last year."

Bilson looked like he really struggled with that revelation, but finally got it under control. "Yes. We have been. But I think I'm broken from them at this point. You need to understand something about this group, though – they are very serious people. We had a consensus. Plans. Influence. Power. Add those together, it's a dangerous combination."

"Why are you telling me this?" I asked.

"Because these people are still controlling you," Bilson said. "Or trying. They want you to lay off China."

I held my breath for a hot second before responding. "I've tried to go along. Get along, these last few months. But letting this sort of thing go...it's not in my nature."

"I know," Bilson said. "But if you do this..." He stopped. Smiled. "*When* you do this...they're going to be upset. You need to know that Chalke is already at her limit with you, or damned close."

"What are you going to do?" I asked.

Bilson paused, thinking. "I'm going to help you." He stared over my shoulder. "I've been doing the wrong thing for a while now." He dropped his gaze to my eyes, and smiled. "I think it would feel good to do the right thing here. Righteous, you know. Truly, not that faux-righteous feeling you get when delivering a sick Twitter burn."

"Wouldn't know about that last thing," I said, and heard something at the window. I turned and found Jian, in pigeon form, scrabbling there. "Excuse me for a second."

"Is that a...are you opening your window for that p – gyahhh!"

Bilson shouted and leapt back as Jian sprouted back into human form, snatching the bedspread and wrapping it around himself deftly as he did so.

"Jian, this is Russ Bilson, political operative," I said, "Bilson, this is Jian, Chinese dissident meta and that white tiger that's been saving me the last few days."

Jian exchanged a look with me, then shrugged. "Nice to meet you. Michelle is on her way. She's less than a mile away, so she will be here soon. Also, she said she might have something for you."

"That'd be nice," I said. "I hate flying blind. Though I'm not flying much these days." I looked to Bilson. "How do we keep our...internal troubles at bay while we go deal with this? I don't want governmental interference."

"Leave your phone here," Bilson said.

"Simple as that?" I asked.

He nodded. "I doubt they've got mine yet, but I'll leave it behind, too, just in case."

"Okay," I said, and looked at Jian. "You got a phone?"

Jian made a face at me. "Yes, but not on me." He looked down, clearly indicating his washboard abs. "You see anywhere I could hide a phone?"

"Prison wallet?" I shrugged.

He shook his head, looking vaguely offended at the suggestion.

"All right, let's get out on the street," I said, keeping my voice down. "I don't want to chance being overheard. But we'll need transport."

"My Maserati's parked outside," Bilson said. Then he frowned. "But it's got a LoJack, and they might be able to track it."

"I guess this rules out a rideshare app, too," I said. "I left my FBI SUV at the office. And it's definitely GPS tracked."

"Michelle has a car," Jian said.

"Guess she's our designated driver," I said, looking at him. "Unless you want to shift into a gryphon and I can ride you bare-back like..." The look on his face made clear that was a firm *NO*. "Car it is, then."

We cleared out of the apartment as quietly as possible, Jian going out the window as a pigeon again, Bilson and I tiptoeing past his phone and shutting the door silently. I had my AR still slung over my shoulder; if Bilson had noticed it, he hadn't said anything about it yet. Maybe he'd just sort of accepted the game we were in.

"This is exciting," Bilson whispered, huffing a little as we cleared the last round of stairs. "Is it always this exciting?"

"For better or worse, yeah," I said, coat dangling behind me as I hit the street, slightly cool morning air washing over me as I left the stuffy apartment. The temp had dropped overnight, even more shocking since I hadn't noticed all those times I'd opened my window for Jian. "The threat of death being elevated tends to cause the pulse to race."

"It's very invigorating," Bilson agreed as a four-door compact SUV screeched to a halt in front of us.

Michelle rolled down the front window, mirrored sunglasses on as she looked out. "'Sup, dudes? Someone order Chinese takeout?"

"You're a laugh a minute, yoga pants." I came around to the passenger side before Bilson could, grabbing shotgun seating placement. "You're in the back, Bilson."

"We're about to face death, aren't we?" Bilson had a trace of a smile on his face as he slipped in the back. "You should call me Russ."

"All right...Russ," I said as we shut the doors. The Washington morning was still dark and the streets calm, near empty.

Jian the pigeon flew above us, visible through the open sunroof, a shadowy outline keeping pace with the SUV from above. "He better not shit on my rental," Michelle said with clear annoyance.

"Where we going?" I asked. It seemed important. Maybe not as important as the fact that Michelle took the next corner at about ninety and almost flipped the SUV, but up there, somewhere in order of importance.

"Port of Baltimore," she said, flipping her unlocked phone at me. "Chinese flagged cargo vessel *Zoushan* left out yesterday for Wenzhou, just a few hours before your raid. Cargo of soybeans and pork." She smiled. "Except it's not actually soybeans and pork."

"How do you know that?" Bilson asked. When she didn't answer immediately, he turned to me. "How does she know that?"

"Michelle's a recovering Triad boss," I said. "She's hooked into the underground, and I'm guessing if she says some shit's being smuggled on that vessel...well, she would know?"

Michelle grinned. "'Recovering Triad boss?' I like that. 'It has been 92 days since our last instance of criminal activity.'"

I checked the chamber on my AR. "Time to reset that counter to zero. But first..." I took a long breath. "...We need to make a quick stop." I thought about it for a second. "And a phone call."

CHAPTER EIGHTY-NINE

There was a helicopter pad not far from the Port of Baltimore. Bilson had made the call, booking the flight as I'd requested, with an insistence on urgency. The rotors were already spinning on the old Kiowa model helo when we pulled up.

"I know I'm probably late to the party in asking this," Bilson said, "but it's my first...uh...raid, so...what's the protocol here?"

I hoisted my weapons, checking my AR sling and making sure my belt held the new addition. It did. Sturdy thing, carrying my two pistols, spare mags, and my newest acquisition. "The protocol is this – I get out to the ship, I drop. Shit goes down, day gets saved, celebrations ensue."

"That sounds...simple," Bilson said.

"Lemme cut you in on a secret – it's never that simple," I said. "Something's bound to go wrong. Which is why you need to observe safely from the shore. See ya, Russ." I gave him a little wave goodbye.

"No, wait!" Bilson charged forward to walk next to me. "I'm not leaving you."

I sighed. "Russ...I'm going into battle here, okay? I know you want to help, but please – what good are you going to do in a fight?"

"I don't know," he said, after a moment of his face flitting around, suggesting he desperately wanted to find an answer to that. "But I *need* to go with you."

"'Need' is probably overstating it," I said. "I like you now, Russ. I like your turnaround. I really like the promise of you helping navigate the diplomatic mess I'm about to cause and maybe subvert your superpals' Network. I would hate to compromise that by getting you killed for no reason, which is what will almost certainly happen if you come with me."

"I can wait in the helicopter," he said. "But I just...I want to be of use."

I caught a look from Michelle with her reflective lenses. "I suppose you want to come, too?"

"Oh, I'm coming," she said, smacking her lips. "My yoga pants and I are not missing this flight."

"How do you and your yoga pants feel about having to answer FBI questions in an interview after this is over?" I asked.

She didn't even miss a beat. "On the other hand, I'm not good with guns, I can't fly a helicopter, and I'm not of much use in a fight, so maybe we call it good with giving you a ride and sending you on your way?"

I looked at Bilson. "See her? She's smart. Be like Michelle."

"Wait." Bilson put a hand on my shoulder. "Without us or even a phone, you're going to be out there on your own." Jian the pigeon squawked overhead. "Or nearly so. What happens if things go wrong?" He looked like he was ready to pop, all that energy, all that motherly worry, nowhere to push it. "I don't know how I could just sit back and let this happen."

I stared at Bilson, then leaned in. "So...don't."

He blinked. "Don't...what?"

"Don't just sit back," I said. "Do what you're supposed to do. What you're good at." He still didn't get it. "Go to your office, call up your press contacts, and push back on this stupid China propaganda bullshit. Tell my story. Get your friends interested in it. Subvert the Network narrative and push some inconvenient truths out there. Michelle, give me your phone."

She looked at me suspiciously from behind those reflective glasses, but offered it to me, unlocked.

I found the record function and turned it on, set it up for a selfie video and hit record. "My name is Sienna Nealon, I'm an FBI agent...well, you know who I am. I've received a tipoff about a Chinese merchant vessel that departed the Port of Baltimore yesterday afternoon with some fifty to a hundred kidnappees on board of the same kind I recovered from the port two days ago. I am currently on my way to pursue this lead. My partner, Xavier Holloway, was shot and killed in what I believe was a Chinese government attempt to keep me from discovering this conspiracy. More ships, more kidnappings have occurred around the United States but haven't been reported because the Chinese government is picking out people who mostly won't be missed. I believe they are taking these people because they have genetic predisposition for metahuman powers that the Chinese government covets after the loss of their own program in 2012." I looked out toward the horizon. "People need to know what the Chinese government is up to. They are the single largest human rights abuser on the planet and almost no one talks about it because they control our corporate media with threats to shut down their access to Chinese markets and Chinese news sources, which would cost these companies billions. This silence cannot be allowed to continue." I looked right into the camera. "So I'm going to make some noise, in my own inimitable way. Good luck ignoring that."

Clicking the record button off, I tossed it back to Bilson. "There. That ought to interest at least a few people. Maybe trend on Socialite or something."

Bilson looked a little pained. "Maybe not Socialite. But you're right – I'll do what I can, my way."

"Good man," I said, and walked away.

"Good luck!" Michelle shouted. "Oh, and Sienna?"

I looked back in time to see that she'd thrown something at me. I reached out and caught it instinctively, only realizing after I had that she'd tossed me her glasses.

She smiled, and it was the kind that crinkled to the edge of her eyes. "Give 'em hell?"

"My own special blend," I said, putting on the glasses. "Locally sourced, artisanal, but definitely not small batch. And I raise every bit of it myself."

CHAPTER NINETY

"I see you're coming loaded for bear," the pilot said as I got into the helo. "Gotta tell you, I haven't taken on a passenger with a weapon load like that since my last tour in Afghanistan."

"You know who I am, right?" I asked, flashing my FBI ID anyway.

"It'd be hard not to know you, ma'am," he said, completely straitlaced and squared away beneath his own ball cap, reflective aviator glasses and headset complete with boom mic. "Where are we heading today? Because I'm assuming it's not just a leisure tour."

"A Chinese cargo ship left the Port of Baltimore yesterday afternoon," I said. "I need to intercept it."

He looked at me levelly. Couldn't see his eyes behind those glasses. Which was probably the same for him. "Why not take an FBI chopper?"

"Because I hired you," I said. Then I looked back at Bilson. "Or my friend did. What's your name?"

"Cayce," he said. It sounded like "Case." "But you didn't really answer the question."

"Because the FBI would like this problem to go away without having to go all-in on it," I said. "There's a diplomatic incident waiting at the end of this particular rainbow if you know what I mean, and they're not keen to bury their noses in that. They prefer the sand."

Cayce almost smiled. "I'm not real excited to get in trouble either, ma'am. Not for a lone fare. And if your cargo ship left yesterday, it could be a hell of a long ways off by now."

I shook my head. "No. They travel at about ten knots, which is around 11 miles an hour. It's 120 miles to the Chesapeake Bay Bridge, and I know the general bearing they'll take after that to Wenzhou." I'd looked it up on Michelle's phone while we drove. "The search radius is going to be small."

Cayce seemed to hesitate. "Okay. Well, I can get you there, but if you get into trouble...I'm not hanging around. I did my time, and I'm not sticking my nose into whatever you're getting into here. Not without knowing what it's about."

"It's about kidnapping and human trafficking, Cayce," I said as he paused, hand frozen on the stick. "By the Chinese government."

I couldn't tell if that registered or not, but Cayce didn't say anything. Just put his hands on the collective and then increased the power to the engine. Pretty soon we were lifting off, the bird coming around to a southeast vector and then leaning hard into the wind as we sprinted over the Chesapeake Bay, trying to find that ship.

CHAPTER NINETY-ONE

Chapman

C*HAPMAN: Has anyone heard from Bilson?*

Jaime waited, staring at the screen.

CHALKE: No. And Nealon is off grid, too. Her phone is at her apartment but she's not answering. At all.

Chapman cursed out loud and pulled up the feed to her phone.

Darkness. And a distant hum. That was all he was getting, and the signal was spotty.

FLANAGAN: What is up with Bilson?

Chapman pondered a course of action on that; he'd had the Escapade app designed at his direction. It was pretty straightforward – mostly. It kept to itself, had top-level encryption, didn't track its users. That last thing would have been easy to pick up, so he hadn't bothered to piss off his would-be colleagues by doing anything that obvious.

But he was the CEO of the world's biggest tech company, owner of both the largest social network and most-used search engine. Those had their own apps, their own EULAs, and their own...quirks. Loudly fussed about quirks, but quirks nonetheless. Like tracking features sprinkled throughout the software.

And for a bunch of brilliant people in their individual fields, the members of the Network were dumb as hell in *his* field.

He pushed a button on the master Escapade program running on his computer. It was a simple bit of programming, not designed to cause a stir. It really didn't do much, even. A little ping, in which the program reached outside its own use of the operating systems of the member's smartphones...

And nudged their FindIt and/or Socialite apps. Every single one of these clowns had at least one of them installed on their phone. Most had both.

The "nudge," as it were, was designed to do one thing. Ping the location systems of said apps, telling them to report in to Socialite and FindIt's main servers. He was looking to add the same functionality with Instaphoto, but that was more of a problem in that – near as he could tell – half the Network didn't use it. Well, it was more of a millennial service.

Location results popped up on a specialized box on his screen in seconds. Chalke was at the Hoover Building; Flanagan, Johannsen, Byrd, and Kory were all at their respective offices in the various boroughs of New York City. Mostly Manhattan, except for that hipster Kory with his Brooklyn address. He was laughable; a tech guy who hadn't even bothered to figure out how the app worked before loading it on his phone. Moron.

Ah, there was Bilson. In DC, no less. And at...

Shit. He was at Nealon's apartment. Or at least his phone was.

Chapman looked around his empty office, contemplating. What could that mean, Bilson's phone being at Nealon's apartment? They'd been working this thing together, sure, but had he gone...whatever the politically correct phrase for "native" was in this situation? "Anti-China," probably.

How could he even share this with the Network?

He couldn't. Not without revealing that he had a way of tracking them.

What could he even do about it?

Nothing, really. It wasn't as though he had tremendous influence in DC. Lobbyists and an office, sure. But real influence...? Someone he could trust to go over there and grab Bilson, shove him in the back of a car, and make him go wherever he wanted?

Well, that was the kind of vulgar exercise that Chapman had never really bought into.

Which left him frowning at the display, deciding how best to handle this little tidbit of information.

He was still considering it five minutes later when everything went straight to hell.

CHAPTER NINETY-TWO

Sienna

"I think that's your freighter," Cayce said as we rumbled across the dark ocean, hints of purple on the horizon indicating the sun might be rising sometime soon-ish.

There were several ships on the water before us, at varying distances. The closest was a cargo ship, for sure, with containers piled up on deck in a tight square. The bridge was on a tower near the back of the ship, facing away from us, and I could see the red flag of China painted across the flat stern.

"I think you're probably right," I said, "but get me a little closer, will you?"

"I'll get you as close as I can without crashing," Cayce said, and there was an edge in his voice. "What you do after that is going to be your business, though, you understand?"

"I understand completely," I said. "Not your mission, not your monkeys. We're copacetic, Cayce. You can drop me off and bail if you need to."

"Thanks for permission," he said, dripping sarcasm. Yeah, he wanted no part of what I was up to. Logical, really; it was the sort of thing a guy could lose his pilot's license for, after all.

"Can you take us in low?" I asked. "I don't want them to see us coming."

Cayce's lips twisted as he contemplated my request. "Best I can do is maybe come in at a forty-five degree angle behind the bridge on the starboard side. They'll have no visual on us, but depending on their radar they may register us. And this thing ain't quiet, so..."

"Got it," I said. "Sweep in on them, drop me on the bow, and boogie."

He nodded, once, and I sensed that was all I was going to get out of him.

The helo dove toward the water, and soon we were skimming the surface, the skids of the Kiowa rolling over the choppy waves. It had a black tint to it, like oil, purple sky barely giving it any light to work with. The *Zoushan*'s superstructure was lit up, as were various points around the railing/hull, and as we grew closer the ship got bigger and bigger.

I'd failed to realize how huge the *Zoushan* was. It was three football fields long, riding out of the water some forty, fifty feet before the deck rails even started. Above that went another five or so cargo containers, layered across the deck in a huge cube of metal stacks filling the entire front of the vessel.

Cayce brought us along the side of the ship and then coasted us to a stop as he banked and came over the bow railing. Using the shipping containers that lined the front as a shield from the bridge of the *Zoushan*, he hovered there.

"You want out, this is your chance," he said tightly. "I'm bailing in five...four...three..."

I didn't need to be told twice. I was out of my seatbelt and out the door before he even started the two count, my AR in hand and my other equipment in my belt. He'd brought us to ten feet over the deck, and the moment I was out and down, the helicopter ducked over the side in a speed run maneuver, bolting off the opposite direction from whence he'd come.

Rising to my feet, I found myself on the forecastle, a mountain of shipping containers rising up in front of me. They were stacked side to side, tight enough that I could barely wedge a hand in between them. It was like a warehouse of metal, and I hurried across the empty forecastle, looking for cover.

Once I was against the shipping container mountain, I eased along it to the side railing. Coming to its end, I looked out and along the railed side of the ship.

It stretched a long damned way, a walking path no bigger than five, ten feet across all the way to the bridge tower. No cover, nothing, for the length of the forward container mountain. A perfect shooting gallery if I got caught out there, nowhere to hide for two hundred yards or more.

A quick trot back to the starboard side of the ship revealed a perfect mirror of a situation. Wide open traversal with zero cover for a long distance. Shit.

I decided to look for a third way, and that meant climbing the cargo containers. Snugging my AR-15 and checking once more along the side route to make sure it was clear of any crew, I started to climb.

It wasn't slow going, but it was delicate work. The only handholds available were the spaces between each cargo container. Each container was approximately eight to ten feet high, so I'd leap and grab, then hang there for a second before leaping again.

Going at that pace, it only took me twenty seconds or so to reach the top of the mountain. Once I had my hands on it, I scaled swiftly, tired of hanging my ass out in the open air, waiting for a guard to come along and drill me.

I rolled onto the top of the container, staying supine. In the distance, across the container stacks, I could see the ship's bridge island, with a huge platform walkway in front of it like a balcony. Someone was up there on the superstructure, and I kept flat, hoping not to draw the eye with movement.

Still, I slowly moved to get a hand on my AR. I didn't want to shoot if I didn't have to, but I also didn't want to get caught out here with no recourse.

A quiet voice in the distance said something in Chinese. It sounded calm, reasonable. Not a shout for help or cry of alarm. That was reassuring. I was at a distance of a couple hundred yards, after all, just a lump on the top of a container. No cause to be worried about lil' ol' me.

I maintained that level of calm until something blew up underneath me like a distant car crash, and the ground dropped from under my back, tipping the world to an abrupt angle.

Sliding wildly, I rolled down the now nearly vertical container roof and bounced into midair. I found myself falling forty, fifty feet, and barely got my feet beneath me before I struck the ground.

I landed hard, but stayed upright. My AR was in my hands in a hot second, knees ringing with pain but not bad enough to dump me over. Nothing was broken, just stinging at the impact. I raised my weapon, looking over the iron sights, pointing it at the ship's superstructure.

Klieg lights switched on around me, stunningly bright, like I was on the fifty-yard line of a football field. I squinted against them, trying to see where I was.

It wasn't at all what I'd expected.

The containers that I thought had formed a solid block on the bow of the ship didn't; Cayce and I hadn't seen it on approach because we'd come in low, below the railing, but they weren't a solid cube of stacked containers at all.

They were a square ring, like an arena, with me in the damned middle.

When I'd been atop the front crate, someone had blown some sort of mild explosive along the seams. Now I could see the damage; every single container around the perimeter of the square had collapsed in, empty, creating a triangular slope to the top level. No matter where I'd climbed up the "arena," I'd have been dumped down here by the trap.

And it was a trap. Several of the bottom-level containers had popped open, and men in black tactical gear – that ubiquitous fashion choice of people the world over who wanted to die at my hands – were out in force. I counted ten, twenty, thirty, with guns all pointed at me. Under the floodlights shining in my eyes I could see some strangely configured weapons. Some had barrels that made them look like toy guns; others were long sniper-looking rifles with strangely fluted barrels. It took me a second to sort it all out in my head.

Sonic weapons.

Dart guns. With either suppressant or tranquilizer in them.

And there, atop the superstructure, two figures.

One was plainly, easily obvious – my old pal Firebeetle. He stared down at me with hard eyes over the lines of Chinese spec ops soldiers, but next to him – oh, next to him...

A grinning man with a wide smile, one that I'd seen oh so recently.

"Yan Liao," I called up to him, keeping my AR pointed in his direction. "Isn't the Chinese government going to be disappointed when you get them implicated in this?"

Liao, clearly not much of an actual diplomat, just laughed in a tone that told me how little he cared about what I thought. "For the prize of Sienna Nealon..." He leaned forward, planting his hands on the railing, and even two hundred yards away his grin shone obnoxiously, "...there is nothing China would not have risked."

CHAPTER NINETY-THREE

Chapman

K*ORY: Something's wrong.*

That was the message that greeted Chapman as he logged into the Escapade app. It boded ill, and set his stomach immediately on edge.

JOHANNSEN: Are you getting this, too?

Chapman just gaped. How could these idiots not share? It wasn't like they were all psychic – put the damned information out there! He started to type that, but Chalke beat him to the punch.

CHALKE: Care to share with the rest of the class?

BYRD: Whut up u guys

God, Byrd. What the hell did he even type with, his tongue?

KORY: The Slack channels my guys are on with reporters from other publications? They're lighting up right now with this video from Sienna Nealon. It's going viral.

Chapman was tapping at his keyboard before he even got done, then dialed his phone with one hand. He didn't wait for the person on the other end to finish answering before he barked an order: "Anything that's got Sienna Nealon's name on it, crush its organic search results. For Socialite, Instaphoto and FindIt. I want anyone sharing it to be deranked to oblivion, you hear me? Make it so their damned mother can't find it – hell, make the posts private and don't let them know it's done. Extinction Protocol."

"Uh, understood," came the reply. Chapman was hanging up before it even finished coming through.

CHAPMAN: I just killed it before it could trend. Anything with Nealon's name on it goes nowhere as of now.

KORY: It's getting passed around pretty heavily among our reporters.

Chapman felt a surge of irritation. What the hell was the point of these people if they weren't going to act?

CHAPMAN: Quash it. Anyone who puts out a story on this is going to get hit with the Nerf bat and watch their post engagements die until they don't even have a publication left. Any blog that puts it out there is going to be seeing organic traffic of their mother clicking their articles and pretty soon even she's going to forget to look at them.

JOHANNSEN: Where is this video coming from, Dave? My reporters can't seem to figure it out.

Chapman was already on it, dialing another number: "A Sienna Nealon video just got posted. Where was it uploaded from?"

Tapping keys on the other end, no talking. Thank God. "Looks like a political account. New Way Forward for America, LLC."

Chapman hung up, cursing a blue streak.

CHAPMAN: It was Bilson. Posted from one of his companies or PACs or fronts.

FLANAGAN: Whoa. What do we do about this?

Chapman only had to think about it for a second.

CHAPMAN: We kick him out. He's gone against the consensus and flagrantly, at that. Seems like he wants to go to war with us.

Chapman's jaw tightened.

CHAPMAN: Let's show him exactly what that means for him.

CHAPTER NINETY-FOUR

Sienna

Yan Liao's laugh rang over the wide arena of cargo containers that penned me in, echoing past all the tactical operators he'd stuck in here with me. It was loud and long and pretty Bond villain-esque, and I didn't hesitate to tell him so.

"You did all this for little ol' me?" I called, still staring at him over the iron sights of my weapon. A hundred-yard shot with a 5.56 was the sort of thing fresh Army privates did in their sleep during basic. "All this kidnapping? Ambushing? Killing? Conspiracy?"

"Not all for you, no," Liao said. "China had need for metahumans with certain powers. They didn't exist on the mainland in the numbers needed, if at all. Why not reach out our hand and pull a few of our former citizens back? They belong to us by rights anyway. As does the future." He leaned over the railing. "The world will belong to China...with your help."

"You think I'm going to help you?" I asked. Didn't put much denial in it, mostly because I wanted to see what he'd say.

"Not wittingly, perhaps," Liao said. "But you will." He gestured toward me. "Do you know how many eggs the average human female contains? How many *your* body contains, with its constant power of regeneration?" He couldn't help himself; he let a grin that could only be described as evil spread across his lips. "When we're done, China will boast an army of incubi and succubi in numbers enough to take over the world with ease."

"Dude," I said, "you have given way, way too much thought to my lady parts, and way, way too little to the other parts of me, which are of much more immediate applicability to your life."

Liao chuckled. "Like your trigger finger? Good luck making that shot before my men drop you." He made a show of looking at his fingernails. "You don't have to be alive for us to harvest you, just so you know. We have medical facilities on the ship equipped to take care of everything right now. But...it could go easy for you. We could treat you like a queen." He shrugged. "Or deal with you like a farm animal." That grin again. "Your choice."

The guys in black around me were moving to my flanks, circling me left and right. I doubted any of them were meta, based on the way they moved. Special forces, probably, but not meta.

"All right," I said, and let my AR-15 drop, safety off, the sling catching it as it fell by my side. I put my hands out to either side. "That queen deal sounds pretty good."

There was a dramatic pause as *everybody* stopped moving. Literally everybody. Liao, Firebeetle – who'd been pushing against the railing, clearly ready to jump over – and all the spec ops guys around me.

Liao was blinking, grin replaced by surprise. "...Really?"

I started to put my hands out in front of me, clearly far from my weapons, palms out. "I mean...why not? I would like to be treated like a queen. For once in my life."

This was failing to compute with Liao. He got a suspicious look. "I don't think I believe you."

"No, really," I said, acting like I was going to get down on my face, just give up and surrender. "I mean, if you're going to breed me like a bitch in heat anyway, why not get everything I can out of it? Oh, and by the by – psych."

I dropped face-first to the deck, caught myself on both

hands, pulling my knees to my chest and spring boarded backward, lashing out with my feet behind me.

The hiss of tranquilizer bullets whizzing by my face was bracing. They'd aimed for my torso but whoops – I wasn't there anymore. Now they were passing through where I'd been a moment before, feathered tails dancing past as I flew backward.

I donkey kicked the container behind me with both feet and it made an almighty, thunderous crunch as I caved in the corrugated metal side. I hit the deck and rolled as tightly close to it as I could–

As a tower of containers started to collapse around me.

CHAPTER NINETY-FIVE

Bringing down the house on yourself is kind of stupid.

But not as stupid as allowing yourself to walk into a ChiCom ambush and letting them harvest your ova from your unwilling body so they could breed an unstoppable army of Sienna Nealon babies.

The container row behind me came crashing down from my little trick, collapsing over me like a bridge falling down. Bullets and darts flew into the falling containers, which shielded me. And fortunately, too, because I didn't have any tricks for dodging a dozen tranquilizer guns and real-deal bullets.

I did have a plan to deal with the sonic guns, though, and I started preparing myself as I lay there, containers slamming over the top of me, my body sheltered beneath two of them like a hobo under a bridge in a hailstorm. There wasn't much I could do besides watch the tower fall.

Oh, and spring out of the way as soon as an escape route was available to me.

I came out from beneath the bridged containers already firing, AR in hand. I moved left and fired in the same direction, opening up on the guys who'd started to flank me before I dropped the stack. If I was lucky, I'd thinned the herd some with my trick, given that a considerable number of these flunkies had been standing in front of me when I brought the tower down.

Drilling Chinese spec op Commies felt like mowing down Taliban in a way; remorse was a thing I saved for people who had souls, not kidnapping bastards trying to harvest my body to aid their hegemonic ambitions. I drilled a spec ops douche with a double tap to the head, watched the pink mist for about a quarter second before switching targets and popping the guy next to him. Then I covered behind a fallen container and kicked it, sending it sliding in the direction of the right-side flank. Screams and crunching followed, filling my heart with joy and the arena with the screams of enemies.

Another ChiComm rounded the corner, blasting me with his weapon as he turned it. It hit me squarely, sending sonic waves through my body.

"Ooh," I said, the wax earplugs I'd packed from my gun range bag securely planted in my ears, "that kinda tickles. Aim lower."

The spec ops dude stared at me, cocked his head, confused.

I shot him. Twice. "Just kidding," I said. "I'll thank you to keep your vibrator away from me. Bad enough you're already after my lady parts, don't try your sonic foreplay on me, Sparky."

Someone appeared next to me and I nearly shot them, stopping myself just in time to realize it was Jian.

Without clothes.

"Hi!" I said quickly, averting my eyes and covering the edge of the fallen container that the ChiComs were hunkering behind. I had a feeling someone would try and sneak around it soon. "What's up?"

"Wanted to make sure you were okay," Jian said. "I didn't see a way out of that for you. That was impressively done. This is a well-constructed ambush."

"Well, I'm not out of it yet," I said. "They're coming after me hammer and tongs here. Or at least tranquilizers and vibrators. Which is alarming in its own way." I fired a burst and looked over my shoulder at him. "You hear what they want to do to me?"

He nodded slowly. "This is a government that will inject a crowning baby with formaldehyde before it draws its first breath in order to enforce their population control laws. It surprises you that they would kidnap the most powerful woman in the world in order to try and breed slaves by extracting her eggs?"

I made a face, firing and taking the top of the head off a Chinese operator who stuck his head out trying to pop me with a tranq dart. "When you put it that way, I'm actually kinda surprised no one has tried it before now. Maybe the rest of the world is just wise to the fact that kidnapping me is opening up a Pandora's box of troubles?"

"Very true," Jian said. "What are you going to do?"

"Slam the lid on their collective kidnapping, human-rights-violating dicks," I said. The floodlights had me in shadow, and the smoke from all the shooting I'd done was clouding the area. I changed mags, slipping the old one in my tactical belt and checking to make sure my new weapon was still resting in my belt. It was. "What are you going to do?"

"Do you want me to fight with you?" Jian asked.

"Unless that helicopter hung around?" I asked. He shook his head. "Then yeah, I could use a hand, since I have no current method of easy extraction."

"Try jumping over the rail?" Jian's voice had a note of amusement in it.

"Sure, turn into a dolphin and I'll ride your bare back to the shore," I said, then blushed because – yeah, dude was naked. "But seriously..."

"You take left flank, I'll go right," Jian said, and I caught him flashing into the air, flapping up and over the container at my back before I heard a roar, distant and dim, through my ear plugs, as he dropped down on the other side.

"Right on," I said, popping another Chinese operator as he tried to bring his gun around from behind cover to dust me. Which was fine. At least I knew what I was doing: breaking out of a damned trap set for me. Probably beat the shit out of a quiet day at the office.

CHAPTER NINETY-SIX

Somewhere ahead, I knew that I had problems coming up. One big one, at least:

Firebeetle.

Where was he? It was hard to say with earplugs in and my gun going off every few seconds as opportunistic ChiCom spec ops guys would try and cut the pie around the corner ahead, thinking they could shoot my metahuman ass before I dusted them. Sometimes they'd fire blind, and get a bullet in the hand for their trouble. Other times I'd pop them with a shot to the head as they barely peered out, trying to get a line of sight to me.

How many were there? No idea.

Where was Firebeetle? No clue.

Were there any kidnappees onboard? Maybe. But not in the shipping containers I'd knocked over, which (thankfully) were filled with actual shipped goods.

It seemed unlikely they were in containers at all; trying to take someone on a sixty-day journey across the sea in one of these things and have them emerge healthy and alive on the other end seemed low odds. These were people the Chinese government wanted alive. I was guessing they were below decks, probably in an area designed for prisoners.

Bullets whistled to my left, cracking into the shipping container behind me as I squatted, AR raised and waiting for someone to step out into my sights. I'd been in place for a minute or two now, though, and a pile of corpses was starting to accumulate where I'd continually ambushed these guys. They weren't stupid, just bold. They had to be getting the clue that I was waiting, so I decided to change things up, meta-style.

Figuring they were stacked up and ready to rush around the fallen container, I leapt on top of it, landing quietly. I swept my gun around, looking for snipers in high positions.

Nothing. That was an oversight on their part, locking the troops in the arena with the lion(ess) and the tiger.

With a couple steps forward, I found myself overlooking five spec ops dudes stacked up, ready to round the corner and bum rush me – if I'd still been there. I couldn't hear them, but by their hand motions they were counting down.

I fired over the edge, pouring bullets down on them fast and accurately. They slumped and fell under my unrelenting spray; only the last of them managed to get his weapon up and return fire, albeit in the wrong direction, before I got him, too.

With a jump, I dropped down next to the fallen. The burnt smell of gunpowder filled the air. I squatted next to the bodies and searched them quickly for grenades and such.

No joy. They'd been given only guns and sonics and tranq guns for this mission. I did grab the tranquilizer gun from one of the guys, though, and slung it over my shoulder in the event it came in handy.

The container tower I'd kicked over had fallen in a zigzag pattern, end to end. I was pretty sure I could hear screaming somewhere on the other side of them, through my earplugs, though I didn't dare pull them out to confirm. I assumed it was Jian at work. Hopefully it wasn't Jian being worked over.

A quick change of mags and I was ready to prowl again. I was fairly certain I'd gotten all the spec ops soldiers on my side of the containers. A bloody ooze spreading on the deck coupled with a black-booted foot sticking from beneath a section of corrugated metal siding told me I'd gotten some more with my container drop.

I put my back against the next container, which had fallen diagonally, separating me from the next section of this makeshift arena. I know what Liao had been thinking: trap her in a big, wide open place with clear sight lines and too many guns for her to be able to fight her way out.

Stupid. There was no place on earth where I wouldn't fight my way out, if backed into a corner like this. Harvesting me? Breeding me like a lab rat?

Damned right I'd fight. To the death.

I readied myself. My pulse was racing. I could feel the anger surging through my veins, dulled by the chill of ice water calm. I fought under that shroud of peace most of the time. Mother's teaching in my youth supplemented by all the fighting and training I'd done in my adulthood left me in battles where I felt mostly calm as I went through them.

Not this time. Something about Liao's plan, Liao's threat, had my heart hammering with pure fury.

Take me prisoner? Turn me into a factory for incubi and succubi to be brainwashed into becoming China's army?

Oh hell no you didn't.

I steadied myself, ready to round the corner, lifting the AR–

When the container I'd backed against slammed into me, knocking me over and trapping my AR against it, ripping the gun from my grasp. I thumped to the ground and rolled back to my feet, stinging from the landing.

A shadowy figure rose before me in the pre-dawn light, lumpy in all the wrong places. The scent of hard metal and diesel oil mixed with another familiar scent that I'd run across in the neighborhood in Baltimore. Sharp pains in my knee stung at me as I stared at my new foe, the silence of my earplugs blotting out the sound of a tiger growling in the distance, preoccupied with destroying foes on the other side of the wall of containers to my right.

This fight was mine.

"Hey, Firebeetle," I said, looking into the shadowy, armored skin of my enemy. "Let's do this thing."

CHAPTER NINETY-SEVEN

Julie Blair

A yawn escaped her as Julie tapped away at her computer. Darkness still reigned outside the Old Executive Office Building, though sunrise was probably close. It never escaped her that she was technically a White House staffer – except she didn't actually work in the White House.

Oh, well. Future goals. Before she left to work in the private political sector.

The mountain of emails she'd started with was...not dwindling. And about the time she made it through these, a mountain would have washed in. The only benefit to coming in this early was that her email volume slowed between midnight and six AM, making this a peak time to dig before the morning rush started.

Julie sighed, coffee in hand. It'd gotten cold already. Oh, well. Time to–

What was this?

The very first email, the one that had just slid into her inbox was from – oh, her uncle Miles. Man, did she regret ever giving him her work address. He was always forwarding crap. At least his emails were easy to ignore. She'd just hit the delete and be on to the next th–

Well, credit to Miles. This one at least had a catchy header on it. Usually it was something that didn't even register before it landed in the garbage bin. Really, she should just mark his address as spam once and for all and be done with it. But she didn't. Because it was her uncle, crazy as he might be. This one, though...

Sienna Nealon delivers a message about China that everyone needs to hear!

Julie couldn't even help it. She clicked, in spite of the source.

Sure enough, the video was exactly what had been promised. She stood on the edge of a dark harbor or something at night, helicopter in the background, and...

Wow.

Julie looked around. Not too many people here yet, other than her and Betsy. She was probably still digging out, too, or working on messaging for something or the other.

Sienna Nealon was going after a Chinese slaver vessel? Julie blinked a couple times. Kidnapping people and taking them overseas? That sounded like slavery to her. Plus, they'd killed an FBI agent?

A moment's hesitation passed, and Julie hit Forward, sending the email along. Someone else had probably passed this along, though, judging from how quiet the floor was – almost no one was in yet – maybe not. Julie stood, determined to follow it up immediately. Who knew if Sienna had any help coming? Based on her message, it didn't sound like it.

Yeah. Something had to be done. Julie felt butterflies in her stomach as she headed toward Betsy's office for the second time this morning. If no one else was here, it was down to her to be the one to do something about it.

CHAPTER NINETY-EIGHT

Sienna

"You cannot defeat me," Firebeetle said, flexing his beetle chest, talking in an accented tone.

"He speaks!" I made a show of gawking, even as I reached behind me, to my belt, for my weapon. "All these battles and you've been a quiet boy. Now you're deciding to pipe up and it's this bullshit?" I made my voice high and mocking. "'You cannot defeat meeee.' Kinda self-serving message there, sparky. You'd probably like it if I just gave up and came along quietly, wouldn't you? It'd save you the trouble of banging the dings out of your armor later, wouldn't it? Ain't happening, though." I smiled.

He set his head, glowing eyes staring down at me. "You must see now...I have been going easy on you. Just enough to keep you hooked so that we could get you here, into international waters, away from backup, from the reach of your government. Now, though, you have invaded our ship. Here...you belong to China."

"I realize maybe you're cool with being the bitch of your bull-shit country," I said, "but I don't belong to anybody. Least of all you and your metahuman slavery and eugenics program."

He circled, and I matched his movement, resting my hand on

the weapon secreted in my belt behind me. "I have bested you every time we fought," he said.

"You have gotten dragged away by a tiger every time you've *ambushed* me," I said. "That's hardly a clear win for you."

Firebeetle looked toward the fallen containers that penned us in. "Your tiger is otherwise occupied. It's just you and me."

There was some snarling and a little whimpering going on behind those containers. Hopefully Jian was doing okay, but I didn't have time to worry about him now. "I'm sure he's fine. And this time? I see you coming, so this isn't going to go like it has before."

"You are as arrogant as any American I have ever met," Firebeetle said. "It is ill founded. Where from springs this overconfidence?"

"I can't speak for my countrymen," I said, "but maybe it's because I've flat-out beaten the ass off anyone who's ever challenged me." I gripped my weapon tighter behind my back.

Firebeetle smiled, and it was an ugly thing; teeth that looked brown, like roach shells. "You've never faced the might of China." And he lunged at me.

I brought around the striking hammer I'd picked up at Home Depot on the way to the helicopter, crashing it into his jaw and sending him spiraling sideways. He hit the deck and rolled a couple times before popping his head up and shaking it.

His head wobbled, his mandible crushed in. His burning eyes floated, wobbly, like he was having trouble seeing me.

"Yeah, and you've never faced the might of Sienna, dipshit." I gripped my striking hammer and smiled, sprinting toward him before he could get up. "You're about to, though."

CHAPTER NINETY-NINE

Chapman

CHAPMAN: *We need to cut off Bilson's access to President Gondry.*

Jaime was typing furiously in about ten different directions. He was giving orders to his companies to keep a lid on the story, he was diving into the Escapade app via his computer screen (a feature only available to him, not the other users), and also texting a couple people to make sure everything was taken care of. He had his headset on, and his plans were coming together quickly.

CHALKE: Already done two hours ago. I own three of Gondry's primary gatekeepers, and I warned them to lock him out as soon as he disappeared from chat.

Chapman nodded. Good for Chalke.

BYRD: u guys is this 4 real

KORY: Can't believe he went this way. Should I cue up some articles about his political activities? Slime him?

Chapman thought about it for a second. The politics of personal destruction was an ugly thing. In this case, it might be a good idea to get rolling on that, in the event it was needed. Or, hell, wanted. He certainly would have liked to see Bilson take a hit for this betrayal.

CHALKE: Write them, hold them. We don't know what Bilson is doing yet, and putting him in the firing line that way will encourage him to escalate this little war. We're not quite to that point yet.

Something about Chalke's calm attitude bothered Jaime. How could they not be at that point yet? Bilson had betrayed them, breaking consensus on China and siding with Nealon, for crying out loud. Wasn't that worthy of some destruction? True, it could cause him to out the Network, but he might do that anyway. Better to neutralize him now.

CHAPMAN: We need to take this guy out of play. He's become dangerous both to us and the agenda. Can you imagine what happens if this China story breaks wide? It could mean war, and not the kind we all profit from. We're talking apocalypse type war. If that means wrecking Bilson, we should do it now and get it over with.

KORY: Might have some bad news. Confirming now.

Chapman's eyes almost popped out of his head. How could Kory post something like that and expect them to just sit idly and wait for his ass to get back to them?

BYRD: ???

FLANAGAN: You can always tell the clickbait site owner by his theatrical headline writing.

JOHANNSEN: I think I know what Kory's got. The story might have gotten to the president.

Chapman's mouth went dry.

CHAPMAN: HOW?!?!?

JOHANNSEN: Not sure. Someone in the White House elevated it, I think. It definitely came to him via the Chief of Staff. Beyond that, I don't know. Probably what Dave is confirming.

KORY: Yes, that's it. You suck for scooping me on that, Johannsen. I was getting confirmation.

JOHANNSEN: Since when does Flashforce care about confirming reporting?

KORY: Eat shit, Johannsen. How many retractions do you print on the average day?

JOHANNSEN: More than the 'none' that you do, since I care about getting stories corrected when we screw up.

CHALKE: Stop it, guys. We have more important things to worry about right now.

Jaime's head hurt. How could Gondry have gotten the story? They'd done so damned much to quash it. He'd used everything in his power to–

A quick sweep of the other search engines showed...yes, the video was trending. That was twenty percent of the internet he couldn't account for. It was quashed on FindIt and Socialite, but...

CHAPMAN: The Nealon video is circulating on other search engines and social networks. There's no keeping it back now. Especially not if the president has it.

Jaime cursed under his breath, slamming a fist into his desktop. His keyboard jumped on the surface. All the power he'd accumulated and he still couldn't quite tamp down the flow of information the way he wanted to.

CHAPMAN: I'm letting my people take the lid off the story. If I can't suppress it, I need to let it go or it'll spawn conspiracy theories in alternative media about how I'm trying to kill it. We'll just have to manage it from here.

FLANAGAN: How should we do that?

BYRD: I'm not on air until 2nite. Wish I could be live rite now. Wud be amazing. Ratingszzzz!!!!!

CHALKE: We control things the same way we always do. Come on, let's start constructing a narrative that makes sense here. One that minimizes the damage to China – and our interests.

Chapman took off his headset and threw it across the room. Everything he'd worked for, everything he'd done, and somehow that little bitch had managed to upset...everything. Again.

He didn't even have it in him to call Huang and let him know what was coming. What was even the point?

It was over.

CHAPTER ONE HUNDRED

Sienna

"You probably didn't have MC Hammer in your country," I said, giving Firebeetle a solid whack across the chest with the big head of the striking hammer. It rang out like steel on rock, a cracking noise issuing forth from his chest plating, spiderweb cracks radiating across his right pectoral, one of a half-dozen such wounds I'd inflicted on his body. Firebeetle flew into a fallen container and caved in the side before hitting the hard deck, face down. "Because if you had, you'd fully understand what I mean when I say that Hammer Time? We stop for it in America."

"I'm not in...America..." Firebeetle pushed himself up, woozily.

"Yeah, you're in international waters," I said, smashing him again, this time across the left pec. A loud cracking noise issued forth, a sweet sound I was starting to love. "You know what that means? You're subject to the laws of the country whose citizen's rights you're violating. Trying to kidnap an FBI agent for purposes of enslavement? I'm afraid I'm going to have to throw the book at you." I leapt after him to where he'd landed and pounded him three times against the deck with my hammer. "Or the hammer, in this case. I–"

I paused, looking at the hammer. The head had cracked, split cleanly along the bottom where it met the handle. "Sonofa. Not exactly Mjolnir, is it?" I turned it over in my hand. The label was still there on the other side of the head, holding it together from falling apart entirely. I laughed. "'Made in China.' Figures."

Raising the hammer high, I brought it down on Firebeetle and split the head off with a mighty blow against his back. His shell was fractured all over, like a boiled egg someone had tapped until it was completely covered with cracks.

He chuckled, lifting his head. "You broke...your hammer."

"Yeah, I should have bought American, I guess." I looked down at him. "If I were you, I'd stay down, Nancy Kerrigan."

Firebeetle looked up at me and smiled through busted teeth. "What are you going to do...now that you've lost your weapon?" He shoved himself up to his knees. "I told you...you cannot beat me. So...what now?" He rose, still wobbling, to his feet. "You didn't break me." He eyed the handle, still clutched in my fingers, his eyes aglow. "You tried. Failed. It will become a pattern for your country. Our ascendancy is guaranteed. You could be part of that." He laughed, low and menacing, fists clenched at his sides. "We have a billion and a half people. Plans that have been laid out for decades. You are a country with the attention span of gnats. Politicians with no more vision than will get them elected. Short-sighted locusts that will consume everything. Like you, with that hammer, striking so hard and fast, with no thought for what you would do when you had wasted against our strength." He laughed now, toneless and loud. "What will you do when you have given it your all, and you have nothing left with which to fight us?"

I just stared at him, haft still clutching in my fingers. "The same thing we always do."

He cocked his head curiously. "Which is?"

"Improvise." I smiled.

Before he could move, I shoved the handle of the hammer

straight into his eye. It didn't stop when it hit the bone at the back of the ocular cavity, and I rammed it clean through into his brain.

Firebeetle froze, jerking in surprise, his remaining eye wide and surprised. As it should, considering I'd just lobotomized him with a hammer. I gave it a quick twist to finish the job, and Firebeetle pitched over, dead.

"See, we Americans are always coming up with some crazy shit to solve our problems," I said, stepping over him as he twitched. "I mean, we're the country of the Shamwow and the Pet Rock. If we can't find a way to kill your ass with what we have, we'll invent a new way to do it. And you can keep that shitty Chinese hammer."

I drew my pistol and stepped up around the last fallen container, out into the open. The tiger noises had not subsided, but I was hard pressed to tell through the earplugs who was winning. I looked back, and could see nothing. The containers hid Jian's battle from my view.

Which was fine, because I had my own problem to deal with. I looked up, up to the bridge island above, where Liao waited, looking over the balcony railing in absolute alarm.

I centered my pistol sights on him. "Don't move, or I'll drop you."

Liao chuckled. "This is a Chinese flagged ship in international waters, Miss Nealon. You are trespassing."

I gave him my sweetest smile. He was standing a good six stories above me and grinning like he'd won in spite of me killing his champion and at least half his army. "You're committing acts of kidnapping and slaving and have threatened me with much worse. I don't know what law book you've been reading, but that's not how international waters work. You're under arrest, Liao."

Liao shrugged. "The people in the hold of this ship are all Chinese nationals. Most have never even been granted asylum in America. None were citizens. We were very careful in that regard."

"Explain Cathy Jang-Peters," I said.

Liao laughed. "Bait. For you."

"Bullshit," I said. "But for a Marine vet, you would have had her."

"Kidnapped in plain sight on an American highway?" Liao laughed again. "True, we would have gotten her, but witnesses would have seen a metahuman in the incident. You would have been called immediately. True, it would have been better if we hadn't lost the furniture store and some of the other links in the chain, but China is prepared to make sacrifices to guarantee our ascendancy." He leaned over the railing and smirked down at me. "That's the difference between us and you. You ride high now and think it will last forever. The wheel always turns in this world, Miss Nealon. Victory goes to the prepared. And you are unready."

"In your case, I think you mean 'the worm turns,'" I said. "And you'd best prepare yourself for the fact that you're under arrest."

Liao laughed, loud and toneless. "You and what army?"

A megaphone enhanced voice blared out over the ship. "Chinese vessel, this is the US Coast Guard. Heave to and prepare to be boarded!"

I half-shrugged. "Not the Army, but..."

Liao's face twitched, and he brandished a badge ID not unlike my FBI one, couched in a leather wallet. "Fine, you get the ship. You can even 'liberate' the passengers. But I still have a diplomatic credential – and with it, immunity." Now his smile twisted to a smirk.

I slid the tranquilizer gun off my back and pointed it up, drawing a bead on him and squeezing a shot in less than a second. It made a popping noise when it fired, almost soundless beneath my earplugs.

Liao blinked, looking down at his hand in surprise. A green feathered dart stuck out of his palm. He stared at it, still leaning on the rail–

Then the drugs he'd meant to use to knock a certain succubus out kicked in on his weak human ass, and he pitched over the railing, weight carrying him into a natural drop.

Liao went splat about twenty feet from me, headfirst onto the metal decking. He twitched a couple times.

"Immunity, huh?" I regarded his body with all the consideration it deserved, given his plans for me. "Too bad it didn't extend to gravity."

And I walked away.

CHAPTER ONE HUNDRED ONE

I found Jian, in tiger form, licking very literal wounds as I came around the fallen shipping container. He was in the midst of a bloody slaughter of fallen Chinese spec ops guys, but it was also clear he'd gotten just about as bad as he'd given.

"Shit," I said, hurrying forward. I didn't have a medkit on me, and wondered if there was even anything I could do. There was a *lot* of blood. "Are you all right?"

"I will be," the tiger said, without turning so much as even his face human.

I jumped back, unused to having a tiger speak to me, albino or otherwise. "Shit!" I said, because...it was a tiger. Talking to me. Sure, I knew it was Jian underneath, mentally, but seeing it was still incredibly disorienting.

"Sorry," he said, not turning human. "This is why I turned into a person to talk to you before. Even with the nakedness, it's less strange, right?"

"Yeah, seeing you sans clothing is definitely more pleasant in general than having a tiger talk to me," I said, "on so many levels." I blushed. "Anyhoo...you'll heal from this, right?" He nodded, his fur matted with Sienna levels of blood. "Can you make it to land in this condition?"

He nodded his big, whiskered head. "Yes. I will. Or I'll turn into a whale and take a nap on the sea floor until I'm better. Did I hear...?"

"The Coast Guard showed up," I said. "My video must have gone viral. Or Bilson got the job done. One of those."

"I need to leave, then," Jian said, lifting up unsteadily on all fours.

"I'd highly recommend that," I said, looking back at the container behind me, which hid the fallen corpse of Liao. "This place is about to become a diplomatic nightmare. You go. I can cover for you."

"Are you sure?" He was so unsteady.

"Yeah, I got this," I said, unsure that I actually had anything, but equally sure that Jian didn't need to go down with this particular ship. Which was my FBI career and possibly my freedom. "Go."

And go he did, turning into that familiar pigeon in a flash, and flapping up, up and beyond the barriers of the containers that had sealed me inside this arena.

I sat down to wait, feeling the subtle motion of the ship coming to a stop, and listening to the shouts – in English – of coasties preparing to board.

CHAPTER ONE HUNDRED TWO

Chapman

CHALKE: Bilson is in the Oval Office RIGHT NOW with SecState Ngo.

That was a nice little bombshell that came out of absolute nowhere, striking Jaime as he was already sitting in despair, watching the Sienna Nealon video trend on Socialite and blow up search results all over the internet.

What the hell else could they do, though? Watch in misery, Chapman figured, and boy, did he have that covered. He was even drinking an organic fruit smoothie in violation of his low-carb policy.

KORY: Release just went out. Gondry is having a press conference at noon to address the incident. My reporters are getting back channel gossip from inside the White House about possible SANCTIONS. On China!

Chapman thudded his head against the desk.

FLANAGAN: Still can't understand how this went down so fast. We blocked this shit!

CHALKE: Someone let it into the system, clearly. I'm on my way to the White House now. So is Nealon, being choppered in from the ship, which is in Coast Guard hands. Will see if I can trace how this happened. For future use, obviously, since this is already borked.

Jaime lifted his head and saw red. His hands typed almost of their own accord.

CHAPMAN: This is vintage Nealon, taking a chainsaw to all our plans. Everything we introduce her to, she screws up. Everything. I've had enough of her shit. I vote we dispense with her the way you've been wanting to all this time, Chalke.

BYRD: uh guys

JOHANNSEN: I agree Nealon's a problem. But she's headed into a meeting with the president. She's highest possible profile right now. You're going to need to do some work on her to bring her low before you try and take her out.

Chapman banged his hand on the desk. That's what they'd *been* doing! They had her in that position just last year, before the stupid Revelen thing blew up on them. How did these idiots not realize or remember that?

FLANAGAN: Agree, it's poor timing. She's at the apex of her power right now. Let her fade some, or find a way to chop her down a few notches, diminish her before we do anything to push her out.

Chapman stared at the words on the screen. He hated them – hated the words, hated this ineffectual group of idiots. They were supposed to be the titans of their industry, the best and brightest all around.

Why, then, couldn't they make anything happen? None of their plans were coming to fruition.

And how was he supposed to explain any of this to Huang?

KORY: There's definitely room to spread some counter takes on Nealon. Put some down markers for pulling her off that pedestal later.

"We've tried that!" Chapman screamed into the quiet of his office. Was everyone in this group suffering from memory loss but him? They'd thrown everything at this bitch in the press, tossed the law at her, kept her a fugitive for years–

And now she was heading to the White House to be feted like a hero. Again.

Chapman looked at his holdings. The stock price had cratered. From what? This Chinese thing, probably.

Would he ever see his deal with Huang go through? He

doubted it. Whatever else happened, he doubted the man was going to be enthusiastic about going forward with their plans at this point.

And Nealon...she was untouchable, at least for the moment.

But Chapman was still furious. Furious, and had resources – and spite – to spare.

CHAPMAN: I want to know who did this. Who brought this to the president. I don't care if it's a damned janitor. I want them fired. I want their family life torched to the ground. I want every friend they've ever had to deny knowing them for fear they'll get the stink of this person's toxic shit on them. If they're married, I want their spouse convinced that the day they met this person was the worst day of their existence, and if they've got kids I want to smear this prole so ugly that in five years they deny even being related to mommy or daddy, with all their memories of their upbringing being retroactively shaded with so much shame that they'll happily tell people their long-missing parent is a scat-obsessed crack whore who only services the homeless at discount prices.

BYRD: lol jesus

CHAPMAN: I'm serious. I want to make this person suffer so much that they regret having been born into the world.

JOHANNSEN: Remind me not to piss you off, Chapman.

KORY: Hahahah, I LOVE this. Sounds like fun.

FLANAGAN: I feel like it's almost a trial. See how much heat we can drop on one person with our all powers combined.

Chapman nodded. It was a trial run, all right. For what he wanted to do to Sienna Nealon.

CHALKE: Yeah, I'm on board for this, and the full heat of the FBI is down for making an example of whoever did this. Let me track them down. Shouldn't be too tough. Then we can let the fun begin.

That made Chapman smile. At least he'd get something out of this fiasco to make up for losing a billion-dollar deal.

CHAPTER ONE HUNDRED THREE

Sienna

"Mr. President," I said, taking Richard Gondry's extended hand as I walked into the Oval Office. SecState Ngo and Bilson were waiting with him, and everybody rose as I came in, wearing the same tattered clothes I'd worn to storm the cargo ship.

"Thank you for coming, Ms. Nealon," the president said, greeting me with a smile. "I know you probably wanted to stay on scene and wrap things up."

"No, it was mostly wrapped up before I left, sir," I said, adopting a kind of stiff, just-short-of-military posture. "We recovered two hundred and eighty-seven prisoners/kidnappees from belowdecks, sir."

Gondry blinked a few times at that. "Good Lord. They really did kidnap that many people."

I shook my head. "That was just one port, sir. I talked to a couple of agents in other offices. There were similar shipments that left yesterday out of New York, LA, Seattle, San Fran, New Orleans. Manifests that look almost the same as the ship I captured. Preliminary estimates from the task force that's forming indicate we could be looking at between 1,000 and 2,000 kidnappees."

You could have heard a fly unzip in the Oval Office after I dropped that particular bomb.

Gondry took it in, barely an emotion to cross his face. He was looking pretty stoic.

"Sir," Bilson said, "we cannot allow this sort of thing to go unanswered."

"Agreed," Ngo said. "Not on our own soil."

"Do you concur, Ms. Nealon?" the president asked, looking to me.

I felt a little poleaxed, being asked my opinion on what was clearly a foreign policy matter. "I don't know that I could justify war over it," I said, trying to be measured in my response, "but I would highly recommend a response that tells the Chinese government that they don't get to do this kind of thing to us and expect business to continue as usual."

Gondry nodded, stroking his silvery goatee in consideration. "I agree wholeheartedly. I've already directed the Secretaries of Commerce and Defense to put together a statement. We won't have war over it, but I can't ignore China while they do these things. They've long turned their nose up against human rights in ways that would make even the most hardened observer do a double-take. It's time we at least have the courage to say something about it, loudly and in a public airing."

I gave a little nod as Gondry seemed to pause, considering something.

The door to the Oval Office swung open behind me, and I turned to find Heather Chalke entering. She paused as she came face to face with me for a moment. Her eyes narrowed – just for a second – before she moved past to talk to the president.

"Sir, I came as soon as I could," Chalke said.

"Ms. Nealon has informed me of the FBI task force forming on this," Gondry said airily. "Good work, Chalke. I'm glad your agency didn't decide to close the file when we thought this was all wrapped up. I'm pleased with your initiative."

Chalke looked like she'd been thrown squarely into a shit heap but was forced to grin and bear it. "Thank you, sir," was all she managed, and boy did it sound like it taxed her to cough that up. "We try to stay in the business of pursuing justice."

"Well, pursue this one all the way," Gondry said, heading back behind the *Resolute* desk. "I want no stone unturned in seeing these people returned to their families. The last thing our country needs is to it hand over asylum seekers to a country that's going to breed them like cattle to build a super army. Which they'll doubtless throw against us in a few years."

"That is their plan, sir," I said, drawing a hot glare from Chalke. "The men in charge of their mission made clear to me multiple times that this was their intent."

Gondry drew himself up. "Good you stopped them, then." He nodded at each of us in turn. "I mean to see you all get credit for this. We're going to draw a line here. The Chinese have pushed us for years. No more taking it." He looked right at Bilson. "You'll see to it that we author a policy that answers the Chinese strategy?"

Bilson nodded. "I will, sir."

"Good," Gondry said, giving us all a curt nod. "If you'll excuse me...I have to prepare for this press conference. I'll be announcing your advancement to National Security Advisor, Bilson, so you'll need to stick around. As to the rest of you – Ms. Nealon? Would you be so kind as to remain for the press conference as well? I want to make sure we recognize your fallen partner."

I shot a look at Chalke, who gave me a grudging nod. "I am at your disposal, sir."

"Excellent," Gondry said, attention on the papers on his desk. "I know you've got a lot to do, so talk to my secretary on the way out. I'm sure we can find you somewhere to work until time."

"Thank you, sir," I said, and motored out the door before the rest.

"Nice job, Sienna," Ngo said as she passed me.

I gave her a nod as she went by. I waited in the secretarial office. I needed to talk to Bilson, but Chalke beat him out the door. "We'll discuss this later," she said, passing me. She looked so stiff it reminded me of a cat with its tail raised.

"I...ma'am?" I asked.

Chalke froze, turning back to me. There was unmistakable danger in her eyes, but it was under control. "Yes?"

"I couldn't just let them get away with killing Holloway," I said.

Chalke's eyes softened maybe a millimeter. "I can understand that," she said, so grudging I knew she was steaming pissed at me. Understanding be damned, I'd still crossed her.

"What do you want me to do now?" I asked, trying to offer a concession.

Her eyes narrowed again, but she spoke very evenly. "It's out of our hands now. The investigation will take its natural course, now that all this additional evidence has been turned up."

"I'll make sure you get the credit for having the guts to follow it up," I said. "Not many people would have done that after the bait the Chinese threw us to try and shut it down."

Chalke hesitated. I could tell she was suffering from a lack of knowledge as to how the last stages of this had played out. Would she reveal that ignorance, here, in the White House, where she might be overheard? "We do what we have to in order to get the job done," she said at last.

"Agreed," I said. "Still, I doubt anyone could have predicted how far they'd go to try and build a metahuman army to replace their losses from Sovereign. Expats, serum, DNA tracking. I know I didn't get a chance to lay it all out before we set out to stop them, but I promise my report will be thorough, and the things they told me while on board their ship...it was a trap. For me. So they could harvest a bunch of succubus eggs."

Chalke recoiled, a look of absolute appall twisting her doll-like face. It passed in a moment, but it was genuine – and horrified. "Good that you stopped them, then." She gave me a nod, then turned on her heel. "Do us proud, Nealon," she said, and then she was gone.

"She'll never admit that she didn't know," Bilson said, slipping up behind me, whispering so low only I could hear him. "And that works to your advantage – for now."

"Congrats on being named National Security Advisor," I said, coolly, and at full volume. "You must be proud."

Bilson smiled, deep, sincere. "It feels good to be in a position where I might be able to tip the scales for the good. For once."

I nodded slowly. "And will you?"

Bilson paused, letting the idea steep for a second. "I will." His smile faded. "Thanks to you."

CHAPTER ONE HUNDRED FOUR

The press conference was a long capper on the end of a long day of paperwork, coordinating, fighting...and of course talking to people.

Honestly, I preferred the fighting.

But as my rideshare dropped me off outside my apartment, thoughts whirling in my head from everything I'd learned and done, I found myself...

Utterly exhausted, of course. How could you go through what I'd been through in the last few days and not be spent?

"Hey," someone said, emerging from the shadows to the left of my building.

I glanced, keeping my hand hovering close to my pistol, then relaxed. "Hey, Michelle," I said as she slunk out of the shadows.

"Saw your press conference," Michelle said.

"Some people might say it was the president's press conference," I said. "Given it was held in the White House Press Room, he was like the keynote speaker, and I was just there to provide...I dunno, color commentary or something."

Michelle snorted. "Yeah...it was *your* press conference. Gondry's fine and all, and I'm sure he'll work really hard at smacking around the Chinese government diplomatically and whatnot, but given that ninety percent of the questions started with, 'Ms. Nealon, Ms. Nealon!'...it was all you. America's got a raging hard-on for you, Sienna. Accept it."

"Ugh," I said, making a sound of disgust. "You say this to me after a day in which the Chinese government sets a trap to turn me into the egg donor of their superarmy?"

Michelle's eyes widened. "Ew! What? Really?"

I nodded. "Sorry. Forgot I hadn't seen you since this morning, before the boat. Their servants left breadcrumbs for me to follow. Not to play into your already-Sienna-centric theme, but...yeah...it was about me, at least in part."

"I shouldn't be surprised," she said, clearly giving it some thought, "given everything my family went through to get out of that country and everything they've done since, but...this is a new low. I hope the president really does sock it to them. Maybe the ruling class over there will learn something."

"Yeah, but it'll hurt the people," I said. "They don't deserve their current overlords."

Michelle shrugged. "Who does?" She shook her head. "Well, I just wanted to say 'bye' before I blew town. I got word that the FBI seized a cargo ship in the Gulf of Mexico. My peeps were on board, so...thanks."

"You're welcome," I said, wondering how much these people meant to her. She'd certainly gone through a lot for them.

Michelle just stared at me. "I like that we've developed this unstated thing where I give you a little help on something but nobody owes any favors once it's done. Let's keep that up."

I laughed. "You go on telling yourself you don't owe me anything, yoga pants. But 'someday – and that day may never come – I will call upon you to do a service for me.'"

Michelle made a face. "Yuck. I don't like that idea, Godmother Corleone. I don't want to contemplate the kind of favor you would ask me for."

"As well you shouldn't," I said, catching a glimpse of a pigeon flying off the building's facade. I could have sworn I saw it dipped its wing at me before it took to the skies. Maybe I'd imagined it, though. "As well you shouldn't."

CHAPTER ONE HUNDRED FIVE

Julie

"Come on in," Betsy said after Julie knocked on the door.

Julie did, indeed, come in, plopping down in the chair before Betsy Suffolk's desk. The comms department offices were quiet after a banner day. The president had undertaken a huge shift in foreign policy after the explosive events of the morning. Julie's inbox was filled, exploding, really. She'd done her best to dig through, but this volume of emails...

Well, it'd take a while. It always did, but...this was more than usual.

"Guessing we're not going to get caught up anytime soon, huh?" Julie asked, tight smile stretching her face.

Betsy looked up, and Julie knew instantly something was wrong.

"What?" Julie asked. The little hairs on the back of her neck were standing up.

"I'm sorry," Betsy said, "there's no easy way to say this." Her eyes, usually rimmed with concern, quick and attentive, looked dull, disinterested. "Julie...you're fired."

"What?" Julie asked. She couldn't have heard that right.

"Yes," Betsy said, and there was a knock at the door.

"I...why?" Julie asked, turning to look. Two guys in black suits were standing there. Secret Service? Why were they...?

"You're going to have to leave now," Betsy said. Julie half expected a joke, for her stern facade to break into a smile, *Fooled you!* and they'd have a laugh.

There was no laughing. Especially when one of the Secret Service agents wrapped a hand around Julie's upper arm stiffly.

"Betsy, what is this?" Julie asked in rising alarm. "What – what did I do?"

"We'll send you the contents of your desk," Betsy said dully.

"I – but – what did I–"

"I'm going to have to ask you to come with me, ma'am," the agent with the grip on her arm said. He started to pull, and she didn't resist.

Walking out, past the rest of the department, all eyes were on Julie. A pall fell over the place, and everyone was watching. Julie trudged in silence, a Secret Service agent steering her toward the exit.

Julie just walked, wide-eyed, trying to process this and keep her feet beneath her as the world seemed to collapse around her.

What was happening?

CHAPTER ONE HUNDRED SIX

Sienna

The exhaustion was really setting in as I opened my apartment door. The place was deathly quiet, save for the refrigerator running, quiet hum of the machinery filling the place where nothing else lived.

"Home sweet home," I said to my empty apartment. I'd left here this morning with an AR-15 slung on my shoulder and big ideas about how I'd finally bust open this Chinese kidnapping case for good.

Now here I was, fifteen hours later, after a raid, a presidential press conference and having done more paperwork than an IBS sufferer at a Taco Bell. If there'd been light in my eyes when the day had started, the disgust with all that the Chinese had planned in the course of trying to kidnap me had stamped it out. I didn't consider myself idealistic, but *dayum*, as the kids say. Their plan was stone cold horrifying, and was still roiling my stomach on a visceral level.

But I had shit left to do before I could sleep. I made my way to the fridge and threw it open, retrieving my phone and hitting the power button.

Sure enough, it lit up. Lucky me. It was durable enough to survive in a fridge all day, though the battery was a little low.

I stared into the screen, knowing that somewhere in California, someone was staring back.

"We need to come to an understanding," I said into the blank screen. "I know you're watching, and I don't care. I'm not trying to thwart you here. China tried to trap me, and they baited it just right. I didn't mean to upset your applecart, and I'm willing to make amends, if you need them." I sighed. "Whatever. Let me know."

I plugged the phone in and then shuffled toward bed, throwing myself into the soft sheets, unworried about my dirtiness, my clothes, anything. I wanted to pass out, and I wanted to do it now. I hadn't really expected an answer immediately in any case, and I didn't get one. That was fine. It could wait until tomorrow.

EPILOGUE

Bilson

Triumphant.

That was what he was.

Russ Bilson stood on the balcony of his DC condo, staring out over the city. It wasn't a penthouse, not yet, but it was one floor below the top of the building. Clear sight lines in every direction for a long ways. Tenth-floor views, which, in a city where the average building was only three, four stories tall, was like being the one-eyed man in the kingdom of the blind.

Bilson couldn't help but feel that glow of ever-present self-satisfaction.

What had he wanted all this time? The National Security Advisor post. Why? So he could do the job. Add some expertise to his portfolio. And after a couple years – and a ton of added connections the world over – he'd come out of it worth millions per year in consulting fees.

Sure, he'd have to leave his current gigs behind for a while. That was okay, though. Hell, it was expected. It'd all be worth it in the end. Power was the game in DC, and he had to admit –

doing the right thing in this case? It had been surprisingly pain-free, in terms of what it had cost him.

He chuckled. Maybe he'd even make a habit of it. It felt good, seeing an unambiguous wrong and stepping in to make it right. Usually his work dealt with a lot more gray. He hadn't seen things this clearly in years.

It was too bad, though, he reflected, looking down at his phone. Breaking faith with the Network had been something he'd done in the heat of the moment, when he realized how calcified their thinking had become. That was Chapman, of course. His billion-dollar deal was clouding his eyes. The rest of them would come around. Maybe Chapman, too. It was hard to say without talking to them.

Bilson pressed his thumb to the screen. It unlocked immediately, his biometrics accepted.

He started to touch the Escapade app, then stopped himself.

No. He'd made his stand. There was no room for regrets, even over the fact that they'd really only clashed over one piece of policy. All their agreements, and it had come to this one bone of contention.

Bilson twisted his lips as he thought about it. A little flash of anger lit him up.

Dammit, they should have listened to him.

He let the phone drop to his side as he looked out over Washington DC. This was going to be his city now. Foreign policy was his fiefdom for the next couple years. "And anybody who doesn't like how I do it can kiss my ass," he said to the empty air beyond the balcony. He didn't shout it, just said it, feeling full and confident.

Bilson's eyes alighted on a rooftop in the distance. It was roughly the same height as his building, and he always regarded it like a distant mountaintop, or a personal rival to his building. How dare it ascend to his heights?

He chuckled. Silly, true. But when you were as ascendant as he was, you noticed your competitive set.

A momentary flash lit up atop the distant building. Bilson barely registered it, a little blink of light and then—

Something struck him solidly in the chest, taking his breath away. A whistling sound followed after–

A bullet?

Russ Bilson looked down at his chest. His pure white shirt was wet, darkening with claret like he'd spilled wine on himself.

He hit his knees, then sagged, cheek landing against the hard concrete floor of the balcony. He tried to take a breath, but it wouldn't come.

It came to him, in those last seconds, as his vision started to darken, just how unfair this was. He'd made it! To the top!

Only to have this happen. And out of nowhere.

No, not nowhere – out of the distance. Taken out by someone on that competitive building...

There was an irony there. And truth, too.

Taken out by a competitor at the moment of his ascension.

How gallingly unfair.

That was the last thought that went through Russ Bilson's mind before he died.

Sienna Nealon Will Return in

CONTROL

The Girl in the Box, Book 38

(Out of the Box 28)

Coming January 2020!

GET IT HERE!

BIBLIOGRAPHY/AFTERWORD

Normally, I don't do this sort of post-book explainer stuff. I mean, I write fiction. Citing sources is a non-fiction beat, the sort of thing I tired of in college and haven't had to bother with lo these many years after graduation. Except...

When I originally came up with the idea for *Dragon*, the concept was simple: Sienna versus the government of China. Not the people – who, like people the world over, are subject to the whims of their government. Sienna respects the people of China like she would any human.

No, the villain here is the government of the People's Republic of China, which (insert editorial opinion) really doesn't act in the best interests of the people at all. No government is perfect, and many are actively terrible. That said, the government of the People's Republic is horrifyingly bad in ways that have often been quietly whispered about and seldom reported in the Western corporate press for fear of adverse consequences landing upon them in the form of having their news bureaus in China forcibly closed by the government. Western films are censored in order to make certain they're fit for release in the Chinese market, which is rapidly becoming the largest film market in the world.

Now that I've made my feelings about the Chinese government clear (as though that didn't bleed through in the story already), here's why I included a bibliography: because in all the chatter of modern life, and in the throes of the (mostly) fictive story I just presented you, it would be easy to assume that all the batshit crazy things I attributed to China in this book were entirely fictional for purposes of advancing the story.

They are not. To my knowledge, China is not kidnapping people outside their own country (mostly, though they absolutely have been accused of it in Hong Kong, extrajudicially), many of the other outrageous activities I mention in this book are alleged to actually happen, most especially the organ harvesting of prisoners.

So, to help separate truth from fiction, I offer this bibliography, with sources cited, as a "Worst of" list when it comes to the shit the People's Republic of China gets up to as they build their hegemony (in state propaganda, they regularly deny being hegemonic, which to me feels like a perfect reason to accuse them of it). Unless otherwise mentioned, the web links below were accessible as of October 2019. Apologies if any are offline when you go to check them now. I'm sure you can search the web for additional horror stories of the PRC's behavior. There is certainly no shortage.

Further apologies to holders of the paperback for this mess; in the original ebook the links are simply presented as links. Here, it's going to be a bit messier.

Haaretz: What goes on inside Chinese gulags - https://www.haaretz.com/world-news/.premium.MAGAZINE-a-million-people-are-jailed-at-china-s-gulags-i-escaped-here-s-what-goes-on-inside-1.7994216?fbclid=IwAR3BzAm_MnBmXKuMsl7rKDG--9gCoMqkeMjbbLlZELu3TKzWPHdfh7yeHjs An absolutely horrific account from an escapee of the hellscape of rape, torture, human experimentation, and possibly genocide. This is literal concentration camp stuff, the darkest corners of the human experience, and it's happening right now. (Note: I received this story on the morning the book went to print, otherwise it would have been more prominently featured in the text. Thanks to J.L. Bryan for bringing it to my attention.) The Washington Post expands on this somewhat with additional accounts: Abortions, IUDs and sexual humiliation: Muslim women who fled China for Kazakhstan recount ordeals: https://www.washingtonpost.com/world/asia_pacific/abortions-iuds-and-sexual-humiliation-muslim-women-who-fled-china-for-kazakhstan-recount-ordeals/2019/10/04/551c2658-cfd2-11e9-a620-0a91656d7db6_story.html.

The Guardian: China pressured London police to arrest Tiananmen protester, says watchdog: https://www.theguardian.com/world/2019/jun/30/political-pressure-before-arrest-of-chinese-dissident-london Not a great look, UK gov.

The Guardian: Organ Transplant studies find that while China gov claims 10,000 organ transplants occur each year, hospital data suggests 60,000 to 100,000 - https://www.theguardian.com/science/2019/feb/06/call-for-retraction-of-400-scientific-papers-amid-fears-organs-came-from-chinese-prisoners

NY Post: Chinese dissidents are being executed for their organs, former hospital worker says - https://nypost.com/2019/06/01/chinese-dissidents-are-being-executed-for-their-organs-former-hospital-worker-says/

The Atlantic, talking in glowing terms about Chinese propaganda being included as a special supplement in the Washington Post. It's Almost Like Being Back in Guomao - https://www.theatlantic.com/international/archive/2010/11/its-almost-like-being-back-in-guomao-updated/67189/

Human Events, also talking about how thoroughly the Washington Post has disguised these "paid supplement" addendums of Chinese state propaganda to their paper: Democracy Dies with Chinese Propaganda - https://humanevents.com/2019/06/17/democracy-dies-in-chinese-propaganda/

Vanity Fair: The Disappearance of Fan Bingbing - https://www.vanityfair.com/hollywood/2019/03/the-untold-story-disappearance-of-fan-bingbing-worlds-biggest-movie-star Fan Bingbing is a Chinese actress who the Chinese government "disappeared" for months after a 2018 tax scandal. Her return was like something out of one of those hostage videos. That whole story is a chilling look into Chinese society, including how Chinese censors can work to completely erase a story in motion and how they will drag dissidents away while on air, disappearing them for months or years.

BBC: Inside China's "Thought Transformation" camps - https://www.youtube.com/watch?v=WmId2ZP3hoc I mean, seriously, after watching that...what the f#*%?

The Federalist: China tries to take Totalitarian Social Control Tactics Global - https://thefederalist.com/2019/08/02/china-tries-take-totalitarian-social-control-tactics-global/ I didn't really hit on the Hong Kong protests in this book, because they were ongoing as I was writing this volume, but there's plenty of fodder there. Helen Raleigh at *The Federalist* has written extensively about China and the protests. Her body of work on the subject can be found here - https://thefederalist.com/author/helenraleigh/

The Federalist: China Rolling Out the Most Massive Population Surveillance System in the World - https://thefederalist.com/2018/11/05/china-rolling-massive-population-surveillance-system-world/ Also not fully explored in this book, but apropos given Chapman's attempts at a Chinese deal - Google has been playing very nice with the Chinese government, creating tools for them to quash dissent. That's in the Guardian, here: Google 'working on censored search engine' for China - https://www.theguardian.com/world/2018/aug/02/google-working-on-censored-search-engine-for-china Wouldn't want to let ideas of free thought or free expression get in the way of making a buck, after all! I'll point out, too, that on many occasions when western corporations have gone into China on these sort of joint ventures, they're often subject to their intellectual property being flat-out stolen by their partners, or are simply forced out. I can't find a good, authoritative source to link to on this matter, so you'll have to do some searching on your own if you're interested in knowing more. It's alluded to in this report (https://www.zdnet.com/article/building-chinas-comac-c919-airplane-involved-a-lot-of-hacking-report-says/) from ZDNet on how China's new Comac C919 airplane is built heavily on stolen technology.

Hand in glove with this cyber stuff, I think I might have mentioned the coming "social credit score" systems briefly in *Blood Ties* earlier this year, but this is a thing that's both horrifying and already coming to the west via Silicon Valley. Yay for technocracy (sarcasm, people. It's my stock-in-trade). Read all about it in Business Insider here: China has started ranking citizens with creepy 'social credit' system - https://www.businessinsider.com/china-social-credit-system-punishments-and-rewards-explained-2018-4/

Another article about the PRC harassing critics, even outside of China - https://www.scmp.com/news/asia/australasia/article/2176618/new-zealand-professor-who-wrote-about-chinas-foreign-influence

New York Times: How China uses high-tech surveillance to subdue minorities - https://www.nytimes.com/2019/05/22/world/asia/china-surveillance-xinjiang.html

Completely unrelated to China, Chapman makes an offhand reference to the City of Baltimore's entire network being held captive by a ransomware attack by hackers – that was a thing that actually happened (via NPR): Ransomware Cyberattacks Knock Baltimore's City Services Offline (https://www.npr.org/2019/05/21/725118702/ransomware-cyberattacks-on-baltimore-put-city-services-offline) Don't click on unfamiliar links in your emails, people. Even from grandma, because she probably knows zip about InfoSec.

If you're into environmentalism at all, China is the world's most prolific, horrific polluter, emitting banned CFCs in defiance of an international ban that they signed on to: USA Today - China is shredding the ozone layer with banned emissions, study says - https://www.usatoday.com/story/news/nation/2019/05/22/ozone-layer-china-emitting-banned-cfcs/3767724002/

Air pollution in China is so bad that a friend's son, trying to leave Beijing, was stuck on a plane, on the tarmac at the airport for nine hours because *they couldn't even see the air traffice control tower* due to the air pollution. This is not uncommon, pollution is at incredible levels in China: You Won't Believe How Bad Pollution in China Has Become - https://allthatsinteresting.com/pollution-in-china-photographs

Some good news in that regard – as a country's standard of living rises, so too does interest in environmentalism. It's kinda tough to care about your air quality when you're foraging to survive or spending 365 days a year growing your food. But there are indications that the government is keen to change this, via Bloomberg: China's War on Pollution Will Change the World - https://www.bloomberg.com/graphics/2018-china-pollution/

If I could take a moment to snarkily editorialize (okay, sure, I've been doing that throughout, but another moment, if you please): I think that while a key reason they are interested in the environment now isn't just because they have air and water quality issues in their country. Skimming their propaganda outlets, as I've been doing for a bit now (it makes me a little nauseous, but it's important for research purposes to see what narratives they're keen to spin), it's very clear to me that in cultivating their English-world content, they understand well the western concerns of climate change and they are very focused on trying to appeal to that market by trumpeting any tiny step or statement, however minute, made by China that would reflect positively on them in this regard in the west. To borrow from Shakespeare, "The lady doth protest too much, methinks." Whatever concerns there are in China about the environment are clearly secondary to their economic ascent, and whatever platitudes they're mouthing in the west about being in sync with western interests they're mostly doing to gin up sympathies while being the largest carbon emitter on the planet. No source to cite here; just my opinion. It's all smoke and mirrors for the most part. They'll talk a great game about being a partner and wanting to change, but they'll keep polluting if it suits their interests. Which it does.

Also, China has funded educational programs called Confucius Institutes across the world, ostensibly to bring the light of Chinese culture, history, and language to the rest of the world. And, frankly, if it was from some country like, say, Micronesia, who doesn't have a record of brutal authoritarian control over its people, I'd welcome the chance to learn culture and language from them. Since it's China, who have a distinctly propagandistic bent to everything they do, the fact that they've opened their Ministry of Truth franchises on a lot of college campuses (500+ of them) across the world...color me worried. Via Politico: How China Infiltrated U.S. Classrooms - https://www.politico.com/magazine/story/2018/01/16/how-china-infiltrated-us-classrooms-216327

Another editorial moment: Usually when I write a book, I try to keep some of themes in the background to serve the story. The story is the thing, because I don't write message fiction. I find message fiction dull and annoying. The purpose of this book is not to say, "OMG! Look how evil China's government is!" (Note again that throughout this book and bibliography, I take great care to put the onus for these terrible acts on the government, not the people of China, who, in my estimation, are one of the longest suffering in the world.) The purpose of the book is to tell a Sienna story with a compelling villain. I have used real-life examples of the People's Republic's acts of actual villainy to make the case, because I'm not going to just gloss over them when they're freely available. But shitting on China's government isn't the point of the book.

It is, however, the purpose of this bibliography.

The fact that western news sources and corporations spend alarming amounts of time actively passing on stories of real, terrible human rights abuses in China is a damned tragedy. Ignoring the plight of the Chinese people because they have corporate interests or sympathies to China's repressive government is disgusting. The American press, in particular, can (and should!) criticize the government of the United States all day long, but can't be bothered to bring up a question at a debate regarding the shocking human rights abuses in China or the incredible, widespread protests for freedom in Hong Kong? They have a population of seven million and *two million people* turned out at one point to protest. (source: The BBC, Hong Kong Protest: https://www.bbc.com/news/world-asia-china-48656471) 'Nearly two million' join demonstration.) Is that not worthy of a question? Or does someone have a China bureau they're afraid will get closed?

Activision/Blizzard bans a Taiwanese player for six months for saying on a company livestream, "Hong Kong! Revolution of our time!" (They'd originally given him a one year ban, then reversed it.) Via IGN: Hearthstone Player blitzchung Responds to Blizzard Reducing His Ban - https://www.ign.com/articles/2019/10/13/hearthstone-player-blitzchung-responds-to-blizzard-reducing-his-ban

Houston Rockets GM Daryl Morey gets scolded and retracts after posting a tweet in support of Hong Kong (and gets blowback from China), via the BBC: Daryl Morey backtracks after Hong Kong tweet causes Chinese backlash (https://www.bbc.com/news/business-49956385). The retraction was like he'd come out of a cultural revolution struggle session. (Source on that extremely dark chapter of Chinese history, via All that's interesting: 44 Disturbing Pictures of China's Cultural Revolution - https://allthatsinteresting.com/cultural-revolution)

The NBA kicks fans out of game for holding Hong Kong protest signs, via a local reporter on Twitter (https://twitter.com/Christie_Ileto/status/1181779722243575809). The NBA wouldn't want to be accused of supporting free people over its own pocketbook, after all.

These are just from the last few weeks, and you could be forgiven for thinking that corporate America was somehow a wholly owned subsidiary of Beijing. Hollywood has been on the Chinese teat for years, as exemplified by...well, a ton of things, including:

The scrubbing of Tom Cruise's character's jacket in the new China-funded sequel to *Top Gun*, via American Military News: Controversy: Did Chinese company censor 'Top Gun 2' flags from Tom Cruise's bomber jacket? - https://americanmilitarynews.com/2019/07/controversy-did-chinese-company-censor-top-gun-2-flags-from-tom-cruises-bomber-jacket/

Here's a litany more – scenes cut from *Mission: Impossible 3*, *Skyfall*, insertions to Iron Man 3, Looper, and the grandaddy of them all, the remake of Red Dawn having the villains switched from China to North Korea(!) in post-production so as not to offend China, via NPR: How China's Censors Influence Hollywood - https://www.npr.org/sections/parallels/2015/05/18/407619652/how-chinas-censors-influence-hollywood

A few years ago, watching the (quite funny) film Game Night, starring Jason Bateman and Rachel McAdams, there's a moment when McAdams, during a compatibility game with Bateman (going from memory here, forgive me if the quote's a little off), squeals excitedly, "China is the future!" Bateman's character hastily agrees.

I nearly vomited in my mouth.

For nearly seventy years, the Chinese government has crushed their own people. Now they're exporting their bullshit autocracy abroad. If China is the future, count me out. But if we don't start through their, "China is awesome and flawless and you should love it with every fiber of your being!" propaganda that's being fed to us, oh, EVERYWHERE, then their real goals and objectives – which are hegemonic dominance of the planet using whatever means they have at their disposal to control public opinion (spoiler alert: there are a lot, as documented here and elsewhere), they *will* be the future.

China's government is trying desperately hard to let you see only the good things about them. Such a pretty country! Such a powerful people! Very true. But there's been a darker side to China all along, one they don't want to show. If there's any great advancement we've seen in civilization these last few hundred years along the climb to where we are now, it's the willingness to introspect on our failures.

There is no country without flaws. None. We all have shockingly brutal horrors in our past, as nations. The beautiful thing about free speech and inquiry is that we can give voice to these – at the top of our lungs, and examine how they've affected us going forward.

China is not subject to this thinking. Their horrors are fresh and ongoing, and no one is allowed to speak of them within their borders and now – now they would like very much for none of you to speak of them, either.

Well, pardon my French (again and again, seriously, sorry, the subject matter just makes me angry), but fuck that. Now you know. Tell everyone. Watch their lips curl in disgust and surprise, because they've probably never heard these things. China's done a fine job keeping it quiet, both on their own and using complicit partners in the west.

Because while the situation is dire in Hong Kong (and China), it really should be the revolution of our time. A billion and a half people without even a basic say in how their lives are run, subject to being thrown in a camp or prison at any moment, and subject to terrible abuse even when they're not in said camps. I wish I had a practical plan I could lay out, some story that would lead to a happy ending for these people. But I don't;

I'm not a policy maker. And I'm drawing to the end of my editorial, so I'll just say this:

Free Tibet. Free Hong Kong.

And someday, maybe, free China.

Robert J. Crane
October 18, 2019

AUTHOR'S NOTE

Thanks for reading! If you want to know immediately when future books become available, take sixty seconds and sign up for my NEW RELEASE EMAIL ALERTS by CLICKING HERE. I don't sell your information and I only send out emails when I have a new book out. The reason you should sign up for this is because I don't always set release dates, and even if you're following me on Facebook (robertJcrane (Author)) or Twitter (@robertJcrane), or part of my Facebook fan page (Team RJC), it's easy to miss my book announcements because ... well, because social media is an imprecise thing.

Find listings for all my books plus some more behind-the-scenes info on my website: http://www.robertjcrane.com!

Cheers,
Robert J. Crane

Other Works by Robert J. Crane

The Girl in the Box
(and Out of the Box)
Contemporary Urban Fantasy

1. Alone
2. Untouched
3. Soulless
4. Family
5. Omega
6. Broken
7. Enemies
8. Legacy
9. Destiny
10. Power
11. Limitless
12. In the Wind
13. Ruthless
14. Grounded
15. Tormented
16. Vengeful
17. Sea Change
18. Painkiller
19. Masks
20. Prisoners
21. Unyielding
22. Hollow
23. Toxicity
24. Small Things
25. Hunters
26. Badder
27. Nemesis

28. Apex
29. Time
30. Driven
31. Remember
32. Hero
33. Flashback
34. Cold
35. Blood Ties
36. Music
37. Dragon
38. Control* (Coming January 2020!)

World of Sanctuary
Epic Fantasy
(in best reading order)

1. Defender (Volume 1)
2. Avenger (Volume 2)
3. Champion (Volume 3)
4. Crusader (Volume 4)
5. Sanctuary Tales (Volume 4.25)
6. Thy Father's Shadow (Volume 4.5)
7. Master (Volume 5)
8. Fated in Darkness (Volume 5.5)
9. Warlord (Volume 6)
10. Heretic (Volume 7)
11. Legend (Volume 8)
12. Ghosts of Sanctuary (Volume 9)
13. Call of the Hero (Volume 10)
14. The Scourge of Despair (Volume 11)* Coming in 2020!

Ashes of Luukessia
A Sanctuary Trilogy
(with Michael Winstone)

1. A Haven in Ash (Ashes of Luukessia #1)
2. A Respite From Storms (Ashes of Luukessia #2)
3. A Home in the Hills (Ashes of Luukessia #3)

Liars and Vampires
YA Urban Fantasy
(with Lauren Harper)

1. No One Will Believe You
2. Someone Should Save Her
3. You Can't Go Home Again
4. Lies in the Dark
5. Her Lying Days Are Done
6. Heir of the Dog
7. Hit You Where You Live* (Coming Late 2019/Early 2020!)
8. Her Endless Night* (Coming in 2020!)
9. Burned Me*
10. Something In That Vein*

Southern Watch
Dark Contemporary Fantasy/Horror

1. Called
2. Depths
3. Corrupted
4. Unearthed
5. Legion
6. Starling
7. Forsaken
8. Hallowed* (Coming in 2020!)
9. Enflamed* (Coming in 2021!)

The Mira Brand Adventures
YA Modern Fantasy
(Series Complete)

1. The World Beneath
2. The Tide of Ages
3. The City of Lies

4. The King of the Skies
5. The Best of Us
6. We Aimless Few
7. The Gang of Legend
8. The Antecessor Conundrum

ACKNOWLEDGMENTS

Thanks to Lewis Moore for the edits, and for soldiering through during a personally difficult time. I appreciate it.

Also thanks to Jeff Bryan, for the proofing, and I'd like to congratulate him on reaching Dad Joke Level: 100. He's really a master of the craft.

Much gratitude to Lillie of https://lilliesls.wordpress.com for her work proofing and compiling my series bible. Her assistance, as ever, is indispensible.

Thanks also to Karri Klawiter of artbykarri.com for the dark and brooding cover. Felt right for the dark themes of this book.

No thanks to the People's Republic of China for all the true horrors they've inflicted on their people, which gave me such fertile ground for this story. I'd rather just make shit up rather than have so many actual bases in fact to work with.

Thanks, though, to my family for making this all possible.

CPSIA information can be obtained
at www.ICGtesting.com
Printed in the USA
LVHW082341160121
676704LV00041B/670